PRAISE FOR STEVEN SPRUILL

RULERS OF DARKNESS

"Spruill spices this clever variation on the vampire theme with exciting plot twists, appealing characters, and a villain one can almost pity. Both mystery and horror fans will enjoy this intelligent and suspenseful thriller."

—*Library Journal*

"The plot is intriguingly complex . . . by adding a noir-crime spin to his medical horror formula, Spruill manages to grab hold of, and ride reasonably high on, the cape-tails of Anne Rice and the current vampire craze."

—*Publishers Weekly*

"Move over Lestat—Merrick, Ruler of Darkness, is on the prowl. Steven Spruill unleashes a hero dark and compelling enough to raise the hair at the nape of my neck and leave me panting for more."

—*Janet Evanovich, author of One for the Money*

MY SOUL TO TAKE

"A Koontz-caliber thriller."

—*F. Paul Wilson, author of The Select*

"Spruill nearly reinvents the form . . . Readers should spend their time with *My Soul to Take*."

—*Washington Times*

"Unusual and provocative."

—*Library Journal*

"Tightly written, fascinating . . . Spruill knows how to portray people and build a story naturally."

—*Booklist*

St. Martin's Paperbacks titles
by Steven Spruill

PAINKILLER
BEFORE I WAKE
MY SOUL TO TAKE

RULERS of DARKNESS

STEVEN SPRUILL

St. Martin's Paperbacks

RULERS OF DARKNESS

Copyright © 1995 by Steven Spruill.

All rights reserved. No part of this book may be used or reproduced in any manner whatsoever without written permission except in the case of brief quotations embodied in critical articles or reviews. For information address St. Martin's Press, 175 Fifth Avenue, New York, NY 10010.

Library of Congress Catalog Card Number: 95-15458

ISBN: 0-312-95668-1

Printed in the United States of America

St. Martin's Press hardcover edition / July 1995
St. Martin's Paperbacks edition / March 1998

St. Martin's Paperbacks are published by St. Martin's Press, 175 Fifth Avenue, New York, NY 10010.

10 9 8 7 6 5 4 3 2 1

To Dr. Nancy Lyon Spruill,
Always so good for what ails me:
manet in aeternum

Acknowledgments

My thanks to the gang of eight—the Gails, McBurnetts, Settons, and Vaughns—for their wisdom; to Mitchell, Pam, and Paul—MDs all—for their expertise; to Don and Marnie, Joe and Claire, and Jeanne, good readers as well as good neighbors, and to Al Zuckerman, who wrote the book on novels.

ONE

*For we wrestle not against flesh and blood, but
against principalities, against powers, against the
rulers of the darkness of this world . . .*
Ephesians 6:12

DURING ONE OF the fiercest windstorms he could remember, Merrick Chapman found himself driving down Katie's street. Startled and dismayed, he pulled over in a dark stretch between streetlights. Overhead, bare branches thumped and clawed each other in the wind. One of them cracked loose and plunged through his headlights to the street, tumbling away in the gale. Worried, he pulled forward. He'd just drive by, make sure the wind hadn't punched out one of her windows or speared her roof with a dead limb from that old oak out back.

As he drew even with her house, Merrick doused his headlights. The branches writhing around the streetlight cast a snarled net of shadows over her small front yard. Like most lots in Georgetown, hers was deep and narrow; the house, an ivy-covered brick Colonial, huddled close to its neighbors. Since he'd left, she'd let the hedge of azaleas under her front windows go.

He decided he liked them untrimmed, a testament to Katie's philosophy of live and let live. *Which, in the end, was all she and I could do for each other,* he thought.

I should never have let it start.

The azaleas thrashed in another heavy gust. Oak leaves trapped there last fall broke free and, as if celebrating their freedom, danced in a mad frenzy before scattering into the darkness. Merrick let his gaze follow the ivy up to her bedroom window. The vines quested across the dark glass like entreating hands. They did not want to be free. They wanted to be inside with Katie.

Merrick gave a pained laugh at himself and looked at the other upstairs window. It glowed with the soft reassurance of a night-light. Behind that window, little Gregory would be asleep in his crib, probably on his belly, his face pressed down among the fanciful black-and-white cows that decorated his sheets. . . .

Headlights blazed against Merrick's front windshield. Instead of passing, the car sat facing him a few yards away. Annoyed, he shielded his eyes. Through the blinding haze, he made out the blue and red bar on top of the other car and his irritation faded. The patrol car drew alongside and the driver curtly signalled him to roll down his window. Instead, Merrick held up his badge. The cop's arrogant expression faded; he touched his cap in salute and drove on.

Merrick turned on his headlights and drove off in the opposite direction. Katie and Gregory were all right. It was after midnight. He should go home, maybe even sleep.

Except he did not want to go home, where no one waited.

He drove down Q Street to Wisconsin Avenue and idled at the intersection. What *did* he want to do? Maybe a cup of coffee at the Little Tavern on M Street. Even this late, there'd be someone there; the grill would sizzle with the homey smells of meat and onions. While he ate, he could enjoy the company of Joe Leaphorn and Jim Chee, the Navajo cops together again in Tony Hillerman's latest novel. Merrick liked the way both characters—and especially Chee, the aspiring medicine man—honored the past of their people. Though they were young, they drew on a wisdom going back hundreds of years, which was no doubt why he felt so drawn to them.

As Merrick started to turn through the intersection, his radio crackled. The dispatcher gave the code for homicide and asked units in the area to respond. With a start, Merrick recognized the address: Massachusetts and Wisconsin—the Washington National Cathedral. He snatched his mike from the dash.

"Regina, this is Merrick. I'll take it."

"What's a lieutenant of detectives doing out on a night like this? On second thought, I don't want to know. By the way, thanks for what you did."

"What did I do?"

"Don't play dumb. I know you got my boy that job at the Giant—Freddy told me the manager said your going to bat for him made the difference. Thanks—I mean it."

"No problem. So we've got a murder?"

"Afraid so. See the man on South Drive."

"Roger, out." Merrick put his magnetized bubble light on top of the car and turned left instead of right. A murder at the cathedral? It set his teeth on edge. Of all the places in Washington, why there? As he drove up the long hill of Mount St. Albans, the wind buffeted his cruiser, forcing him to clench the wheel again. At the top of the hill, he turned into the cathedral grounds. Floodlights bathed the massive west facade, except where fog streaked across the tops of the twin towers of Peter and Paul. Bearing right onto South Drive, Merrick skirted the towers then slowed as he saw a man in a dark coat on the cathedral's south lawn. The man took a tentative step toward him, peered at the bubble light on top of the cruiser, then waved him over. Merrick unclipped his flashlight from under the dash, got out, and walked up the slight rise toward the cathedral's long south face. The man hurried to meet him, or maybe to escape what lay behind. He was about sixty, a kindly wrinkled face, drawn tight with a horror that made Merrick's heart sink.

"I'm David Monroe," the man said, "a priest here. I found the body. It's over there." Without looking, he pointed at some tall box elder bushes tucked into the corner formed by the back of a tower and the south wall.

"Detective Lieutenant Chapman." Merrick showed him his badge.

"It's horrible," the priest said. "A young woman. She—" His chattering teeth stopped whatever he'd been about to say.

Merrick heard a hiss of tires on South Drive and turned to see a patrol car pull up behind his cruiser. The same cops he'd just encountered down in Georgetown got out. He waved them into position, one against the wall of the cathedral, the other at the edge of South Drive.

Turning back to the priest, he said, "Can you show me?"

The man glanced fearfully toward the bushes. "I . . . yes, of course." He led the way.

Merrick shined his flashlight down to where the priest pointed. The leafy branches broke the body into a mosaic of impressions—a chalk-white face, a stiff bib of blood on a smart teal sweatshirt . . . *God, her throat!* The sight of the woman's ragged, chewed skin shocked Merrick; he jerked his head back to choke off a groan. Switching off the flashlight, he let a merciful blanket of darkness cover her again. The branches of the box elder churned and rattled in the wind. Merrick leaned into the gusts, shuddering. How many times before had he seen this? He watched for it always; in a way, he lived to find it, and yet the shock of these first moments never seemed to diminish. *It begins again.*

"Are you all right, Detective?" the priest called, behind him.

"Yes," Merrick answered. Struggling to collect himself, he gazed at the cathedral. Under the floodlights, the limestone glowed white as old bone. The cop from the patrol car gripped the bill of his hat and huddled beneath a stained glass window of the clerestory. Above, the row of flying buttresses that joined the clerestory to the central nave had vanished in a streamer of fog. The fog itself seemed to moan as the wind that drove it writhed through the hidden stone arches. Higher up, the mist shredded into patches that raced across the pinnacles of the cathedral. Merrick wished the damned wind would stop or at least die down. Mount St. Albans was the highest point in Washington, and it figured that the gale would be worse up here, but suddenly it seemed more than a wind. It sounded as though the hill were letting out an anguished scream. Sacred ground had been profaned.

Another gust shook the box elder, bringing to Merrick the faint smell of decay. He flipped the flashlight on again. Jogging clothes and shoes. Auburn hair. Mid twenties; lovely—before someone had gone after her with his teeth. The blankness of her expression pierced Merrick. Once there had been a person inside, but now the body was empty. Even so, it spoke to him. Her Nikes, toed in by death, told of energy and self-discipline.

Merrick drew a ragged breath and dragged his palms down his cheeks, scouring out the bite of the wind. Thunder rumbled overhead.

"What could make someone do this?" the priest asked in a choked voice.

Merrick turned. In the ghostly bounce of light from the cathedral, the man's kindly face looked almost as white as the corpse's. It seemed to float bodiless in the night, his dark clothes blending with the dense grove of trees beyond South Drive. His eyes looked puffy and Merrick realized finding the body had made him weep.

"Nothing could *make* someone do it," Merrick said. *"Nothing."*

The priest edged away from him and Merrick realized his voice had come out in a snarl. His face felt tight as a mask across the bones. He raised a hand in apology and the priest's shoulders dropped a little.

"Why here?" the priest muttered. "Did the killer want to leave a message?"

"Maybe it was just convenient," Merrick said, though he had been wondering the same thing.

"Do you think we can keep this out of the papers?"

"Who have you told?"

"No one. I'll be informing the bishop in the morning, of course, but he more than anyone will want it . . . contained."

"I understand," Merrick said.

"It's just that this place is a monument to beauty and purity. We don't want it to become a magnet for ugly curiosity."

"No. And I don't want to start a panic."

"But if the same killer strikes again, we'll have a responsibility—"

"Yes."

Thunder growled again above the thick clouds over the cathedral as if looking for an opening. The priest clutched his collar to his throat and peered up. "Strange," he murmured. "I've never seen it like this."

"I'm surprised anyone would be out walking so late on such a night," Merrick said without looking at him.

The priest grunted. "It wasn't for fun, I can tell you that. I was worried about the stained glass. My hat blew off into the bush and when I went to get it . . ." He grimaced.

Merrick forced his mind onto the question that mattered: How long had the body been under the bushes? They were very thick, making it impossible to see her from the sidewalk that encircled the cathedral. There wasn't much smell, but the last few days had been cool and overcast, which would slow decomposition. The blood was dry and brown. She might have been there a couple of days, Merrick guessed. Every passing minute the trail would get a little colder. But if the killer of this woman was what Merrick thought, there *would* be other victims, more trails that only he could follow.

Headlights swept up South Drive. The evidence van and,

behind it, the long black Chrysler of the chief medical examiner. Dr. John Byner slid from behind the wheel and strode up across the grass, his medical bag swinging in his hand. Byner was a short, powerful looking black man with the sloping shoulders and economical gait of a boxer. He nodded at the priest and Merrick. "Gentlemen. A foul night. I guess winter's trying to make a comeback."

Merrick led him to the box elder bush and pulled back the low branch that hid the body.

"Wait for us, Doc," said one of the lab techs, hurrying up the slope.

"Always," Byner said, but he did not wait. "Shine your light around her neck and shoulders there."

Merrick did it.

Byner swore and Merrick saw the look of horror on the pathologist's normally stoic face.

"I'm sorry. I should have warned you—"

Byner gave his head a quick shake. "I've seen biters before, but . . ." He cleared his throat; studied the ground within the circle of light. "What I haven't ever seen is skin this white. He must have bled her dry. So why does the grass look so clean? She could have been killed somewhere else then dumped here—except . . ."

Merrick saw what the ME was looking at. There were a few bloodstained tips of grass around her neck, but not many, not enough.

"Sweep that light out a bit."

Merrick played the flashlight beam around her body.

There was no further sign of blood in the grass.

"Damn," Byner said. "Clearly, she was still hemorrhaging when she fell or was dragged here. So where's the rest of it?"

He drank it, Merrick thought. Then he licked what was left off the grass. Despite his repugnance, he felt the dark compulsion of the hunt stealing over him.

A psycho who imagined he was a vampire might taste her blood, but he couldn't drink much. How many quarts before the heart stopped pumping it out? Two, three?

Merrick cautioned himself. It was still possible this was a normal killer who had managed to drain the blood off some other way, leaving only that small final spill around her neck. . . .

An image of the gushing blood struck Merrick. Quickly, he suppressed it, but his throat crawled with a sudden, perverse thirst. A powerful urge to flee seized him. He didn't have to stay here.

He could go back to his car and drive off into the night, keep going until the city was far behind.

Byner looked up at him. "Are you thinking what I'm thinking? That this might be the same sick bastard from twelve years ago?"

Merrick's first reaction was that the question was foolish. The killer from twelve years ago would never come back here . . . but Byner had no way of knowing that.

"It's possible," Merrick said, "but let's not jump to conclusions."

"Right."

Byner returned his attention to the corpse, starting the minute inspection duty demanded. Merrick stared down at the pathologist's back, unable to break free of the thought Byner had planted. The killer from twelve years ago? Surely not, and yet the idea clung with a strange, irrational force, making his hackles rise.

Merrick felt himself backing away from the bushes. Instead of fighting it, he retreated across the lawn until he could see everyone, the priest, the lab team, Byner, huddled around the box elder bushes. Turning in a slow circle, he probed the dark line of trees across South Drive, then the road itself, then the long stone flank of the cathedral. Nothing. He focused on the cathedral wall, searching the pale stone, the stained glass windows. The fog had blown off and he could see the flying buttresses now. Gargoyles jutted from the base of each arch. Merrick searched the hideous faces. . . .

There!

His breath caught in his lungs. He stared with a dread fascination at the gargoyle. It was the closest one to the victim, in direct line with the bushes. It seemed to peer down at her, mocking and lascivious.

The white limestone of its muzzle had been stained a rusty red.

Merrick felt a shock in his stomach. His fingertips pulsed and began to ache. He checked the knot of men clustered around the bushes to make sure no one was looking his way. Then he sprinted across the lawn and leapt the twenty feet to a molded three-inch ledge in the stone. Gripping the arch of a window with one hand, he found a slight seam between the huge blocks with the other. The limestone felt gritty against his palms. Fingertips hooked, he scrambled up the face of the cathedral, feeling his way to the base of the flying buttress. With a final effort, he pulled himself onto the horizontal surface fifty feet above the ground. The wind screamed down the tunnel of stone, whipping his coat around him. Hooking a leg over the gargoyle, he straddled it. He leaned close to the hideous stone muzzle and sniffed. Yes, dried blood—from the dead woman, he was sure.

A powerful sense of foreboding gripped Merrick. Above the treetops, he could see down the long slope of Mount St. Albans. The lights of downtown Washington glimmered with sweet serenity. If the people down there knew what stirred among them, a terror they had never known would grip them. They would fear to go outside, to be alone, even to sleep. Not a sick bastard who thought he was a vampire, no. And not a vampire, either. Vampires did not exist. What *did* exist was infinitely more dangerous than the myths it had spawned.

Below, the priest stepped back from the crowd and looked up toward the gargoyles. Reaching out mentally toward the man, Merrick found where his image would fall and pinched off the capillaries feeding the priest's visual neurons, adding second blind spots to the normal ones where the optic nerves exited his eyes. The priest gazed up toward him for a second. The staring eyes filled Merrick with a superstitious dread, even though he knew they saw only stone—that the priest's visual cortex was filling in the blank spot from surrounding context just as it constantly did for the eyes' normal blind spots. After a minute, the priest gave his head a befuddled shake and turned back to the lab team.

Merrick sniffed the bloody muzzle of the gargoyle again and his foreboding deepened. Why had the killer smeared the blood here? His kind usually tried to avoid detection. They took runaways, or covered their spoor by putting bodies through an auto crash, or simply buried their victims where they would never be found. But not this time. This blood, so high above where a man could reach with a ladder, proved that the body below was not the work of an ordinary killer.

Merrick rammed his palm against the thick muzzle of the gargoyle. Scouring the rough stone, he broke the dried blood into a dark powder that blew away in the wind. When nothing was left but a faint stain that would be invisible from the ground, he jumped from the gargoyle. As he hit the ground, his legs flexed like a cat's. His bones and muscles, so much stronger than a normal man's, absorbed most of the impact, passing the rest on to his rolling shoulder. As he sprang up, a sudden, powerful conviction filled him that the blood on the gargoyle had been meant for him personally, a bloody stone gauntlet flung in his face.

A cold fury filled Merrick. You *are* back, he thought. *How dare you?*

TWO

DR. KATHERINE O'KEEFE hunched over her microscope. The red blood cells wavered and blurred. She could feel the fatigue eating at the sinews behind her shoulder blades. Her eyes itched and her lungs felt stale, as if she'd been breathing the same air over and over. Long day.

How about a hit of Dex?

For a second, she could almost feel the smooth, slightly bitter tablet resting, full of promise, at the back of her throat. The sudden, faint echo of desire chilled her. Would the day ever come when it left her entirely? She hadn't touched the stuff for nine years, not since her first year of residency. She should never have touched it at all, not Katie O'Keefe, who didn't even like to take an aspirin. But that first year, near the end of a thirty-six-hour shift, she'd fallen asleep listening to a patient's heart and woke up only when her head hit the edge of the examination table. She would never forget the panic and desperation, the certain conviction that she wouldn't make it to her second year without help. She'd promised herself to keep it under tight control, just the odd hit every now and then on the worst nights. Two months later it was a regular thing, two or more tablets a night, Dexedrine, Ritalin, Amphedroxyn—whatever she could get. So she'd taken three days of sick leave and cut herself off. For a week after she got back she was sure everyone could see the small tremor in her hands. Her throat crawled with longing every time she passed the drug cabinet. But she'd stuck her hands in her pockets whenever she could and pushed through the black walls of fatigue until the dependency withered away, leaving only this occasional ghost of longing, because it seemed a part of her brain would never forget the rush.

Never again, Katie thought.

Pushing back from her microscope, she stood and stretched her arms toward the ceiling, sucking in a deep breath that smelled faintly of paraffin. The clock above the lab door caught her eye: 7:15.

She thought of little Gregory at home. Right now, her mom would be giving him his bath. Time to call it a day, Katie decided. She felt an immediate lift at the thought of picking up her son, smelling the soap on his skin, hearing his happy jabber. He was learning new words at an amazing rate and his sentences were getting longer and more polished every day. Hard to believe he was only two.

Filled with renewed energy, Katie pulled off her lab coat and headed for the door. The phone rang. She hesitated, her hand on the knob. Let one of the techs get it, she thought. The phone went on bleating behind her, urgent and accusing. With a sigh, she gave in. "O'Keefe."

"This is Rosa on Three East. Glad I caught you. Jenny Hrluska is asking for you."

Katie's resentment at the call vanished. Jenny was one of her favorite patients—a sweet young girl who was facing leukemia with more courage than most adults. "Any change?"

"Not really. The rash may be a tad worse. She seems to be having some pain in her arms, though she denies it. I think she's just scared. I tried to reassure her but none of the rest of us seem to have your touch with her." Rosa said it with good-natured envy. "Oh, one other thing—she keeps saying she's hungry. We hear it almost every time we go in, now. We've tried bringing her everything from cottage cheese to pizza to cake, but she takes a tiny bite and leaves the rest. I've never seen anything like it."

"Okay, I'll be right up."

Katie headed for the elevators, mystified. This strange hunger of Jenny's—what could be causing it? The girl had just endured full courses of radiation and chemotherapy in an effort to kill the stem cells that were producing her cancerous leukocytes. The treatments had caused the usual side effects of nausea and loss of appetite. But at the same time, paradoxically, Jenny had started to report hunger pangs, which had become more and more frequent. Nauseated but hungry. It was baffling.

Katie recalled the one similar case she'd been able to find—a thirteen-year-old boy reported in the *New England Journal of Medicine*. The article's author had described the same bizarre hunger and failure to respond to treatment that Jenny was showing. The writer had concluded that it might be a rare new strain of childhood leukemia and that further study was needed. A futile plea if ever there was one—research funds rarely got diverted from heart disease, AIDS, and the prevalent forms of cancer for an anomalous case, no matter how curious. Ultimately, the article had disappointed her. Though it described the strange hunger pangs, it did not suggest any cause or treatment. When she'd called the author, he'd told her, rather curtly, that the boy had died and he had no idea why—the worst thing a patient could do to his doctor.

Katie had a chilling presentiment that Jenny, too, was dying. Medically speaking, it was too early to say that, but the stubborn refusal of Jenny's blood count to improve was very disturbing. Along with chemo and radiation, Jenny had been treated with antibiotics, transfusions, and cerebrospinal fluid injections. Under such an onslaught, her symptoms should have diminished by now. Twenty years ago, one out of four children survived leukemia but the number was now almost two out of three. Most patients like Jenny would need hospitalization for a few weeks. Jenny had been in her bed almost three months.

It was frustrating as hell.

At the nurses station, Katie shrugged into a sterile gown, gloves, and a surgical mask. In Jenny's room, the light was low, the air fragrant with lotion. One of the nurses must have just given Jenny a rubdown. Everyone loved the girl. Katie walked to the bedside with a smile, knowing it would show in her eyes even though the mask hid her mouth. "Hiya, Kiddo."

Jenny smiled back, revealing a row of braces. "Hi, Doctor O'Keefe. Thanks for coming."

Katie nodded, hiding her distress at Jenny's terrible paleness, which seemed to worsen every day now. Even in her illness, she was a pretty child, just starting to bloom at age twelve. Her silky, blonde hair, thinned by the chemotherapy, stuck to her forehead. Her blue eyes were clouded with fear. Katie's heart went out to her. Jenny should be going to slumber parties with her pals, plotting how to interest some cute but oblivious boy in her class. Not lying there barely able to rise, not after all these weeks. Katie stroked Jenny's arm, hating the barrier of the gloves. But she dared not take them off. The cruelest irony of leukemia was that the swarming white blood cells did not work properly, leaving the body horribly vulnerable to infection.

"So how was your day?" Katie asked.

"Pretty good. Mr. Chapman visited me."

Katie's heart quickened. *Merrick!*

"You know—the policeman who comes around to see the kids," Jenny said, apparently mistaking her silence for lack of recognition.

"Yes. Did he do some magic tricks for you?"

"Uh-huh. A card trick. He's really good."

Especially his disappearing act. Katie caught herself. Breaking up had been as much her decision as Merrick's—maybe more. It had been for the best. She just wondered if he still missed her. She certainly missed him.

Putting Merrick out of her mind, she inspected the pinpoint rash on Jenny's skin and felt a small relief. It did not seem worse. The red and dark speckles were caused by bursting capillaries, a common complication of childhood leukemia. Still, the rash could be a sign of deeper, internal bleeding, and that would be a real problem. She'd have to reduce the indomethacin dosage, which would mean more pain in the joints of Jenny's arms and legs. Fighting leukemia was always a delicate balancing act, since most of her drug weapons against the disease could also aggravate internal bleeding. The next step along the tightrope would be to increase the platelet transfusions and hope Jenny's clotting would improve.

"So how are you feeling?"

"I'm fine," Jenny said with a wan smile, this time keeping the braces hidden. "You look so pretty tonight."

"Just tonight?"

Jenny gave a faint giggle and her cheeks flushed slightly. "No, every night. I wish I had hair like yours. It's so thick and dark."

"That's funny. I always wanted to be a blonde."

"And your eyes are beautiful," Jenny went on, "even without mascara."

"Hey, no fair. I came here to cheer *you* up."

"I bet I know how come you don't wear mascara."

"How come?"

"Because it gets on the microscope."

"Good guess," Katie said approvingly. She had the sudden sense of Jenny lying there day after day, thinking about her, fantasizing herself out of her sick bed and into a life that, to her young mind, actually seemed glamorous.

A life she might have no chance of living.

"The nurse said you wanted to see me."

Jenny hesitated. "Well, it's just that I feel so weak. I'm hungry a lot but when I eat it doesn't help. I still feel hungry. I was wondering if you'd figured out why."

"I'm still stumped," Katie admitted.

"Oh!" Jenny touched a hand to her lip.

Katie saw that her nose was bleeding, another sign of the thrombocytopenia that caused her rash. Feeling a surge of frustration, Katie took a cotton swab from the drawer of the bed table and held it against the nostril. "I think it's a little one," she said. Jenny tried to smile, but looked frightened. Hoping to distract her, Katie said, "What's been happening on your *Cheers* reruns?"

"I dod't doh," Jenny said, nostrils clogged by the swab. I havid seed id lately."

The answer worried Katie. *Cheers* was Jenny's favorite show. "I hear Sam Malone wears a wig."

"Doh!" Jenny said.

"Yup."

"He's too old for be adyway."

Katie eased the swab back and saw with relief that the bleeding had stopped. "There. All over."

"Am I going to die, Doctor O'Keefe?"

Katie took Jenny's hand. The question did not startle her; she had heard it too many times before from young patients. But it did sadden her, and make her angry all over again at the horrible disease. "Jenny, dear, if I think you're going to die, I promise I'll tell you. You're very sick—you know it and I know it. But almost no one your age dies of this anymore."

"You promise you'll tell me?"

"I promise."

Jenny looked away. "I want to know ahead of time."

Katie felt a gloss of tears forming on her eyes. She blinked them back and bent over the bed, gently moving Jenny's arms as she watched her face. "Hurt?"

"A little."

"Are you hungry right now?" she asked.

"Uh-huh."

"What for?"

Jenny's eyes went distant. "That's just it. I don't *know.*"

"Ice cream?"

"Uh-huh."

"Anchovies?"

Jenny made a face. "Eeeeuw, no way."

"Remember, if you think of what you'd like—anything— give the nurses a call and they'll get it for you. I'll keep trying to figure out why it's happening."

"Okay."

At the door, Katie turned back and gave her a little wave. Jenny fluttered a hand weakly, then licked at her upper lip, where the blood had been.

As Katie walked away down the hall, she felt a peculiar uneasiness. Jenny's eyes—they'd looked almost rapt as her tongue sought out the blood. The disturbing image clung for a moment, then yielded to thoughts of Gregory. At once, Katie's mood lifted. Here I come, Angel. I'll kiss you on top of your head like you like, then you can sit on my lap and I'll read you a story.

As she passed the nurses station, Rosa leaned across the counter, holding out a phone receiver to flag her down. "For you," she said. "A Doctor Byner."

For a second, Katie considered not taking the call. Then, controlling her impatience, she took the receiver. "This is Doctor O'Keefe."

"Doctor," said a deep voice with a Southern accent, "I'm John Byner, chief medical examiner for DC. I know it's after hours, but I need a favor. I've been doing an autopsy and some- thing rather strange has come up."

"I'm not a pathologist."

"I realize that, but I need the opinion of a hematologist, and you're one of the best. I was impressed by your recent article in *JAMA.* In fact, your discovery of a new blood antigen may be relevant to my case."

"So what's the problem?"

"I'd rather not say over the phone. Could you come over to my lab in the ME's building? There's a patrol car waiting for you at the main entrance of your hospital."

She laughed in spite of herself. "Pretty sure of yourself, aren't you?"

"Please, Doctor. It's important."

Katie hesitated, intrigued. She glanced at the clock in the nurses station. Five after eight. "How long will this take?"

Byner hesitated. "Not long at all. A quick look at a specimen and your opinion, that's all. Fifteen minutes at the most."

She'd still have time to read Gregory a story. "All right."

"Terrific. Thank you, Doctor. We're in room twelve, the basement."

As Katie walked out the hospital entrance, she was surprised to see that it had been raining. Fortunately, the fierce winds of last night had died away completely. The headlights of a waiting patrol car poured like liquid silver along the wet pavement of the parking lot. The driver, a woman cop, said a neutral hello, and let it go at that. Probably resented being ordered to chauffeur duty. Katie couldn't blame her. The cop turned on Reservoir Road, passing the quarter-mile sprawl of the hospital. As they drove into the heart of Georgetown's business district, Katie cracked the window, watching the knots of people stroll along the sidewalk. The glowing fronts of art galleries offered tantalizing snatches of color, though most of the canvases were too small to see properly from the street. The eating places were in full swing. Passing Geppetto's, Katie smelled pizza in the cool humid air. On the other side of M Street, a forsythia bush bloomed yellow in the lighted portico garden of the Four Seasons Hotel. It's spring, Katie thought. I knew that, but not really. I've got to start coming up for air.

She found herself taking a deep breath and smiled. Work *had* been keeping her ridiculously busy—riding herd on residents, the follow-up paper on the new antigen for *JAMA*. But her social life? Nothing serious, or even interesting. It was time she started looking around again and stopped comparing each of her occasional dates to Merrick Chapman.

The car left the bustle of Georgetown. As they passed George Washington University to the south, Katie's mind went back to the night she'd met Merrick in GW's emergency room. She'd been called in for a consult on a poison victim Merrick had brought to ER. She remembered feeling impressed that Merrick had stayed with the man instead of just dumping him off. He'd asked her a bunch of questions trying to find out what the poison was, but he hadn't written anything down, instead gazing at her as though he was recording her along with her answers. Her heart had begun to beat its way up toward her throat. In a stroke of boldness, she'd asked him out for coffee, and that had been the start. . . .

But it was over now.

Right, Katie thought. So why are you thinking about him? Her lingering attachment to him aggravated her. After more than two years, she should truly be over him. It was just that he was so much more vital and impressive than other men, so strangely intense. . . .

The patrol car turned at Fourth Street and, a moment later, drew up in front of the Medical Examiner's building. The brick front glistened from the rain. Hurrying inside, Katie descended the stairs to the basement, pursued by the echo of her heels clicking along the empty corridor. When she got to Room 12, she walked through the open door and stopped, startled. Merrick was standing at a lab bench, towering over the man in the white coat beside him. As Merrick turned, his eyes widened. Clearly, he was surprised to see her, too.

He still looked very fit; living without her certainly hadn't made him go to seed. Tonight he wore a leather flight jacket. Though winter was barely over, he was tanned. Meggan, her best friend at the hospital, thought he looked like a young Sean Connery, the lean, intense version of the early James Bond movies. In purely physical terms, Meggan was right, though Merrick was bigger. And, oddly, despite his youthful physique, he reminded Katie more of Connery now—something in his expression, perhaps. His eyes, his eyes. . . . Sometimes they reminded her of a professor emeritus she'd had in med school, a man who'd practiced medicine for fifty-seven years, first in Detroit's inner city, then Appalachia, then Bangladesh, and finally Somalia. There was something very powerful, very knowing in Merrick's eyes—and it hadn't lost its effect on her. Gazing at him, she could feel her heartbeat picking up.

"Katie, what are you doing here?"

The man beside him turned. "Ah, Doctor O'Keefe. I'm John Byner. You two know each other?"

"We've met," Merrick said, a touch drily.

Katie stepped forward to shake Byner's hand. He was a muscular black man with streaks of gray at the temples and a weary, almost haunted expression. It was a look she often saw on the faces of her residents, except that Dr. Byner was over forty and trapped not in a few years of training but in rotations of murder and mayhem that never ended.

"Thanks for coming on such short notice," Byner said. He turned to Merrick. "I called Doctor O'Keefe just after I phoned you," he explained. "We need an expert, and she's the best around."

"I can't disagree with that," Merrick said.

Katie wondered what was the matter with Merrick. He was glad to see her, she could tell, but he seemed also to wish she weren't here. For a moment, neither man said anything, and Katie realized that both were, for some reason, reluctant to proceed. Her nose prickled with a faint smell of formaldehyde. A ventilation fan rumbled to life on the other side of the wall—that must be where they did the autopsies.

"So how are you doing?" Merrick asked her.

"I'm fine. You?"

"The same. And Gregory?"

"Great."

"That's good." The faint lines around his eyes deepened in a genuine smile. She made herself look away, at Dr. Byner. His weary brown eyes were filled with curiosity. Clearly, she and Merrick had more than "met," and he was probably wondering what the story was.

"It's late," Byner said. "Lieutenant, why don't you summarize the background for Doctor O'Keefe, and then she can have a look."

Merrick blew out a breath. "All right. Doctor Byner is doing the microscopic exam on a murder victim discovered on the National Cathedral grounds last night. A young woman. Her throat was torn open. She died from loss of blood. A fair amount of blood seems to be missing."

"Torn open? by what?"

"Human teeth," Dr. Byner said.

Katie felt a sudden, sour weight in her stomach. She was glad she hadn't had dinner. "I'm surprised it wasn't all over the news today," she said, imagining what the tabloids would do with it: VAMPIRE STRIKES AT CATHEDRAL. Not that you needed vampires for this kind of sickness. Reality, unfortunately, could be worse than any myth.

"We've been able to keep it quiet, so far," Merrick said. "A priest found the body in some bushes beside the cathedral.

She was under the low branches, completely hidden. Doctor Byner estimated she had been dead two days.''

Byner gave his microscope an oddly strained glance. ''Doctor O'Keefe, I've got some unpreserved blood here taken from the wound. I'd like you to look at it, please.''

Katie walked to the scope, feeling a touch of foreboding. Something was bothering both men more than they cared to let on. She looked through the scope. The first thing she saw was the expected mass of shriveled RBCs. Something near the bottom of the slide caught her eye. In the midst of the ruptured and crenated red blood cells sat three that looked like they'd just been drawn from a living body a minute ago. They were round and plump, very pink, with none of the central pallor of RBCs that had given up their oxygen.

Incredulous, she looked up at the two men. ''Come on, what is this?''

''I was hoping you could tell us,'' Byner said.

''The victim has been dead for three days?''

''That's right.''

''And she was lying outdoors in some bushes for two of those days?''

''Correct.''

Katie shook her head. ''Doctor, you know as well as I do that red blood cells exposed to the elements stay fresh only a few minutes.''

Byner and Merrick exchanged a glance.

''What?'' Katie said. ''Come on, you two. Out with it.''

''I typed the victim's blood, of course,'' Byner said. ''Those three cells you just looked at don't belong to her.''

Katie's neck prickled. ''Then they must be . . .''

''That's right,'' Merrick said softly. ''They're the killer's.''

THREE

KATIE LOOKED THROUGH the microscope again, astounded by what she was seeing. The killer's cells should not look like that—not after three days. The shriveled RBCs of the victim all around the killer's plump ones drove the contrast home even more dramatically.

"There's something else you should know," Dr. Byner said. "In a lobe of the victim's left ear, I found a small pool of the killer's blood—enough to run tests on. When I did, I found no serum, only the blood cells themselves."

"The serum must have evaporated while she was lying exposed for three days," Katie said.

"Yes, but what puzzles me is that the cells showed no signs whatsoever of clotting. If the serum held platelets or anticlotting factors, they didn't work."

Katie shook her head. "That's nuts."

"Indeed it is."

Merrick looked at her and then Byner. "You're saying the killer is a hemophiliac?"

"It looks like he *should* be one," Byner said, "but he isn't—can't be."

"Please explain," Merrick said.

"Well, for starters, if the killer were a hemophiliac, we'd have found a lot more of his blood at the scene. Even a small wound can kill a hemophiliac because he just goes on bleeding until he sinks into shock from blood loss and his heart stops. If our killer's blood didn't clot, we should have found a lot more of it, and maybe his body, too."

"So why didn't we?"

"I don't know." Byner's shoulders sagged. He leaned back against a lab table.

Katie looked at the killer's cells again. For a second they seemed to blur. She realized the same thing had happened the first time she'd looked at them. Raising her head, she pressed a finger gently to each eyelid, then looked again. The cells still appeared blurred at the edges. She felt her pulse pick up. "Doctor Byner, when you looked at these, did you see a very faint corona around the cells?"

Byner straightened, alert again. "Sometimes I thought I did, but I'm not sure. Shouldn't be anything there."

"It could be some sort of protective membrane. Have you run an IE?"

"Don't have the equipment," Byner groused. "This is Washington, DC, the last colony. Around here a rack of new test tubes takes an act of Congress."

"What's an IE?" Merrick asked. His gaze held her and she saw the old desire, felt an answering hunger for him.

"Immunofixation electrophoresis. It might tell us whether these cells have some extra proteins or antigens not found on normal RBCs."

"Antigens?" Merrick said, still gazing at her. "They're what causes rejection when the wrong two people mix their blood."

"Right." She wondered if he intended a double meaning. His eyes gave no hint. If only what had happened to us were so easy to understand, she thought. "Antigens don't always cause bad reactions, though," she went on. "For example, a person's body doesn't reject its own inborn antigens. Those antigens are basically proteins, and we don't really know why they exist, what function they serve. I'm only guessing, but maybe there are some weird proteins on these RBCs that have somehow kept them fresh." She wished he'd look away.

"Mind if I take a peek at those cells?" Merrick asked, and she realized he had sensed her discomfort.

She nodded at the scope. As he bent over it, she could smell the leather of his jacket. She had a powerful urge to put her hand on his shoulder. Instead, she stepped back a little, saying, "See those three cells that are plump and red?"

"Yes. But I don't see any corona. They *are* much redder than the other cells, though."

"That's probably from the hemoglobin. I'm guessing from the rich color that the cells are still carrying oxygen after three days, which should be impossible."

"So this is arterial blood."

"Yes," she said, impressed. For a cop with no formal training in biology, he was quick on the uptake. She remembered how Merrick was always surprising her. Like the time he sat down at her piano and started playing Rachmaninoff's Prelude in G Minor. They'd only been dating a few weeks, and he'd said nothing about being able to play. She had mentioned that the G Minor was one of her favorites, and he'd just sat down on the bench and started playing the flowing and difficult middle movement with uncommon accuracy and great sensitivity. It knocked her over. Each new ability she glimpsed in him, each bit of arcane knowledge, was all the more impressive because he never showed it unless there was a reason. . . .

Katie caught herself. It was really not helpful to keep thinking about Merrick that way. She turned to Byner. "Is there anything else you can tell me that might shed light on this?"

He looked at the ceiling a moment, eyes narrowed in concentration. "Nothing directly."

"How about indirectly?"

"Well, the killer bled, but not because his victim scratched him. There was nothing under her nails. I expected to find tissue and blood—or fabric—because there are no ligature marks on her wrists and no sign of blunt force trauma on the head or cervical vertebrae. No evidence he knocked her out some other way, either—no needle marks and nothing in the blood chemistry. The only wound was on her throat. He really tore that up—"

"Doctor, please," Merrick cautioned.

"That's all right," Katie said. She *did* feel a little queasy, and maybe it showed on her face, but she wasn't about to throw up or pass out.

"The point is," Byner said, "the victim should have scratched hell out of him, hit him, done something. There should have been *some* sign of a struggle."

"If she didn't scratch him," Katie asked, "why did he bleed?"

Byner shrugged. "I couldn't begin to guess. There's no evidence on that."

Merrick grunted. "And not much on anything else, either. Just a few odd RBCs that raise more questions than they answer."

Katie looked at him, surprised. Didn't Merrick realize that these blood cells were a lot more than just odd? The more she thought about it, the more intrigued she became. The cells might lead to some very exciting discovery. In science, things that didn't act like everyone thought they should often caused quantum leaps in knowledge once they were understood.

"I've got to study these cells," she said.

"I was hoping you'd say that," Byner replied. "Your lab at Georgetown is a lot better than ours here."

"Hold on, you two," Merrick said. "We can't let these cells out of here."

"Why not?" Katie asked, turning on him. "I know how to take care of a blood sample—"

"Sure, but stop thinking like a scientist for a minute. Imagine if the media got hold of this—KILLER'S BLOOD CELLS WON'T DIE." Merrick grimaced. "By comparison, Barnum and Bailey would look like a firm of CPAs."

Katie stared at him, nettled. "I'm not going to talk to the press or anyone else."

"I know. But the more these cells get around, the tougher to keep the lid on."

Byner said, "We don't have much choice, Merrick. I've done as much as I can, here."

"Aren't your tests likely to destroy the sample?" Merrick asked Katie.

"Yes," she admitted.

"Well, that's no good. If I catch a suspect, I want to be able to compare our sample to his blood. We can't do that if it's been destroyed."

"Look," Byner said impatiently, "we don't need to compare two physical samples directly, we can compare any new RBCs to the recorded results of Doctor O'Keefe's analyses. Hell, we don't even need that. If you catch a guy whose arterial blood is still fresh and oxygenated after three days sitting out on a slide, he's your man. This bastard may look as ordinary as your next-door neighbor, but his blood is unique as far as we know. And if Doctor O'Keefe can run these cells through the paces at a top research lab, we may be able to give you pretty good guesses about some of his other characteristics. This is your case, Merrick, but the forensic end is mine, and I say we do it."

Merrick stared at him a minute. "I'll make a deal with you. She takes the cells, but you both agree to keep this strictly between the three of us for the present."

Katie said, "Wait a minute. I'll need help."

"Help with what?" Merrick's voice rose a notch. "How many people does it take to lift a tube of blood?"

"I could run the tests myself," she said, "but I'll still have to interpret the results. Much as it would fascinate me, it won't do *you* any good to know that the killer has a biologic preservative in his blood, or such and such a protein on his cells. What you'll want me to tell you is how he got the way he is. Was he involved in a nuclear reactor accident? Did he have an atypical reaction to chemotherapy? Was he part of some secret lab experiment in genetics? We're talking a load of additional research that might range into God knows what. I do have one or two other duties at the hospital, you know. If you want my report in the next month, I have to have help."

Merrick gave her a look of total exasperation. "Katie—"

"I'll use a resident I know I can trust absolutely. His name is Art Stratton. He's very quick, an excellent researcher. If I tell him to keep quiet about it, he'll keep quiet."

"Come on, Merrick," Byner said. "That's not an unreasonable request."

Merrick gave Katie a long, hard look. "You, me, Doctor Byner and your resident. That's it. *No one* else is to know about this."

"Agreed," Katie said.

Merrick transferred his gaze to Dr. Byner. The pathologist hesitated, then nodded. "I'll put three mils of the blood in a cold pack for you, Doctor O'Keefe. And you'll need a ride home." He glanced at Merrick, who said nothing. "I'll arrange another patrol car for you," Byner offered finally.

Merrick blinked, as though coming out of a trance. "No, that's all right. I'll drop her off."

Gee thanks, Katie thought, a little hurt. She knew she had no right to be. They'd both agreed over two years ago that the pain would only be greater if they strung it out by finding reasons to be around each other. That was just as true today. No matter how much she wanted to, the last thing she *needed* right now was to get into a car with Merrick and drive off into the night. "I'll take a cab," she said to Dr. Byner. "I'll include it in my bill."

Gregory was in bed when Katie got home. Disappointed, she put the Styrofoam cold pack with the killer's blood cells in the basement refrigerator, then allowed her mother to lead her into the kitchen. Mom fussed at the microwave for a moment then produced a steaming plate of chicken and greens, one of her own recipes, called *Poulet Baton Rouge.* Katie ate slowly, savoring the Cajun spices, letting them do their wonderful, head-clearing magic on her. Her mother watched her eat with a satisfied, maternal air. Katie noticed that she'd done her hair, cutting and perming it herself with her usual competence. In jeans and a tweedy jacket, Audrey O'Keefe looked the image of the English Lit professor she had been at Brown. At the same time, since her retirement, some of Grandma Guillemin's expressions had been creeping back into her speech, hints of the rich patois of the bayous. O'Keefe might be Audrey's married name, but those dark brown eyes and Gallic nose had not been made in Ireland.

"You skipped lunch again, didn't you?"

"I had a salad," Katie said.

Mom arched an eyebrow, but before she could launch into her nutrition lecture, Katie said, "So how was Gregory today?"

Derailed, Mom broke into a smile. "Oh, you'll never believe what he did."

"What?"

"A little before lunch, I heard some stealthy sounds in the pantry. When I pulled the curtain back, there he sat with a jar of my strawberry preserves. Talk about caught red-handed, it was all over his fingers, not to mention his mouth. I asked him what he thought he was doing and he said, calm as you please, 'My mommy says dis jam is good for me.' "

Katie grinned, then burst out laughing. "What an alibi." She sobered. "I miss everything. I wanted to read to him tonight. Then I . . . got delayed." Thinking of the killer's blood cells now in her basement, Katie felt a pang of unease. They were fascinating, and quite harmless in themselves, but she would breathe easier when she got them out of the house tomorrow.

"You go up and see Gregory," Mom said. "I'll clean up here."

Katie hurried upstairs, trying not to feel guilty about leaving the dishes. Since she'd had her mother move in with her everything had been so much better. She paid her to take care of Gregory during the day, but didn't want her duties to extend to things like fixing dinner and cleaning up in the evening. On the other hand, every time Katie tried to put a stop to it or hire extra help, her mother reacted as though she were about to lose a sacred right.

Katie tiptoed into the nursery. Gazing down at Gregory in his crib, she felt a surge of love. He looked so small and vulnerable. As she watched, he sighed and turned over, pulling the blanket with him. Mickey Mouse and Goofy smiled up from his rumpled PJs. Thinking of the strawberry preserves, Katie wondered if it was Gregory's first fib. No, last month he'd said he didn't break the vase. . . .

What was she doing adding up such things, anyway? Weren't all children in their terrible twos pretty loose with the truth? I'm thirty-three, Katie thought, and I still don't know the truth half the time.

She bent over Gregory and kissed his head, the straight dark hair so like his father's. Thinking of Merrick brought an ache that had been renewed by his nearness tonight. If only they could be together. Gregory needed him. . . .

Katie caught herself. It was she who needed Merrick, not Gregory. What Gregory needed was love and care, and he was getting plenty of that from his mom and grandma.

Relax, Katie thought. I'm doing the best I can. Gazing down at her son, she felt an irrational stab of fear for him. It was the murder, she knew. Even though she had not seen the body, she could not stop imagining it. What kind of human being could kill with his teeth, tearing open a person's throat? She shuddered. Bending over Gregory, she smoothed a damp lock of hair from his forehead. Tonight, the world seemed too terrible for children. I'm afraid for you, little boy, she thought. My son. You're so dear. If anything happened to you I couldn't bear it.

She felt a pain in her knuckles and realized her hands had locked together fiercely as if in prayer. Unable to help herself, Katie scooped up her son and hugged him to her. He stirred, but went straight back to sleep, his head a warm, precious weight on her shoulder. A terrible premonition that he was in danger from something she could not see or even imagine passed through her. It's the murder, she told herself again. It's spooked me, that's all.

But the fear did not fade.

FOUR

WHEN HE LEFT Byner's lab, Merrick drove from the morgue down Fourth Street and then along Constitution Avenue. The black pavement, damp from the rain, gleamed under the ornate old streetlights. The Washington Monument slid past on his left and then, on his right, the giant sculpture of Einstein. The great scientist hunched over in thought, as if he were pondering the Vietnam Veterans Memorial hidden by the grassy banks across the avenue. Though Merrick could not see it from the street, he felt the weight of the long, black wall of stone. On its glossy surface were etched the names of nearly fifty-eight thousand dead—perhaps five times the number killed by the ancient creature he now hunted.

With an effort, Merrick relaxed his shoulders, loosened his fingers on the steering wheel. He took the Roosevelt Bridge across the Potomac. As he neared the Virginia shore, he could see the dark treetops of Roosevelt Island clawing up toward the bridge.

The hemophage had bled on his kill. *Christ!*

Merrick slapped the steering wheel. Bad luck, Byner calling Katie in. If only there had been some way to detect the RBCs myself, he thought, while I was at the scene. Then no one else would have seen them, much less a police pathologist and a hematologist. . . .

Katie.

His body ached from being so close to her; his longing for her was incredibly intense. She was so beautiful. She'd let her hair grow longer and it looked terrific, dark as a raven, with rich red undertones. He had scarcely been able to look away from her eyes, wondering as he had so many times what rare gene had made them that exotic violet color. She'd smiled tonight when she first saw him. How it had warmed him, that wonderful smile, a bit lopsided, completely artless. Without trying to look beautiful, Katie was. But it was her inner beauty that he loved most. Her kindness, her even temper. Katie was cursed with the gift of understanding. God, he missed her. And she missed him, he could tell. He wished she did not. If she would just hate him and be done with it, it would be, if not easier, at least quicker.

She'll be in danger, Merrick thought grimly, if the hemophage learns she has his blood.

He wondered again if he should take the blood. Simple enough—just go to her house tonight, switch it for a sample of normal blood and do the same in Byner's lab. . . .

But it was already too late to gain much by stealing the cells. Katie and Byner had had a microscopic look at the blood's main structural difference from normal blood. They had already discovered two of the blood's most important secrets—its membrane and its impossible freshness. Anything further they might learn could hardly worsen the disaster now waiting to happen if they talked to anyone else about the blood.

Which was exactly what they *would* do if they detected the switch. And who else but him could they suspect of stealing the blood? *He* would then become the focus of their speculation— which was more dangerous than what they might learn from the blood cells.

Finally, even if he got away with the switch, it would do nothing to protect Katie if the killer learned she was studying his cells—with her believing she had the killer's blood, so would the killer.

Frustration gripped Merrick. There wasn't any quick way out

of this. If taking the blood wouldn't work, the only course left was to minimize its impact. And the best way to do that was to catch this hemophage quickly.

I need Sandeman, Merrick thought.

His sense of urgency sharpened and he stepped on the accelerator. The houses thinned out as he drove deeper into Virginia. The rain started again, a fine drizzle that blurred approaching headlights. Merrick tried to let his mind blur, too, just drift in the warm cocoon of the car.

Is it really you, Zane?

Merrick pushed the question from his mind. He did not want to think about who the hemophage was. At the cathedral, he'd jumped to a conclusion, even though it was exactly what he'd warned Byner not to do. Nothing was proven. He would see what Sandeman thought.

Merrick left Route 50 and turned onto a narrow country road that had changed little in a hundred years. Nothing but fields for awhile, then Nathan's general store glided by on his right, its round Coke emblem glinting orange under the naked bulb of the bug light. It reminded him of the blood cells under Byner's microscope.

With an effort, Merrick blanked his mind again. The road grew even narrower as the fields gave way to woods, and trees crowded up to both shoulders. Slowing, Merrick found the turnoff, a slight gap in the woods. The cruiser's headlights bleached a swath of bushes and weeds, throwing tangles of black shadow back to slide across the trunks. Dousing the headlights, he followed the deep twin ruts on their winding course between the trees. His eyes adjusted at once, eating up the infrareds, turning the night into a shady afternoon only slightly blurred at the edges.

After about a mile, he parked and got out to walk. The weeds pulled at his pant cuffs, soaking his socks. The damp bark of the oaks gave off a bitter, wet-worm smell. He heard the chill, liquid cry of a whippoorwill and shivered. The property had been his for a hundred years, but he would never feel at home here.

Merrick found the small clearing defined by the four old oaks that formed a natural square. His heart raced with a mixture of anticipation and dread. It had been too long since he'd seen Sandeman.

But to see Sandeman he must see the others, too.

Merrick's gut tightened and the muscles of his neck and shoulders clenched. He stood a moment, breathing deeply, trying to prepare himself for what was coming. He swept away the damp leaves in the center of the clearing. Groping the sod until he found a seam, he felt for the iron ring beneath . . . *there.* He pulled up the trapdoor, with its load of earth. Beneath, the platinum iridium gleamed redly in the light of the clearing. Merrick dialed the combination and the door yielded, swinging down smoothly on its hydraulic hinges. A soft, bluish light, keyed to the door, flowed up from below. Halfway down the ladder, Merrick paused to push the massive door back up into place. He gave the inside dial a spin to make sure it locked again.

The anteroom smelled faintly of mildew and damp cement from the reinforced concrete. Merrick tasted bile and swallowed hard. Always that same smell just before he saw them. How he hated it.

Merrick dialed the combination on the anteroom's door and it swung open, activating more blue lights in the large vault beyond. He tried to look straight ahead. Still he saw them, from the corner of his eye, blurred ranks of bodies. He forced himself to face them, the seven men and four women lying with utter stillness on their cots, arms at their sides, heads cocked forward on the pillows. Long white hair fanned out around the withered faces. Most of the eyes were open. They seemed to be staring at him. Under the indigo light, their skin glowed coldly. They made him think of pharaohs in an ancient embalming chamber, rulers of darkness struck down by a mysterious plague. Struck down, but not dead, Merrick thought.

And I am their plague.

Keeping his eyes on the single door at the far end of the chamber, he forced himself forward down the aisle between the two rows of cots. Mindful of the three phages locked behind steel doors on either side of the central vault, he tried to make no sound. Last time he'd been here, those three were still too strong to transfer to the common ward, where they would have direct access to the anteroom door. If he wasn't quiet, they would hear him, and he really did not want that. As he crept between the dying hemophages in the commons, Merrick wondered if even they might be able to sense him. None had the strength to move in any meaningful way, or he'd not have transferred them here. They looked unaware and helpless, but even now, their uncanny predator senses might still be sharp enough to sense him. The thought made his spine crawl.

One of the bodies drew a single shuddering breath. Dread froze him in mid step. He closed his eyes a second, then looked down. The bony, withered phage looked like the "ice man" found a few years ago in the Italian Alps. Merrick remembered the shock he'd felt at seeing the photo on the cover of *Newsweek,* the weathered bronze skin, the striking blue eyes, still intact after five thousand years. He'd read the article with an alarm that had faded only when he realized the scientists had no real idea what they were prodding and probing. They knew the body's incredible age but, at a loss for any other explanation, they'd attributed the incredible preservation to the glacier under which the corpse had lain for so long. They had no inkling that their find was not an ordinary man, that it had lived for years under the avalanche that must have trapped it long before the glacier descended. And why should the scientists know? How could they conceive of their treasured "early man" needing neither food nor water but starving, oh so slowly, for lack of blood?

Merrick forced himself to take the grooved hand in his. It was cool but not cold. The hemophage's ice blue eyes gazed into his. Merrick could sense the life still lingering in them. Tiny match flames seemed to flare deep in the pools of blue. Suddenly, the eyes glared with an incandescent hatred. The withered lips moved slightly then went still.

"I know," Merrick whispered. "But I couldn't let you go on. Three thousand people you slaughtered before I tracked you down and stopped you."

And now I must hunt a new killer, he thought, and bring it here—a hemophage so desperate from hunger that its nose bled. Why? Had it been trapped for awhile?

One thing was certain: It wasn't hungry anymore.

Merrick returned the skeletal hand to the cot. He forced himself to check each of the bodies. Two were dead, finally and at long last, though their bodies would not begin true decay for centuries. At least he could bury them now. The rest were still alive.

Merrick crept to a side wall of the vault and leaned against one of the doors to listen through the steel. For a moment he heard nothing. Then a foot scraped on the other side of the door, the dry rasp of calloused skin on cement. He remembered catching this hemophage in a marsh outside Norfolk. It had been preying on runaway kids.

As Merrick listened through the door, the phage started mumbling, chanting a phrase over and over again in a language Merrick did not recognize. Unnerved, he backed away from the door.

I should check the other cell, too, Merrick thought.

Next time.

Hurrying to the door at the end of the vault, he eased the key into the lock. The door yawned open silently on its oiled hinges. Relief filled him as he slipped inside and closed the door on the chamber of horrors behind him.

He turned to Sandeman. The hemophage lay on his cot, surrounded by his precious books. His stillness was absolute. Merrick's heart sank. Kneeling by the bed, he picked up Sandeman's wrist. At first, he could find no pulse, then he detected a beat, faint and very slow. Relieved, he studied the head on the pillow. The face was lean and aristocratic, the skin stretched like parchment across the prominent bones of cheek, forehead, and jaw. Sandeman's hair had turned a snowy white. It had thinned a little and grown longer, halfway down his neck now. Laugh wrinkles at the corners of his eyes gave him a kindly, almost saintlike aspect.

And what was Sandeman, if not a saint?

Sandeman's eyes popped open. "What are you staring at?" His voice was rusty with disuse.

Merrick grinned.

"Help me sit up."

Merrick did, his grin fading as he felt the thinness of the phage's arms. Since Sandeman had first entered the vault last year, his muscles had slowly wasted away, leaving the sharp edges of tendon and bone. How much longer would he be able to move? Merrick remembered the wiry but strong Sandeman of a year ago, a hundred years ago, three hundred. Always an elegant dresser. Hanging out with another phage whenever he could. An agreeable, learned man who wanted desperately to stop himself from killing but could not.

And so, by his own choice, the vault now did it for him. He, alone, among all the phages, was here of his own will.

Sandeman eyed him. "What's so awful," he asked, "aside from what you're looking at?"

Merrick pulled a folding chair over to the bedside and sat down. He told Sandeman about the cathedral murder—the hemophage blood found on the victim. Sandeman listened, eyes closed, then said, "So now your Katie might discover us. I told you it was *byezumnay* to fall in love with a blood doctor."

Crazy. Merrick remembered that Russia was the last place Sandeman had lived before the vault—five years outside Moscow and Leningrad, feeding from the throats of former KGB interrogators. Merrick couldn't recall exactly when he, himself, had learned that particular language. He said, "Katie would have been called in whether I knew her or not."

"What an uproar it could cause if we were discovered," Sandeman murmured. "I'm past being threatened by anything, and yet it chills me. But tell me, my friend, why would *you* care? If our fellow humans without the gene learn about us, they'll hunt hemophages down and destroy them—which is exactly what you've been doing."

"I hunt them only if they kill."

"All hemophages kill."

"You don't. I don't."

"We're the only ones."

"You don't know that. There may be others. What I do know is that we are not animals. We can control ourselves. It's what we *do* that counts, not what we 'are.' " Merrick's face began to burn with indignation. "I can think of nothing more monstrous than hunting down and exterminating a whole race purely because they were born with a certain gene—"

Sandeman held up a hand. "On that we agree, my friend. The history of normals is tainted with that very crime. If they ever found out about us, they'd be so terrified they'd bury you with all the rest, and nothing could be more unjust."

A familiar foreboding touched Merrick. Even if normals didn't manage to catch and bury him, he'd be a pariah, living out his centuries alone. It was his worst nightmare.

"The killing at the cathedral," Sandeman said. "Something else is bothering you about it."

Merrick wondered what he would do without this dying man, so perceptive, so different from the others in the vault. The one soul in all the world I can talk to, Merrick thought. He said, "The killer smeared his victim's blood on one of the cathedral gargoyles."

Sandeman's eyes widened.

"If I hadn't removed it, and Byner or his technicians had seen that blood and matched it to the victim, it could have caused quite a stir. The gargoyle is at least fifty feet up, well beyond the reach of the tallest ladder an ordinary man could carry around with him. And what kind of killer would want to be encumbered by a ladder?"

"Do you think he did it to toy with the police?"

"Not likely," Merrick said. "I've never encountered a hemophage who feels the need to show himself superior to a nonphage. None of us craves discovery."

"Why, then?"

"I think he left the blood for me to see. I think he was challenging me."

"So do I."

Merrick's neck prickled with a powerful sense of menace. He had not expected Sandeman to agree so quickly. "If I'm right, the killer is not just any hemophage. He is a phage with a personal grudge against me. He hates me."

"*Nyeudacha!*" Sandeman's face tightened. "Zane."

"Yes."

"But didn't you run him out of Washington ten years ago?"

"Twelve. I was living in San Francisco, but when I saw the story in the *Chronicle*—VAMPIRE KILLER TERRORIZES NATION'S CAPITAL—I moved to DC. I got close enough to see him then. It was Zane, I'm sure of it. But, as always, he ran before I could—"

A sudden, muffled scream penetrated the room, stopping the words in Merrick's throat, raising the hackles on his neck. The scream went on and on, undulating, fading, then renewing itself. The rage in the cry set Merrick's nerves on edge. He found Sandeman looking at him with an opaque expression. Then Sandeman closed his eyes and took a deep breath.

"Is that—"

Sandeman raised a hand, cutting him off. His eyes remained closed. Merrick wondered if there was much screaming down here. However much there might be, it could not begin to compare with the screams these prisoners had stopped in the throats of their innocent victims.

Still, how awful for Sandeman.

Merrick studied the other phage. His face seemed stiff with concentration. Abruptly, the scream ended. Sandeman sat motionless a moment longer, then opened his eyes.

Merrick started to say something, but Sandeman cut in. "If Zane has returned, you have my sympathy. But you didn't come here for that."

Realizing Sandeman did not want to talk about the scream, Merrick said, "I need your help. You know Zane better than I."

Sandeman's gaze slid away. He looked uncomfortable. Why? Merrick wondered. Sandeman fumbled up a leather-bound volume at the foot of his bed and paged through it with a trembling finger. Merrick read the gold embossed title: *Crime and Punishment*. Sandeman's sudden interest in the book seemed feigned. Merrick said, "If you could just—"

"I really don't know Zane that well," Sandeman said. "Our

paths crossed now and again over the years, that's all.''

"I only need the answers to two questions."

Sandeman put the book down. "If I can."

"Do you think Zane knows I'm still here in Washington?"

"Yes. I gathered that he always keeps track of where you are."

Merrick shook his head, perplexed. "Then why on earth would he come back?"

"Because something has happened to make him believe he can defeat you."

A chill ran up Merrick's spine. Zane was very powerful, very capable. But he had always run. No, it didn't make sense. "You're just guessing, right?"

Sandeman's face remained grim. "I last saw Zane a little over a year ago, in Leningrad, shortly before I came to you and asked to be put here. He was working on something—a new weapon, he called it."

Merrick's unease deepened. But he said, "Does he think he can shoot me with a silver bullet?"

Sandeman gave him the barest of smiles. "At the time, I assumed he meant a weapon against normals. If he had anything that would kill one of *us* quicker than this room, I'd have begged him to use it on me."

The longing on the other phage's voice pained Merrick. Quickly he asked, "Did Zane describe this 'weapon'?"

"He wouldn't say much, but I gathered it involved Influence."

Merrick frowned. *Influence*—the term phages used for their inborn ability to regulate blood flow in their victims. That ability, together with great muscular strength and cells that repaired themselves almost at once from injury or aging were the three biologic pillars of hemophagia. Remove them and, except for extra-keen senses, you'd have a normal human, in terms of ability. But the capacity to Influence blood seemed to be limited to the capillaries of the retina, vessels in the brain stem, and the constriction or dilation of major veins and arteries. All phages knew how to do it—and how to fend it off.

Merrick shook his head. "Even if Zane has learned to increase his powers, Influencing normals is not the same as Influencing another phage."

"Not the same," Sandeman agreed. "But Zane may have learned to do it."

"Not to me."

"How can you be so confident?"

Merrick did not answer.

Sandeman studied him for a moment, then said, "One of my phage friends told me a story a few years ago—right after the Russian Revolution I think it was. About how the *ubeytsa* Merrick hunted down and buried fifteen phages at one time."

Assassin. The irony of it made Merrick grunt. *"They* were hunting *me."*

"Then it's true," Sandeman whispered.

Merrick felt strangely uncomfortable. He had never told the story to anyone. Who was there to tell? The ones he needed to know, all knew it. He said, "There were ten of them, not fifteen. They banded together to try and take me out."

"And you defeated them all."

"Not all. Nine of them. And not all at once, either. They made a mistake. They knew that, between them, they had more than enough strength to overcome and bury me. Of course, ten phages in close proximity create an aura so powerful even normals can sense it. They knew I would feel them coming, that I could sense them and they couldn't sense me, but they didn't realize what an edge that gave me. They were confident as a pride of lions on the prowl. But as long as they stayed together, I never let them close. After awhile, they were forced to split up to increase their chances of finding me. Then I went after them. I was able to pick them off, one by one, and bury them. When only three were left, they gave it up and fled. Within the next few years, I tracked down two of those."

Sandeman swallowed. "And the other?"

Reluctant, Merrick did not answer.

"You let the last one go so he would spread the word," Sandeman said with dawning recognition. He looked away, and there was fear in his eyes. Merrick felt a sorrow so sharp he could not speak for a moment—the one friend in all the world who could understand, and instead it terrified him. "They *were* out to destroy me, Sandeman."

"Because they knew you would try to destroy them."

"That's different. They were all killers."

"They were predators, doing what nature intended."

With an effort, Merrick controlled his exasperation. "Nature doesn't *intend* anything. Nature just is. It has no morals, no special plan for the human race, hemophage or otherwise. All of us have to decide what we will be and to hell with nature."

"You make it sound so easy," Sandeman said softly. "I

tried, God, how I tried—no, *look* at me, Merrick! I believe, just as you do, that it is wrong to kill another human being. I fought it, so very hard. You fight it, too, don't you, even now? Every time you draw their blood you hunger to kill them, but somehow you don't. You fight and you win. The rest of us aren't as strong as you. Not me, and not Zane.''

Merrick shook his head. ''Sandeman, you are *stronger* than me. You are *dying* to save them. And don't compare yourself to Zane. He has known about transfusion since it came into common use with normals, and he kept right on killing.''

''Would you feel differently if you knew he had tried to stop?''

Merrick looked at Sandeman, feeling a stir of hope. ''Did he? Do you know?''

Feebly, Sandeman raised a hand. ''No. I'm sorry, I didn't mean to give that impression. I don't know—one way or the other.''

The quick denial left Merrick deflated. ''Zane loves killing,'' he said bitterly. ''Why would he try to stop?''

''For you, perhaps.''

Merrick gave a harsh, disbelieving laugh. ''He hates me.''

''And how do you feel about him?''

''How I feel is irrelevant. He has murdered thousands of people. If I don't stop him, he'll murder thousands more.''

Sandeman sighed. ''There are over five billion people on this planet. Mankind did away with the last saber-toothed tiger thousands of years ago. Two million people starved to death in the Sudan last year. You don't have to kill, and I don't have to kill—now that I'm locked away in here—but maybe someone *does* have to kill.''

''Not around me.''

Sandeman gave a frustrated grunt. ''Ah, Merrick, Merrick. You're a strange one all right, a wolf who guards the sheep. Damn it, you crazy bastard, why does that make me want to swear and hug you at the same time?''

Merrick grinned, and Sandeman broke down briefly with a pained smile of his own. ''Do you know why you do it, Merrick? Why you keep hunting them down and killing them?''

Merrick's grin faded. ''Yes. And if you are my friend, you will say no more about it.''

''You know I am your friend,'' Sandeman said softly.

Merrick's flash of anger faded and he touched Sandeman's withered arm in apology.

Sandeman cleared his throat. "All right. What will you do about Zane, then?"

"Find him—as quickly as possible."

"And if he is hunting you, too?"

"That would be a mistake. As you say, for five hundred years I've hunted the hunters. None has ever beaten me."

"Except Zane," Sandeman murmured.

Merrick stared at him.

"He's evaded you," Sandeman explained. "Time and again. Has any other phage you hunted done that?"

"No," Merrick admitted.

Sandeman closed his eyes. For a moment he said nothing. "Why do you think he is always able to slip away from you?"

A pain welled up at the base of Merrick's throat, driven by a deeper ache, the old love of Zane throbbing suddenly in his chest like a second heart, dense and black. How many people had died because of that love?

Needing to move, Merrick got up and paced the small cell. It only made him feel more trapped. Zane, empowered by new skills, back to challenge him—it was possible. Such a Zane might indeed be a real threat. I won't be able to sense a lone phage coming, Merrick thought. I'll have to depend on my eyes, nose, and ears. Under the right circumstances, Zane could be three feet away before I knew it. Then everything will come down to what this new skill is—if, in fact, it exists. Might Sandeman know more about it, something he hasn't told me yet?

Turning back to the other phage, Merrick saw that he had slumped back against the wall, asleep or unconscious. He's so weak, Merrick thought with dismay. If he's right about Zane, I'll need him more than ever before—his wisdom, his moral support. But he is fading.

And then I will be alone.

Merrick eased his friend down onto his cot, lifted his head and slid the pillow under. As he straightened, Sandeman's eyes opened and he caught Merrick's wrist in a feeble but determined grip. "I'm glad you came to me," he murmured. "Before you go, one thing more: Whether Zane has a new weapon or not, he is no ordinary phage. Never forget he was born with one very important edge none of the other 'hunters' have had. You for a father."

FIVE

KATIE FELT A vague uneasiness as she waited for the elevator in the hospital lobby. She wished someone else was around. Even at 5:00 A.M., there were usually a few people taking a break on the lobby sofa—family members keeping a vigil for a loved one in ICU or the emergency room.

Katie eased her grip on the cold pack. It was not heavy, and yet the killer's blood had a psychological weight of its own. She realized suddenly that she'd been jumpy ever since she'd taken the pack home last night. First her fears about Gregory and later the nightmare. She shuddered, seeing again the image that had jerked her awake. A man with red teeth—

"I don't believe this! You beat me in again."

Startled, Katie turned. "Meggan!"

Meggan Shields, MD, FACS, looked her usual gorgeous self, long blonde hair carefully brushed, just the right shade of lipstick, perfect makeup. Katie wondered why she bothered on work days. In a few minutes, that beautiful hair would be pinned up under a surgical cap as she cut into someone's ear, nose, or throat. The only part of Meggan's face people would see for most of the morning was her eyes.

Meggan pushed the Up button. "What if Admin hears a hematologist is beating their surgeons in to work?"

"Maybe they'll start diverting some of your exorbitant salaries to us."

Meggan brightened. "That reminds me. Have I got a guy for you—"

"Wait," Katie said with a laugh. "How could your exorbitant salary remind you you've got a guy for me?"

"Because this guy probably doesn't *have* an exorbitant salary. He works on Capitol Hill for Senator Mikulski, and staffers work as much for glory as for cash. We just met him last night. Wolves at the Door was on video at The Tombs and he was alone at the next table. His name is Myron Lane."

"Myron?"

"Don't laugh. The guy's got a smile like Harrison Ford and he didn't once talk politics. He likes—get this—*Rachmaninoff!*"

"Don't you mean Rock-maninoff?"

"He wasn't even watching the video," Meggan protested. "He was only there so he could meet a nice hematologist."

"No doubt." Katie listened to the distant clack of the elevator cables, wishing the doors would open.

"How about just saying hello to him a week from this Saturday night," Meggan suggested. "We're having a party to christen our new house—actually our exceedingly old house—in Fairfax. You'd like Myron, I promise. No ponytails, no little round glasses. Looks like he plays rugby."

"Rugby and Rachmaninoff," Katie said.

Meggan sighed.

Katie realized how sour she'd sounded. "Sorry."

"No, no. I'm being a pest, I know."

"You're not a pest. I appreciate it, but I just don't have time to think about men right now."

Meggan gave her a shrewd look. "You ever see Merrick anymore?"

Katie hesitated. If she mentioned last night, she'd never shake loose. "Now and then."

"But not to date."

"Don't worry about me. I've dated plenty since Merrick."

Meggan frowned thoughtfully. "Hmmm, plenty . . . have I met him?"

"Cute." Katie aimed her index finger at Meggan and dropped the hammer.

Meggan smiled, then grew serious. "I know you're not over Merrick. But Katie, there are only two choices: Go back to him or forget him. Decide and do it. More than two years is a long time to go without love."

"You make it sound so simple."

Meggan shrugged, patted Katie's shoulder. "So whatcha got in the cold pack?"

"Blood, what else?"

Meggan laughed. "What a team. I spill it and you chill it." The elevator doors rattled open.

"I'm going down," Katie said.

"So. Will we see you a week from Saturday night?"

"I'll let you know."

Meggan made a face as the doors closed.

As Katie walked away from the elevator in the basement, Meggan's advice circled in her mind. Decide and do it. How like a surgeon. Whereas, Katie thought, I put things on glass and study them. Maybe I've studied this one long enough. Meggan's wrong—actually, there's only one choice: Forget Merrick and move on. I can. And I will.

As soon as I've finished working with him on this case.

Unlocking the door to her lab, she stepped into its cool silence. The thermostat and light controls were still on their night setting. She stood a moment, savoring the faint, clean tang of bleach that rose from the spotless black lab benches. Byner was right, in addition to the hospital's regular hematology lab, Georgetown did have one of the better blood research labs in the region. As the newly minted chief of Hematology, she had control of this lab and the smaller electron microscopy chamber next door. No one else was scheduled to run any research projects here in the next two weeks, so she'd have the place all to herself. In these two rooms, she was confident she would unlock the mystery of the cells.

All she had to do was find the time.

Katie locked the cold pack away in the cooler, picked up the wall phone, and dialed Three East to ask for Art Stratton.

"He's in his on-call room," the nurse said. "We made him knock off for an hour's sleep. I never saw any resident work so hard."

Katie thanked her and hung up. Clearly, the nurses liked Art—not only were they letting him get some sleep, they were defending it to his supervisor. Katie was pleased to see that Art was mastering the task of making a hundred decisions an hour without treading on the toes of the nursing staff. Art's laid-back California style no doubt helped, and it didn't hurt that he resembled the drop-dead handsome Dallas Cowboys quarterback, Troy Aikman.

Katie dialed Art's on-call room. As she waited through eight rings, she recalled the coma-like sleep of her own residency. You never got a full night. You passed out for a few minutes whenever you could, sinking like a stone, deeper than dreams. Waking up was like trying to raise yourself from the dead. . . .

Katie felt a momentary clamor in her veins, a ghost of the old amphetamine hunger. As foolish as it had been to take the pills, she had never again felt so awake, so aware as she had those few months during her residency. A lot of residents made the mistake; she hoped Art would not be one of them. If you never started, you would never miss it—the powerful, super-alert feeling, the bright, sharp edge on everything you looked at, the confidence, the utter certainty that you could handle whatever came your way.

"Stratton," mumbled a voice ragged with fatigue.

"Sorry to wake you, Art. But I need your help with something this afternoon, which means you'll have to get rolling a little early."

There was a slight pause on the other end, and she knew he was struggling to remember who he was and why he was stretched out on a narrow bed in a closet-size room. She visualized him lying on his cot, head propped on an elbow, thick blond hair ruffled from sleep, those striking blue eyes still half dreamy—

"Okay, Katie, shoot."

"I've got some odd RBCs—I'll explain more later. I'm going to run some tests this afternoon, and I'll need your help with a library search."

"Sounds interesting."

"It is. Since you'll be doing the reading, I'd like you to be in on the testing. If we both gun it, we should be able to meet in the lab around three."

"Great!" Art sounded as if he really meant it. Evidently no one had told him that residents were supposed to act like martyrs when handed extra work.

"One more thing, Art—and this is very important. Don't mention this to anyone."

"Trying to beat someone into print?"

"Not exactly. I'll explain this afternoon." Katie started to hang up, then remembered herself in Art's place—twenty-six and going on seventy. "You up?" she asked.

"Yeah."

"Get out of bed and stand up, Art."

He laughed. "Okay. I'm standing. Good-bye."

Back on Three East, Katie went to check on her two most perplexing cases, Jenny Hrluska and Rebecca Trent. Jenny appeared about the same as yesterday evening—achy joints, no more nosebleeds, but still reporting the strange hunger. Discouraged, Katie headed for Rebecca Trent's room. Rebecca was sitting on her bed, bent over in such concentration that she did not look up. Katie saw that she was painting her fingernails a bright red. Rebecca's nails were brittle and furrowed with age. She was very small and thin, with gray hair, wrinkles, and an osteoporotic hunch. What concerned Katie even more were the things no one could see—severe atherosclerosis and early stage kidney failure. Looking at her, Katie had to remind herself that Rebecca was only nine. She would die of old age before she could reach her teens, killed by progeria, a disease as vicious and baffling as it was rare.

"Pretty sporty," Katie said.

Rebecca still did not look up from her nails, and Katie remembered that she was beginning to suffer hearing loss. She said it again, louder.

Rebecca looked up with the stiff-necked care of the old. Her smile made the round, wrinkled face beautiful. "I thought they needed a bit of color," she said.

"I like it—it looks like bluuuud."

Rebecca gave a raspy giggle. "So how's the latest rat?"

"I'll have to check with Doctor Stratton, but as of yesterday, no change."

Rebecca sighed. "So much for Fraction Six."

"Maybe not. There's still time." Katie kept her voice bright, knowing that Rebecca was more than disappointed. A smart child, she understood the experimental strategy very well, and each time a new serum fraction was extracted from her blood, her hopes rose. She knew that if the rat receiving the injection showed signs of rapid aging, it would be a first step toward understanding just what caused the rare and terrible disease that was killing her on fast-forward.

"So you going to try again?"

Katie went to her, giving the hunched shoulder a light squeeze. "That's why I'm here."

"Aiieee," Rebecca said. "The needle again." But she smiled, clearly fighting to keep her spirits up.

"You want to call the vampires or shall I?" Katie asked.

"I'll do it," Rebecca said. She pushed her call button and spoke into the intercom and, a moment later, a nurse bustled in and drew off ten milliliters of blood.

Katie walked the sample down to Hematology for centrifuging. As she handed it over to the tech, she tried to muster some optimism, but it was getting harder and harder. Age was ravaging every cell in Rebecca's body. A defective gene was no doubt the initial cause. But just as surely, Rebecca's blood was involved. Blood washed past every cell, pouring in nutrients and carrying out waste. It was the body's river of life—and death.

Katie was convinced that somewhere in that great river were clues to what was killing Rebecca—perhaps the lethal agent itself. Proving it was devilishly difficult. If she had been able to inject a rat with Rebecca's whole blood, and it caused rapid aging, it would prove she was on the right track, even if she wouldn't know which factor in the blood was responsible. Unfortunately, injections of whole blood into rats, even from a healthy person, caused immediate toxic effects so pronounced they'd mask any aging effects. So instead, Katie had to go through a laborious, multistep process. First she would extract a biochemically simple fraction from healthy blood and make sure it caused no toxic effects when injected in a rat. Then she would extract the same simple fraction from Rebecca's blood and inject it into another rat. She would monitor the rat for ten days. If nothing happened in the first two days, she would start the process over again with a different rat. Even running fractions concurrently, it was a slow, time-consuming process. So far, she had investigated six different fractions of Rebecca's blood.

Maybe this seventh one would be the charm. What a fantastic breakthrough that would be. Then she could try to modify a dialysis machine to filter Fraction Seven out of Rebecca's blood.

Walking back from the lab, Katie wondered for the hundredth time whether she should be spending so much time and energy on progeria. The condition was so rare that most doctors went their whole careers without seeing a single case of it. Maybe

she should be looking for a cure of aplastic anemia or acute mye-
logenous leukemia instead—diseases that claimed tens of
thousands more lives than progeria. . . .

But when she thought of Rebecca sitting on her bed, a sweet
old lady of nine, fighting the marks of age the only way she knew
how—with red nail polish—Katie felt a surge of determination.
Rebecca is not going to die, she thought stubbornly. Not if I can
help it.

By the time Katie finally got to the research lab, it was nearly
four. Art was sitting with his feet up. He looked pointedly at his
watch.

"You just ran down the stairs," she said.

He gave her a mystified frown. "How did you know?"

"Aside from the fact that you're struggling not to pant, if
you'd been here more than five minutes, you'd be asleep."

"As usual, Holmes, you amaze me."

"Thank you, Doctor Watson."

Art gave her his lazy, half-lidded smile and it occurred to
her that he never looked tired because his eyelids were seldom
more than half open anyway. The relaxed look was an asset in
dealing with edgy patients—as long as he didn't learn to actually
sleep with his eyes open. She'd seen residents do it; had done it
herself—until the amphetamines.

"So what's the big secret?" Art asked.

Katie told him. By the time she'd finished, he was sitting up
straight, a fascinated expression on his face. "Blood cells that can
lie out in the open for days without deteriorating. This I've got
to see."

"And so you shall." Taking the cold pack from the lab
refrigerator, Katie was relieved to feel none of the unease that
had plagued her earlier; instead, an eager anticipation filled her.
A little detective work suited her mood exactly.

"So what's the plan?" Art asked.

"The police are hoping these RBCs will lead to some edu-
cated guesses about the killer's background," she said, "where
he came from, what he might have been exposed to, things like
that. We've got to keep that in mind and not get too carried away
on the cells themselves. But for starters, we do need to find out
as much as we can about them. I'm especially interested in the
platelets. Doctor Byner didn't find any trace of them or of any

other clotting factors, but I find it hard to believe that the killer's blood doesn't clot.''

"No kidding. So we run a complete blood count first?"

"Right. And then an IE to look for any weird proteins." She picked up a slide with some of the blood cells Byner had taken from the smear on the victim's shoulder. Carefully, she dribbled Isoton III solution across the slide, rinsing the cells down through a glass funnel into the five-milliliter tube, then fitted the small test tube up under the pipette that dangled at the center of the CBC analyzer. The machine hummed and clicked as it sucked up the suspension of RBCs and sped it from station to station through plastic tubes deployed across its front.

"Watching this thing work," Art said, "is enough to make you give up eating spaghetti."

The way the thin plastic tubes twisted and turned did resemble stray strands of pasta on a big silver platter. "More like vermicelli, I'd say," she offered, "with the red sauce inside instead of out."

The machine's CRT screen winked, a smear of green on black, then began displaying information. Katie leaned forward. Data began to march in orderly rows down the monitor screen. She scanned down the list to platelets.

The count was zero.

Katie felt again the consternation of last night. A killer whose blood did not clot had bled—but only a little.

"Unbelievable," Art whispered. "And look at the hemoglobin."

Katie saw with a jolt that the value for hemoglobin was also zero. "That's impossible," she said. "There's got to be hemoglobin. That's one of the main reasons for having red blood cells—to get oxygen to the body cells."

"Maybe the machine's run out of lysing agent," Art suggested.

"I topped it up yesterday. The lysing agent didn't work. It didn't break up the cells."

"Katie, you're talking about ammonium salt and potassium cyanide."

"Okay, but it's also true that these cells still look fresh after four days with no preservative. That implies something is protecting them."

"Maybe it's that extra membrane you thought you saw in Byner's lab," Art said. "But what kind of membrane could hold off a lysing agent?"

"I don't know."

"Let's look at it under the electron microscope."

"I was going to run some protein tests first," Katie said, "but you're right. Before we do anything else, we need a better look at that cell wall."

It took her only a moment to isolate a few RBCs on another slide. Entering the dim room that housed the university's electron microscope, Katie felt for the switch. The fluorescents flickered on, revealing the scope's huge central shaft that reached up almost to the ceiling. Its rings, controls, and viewing port made it look like a massive sculpture, something alien and powerful, a metallic totem pole left by some advanced race. The scope could make even an infinitesimal virus look huge. If there was an extra membrane on these RBCs, the scope would show it.

Art transferred the RBCs onto the scope's slide—actually a small, thin grid made of gold. Eager to see the cells, Katie decided she would try them without staining them, first. Inserting the grid through an air lock into the microscope's vacuum chamber, she hit the switch that powered the scope. With a soft hum, the gun at the top of the scope poured a thousand-kilovolt stream of electrons down through condensing lenses and then the RBCs. Bending over the leaded glass eyepiece near the bottom of the scope, Katie looked into a world measured in billionths of an inch. The fluorescent screen triggered the usual slight itch in her eyes. Two red blood cells sat near the center of the viewing field, looking big as balloons—

And there it was—a dense, perfectly smooth membrane around each cell!

"What?" Art said, and she realized she'd sucked in a breath. No red blood cell she had ever seen possessed such a membrane. Where had it come from? What was it composed of?

She moved aside for Art to take a look.

"Christ!" He stepped back and stared at her. His eyes were all the way open.

Reclaiming the eyepiece, she stared at the membrane. She wished the scope could give her color, but the wavelength of electrons was too much shorter than visible light, showing the membrane as a black ring around the grayish mass of the cell. It looked totally solid, but she knew it must be selectively permeable, or the RBCs wouldn't be able to pick up wastes or release nutrients and oxygen into the body cells. As she watched the membrane, Katie saw with surprise that it was starting to change. "It's getting thinner," she exclaimed, "and darker."

"The electron beam is killing it," Art said.

"I don't think so."

Astonished, Katie watched the cells for another two minutes. They remained round, showing no sign of rupture. The darkening of the membrane suggested that it had just grown denser, probably in response to the onslaught of electrons. "Incredible," she said. She straightened and looked at Art.

He took her hands, grinning. "Incredible is right. You're going to be famous."

"Art! I told you, we can't talk about this to anyone."

"I understand, but Katie, you know this will have to come out eventually, and you'll be the one who discovered it. . . ."

As he went on talking, the pressure of his fingers began to register. Her hands felt suddenly warm where he was holding them. Gently, she pulled them free. Her mind spun with excitement. Art was right—they had just made a stupendous discovery. The membrane had to be a complex protein produced by a gene. Either it was a normal gene or one that had been altered in some way. If the gene was normal, it must be extremely rare or blood cells like this would have turned up before now. There were an estimated hundred thousand human genes, and so far only a few had been identified. The other possibility was that the gene had been altered by something in the environment. Either way, these RBCs could only have come from one of a very few people on earth.

And the question is, Katie thought, how can I use this information to help Merrick find him?

Her unease returned in a rush. The man who'd shed this blood had killed a woman with his teeth. I want to help find him, she thought. But I don't want to see him. Not ever.

SIX

When Katie took the cells back into the research lab, she was startled to find Merrick waiting. Art started to say something about the lab being for authorized personnel only, but Katie caught his arm.

"Art, this is Detective Lieutenant Merrick Chapman. Merrick, Doctor Art Stratton." Watching the two men shake hands, Katie remembered how reluctant Merrick had been for anyone else to know about the cells. But he gave no sign of it now.

"Katie speaks highly of you," he said.

Art shot her a gratified look.

She put on her stern supervisor face. "Don't let it go to your head."

"So," Merrick went on, "what have you two found out?"

Katie told him. He listened intently. When she'd finished, he asked, "How does that help us find the killer?"

"The membrane might come from a mutated gene. A common cause of genetic mutation is radiation. There's a lot of literature on the subject." She turned to Art. "Check and see what types and dosages of radiation have caused changes—any changes—in RBC structure. Then cross-reference to date and location of nuclear reactor accidents. A long shot, but it could give us a lead."

Nodding, Art took a pad of paper from his lab coat and scribbled briefly. The silence stretched to the point of awkwardness. Merrick gazed at Katie. From the corner of her eye, she was aware of Art staring at Merrick.

"Got time for a cup of coffee?" Merrick asked.

Reasons why she shouldn't jostled each other in her mind, but she said, "Why not?"

Art cleared his throat. "Gotta run. Nice meeting you, Lieutenant."

"Likewise, Doctor." Merrick shook his hand again and watched him leave. "Seems like a smart young man," he said. "A shame he's so homely."

"Merrick," she said, amused, "he's my resident. Clinical supervisors do not allow the homeliness—or incredible hunkiness—of their supervisees to influence them in any way."

Merrick gave her a fleeting smile. "Aren't ethics a pain?"

Sitting across from Merrick in the sidewalk café, Katie was glad she'd agreed to come. Just because they weren't dating anymore didn't mean they couldn't have a cup of coffee together. She hadn't left work before five o'clock in weeks; it felt good to sit here on a balmy late afternoon doing nothing important. Sunshine slanted along the cobblestones of Q Street, making the old trolley rails gleam like hammered silver. A robin so fat it looked like a sweet potato with wings hopped along the strip between sidewalk and street, its cocked head surveying grass that was shedding its winter paleness for a hopeful green.

Katie realized that, even though she was very aware of Merrick, she was avoiding looking at him. Silly. Sipping her coffee, she appraised him over the rim of her cup. He was leaning back in his chair, his face tilted toward the sun. The breeze ruffled his thick brown hair. In his faded jeans, black T-shirt, and blazer he looked relaxed and carefree, like a man on vacation. Only the faint crease between his eyebrows told her he was troubled. By her report on the blood? Or by how little help it was?

Opening his eyes, he caught her gazing at him. He smiled, the wonderful dimpled smile she still saw sometimes when she closed her eyes in bed at night. Her answering smile felt awkward. It was just so strange to sit here with him. If this were three years ago, she'd lean across right now and kiss him.

But it wasn't three years ago.

Merrick leaned toward her, and for a second she thought he was giving in to the same impulse. But he did not kiss her. He said, "I want you to be very careful." His voice was so low she could barely hear him. She realized he was concerned about being overheard. She glanced around. The closest person was an old man three tables away, who was certainly out of earshot even if he wasn't hard of hearing.

But, to humor Merrick, she kept her own voice low. "What do you mean?"

"This is a very vicious killer," he murmured. "A psycho who thinks he's a vampire. Obviously, he's obsessed with blood. If he somehow found out you had some of his, there's no telling what he might do."

Katie remembered the spooky moment in her lab, her fear that sooner or later she might have to face the killer. A chill rippled over her skin. "How would he find out?"

"Three people can keep a secret—if two of them are dead. Four of us know this one, possibly more, if any of Byner's forensic technicians got wind of the cells before he showed them to us. Some killers are very adept at keeping track of their cases. They hang out at the precinct or at cop watering holes, eavesdropping on the gossip. If this killer finds out the police have his blood and have farmed it out to an expert, he could track you down." Merrick eyed her. "I don't suppose I could persuade you to turn the analysis over to another hematologist?"

Katie stared at him, indignant. "No, you could not. No one else can do more for you than Art and I will—"

"I don't question that—"

"Besides, what I saw in Byner's lab and again today under the electron microscope is fascinating beyond anything I could have imagined. I feel the way Antonie van Leeuwenhoek must have when he became the first human to actually see a bacterium. There's no way I'm letting anyone take this away from me."

Merrick leaned forward. "Even if it puts you in danger?"

Katie studied him. "Why are you trying to scare me?"

"Because I care about you." He looked flustered, as though she'd backed him onto forbidden ground. Which, in a way, she had. Suddenly she was tired of the pretense, the burden of acting like they had not once been lovers.

"I still care for you, too," she said. "Let's not turn that into a barrier. Maybe we can't live together, but surely we can work together."

"Katie, damn it. . . ." He took a deep breath. "Yes, of course. We can work together."

"Good."

He stared off across the street again and she could sense his pain, mirroring her own. This was insane. She didn't just care for him, she loved him.

But their relationship had been doomed from the beginning by one inescapable obstacle: She wanted children, and Merrick did not. On that issue, there could be no compromise, no common ground. Even so, they had tried to find it. She could recite their countless agonized discussions from memory: *Katie, I won't have kids if I can't be there for them. And I can't. I put in long hours, lots of evenings and nights. I'm in homicide. What if I were killed?*

That doesn't stop other cops from having families. And you know you love kids—you can't stay away from the ones on my ward. Wouldn't you love one of your own?

The issue isn't what I love, but what's best for the child. . . .

Around and around they'd go, neither of them yielding, no way to satisfy both. Finally they'd accepted the inevitable, and tearfully ended the relationship. Two weeks later, she'd learned she was pregnant. Somewhere near the end of their affair, one of Merrick's condoms had failed him—and presented her with the precious gift of Gregory.

So now here they were, the three of them, in this strange wobbly orbit around each other. Every month Merrick sent her a check for Gregory's support, more than he could afford or she needed. He'd swoop in and visit his son, but always while she was at work. How that hurt. Yet, in a way it kept her hope alive, too. He seemed afraid that if he let the three of them come together, even for a few minutes, he wouldn't be able to pull away again. Why else would he refuse to let Gregory be told he was his father? It was as if the word *Daddy* from his son's mouth would break the last of his resolve.

And now, over the past few days, she'd seen that he still cared for her, more than cared. So why couldn't they all be together as a family? What was he so afraid of? There was something else, she felt sure. A reason he had never allowed into their discussions. Something with such power over him that it could make him give up everything he seemed to want. . . .

Katie felt a familiar frustration. Merrick *had* given her up, and that was that. Any further move had to be his. And she must stop waiting in the back of her mind and heart for it. She needed to make the final emotional break with Merrick and start some serious socializing with other men.

Something made Katie notice the old man sitting a few tables away, again. He seemed to be discreetly watching them. He was rather handsome, with thick white hair and a leathery, seamed face. In forty or so years, Merrick might look much like him. Will I still know Merrick then? Katie wondered.

She reached across and took Merrick's hand. The old man smiled and looked away reflectively, as if he might be remembering some old romance of his own.

"Do you still have the .357 magnum I gave you?" Merrick asked.

"Sure. Why?"

Pulling his hand away, he took something from his coat, a glossy green card, and she recognized the visitor's pass to the police firing range. "I want you to put in some practice time." He shoved the pass across the table.

"I do wish you'd stop trying to scare me."

"Promise me."

Katie had never seen him look so serious. She remembered her nightmare, the faceless man with red teeth. The slanting sunlight suddenly lost its warmth. She picked up the pass.

The old man watched Merrick and the woman talk, feeling a mixture of triumph and wariness at being so close to his father again. He'd outsmarted the old bastard—so far.

But what if Merrick took a closer look?

Zane's uneasiness deepened. Six months without blood had not only aged him—he hoped beyond recognition—it had weakened him. He'd be no match for Merrick in his present condition.

He sipped at his cappuccino, letting its heat soothe him. He was giving Father too much credit. Because of the blood on the gargoyle, Merrick knew the cathedral killer was a phage, and he must suspect the taunt had been left by his son. But he couldn't be sure. Theoretically, it could be any phage—they all had a reason to hate him. All knew how Merrick had dealt with the ones who had banded together to hunt him. No one knew where they were buried, but every phage could imagine what it would be like to be one of them—to lie under a ton of earth, dying ever so slowly from lack of blood. . . .

Shuddering, Zane blocked out the horrible image. We all hate Merrick, he thought, but we fear him even more, and he knows it. So if one of us finds the courage to taunt him, he must look for the one with the strongest hate. Even if he suspects it's me, what he cannot know is that I look old. He would never believe that I—or any phage—could have the discipline to tear that woman's throat and not drink the blood, much less to abstain for six months.

Zane smiled, thinking of the trick he'd pulled with the teeth. His smile faded as he remembered how perilously close he'd come to drinking anyway, even though it would have undone months of sacrifice and planning. The killing was the strongest part of the compulsion, but to do it without feeding was like chewing without swallowing. He still wasn't sure how he'd managed to hold back, to collect the blood in a basin and flush it away in a storm sewer. But he'd done it.

Zane felt a fierce pride. I'm as strong as you, now, Father. In fact, stronger—

He tensed as Merrick turned in his chair and glanced around the café. Merrick's eyes centered on him and Zane felt himself freeze. He looked down at the table, keeping utterly still. The aged skin and white hair that a moment ago had seemed such a foolproof disguise suddenly felt horribly transparent. A single movement could betray him—a turn of the hand, a way of tilting his head that he was unaware of, but that his father would recognize. Seconds crawled by. Unable to bear it any longer, Zane glanced up, and found that Merrick was no longer looking at him. He was talking to the woman again. A huge relief swept Zane, making him want to laugh. *He looked right at me and didn't know me.*

And I was afraid.

Zane's relief evaporated; he clenched his teeth with exasperation. He must do better than this. He had reacted not like a hunter, but like prey. Under the circumstances, not moving had been correct, but the fear must go. Fear poisoned the wits, paralyzed the muscles. Unless he could conquer it, he'd have no hope of taking Father. . . .

And such negative thoughts must be banished, too. Self-doubt was as dangerous as fear. I *am* strong, Zane thought. Strong enough not to drink and daring enough to smear her blood on the gargoyle. Looking like an old man, I could simply have sneaked quietly into town and watched Merrick all I liked. I'd have been the furthest thing from his mind. Instead, I stood up to the old monster and sent him a message.

Zane felt his confidence rise. I'm through running. I'm back. And this time, *I* will have the edge.

The woman laughed at something Merrick said. Zane felt a distracting tug of curiosity. She was pretty. What was her connection to the old bastard? Were she and Father just friends, or something more? A moment ago, she'd grasped his hand briefly, but that could mean affection, reassurance, even aggression. Zane wished suddenly that he could hear them, but they were speaking too softly, and the blood deprivation of the past six months had diminished his supernormal hearing to the point that it was barely better than a normal's. Though their faces were close, they seemed tense. Again, ambiguous. They could be whispering endearments or arguing, keeping their voices low because they didn't want to make a scene.

There's too much I don't know about normals. All I've ever needed to know was how to get them alone.

Zane watched Merrick and the woman, focusing on their interaction. Father was leaning back in his chair, listening to her. His eyes never left her face. There was a strange intensity there. He does find her attractive, Zane decided. At the very least, they know each other well.

Might he even be in love with her?

Zane felt an anger so intense that it brought a strangling pain to his throat. Love, oh yes, *love,* the heart of Father's delusion, the soul of his treachery—especially romantic love. Century after century, he kept falling for normal females. Giving himself heart and soul to a woman was the chief reason Father had turned against his own kind. How could he imagine himself loving one of these sheep while he hunted his own kind? Judas, Zane thought. A king among phages. You should be the greatest, most terrifying predator the world has ever known. Instead, you pervert yourself and betray your own kind.

Zane watched as Merrick motioned the waitress over, paid for the coffees, and walked the woman out of the café. The couple headed back up the street toward where they'd parked. Zane dropped a five on his table and strolled to his own car, across from the café. No need to hurry—the street was one-way and they would have to pass him. He got into the rented Nissan, started the engine, and then watched the rearview mirror until

Merrick's unmarked cruiser drove past. Pulling out, he followed them. Would Merrick take the woman home with him now?

No, he was turning back off Wisconsin into the residential section of Georgetown. After only a few blocks, Merrick stopped in front of a two-story brick house with a small front yard and a larger, fenced backyard full of tall, skeletal oaks and smaller, budding maples. Merrick walked the woman up to her door, gave her a quick kiss on the cheek, then headed back for his car.

Decision time: Go on following Father or stay here and try to learn more about the woman? The kiss lingered in Zane's mind. Quick, but hardly perfunctory. I know where Merrick lives, Zane thought. I can pick up on him there, later.

Zane watched Merrick's car pull away. He sat in the deepening shadows, while the streetlights came on and the alleys between the houses sank into darkness. He waited patiently until ten-thirty, then got out and scanned the close-set houses, glancing at each lighted window. He could see no one looking out at him. Slipping between the woman's house and the one next door, he circled into her backyard where the thick trunk of an oak tree gave him good cover. A quick survey of the back wall revealed an open upstairs window. And the house was brick.

Zane smiled. What could be easier?

He started up the wall, hooking his fingertips and toes into the mortar seams with practiced ease. But after only a few feet, he felt strain in his arms. Cursing his weakness, he labored up the wall, taking it slowly. By the time he reached the window, he was sweating.

He crawled through into a bathroom—black-and-white tiles, cracked in places, a small sink, the smell of soap and wet towels. The woman must have taken a shower. Zane held a towel against his face, smelling her, a pleasant fragrance, like clover. He ran his hand along the shower curtain draped inside the tub. Tiger lilies marched across the plastic. A drip pinged steadily against the drain. The humid, intimate warmth of the room charmed him and he decided to wait here a moment and listen. Faint sounds came from below. Two women talking. The voices stayed in one place. He could look around.

Outside the bathroom, down a narrow, dim hall, the first door he came to was open. Inside he found a small den dominated by a rolltop desk strewn with papers. Hanging on the wall were several framed certificates—a medical degree and, next to it, a board certification: Dr. Mary Katherine O'Keefe—

Hematologist?

Zane stared at the document, astonished. This made no sense at all. Why would Merrick have anything to do with a blood doctor?

As long as he doesn't bleed into her hanky, Zane thought, he's in no danger from her. All the same, why take even that small risk? Maybe they have a professional relationship—homicide cop, blood expert. That would make sense. But does it explain them being in the café together?

As Zane turned to look around the room, a floorboard creaked under his foot. Holding still, he listened. Downstairs, the murmur of voices stopped. Footsteps climbed the stairs. With a silent curse, Zane backed across the room, easing his feet along the old floorboards, flattening himself against the wall. A woman appeared in the doorway, not the doctor, older. Smartly dressed, strong Gallic features. Zane watched her eyes, constricting the retinal capillaries precisely where his image fell. Her gaze swept over him, hesitated, and returned with a blink. Zane felt a slight uneasiness, then reminded himself that only another hemophage could detect and defeat Influence. Normals might experience blurred vision or a momentary blank spot while the brain struggled to fill in with surrounding context, but they had no way to know what was really happening to them. He was a bit off his form these days, that was all. As soon as he'd fed again. . . .

The woman shrugged and backed out of the room. Zane held still until she'd returned downstairs. So wary—it might have been amusing to let her see him. But he was not here to play games, he was here to learn about this friend of Father's, this blood doctor.

Zane slipped down the hall into what looked like the master bedroom. By its smell, he could tell it was the doctor's. Settling into a wing-backed chair in one corner, he surveyed the room, trying to get a feel for her. There were girlish touches—flouncy lace at the window and a pink carnival-prize bunny on a shelf. But the bedspread was a sensible, quilted blue and the walls a plain cream color—no flowery wallpaper for the doctor. The room was neat, but not obsessively so. Her makeup table held a hairbrush and a few bottles of the mysterious ointments women put on their faces. He had never been in a woman's bedroom with so few bottles. Apparently, this woman did not linger over her appearance.

Something about the bed caught his eye—pillows only on one side. Interesting. She slept alone and did not care to pretend otherwise to herself.

Zane heard footsteps on the stairs again, this time a lighter tread. The bedroom door opened and the doctor walked in. He felt a light charge of curiosity. What did this one do when she thought she was alone? Talk to the pink bunny? Turn the radio on and pretend to conduct the orchestra? Zane readied himself to rise from the chair in case she came close enough to bump into him, but she did not. She slipped out of her bathrobe with the economical movements of the weary. Her gaze idly swept the room, passing over him without even a flicker of hesitation.

She was wearing only panties and the sight of her body began to arouse Zane. She was a splendid-looking woman—slender and pale, with long, graceful legs. Her breasts were small and perfect, with no hint of sag. He could see a faint tracery of veins on them, could sense the easy, sweet slide of blood through them. Excited, he rose and slipped across the room until he was close enough to touch her.

Turning away from him, she sat down at her dresser and began to brush her hair, releasing its slight oily scent to him. The smell was oddly carnal. Each brush stroke briefly revealed the long, slim column of her throat, the vein pulsing there. His sexual desire began to fade under another, darker, lust. Involuntarily, his lips drew back from his teeth and he felt himself leaning toward her.

Again, as if by instinct, she moved suddenly away from him, rising and padding into the bathroom. He used the moment to try and regain control of himself. He must not feed, not yet. But even now, with her in another room, he was too aware of her. His blood sang in his ears as he listened to the familiar sound of a woman brushing her teeth. Ah, now she was coming back to him.

Zane stepped back as the woman pulled on her nightgown and crawled into bed, dropping against the pillows like a stone. The loose way she fell back triggered a hundred images in his mind, a hundred women falling back as he cut off the blood to their brains. The images, so deeply ingrained in his brain, inflamed him, pulling him into the familiar, lethal cycle. He found himself leaning over her, gazing at her throat. His own throat ached with hunger. He could smell her blood.

He wanted it.

Closing his eyes, he tried to think of something else.

And then he was leaning down, his teeth inches from her smooth throat—

NO! YOU MUST NOT FEED YET!

Zane reared back, clenching his teeth. The woman started to

stir awake and he dilated her jugulars, throwing her back into sleep. Desperately, he put a hand on her breast, feeling its warmth, the slight, unconscious hardening of the nipple. His lust to kill her faltered for just a second, interrupted by a flash of sexual desire. It freed him just enough. At once, he fled.

His hands shook as he lowered himself out the bathroom window. The need to hurry drove him; he wanted to drop to the ground, only two stories, but he wasn't sure his bones would bear up in their depleted state. Climbing down the wall, he almost lost his grip on the mortar seams and fell. He dropped the last ten feet to the grass, staggered up and ran to his Nissan. He slumped in the seat, panting, feeling his heart pound. That was too close. He'd almost fed, and he must not—not until he'd finished stalking Merrick, memorized his habits and patterns, identified his weak spots.

Zane looked up at the woman's bedroom window. He hated her suddenly, for being unattainable, even for a night. *Do* you love her, Father? If you do, I'll make you—and her—sorry.

Katie gasped and sat up, blinking in the dark bedroom. *What was it?* A nightmare? But she could remember nothing. Feeling a tingle in her breast, she touched the nipple. It was hard. Suddenly she was aware of the smell of sweat. But she was not perspiring. Fear surged in her, making her heart pound against the mattress.

She got up, pulled on her robe, and went to the window. Below, a car sat at the curb under the streetlight. In the bright flow of light she could see the steering wheel and a man's legs. As she watched, hands, heavily veined and grooved with tendons, reached up and gripped the wheel. Just an old man sitting in his car. Odd. But, still, nothing to worry about.

The car pulled away, slowly. Katie remembered the handsome old man in the café. Without knowing why, she shuddered.

SEVEN

KATIE WOKE UP thinking about the blood cells. Cracking an eyelid, she checked the clock on her bed table. Five-oh-two—she had another half hour. She closed her eyes again, but sleep refused to return. Her mind buzzed with anticipation. If she got to the lab early, she'd have time to check the cells before she started work.

Switching off the alarm button, she got up and trudged into the shower. As she toweled off and dressed, the aroma of brewing coffee drifted up into the bedroom. She inhaled deeply, feeling her blood quicken at the promise of caffeine. It was not altogether a pleasant feeling, reminding her of the way she'd once felt about amphetamines. Not the same thing, not by a long shot, but she didn't like having to assure herself of that each morning.

Downstairs, she found her mother sitting at the kitchen table in her peach Christian Dior robe and slippers, reading the *Post* through her half glasses.

"Did I wake you?" Katie asked.

"Morning, dear."

Katie smiled. Her mother might be an early riser, but conversation was anathema to her until her cherished newspaper had kick-started her brain. Katie poured a mug of coffee and dropped a slice of cinnamon bread into the toaster. She decided to make herself wait for the first sip until the toast popped up. To take her mind off the delay, she paced the kitchen, making plans. The electron microscope hadn't damaged the cells at once, but they may have deteriorated overnight. In a way, she hoped so. She wanted to rerun the hemoglobin test, but it wouldn't be any use if the membrane was still strong enough to repel the lysing agent—

"I don't believe it!" Mom said.

"What?"

"Neddie Merrill made the paper!"

Katie tried to place the name. Mom held up the style section. After a second, Katie recognized the photo above the fold. "That old woman who used to live up the bayou from Grandma Guillemin?"

"Bite your tongue—Neddie's only a few years older than I am."

The toast popped up, filling Katie's head with the mouth-watering fragrance of hot cinnamon. She spread on a touch of margarine and nibbled at the crust; only then did she allow herself a sip of coffee. As always, it was good but just the barest bit disappointing.

"You won't believe this, Katie. Seems Neddie's been using her 'special powers' to help the police solve crimes." Mom looked up, gazing over the tops of her half glasses with the faraway look of memory. "Neddie Merrill. When I knew her, she was a *traiteur,* a sort of folk doctor who treated snakebites and fevers with herbal remedies. On the side, she raised red-eared sliders—you know, those little turtles they sell in pet stores. The psychic stuff, treating spells, as she called it, was only a small part of her work."

Mom looked down at the paper again, scanning the columns of print. "Evidently, Neddie's clairvoyant side has started to blossom. According to this, she started helping the local sheriffs in Bayou Sorrel and Plaquemine. Then, about a month ago the Baton Rouge police gave Neddie a bullet from a murder victim. She held it, then informed them the murderer had killed himself. Using her description of an abandoned shed along Little Bayou Pigeon, they found his body. The gun in his hand was the murder weapon.''

"Amazing," Katie said, wiping the toast crumbs off the counter into the open dishwasher. She thought: but not as amazing as RBCs that won't deteriorate. Maybe I should give the blood to Neddie, let her find the killer. Katie smiled, imagining what Merrick would say to that.

"Little Bayou Pigeon," Mom repeated softly. "When I was just a girl, your Grandma Guillemin used to row me out there in the scow to help her trap crawfish."

The wistful note in her voice caught Katie's attention. Leaning back against the dishwasher, she eyed her mother. During all her years teaching at Brown, Audrey O'Keefe, PhD, had nursed the idea of returning to the bayou country after she retired. Instead, she'd agreed to come here and help with Gregory. She'd insisted it was what she wanted, but was it really?

Afraid of the answer, Katie tried to put the question from her mind. She stowed her mug in the dishwasher, denying herself even a glance at the half full coffee pot, and tiptoed upstairs. Gregory was still asleep. She leaned over and gave him the gentlest of kisses so his grandma could have a few more minutes of peace. When she ducked into the kitchen to say good-bye, her mother was sitting at the table, gazing at the fridge, the dreamy look still in her eyes. Katie wanted to let it slide, get off to work, but she knew if she did, her worry would only deepen.

"You still miss the bayous, don't you?"

Mom's eyes focused on her. "Oh, I've got fond memories, sure. Mist rising off the lagoons in the morning, making the water hyacinths shimmer like lavender gems. Late afternoons, the sun slanting in just right turns swamp water into molten gold. Sometimes you can smell the cypress oil in it, a delicate piney scent. At night, the crickets and frogs start up the sweetest lullaby. . . ." Mom gave the paper a smart shake and folded it up briskly. "Listen to me. Looking back sets one foot in the grave."

It was one of Grandma Guillemin's pet expressions. For a moment, despite the elegant robe, the professorial glasses, Katie could see Grandma sitting there at the table.

Mom stood. "Believe me, Katie, dear, I couldn't be happier than I am right here, with my daughter and grandson. Babies beat bayous anytime."

Katie pulled her into a hug. Mom hugged back with an urgent fervor, then pushed off gently. "Best get to work, Doctor O'Keefe."

"Aye, aye, Doctor O'Keefe."

Katie got in too late to check the blood cells but in time for the charge nurse's summary of the night shift. The nurse told her Art had gone down to the cafeteria for breakfast, and wanted her to join him there for a minute if she could. Curious, Katie took the elevator down. She spotted him at a corner table. An older man sat across from him, sipping coffee, and glancing around as Art talked.

Art waved her over. "Katie, thanks for coming. I wanted to introduce you to my father, Alexander Stratton. Dad, this is my clinical supervisor, Doctor Katie O'Keefe."

"Doctor, a great pleasure to meet you." Alexander Stratton stood and shook her hand. He was a bit taller than Art; she could see where Art got his good looks. Alexander was a mature version of his son, his blond hair still thick but streaked at the temples with white. His suit, a subdued blue pinstripe, was beautifully tailored, making him look almost as lean as his son. She detected a subtle hint of cologne. Katie remembered Art telling her that his father was a partner in a prestigious California law firm.

Alexander pulled up a chair for her. As she sat, she saw that Art's eggs and orange juice were barely touched. He sat back in his chair, fingers laced around one knee, and anyone who didn't know him would think he was relaxed, but Katie knew better. He'd shown this same deceptive calm his first day on hematology, when she'd sat him down at a microscope and quizzed him for an hour on difficult slides. He'd shown it again the first time he ran a bone marrow extraction, and she still saw it in the moments before he had to tell parents their child was dying. This encounter with his father must be terribly important, even intimidating, to Art, she decided. When she came in, he'd been talking with unusual animation while his father's gaze slid around the cafeteria. Art seemed desperate to impress him, and his father seemed unaware of it.

"My son didn't tell me his boss was so attractive."

"Thank you," Katie said. "That's because clinical supervisors, seen through the eyes of residents, tend to resemble tyrannosaurs."

Alexander smiled.

Struck by an idea, she turned to Art. "Pediatrics just admitted a baby with SCID. They think it's a case of adenosine de-aminase deficiency. They asked me if I knew anyone at NIH they could consult on the case. I told them you knew a lot about ADA deficency.''

Alexander looked interested. "SCID," he asked, "is that Sudden Crib Infant Death?"

"No." Wisely, Art did not smile at his father's error. "It stands for Severe Combined Immunodeficiency. The disease is present when the victim is born, and it's usually fatal, but we've had some success fighting it with bone marrow transplants. ADA is a particular form of it, where a certain enzyme is missing. I just attended a seminar on it. NIH is working on a gene replacement therapy. . . .''

Katie listened as Art explained the disease and treatments to his father in the kind of clear language the lawyer in Alexander would have to appreciate. Alexander nodded and asked several questions, all of his attention on his son, now. Clearly, he was impressed with Art's knowledge. Katie could see Art relaxing. He even took a few bites of his eggs between sentences.

What was it about fathers? Such awesome emotional power they wielded, probably without even knowing it most of the time. Watching Art and Alexander, she felt a twinge of envy. She wished she could sit down with her own father. She knew almost nothing about Preston O'Keefe. He had died of lung cancer before she was old enough to talk. Katie had only the vaguest memory of a tall man who smelled of tobacco; of a cheek that had prickled against hers, probably when he'd hugged her. She wished she could remember the hugs, but she could not.

Art glanced at his watch. "Dad, I'd better get over to pe-diatrics, and I know you've got a plane to catch."

Alexander looked at his watch, startled. "You're right. I do have to run." He stood and shook her hand, then his son's, hes-itating, then drawing him into a quick hug. "A pleasure to meet you, Doctor," and he was off.

Art said, "Thanks."

"What for?"

"For making me look good with Dad."

"You're the one who did that."

He looked at her, and she glimpsed something in his ex-pression she had not seen before. For a second, it eluded her and then she remembered where she had last seen the look: in Merrick's eyes, the night they first began to fall in love.

Oh, no, Katie thought.

* * *

Merrick briefed the team of detectives Captain Rourke had assigned to help him with the cathedral murder. He spoke with an easy, informal air, sitting on the edge of his desk to help hide the tension that gripped him. As he looked at the faces in front of him, a flash of déjà vu took him back more than a hundred years to another squad room. London: 1888—the year of the eights. Not for another thousand years would three infinity symbols line up again—but it was to eternity that a hemophage had, in 1888, sent five Whitechapel prostitutes.

Merrick remembered leaning against a desk, heavier and more richly carved than this one, facing three rows of bobbies. Standing at attention, dressed in their heavy black uniforms buttoned to the neck, the bobbies had looked different from these men who now lounged around this office in their sport coats and Rockport loafers. But his task had been the same: to keep them away from the killer.

It had not been easy. It was a bloody autumn for the police. The killer had been wantonly vicious, had taunted them with notes signed "Jack the Ripper," and they were determined to hunt him down. Such sensational, panic-mongering killings were rare for a hemophage, but this phage had been inexperienced—barely fifteen years old—and poisoned by hate. His father, a working-class normal, had gone insane and then died of syphilis contracted from a prostitute.

It took me ten weeks from the Ripper's first murder, Merrick thought, to catch and bury him. Zane is not some green cub—how many people has he killed in five hundred years? Probably over ten thousand. I've hunted him many times and never caught him.

Merrick's stomach knotted. Time was wasting. He needed to be out there hunting.

But this was important, too.

"By now," he said, "you all know that the dead woman, Sheila Forrester, was a niece of the British Ambassador."

One of the detectives groaned, and Merrick asked: "You have a problem?"

"No. I love heat from on high."

"The only heat you have to worry about is from me," Merrick said. "Ms. Forrester jogged regularly near the cathedral. So I want you people to canvas the neighborhood up and down Wisconsin around the cathedral. Talk to everyone, and I mean in depth. Someone may have seen something but be unable to remember it without prodding.''

More groans. Sifting an entire neighborhood for crumbs of information rated somewhere between filling out paperwork on shootings and sitting through all-night stakeouts in the dead of winter. Merrick hated having to put them through it. It was a complete waste of their time. The killer was a hemophage. No one would have seen anything. But it would keep his squad out of his way—and alive. If they came too close to the killer, they would not solve the case. They, too, would die.

But he mustn't be too obvious about putting them off the scent, either.

Merrick felt a keen frustration. How many times had he walked this same tightrope since the 1680s, when he'd taken that first primitive police post as reeve of Berkshire? Whatever passed for the police department in an area had always been the best place for him to sniff out hemophages. It was also the most likely place for normals to get *his* scent. These men and women sitting in front of him now were far more dangerous to him than any other normals. Suspicious by nature, the best of them could be uncannily perceptive. They would be watching to see how he ran the investigation. If anyone guessed he was trying to keep his own detectives out of the killer's way, it could be the first step to his exposure.

And there could be no question how these detectives would react to an imposter hiding among them—a born killer. If they could not catch and destroy him, they would hound him, broadcast his face in every city, exile him to a permanent life of solitary running—

Dread rose in Merrick. He fought it down. In twelve years here, he had made no mistakes, and he would make none now. And he would never go back to the frustration of the old days, when he'd had only his own resources to draw on. How many phages had he missed in those days, hunters so subtle in the way they killed that no one even knew a murder had been committed? Information was his only hope of catching most phages, and working inside a modern police department gave him access to information he could get no other way. It had become his narcotic, this stream of high-grade data so empowering and addictive he could not imagine being without it: statistics on runaways, missing persons reports, patterns of wounds in traffic fatality reports. In the twelve years since he'd come to Washington, he'd used the knowledge hidden in these sources to bring down fourteen hemophages. He'd buried each of them before anyone in the department knew what was happening.

Unfortunately, it was too late for that this time. Even if he caught and buried this phage, for months afterward the detectives in his squad would go on hunting for a suspect. Over a hundred years had passed since "Jack the Ripper" and people were still trying to find out who he had been.

"Any questions?" Merrick asked.

"Any sign the killer molested her?"

"None. But that doesn't rule out sexual motives, as you know." Merrick felt a twinge of guilt. Zane always killed attractive young women of child-bearing age, but there was never any evidence, even in the lab, that he interfered sexually with his victims. Still, time the squad wasted pursuing it would help keep them away from Zane.

One of the men in the rear straightened against the bookcase. "What about VICAP?"

"Nothing yet. I requested the usual search, but they haven't gotten back to me. If they find this killer's pattern in their national data base, I'll let you know."

"How come you get to do all the fun stuff?"

"Because I'm the lieutenant. I thought you knew that. All right, hit the bricks."

When they were gone, Merrick slid off the corner of his desk and walked to his window, gazing down at the traffic on V Street. *The fun stuff, right.* Like trying to figure out how to contain and minimize the blood report Katie would be making to Byner. Merrick felt the hairs prickle on his neck. Zane, he thought. How could you be so *careless*—?

He caught himself. He had no proof yet that the killer was Zane. It was one thing to send his men on a wild-goose chase, and quite another to go galloping off himself. The flagrant "vampire" murders Zane had committed here twelve years ago did not mean it was him this time. He had a rational motive then, Merrick thought—to disrupt my life. I'd just made homicide detective in San Francisco. He knew I'd have to quit to come after him, and once I'd done it, he ran. This killer isn't trying to lure me anywhere. This is my turf, and he's taunting me, which is not rational. It could be another phage like the Ripper, still young enough to carry a grudge from his life before the change—and too young to have heard about Merrick the "assassin."

But I watch the hospitals. There's only the one new phage right now, and she's dying quietly in her bed. . . .

Merrick heard footsteps down the hall. John Byner appeared in his doorway and started to knock, then dropped his fist as he realized Merrick was already looking at him.

"We need to talk," Byner said.

Merrick felt a sharp foreboding. "I'm always glad to see you, Doc. How's John junior?"

Byner's worried look eased. "Doing great. By the way, he wants to know if he can keep the books a little longer. He hasn't finished the Chaucer and he wants to reread the Dickens but right now he's busy studying for finals."

"Tell him to keep them as long as he wants."

"Thanks." Byner eyed Merrick. "You're a good influence on him."

"He's a good influence on me."

Byner drifted to the wall of books. "Have you read all of these?" He pulled out the thick volume by Kraft-Ebing. *"Psychopathia Sexualis.* I haven't seen this thing since med school. Don't loan him this one, all right?"

Merrick smiled.

Byner slide the volume back in, stood in front of the window, and fiddled with his hands behind his back.

"Come on, John. Whatever it is, it can't be that bad."

"I just called Doctor O'Keefe at the hospital. She mentioned she'd spoken with you, too."

Merrick's foreboding deepened. Byner measured him with a sidelong glance. "Now don't laugh. But this man you're hunting . . . I'm starting to think he . . . might not *be* entirely human."

Merrick felt a cold rush in his veins. He kept his voice calm. "Surely Doctor O'Keefe didn't tell you that."

"Not in so many words, but—"

"I believe she mentioned a possible radiation mutation," Merrick said, "in a gene that determines the killer's blood characteristics."

"Mutation, hell. Damn it, Merrick. She poured a thousand kilovolts down on those cells and they didn't wilt. If that blood is from a man, I've never seen one like him."

"So what are you saying? That he's a vampire?"

"Go on, laugh," Byner muttered.

"I'm not laughing. But only because I try to be unfailingly polite."

Byner blew out a breath and collapsed into a chair in front of the desk.

Merrick said, "The killer's got unusual blood, that's all. In due course, we'll know why. If not a radiation mutation, it will be some other reasonable explanation. Listen, John, I'm going to catch this murdering bastard, and when I do, the last thing we need is for the prosecution's chief medical witness—and maybe the whole trial—to be compromised by sensational press coverage of the killer's blood.''

''We could call in some people from NIH and swear them to secrecy.''

Merrick's stomach felt suddenly hollow but he kept his voice calm. ''Come on, John. We live in a town where sworn secrets are leaked every day. Every person we bring in drives up that risk. Home runs aren't hit by committees, they're hit by individuals. Doctor O'Keefe is as smart as they come. Give her a chance.''

Byner gave him an appraising look. ''You got something going with her?''

Merrick hesitated. Byner could learn the truth easily enough—and might know it already. ''We used to date. Now we're just friends. In any case, you're the one who called her in. The point is, you were very right to do so. You know her work. They don't come any better. She *will* solve this. Just give her some room.''

Byner looked skeptical but he nodded. ''All right. We'll keep it just with her—for the moment, at least. But this is one very hot potato, Merrick. You keep trying to hang onto it and it'll burn us both.''

''Understood.'' It was time to get Byner out of here, before he changed his mind. Merrick took a Macanudo panatella from his jacket pocket.

Byner gave him a horrified look. ''You're not going to light that thing.''

''I find it smokes better if I do.''

''I'm out of here.''

Merrick put the cigar down and walked him to the door. Turning to face him, Byner said, ''Catch this sicko, soon, Merrick.''

''I will.''

At the door, Merrick saw Captain Rourke, bearing down fast. Byner had to step against the wall to make room for Rourke to get by. Before he entered Merrick's office, the captain glanced after the medical examiner. ''Did I hear Doc telling you to catch someone?''

Merrick shrugged.

"He stole my line," Rourke said.

Merrick saw that the captain's homely, basset-hound face was redder than usual. His neck bulged over his collar; the white shirt strained to contain his massive chest and belly. Rourke liked to joke that his wife didn't have to iron his shirts, that wrinkles had no chance around him. What wasn't so funny was that he was a stroke waiting to happen. Merrick could feel it whenever he was around the man, could actually hear it—the blood hissing through Rourke's clogged carotid arteries. It made him sad. Rourke was a decent man and he wished he could warn him somehow.

Rourke eased himself down on the radiator cover and hitched his pants up. At once, his belt slid back down, vanishing under the curve of his belly. "At the risk of sounding repetitive," he said, "you do have to catch this sicko—and might I add, quick. The old limey bird is pressing hard about his niece's murder, and I can't say I blame him. The killing is still under wraps, but he'll leak it the second he thinks we're bogging down." Rourke eyed him. "So how we doing?"

"Come on, Captain."

"I know, I know. You just started." Rourke sighed. "Look, you know how I hate looking over my detectives' shoulders—"

"I've always appreciated that."

"But you gotta understand, this time is different. If we don't crack this in the next few days, the ambassador will have the commissioner, the mayor, and probably the president of the United States breathing down my neck. I've got no choice on this one. I want to know everything you know, as soon as it happens. Clear?"

"Clear," Merrick said.

"So, I repeat, you got anything yet?"

Merrick tried not to think about the blood cells. "No."

Rourke's face got a little redder. "I'll say this for you. You don't sugarcoat anything. I hate that."

Merrick smiled.

"Keep me posted, hear?" Without waiting for an answer, Rourke lumbered out of the office.

Merrick swore softly. A decent man, but also one who always covered his ass. If Rourke found out about the blood cells, he wouldn't just call in a few blood experts from NIH, he'd brief his superiors up the line. With a hard-nosed medical examiner and an eminent blood researcher to back it up, the story would hit the newspapers, starting with the *Washington Post,* and spread to other big papers of the legitimate press, a radically different springboard than the tabloids, where such things usually played. The fact that the blood had come from a vicious murderer would add fuel to the fire—especially if there were more killings. Nothing captured public attention or inspired fear like the search for a serial killer. And this killer was operating in the nation's capital, a regular source of news for the nation and the world. Merrick had never known so many adverse factors to converge before.

Not entirely human. Merrick remembered Byner's words, with a chill.

The clock was ticking.

If I catch the phage quickly, Merrick thought, before he kills again, Byner's urgency about the cells will fade—and so will Katie's. But if I don't—if he kills again—all bets will be off.

Merrick felt the tension building between his shoulder blades. Byner and Rourke were now the deuterium and tritium in a hydrogen bomb. Keep them apart and all you had was a case of nerves. Combine them and the bomb went off.

Would you agree to a simple blood test, Detective? That seems a reasonable request. . . .

And then the running.

EIGHT

"YOU WANT JUST the guests who have paid or are paying cash, right, Detective?"

"Right," Merrick said.

"My assistant is bringing them. It might take a few minutes."

"Thank you, Mr. Randall." Merrick could smell the man's blood, a good scent like warmed Camembert. It was the gene, he knew, telling him it was time to feed. A familiar melancholy settled over him, but he managed to smile as Randall joked about a Shriner's convention that had just left town after annihilating the hotel's supply of bar snacks—even the Brazil nuts.

"Must have been locusts in a previous life," Merrick said.

Randall laughed. Despite his thinning, sandy hair, he seemed young to be a manager, and refreshingly unpretentious. He wore his good Brooks Brothers suit as if it were jeans and a sweater.

His office sported cactus instead of ficus, football players instead of the usual insipid hotel art.

Merrick pointed to a framed photo on the desk. "Your kids?"

"Nieces. I'm not married." Randall picked up the photo and gazed fondly at it. "I couldn't be prouder if they were mine. Marly, here—the taller one—just built her own computer from a kit. Her sister Tory plays a hot trumpet and a mean game of chess. They're my oldest brother's kids, live up in New York. I see 'em every couple of weekends. You got any kids, Detective?"

"It could well be."

Randall laughed again. Merrick could see the carotid artery pulsing on his neck, feel his own nerves phasing on the rhythm. He was aware of the empty transfusion packs he'd zipped into the lining of his coat a few days ago, when he'd realized it would soon be a month since he'd fed. The need began to arise every two weeks, but his loathing of it always made him put it off. Now the hunger was strong, impossible to ignore. As always, this first moment when he knew he must surrender made his stomach feel hollow with fear. As powerful as his need for blood was, he knew that when he actually stood over his victim, his lust to kill would be even stronger. There was never a feeding where he did not struggle for control. Would this be the time he finally lost it?

The fear swelled, striking through him so furiously that he had to swallow to stop from groaning aloud. I'll wait another day, he thought. I don't have to feed. Not yet, not today.

Randall held the photo of the two girls across the desk to him. "I took this picture myself," he said, "last time I was in New York."

Reaching out to take the photo, Merrick saw the faint scoring across the back of his own hand that, in a few more weeks, would begin to deepen into wrinkles. He had slept six hours last night. There was a faint ache in his ankles and hands from when he'd scaled the cathedral wall. For every day he waited, the deterioration in his cells would accelerate. No one would notice any change in his appearance for several more months. But what if he came to grips with the phage in the next few days—a phage who had just fed? How much of a deficit in his hearing or eyesight, how much weakening in his muscles, would be too much?

Merrick wondered if Randall lived in the hotel. It would be convenient from him. *And for me.* He gazed at the photo. The girls were both smiling indulgently, clearly fond of their doting uncle. He handed it back. "It's a nice picture."

Randall smiled proudly, then sobered. "Speaking of pictures, do you have one of the man you're looking for?"

Merrick pulled the drawing from his coat pocket. Created by a police artist from the fragmentary memories of two survivors, it depicted a serial killer who liked to bite his victims' throats. The man was last seen in Baltimore, about thirty miles away. The blood of his victims was always found around the bodies, which meant he was not a hemophage, but if he happened to be staying at the hotel, Merrick would gladly arrest him.

Randall gave the drawing a long, careful look. "Doesn't look familiar. But I'll show it around to the staff and call you if anyone recognizes him."

"Thanks."

"No problem. By the way, if we get lucky with the video-tapes, can you keep it out of the papers that I let you see them? Most guests don't realize we record them as they register, and I'd just as soon keep it that way."

"No problem." *Because, even if I see Zane on the tapes, I wouldn't let on to you.* Merrick wished the assistant would hurry. If he could get away quickly, before he formed a plan of attack on Randall, maybe he could put off feeding a bit longer. And time was wasting. He had hoped to cover ten hotels before evening, when the managers turned things over to assistants and went off duty; so far, he'd managed only six out of more than thirty within a five-block radius of the victim's apartment. Even if he could cover every hotel in the city, there was no guarantee he'd find Zane. Still, until he got a lead, it was his best bet. Phages rarely killed where they lived. They traveled to other cities and holed up in hotels. They paid for everything in cash, never leaving credit footprints while they were in their kill zone.

With a soft knock, the assistant came in. She was a tall, slim woman with dark hair. Her fingers lingered a second on Randall's as she handed him four videotape cassettes. Ah, Merrick thought, and was happy for the man.

The assistant said, "Only six people have paid in cash the past two weeks. We don't get that many as a rule. Two of them are on the first tape, two on the second, and one each on the last two."

"Good job," Randall said.

"The first two I'll show you are still with us." She put the tape into a VCR on a corner table, turned the set on, and pushed play. The image of a bald man in his sixties froze on the monitor. Looking at it, Merrick felt an eerie foreboding. This is what will doom us all one day, he thought, if the normals ever find out about us. Bloodless videocameras, immune to our Influence; surveillance systems in every home, on every street. First they will drive us into the Third World; then, as India and China and Africa are forced to modernize, into New Guinea, the Amazon jungles. And when phages have drained the blood from the last lost tribe, we will all die slowly and horribly, like Sandeman. A chill crawled along Merrick's spine.

"Detective?" Randall prompted.

Merrick blinked at the screen. "No," he said.

The woman hit fast forward, watching the index counter. Another man, mid forties, wearing a cowboy hat.

"No."

None of the other four was Zane, either. Merrick felt a strange mixture of relief and disappointment. Randall gave him a sympathetic grimace. "Sorry."

"I appreciate your help." Merrick shook Randall's hand, thanked the woman, and walked out of the office. Instead of leaving the hotel, he found a marble pillar in the lobby that would hide him while he watched the door to Randall's office beside the main desk. Leaning against the cool marble, he felt a pulse of dread in his stomach. He focused on the tenuous inner bond he'd tried to build between himself and Randall in the few minutes they'd been together. A nice young man, a good guy who loved his family. His death would bring great pain to other people. I will not kill him, Merrick thought. I *must* not.

He forced the tense muscles of his neck to relax. Glancing through the revolving door of the entrance, he saw that night had fallen. Cabs rolled through the hotel's front portico, their daytime grime masked in the dazzling reflection of marquee lights. A couple in evening clothes strolled through the lobby toward the hotel restaurant. Merrick shook his head, frustrated. The day had sped by too quickly and he had accomplished nothing. A phage could kill day or night, but darkness made it easier and was therefore preferred. Would there be another killing tonight—one he could have prevented if he'd covered more ground this afternoon?

A couple hurried past him toward the check-in line at the front desk. Judging from the rumpled, off-kilter look of their clothes, they'd just endured hours in cramped airline seats. Their two boys horsed around behind them. Merrick watched them with a mixture of pleasure and regret. How many children had he fathered? Not all that many, considering his age. Only two were alive today—Gregory and Zane. One he must give up, the other, destroy.

Merrick's throat tightened in grief. He remembered Zane as a little boy, still as normal as these two: Zane's cheery, round face, the wild cowlicks that found a different haven every day in his thick brown hair. He always had lots of friends, Merrick remembered—even boys older than him. But we were together a lot, too. Like that time I carried him into the deep woods with me. He'd been begging for months to go explore, but now that he was finally out there, he was scared. His arms were so tight around my throat I could hardly breathe. I told him I wouldn't let anything happen to him, and he relaxed. He trusted me.

Why couldn't I save him?

At the check-in counter, the shorter boy tagged the bigger one. His brother lunged at him and they chased off across the lobby. As the boy in the lead pulled away, he started making faces over his shoulder, unaware he was veering off toward an old man with a cane. Merrick winced, but at the last second the man stepped back and the kid missed him. Then the mother caught up and marched them back toward the desk. As she passed the old man, she murmured an apology. He waved it off rather brusquely. Merrick's interest quickened. There was something familiar about the man. . . .

He was at the sidewalk café yesterday, Merrick realized with surprise. A few tables away from Katie and me. No cane, and he wore baggy pants and a jacket, not a suit, but it's the same one, no question. Strange.

The old man shuffled toward the exit, pushed through the revolving door, and made his way slowly to the line of cabs. Merrick glanced back at the main desk in time to see Randall emerge and head toward the elevator bay.

Hurry!

One of the closing doors caught Merrick's shoulder as he slipped into the elevator with Randall. The doors rebounded, opening all the way before they rolled shut again. Frowning, Randall took a notebook from his coat and scribbled briefly. Merrick eased back to the far wall of the elevator. The small effort of Influencing Randall's retinas attuned him to the man's blood again. In the boxed-up air of the cage, the scent was powerful, intoxicating.

Randall got off on the twelfth floor and walked to the end of the hall. Keeping a few steps behind, Merrick began delicately constricting capillaries in the man's brain stem. He was rewarded by a yawn as the manager fumbled out his key and opened the door to a corner suite. Merrick squeezed down some more. Randall shuffled inside and leaned against the wall of the foyer, yawning again, giving Merrick the time he needed to slip past. Randall closed the door and slipped the chain lock into position. Trudging into the living room, he dropped onto a couch, picked up a remote control, and flipped on the television. Merrick continued to narrow the brain stem capillaries a little at a time. After a few minutes, Randall's eyes slipped shut and he sank into a deep, narcotized sleep.

Merrick looked quickly around the apartment. On an étagère by the window, he saw another, larger photo of Randall's nieces. He took it from the stand and placed it where he could see it, on Randall's lap. He could feel his heartbeat accelerating, but he made himself relax and move slowly, knowing if he allowed himself the slightest haste, he could slip too easily into frenzy when he saw the blood. Shrugging out of his sport coat, he unzipped the bottom fold of lining and took out two vacuum transfusion packs and a needle. He fitted the needle to the short plastic tube of one of the packs. Elevating Randall's foot onto the hassock to minimize bruising, he rolled the man's sock down his ankle. His hands began to tremble and he stopped to take a deep breath, pressing his palms together until the tremor stopped.

He slipped the needle into the big vein behind the ankle; Randall did not even twitch. Keeping his eyes off the transfusion pack, Merrick stared at the photo of the two girls. This is a good man, he thought. He loves his nieces and they love him, need him. That woman—his assistant—needs him, too. . . .

Ah, he could feel the pack swelling warmly against his hand. He wanted it so much, *WAIT!*

He was forced to look down to change packs. A trickle of blood escaped as he fitted the second pack to the needle. Merrick pinched his eyes shut, but still he could see the red ribbon of blood, feel the answering boil in his head. Staring at the picture of the girls, he imagined them coming through the door, throwing their arms around their uncle.

The second pack filled.

Merrick had to look at the ankle again to clean up the tiny spill. The blood's glossy, rich redness burned into his brain like a hot wire. A killing rage flashed through him. He lunged at Randall, then twisted away. Lurching to the bathroom, he splashed his face with cold water, rolled up a wet washrag, and clamped it between his teeth.

Back in the living room, he replaced the picture on the éta-gère. His teeth ground savagely on the washrag, as he stuffed the two bulging transfusion packs into the secret pocket. He fled the suite. Even in the hall, the urge to go back and tear open Randall's throat filled him. He hurried to the stairwell, spat out the washrag, and retrieved one of the transfusion packs from his coat. Uncapping it, he put it to his mouth and drank, squeezing the bag, feeling the hot fluid shoot down his throat.

In seconds, the urge to kill eased. He felt a rush of physical vitality. He was strong as a lion. The dim light of the stairwell blazed like a noonday sun. His hearing sharpened, bringing him the feathery rustle of a roach scurrying across the landing one floor down. He could smell a smudge of chocolate on a Snickers wrapper someone had dropped on the steps. Holding his hand in front of his face, he saw that the back of it, smooth as a peach, glowed like a baby's skin. How could such tender flesh cover such hideous evil? He cursed the sharpening of his senses, which only showed him his depravity more clearly. If only he could die, could cease to exist between this second and the next.

But there could be no such mercy for him. Even if he were to sever his own head, the stump of his neck would seal at once, and his remaining skin would drink the meager oxygen he would need directly from the air and pass it to the capillaries. The mus-cles of his cheeks and forehead would contract involuntarily, pumping his remaining blood. He would live on, conscious and aware, but helpless, for many months. And if someone found him . . .

Merrick shuddered. What a monstrous abomination he was, the true Merrick, behind all the civilized manners, the hopeless efforts to be a normal, decent man. He hated himself, as he hated all the other blood drinkers like him, with a hot and bitter ferocity.

Do you know why you do it, Merrick? Why you keep hunting them down and killing them?

With a fierce growl, Merrick clapped his hands over his ears, trying to shut out Sandeman's voice in his mind. It doesn't matter why, he thought. We deserve to die—all of us.

Returning the empty transfusion pack to the lining of his coat, Merrick hurried back to the elevator. He was acutely aware of the remaining pack, a warm weight that nudged his hip with each step. He wanted it, too, though not as much as he had wanted the first. He must drink it in the next few hours or it would begin to deteriorate, but he would wait as long as he could. A small token of resistance, but every act of self-control strengthened him, he knew, just as the slightest unnecessary surrender would weaken him.

He lengthened his stride, seized by a primitive urge to escape. He had not killed Randall, but the gene did not know that. Once outside the hotel, he felt safer. Inhaling deeply, he drew the cool spring air into his lungs. Its sweetness mocked him, sending another spasm of self-loathing through him. If he had work to occupy him, it would help, but he did not. There was nothing to do now but wait and hope his quarry would not feed tonight, too. Tomorrow, when the managers came back on duty, he would get an early start on the remaining hotels.

Merrick stood beside his car, wishing it could carry him away from himself. He pictured himself speeding down a dark, straight road, feeling himself bleed out behind until there was nothing left but his hands gripping the wheel.

Where *could* he go, what could he do that might make him feel better? Somewhere in him there was some good, surely. He thought of Jenny Hrluska, dying in the hospital with no one to help her—no one who understood. He checked his watch. Eight o'clock. Visiting hours were over. But he was not just any visitor.

As Merrick walked past the nurses station someone called out to him. Turning back, he saw it was the charge nurse. "Good evening, Shirley."

"And where do you think you're going?"

He managed a smile, knowing her bark was worse than her bite. "I thought I'd look in on Jenny."

"Not without a mask and gown, you won't."

Shirley helped him slip on the baggy gown, mask, and rubber gloves. "We're letting her parents stay after-hours now. They just left to get a bite to eat. I think she's sleeping now. Don't stay too long."

"She's getting weaker?"

Shirley nodded sadly.

Still, he was unprepared for how bad it was. Jenny's skin was white as chalk. She crouched like a supplicant, supporting herself on shins and forearms, her cheek pressed into the bed. Her hunched, thin body panged him. A buried memory surfaced, of lying on the straw mattress at the back of his family's hut, his whole body aching. The leukemia would torment his joints so fiercely that he would shift around gingerly in a desperate effort to ease the pain. Sometimes he would finally find sleep in the same unlikely position Jenny was in now. His throat clenched as he gazed at her. If only he could believe she did not have the gene, that treatment might yet help her. But he had lost that hope weeks ago, when her telltale hunger pangs had started. Children with other leukemias sometimes failed to respond to treatment, but only in hemophagic leukemia did you see this constant strange hunger and thirst that could not be satisfied. The fact that both her parents were normals had not saved her, any more than it had him. Most phages whose family trees he had researched were born to two normal carriers. Clearly, the gene was recessive, or Zane would not be the only phage he had ever fathered. Not just recessive, rare.

But not rare enough.

Jenny opened her eyes and cried out.

"It's Merrick," he said.

Sagging, she gave him the ghost of a smile. "I thought you were Doctor Giggles."

A character from a B horror flick. They'd discussed him last time—how in her dreams she kept seeing Dr. Giggles in his mask and gown, coming after her with his scalpel. There was a strange, sad quality in the way she described it, as though a part of her would welcome it.

Merrick remembered how he had prayed to die.

"Actually," he said, "I'm Doctor Googol."

"A very large number," Jenny said. "Ten to the one hundredth."

"Where did you learn that?" he asked, surprised.

"In a comic book." She coughed, her body arching, hands clawing into the mattress.

Merrick looked around desperately for something to distract them both. He saw the Barbie doll sitting on Jenny's bed table. When he'd asked her about it last week, she'd acted embarrassed, said her mother had brought it in without asking and she didn't play with dolls anymore. But it was still there, wasn't it? And some time in the last week, the doll's clothes had mysteriously changed.

"I see Barbie is wearing a prom dress now," Merrick said.

Jenny raised her head. "Oh, that. I got tired of looking at the bathing suit. I had Mom change it for me." Another spasm of coughing doubled her over. When she was finished, she rubbed at her eyes. Her movements were so feeble and uncoordinated that Merrick felt tears spring into his eyes. Thinking of the second transfusion pack, buried under the gown and coat, he felt a sudden, fierce desire to give it to her. He saw that Jenny's nostrils were flared and her eyes were questing with new alertness. Was she subliminally aware of the blood? He should not have brought it in here.

"I'm so hungry," she said.

He nodded.

"But everything I eat tastes terrible, because of the radiation, Doctor O'Keefe says. I'm thirsty, too. I drink like a fish and I'm still thirsty."

"It's part of the sickness." Silently, Merrick cursed the gene. Why Jenny? To die or to kill—what cruel god had given only these two vile choices to an innocent child?

"Doctor Googol, am I dying? Doctor O'Keefe doesn't want to tell me, but I think I am. I need to know."

"We're all dying," he said, though it wasn't quite true.

"You know what I mean. Am I?"

"Yes, you are."

"Oh." Her bleak expression nearly broke his heart. After a minute, she said, "It's going to be rough on Mom and Dad."

"I know. But they'll be all right after awhile."

"Are your parents still alive?"

"No." Merrick wondered at the question, then understood. Though he listed his age as thirty-five—and looked around thirty to most people—to a twelve-year-old, he must seem, if not ancient, old. He thought of his father. The memory that had stayed sharpest over the centuries was his father's agony—the village healer who could not save his own son.

"I wish I could crawl away somewhere," Jenny said, "so my parents wouldn't have to watch."

Merrick looked at her, startled. It was exactly how he had felt. And, in fact, he had done it. Tormented by the soft sobs of his mother in the hut's other room, he had waited until she left. Then, dragging himself from his bed, he'd managed to stagger off into the woods behind the village. He remembered lying in the bushes beside the path, gnawing the branches, chewing on the grass beside his face, still trying to satisfy his hunger. Dying, but ravenous.

He'd heard the shouts then, faintly. At first he'd thought it was a dream, but then he'd felt the ground throb under him with approaching footsteps. Through the tall grass, he'd seen a man run in panic down the path toward him. Two men in ragged clothes chased him. One of them had a knife and the other a stick. They caught the stranger only a few feet from him. Hidden by the grass, Merrick could only watch in horror as the two high-waymen clubbed the other man to the ground. They stripped his clothes off and took his leather purse. And then they cut his throat.

As they ran away, Merrick pushed his head above the grass. He saw the torn throat, the gush of bright arterial blood. The most peculiar feeling swept him. Suddenly he found himself on his hands and knees, crawling toward the dying man. A feverish strength filled him. He clamped his hands over the man's throat, thinking he wanted only to stop the bleeding, as he'd seen his father do, but then he was licking his palms, falling on the man's neck and sucking at the pumping wound as he felt the incredible rush for the first time. He rose from the corpse, appalled at himself, and ran in panic through the woods.

He had never let himself go near his parents again.

"I don't want to die, Detective Chapman."

"I don't want you to die, either." He stroked her back with his gloved hand. He was conscious again of the blood against his hip. All he had to do was give it to her and she would live.

And hundreds, perhaps thousands, of others might die.

Maybe I could teach her to use the transfusion packs—

He remembered himself only an hour ago, lunging at Randall, filled with the frenzied desire to kill him. Only by the barest thread had he held back. Each time, only by the barest thread. And what about Sandeman, dying a prisoner in an underground vault because he could not hold back, because once he saw the blood he had to take the life, too. If I gave Jenny blood, Merrick thought, and then couldn't stop her from killing, I'd have to put her in the vault. Her death then would make what she is going through now look swift and merciful.

If I could just believe I'd be able to help her. . . .

But if I couldn't save my own son, who I loved more than anyone in the world, how could I hope to save this young girl I barely know? And with Zane, the task was easier than it would be with Jenny. The idea of developing a transfusion technique hadn't even entered my mind yet. I was just trying to get him to kill only the most deserving—thugs, murderers, rapists. From the time I gave Zane blood to when he ran away from me at eighteen, I tried everything I knew. Five years I reasoned with him, begged him, even physically restrained him. And every chance he got, he killed innocent young women.

A terrible, helpless anger settled over Merrick. Beneath his stroking fingers, he felt the bones of Jenny's spine, prominent against her shrunken, blood-starved skin. He could not help her.

He wanted to scream at someone, to plead her case, to die instead of her. But there was no one to scream at, no one to hear him plead. And he could not die, because even he was not as strong as Sandeman.

Not yet.

NINE

ZANE FOUND HIMSELF in an alley that seemed to have no end. He felt very uneasy. Towering walls rose on either side of him. The darkness was so deep that even his sensitive eyes could barely make out the ground. There was something familiar about the place. . . .

He realized he was having the nightmare and his uneasiness deepened into dread. Wake up! he commanded himself. His eyes felt open but he knew they weren't, not really. He strained to get the lids truly apart. Hazy coronas of light flickered briefly, then faded, leaving him still in the alley. A low babble rose in the gloom ahead and then flashlight beams lanced from the darkness—at least thirty lights, maybe more. In seconds, the crisscrossing beams found him and a shout went up. He cut off all blood to the retinas of the men in front, but the crowd pushed forward, the walls channeling them toward him like a horde of blinded, crazed rats. He struck at their brain stems, but their sheer numbers diluted the blow; a few fell and the rest kept coming, their shouts turning savage with excitement. It was almost as if they already knew about phages, knew what he was. How could they know? Had he made a mistake?

Wake up!

Zane tried to move his head and shoulders, to break free of the nightmare, but he remained in the dark alley. Now men were running at him from the other direction, too; the only way out was up the walls. Fear sharpened his senses, helping him find the small seams he needed. The mob below shined their flashlights up, spilling his shadow up the wall ahead of him. He saw that the summit was crowded with men, too.

"There he is!" someone shouted from above.

Panic swept him as he realized he was trapped. He tried to veer away, crawl sideways across the wall, but suddenly the surface became smooth as glass. He felt himself sliding down the surface, then pitching away from the wall into a giddy free fall. A net closed around him, breaking the fall as it entangled him. The men swarmed over him like ants, wrapping the net more tightly around him. He struck out with his mind and his fists, but they kept piling on top of him. As quickly as he broke one strand of net, they threw another over him. They carried him from the alley into a vacant lot. There, under blazing arc lamps, he saw a deep pit ringed with bulldozers. Horrified, he screamed, "Don't do this! Please, *Please!*"

They swung him over the edge, down into the pit. Tangled in the net, he could not get his feet under him. The bulldozers started up with a beastly grumbling roar and he felt the dirt pelting down on him. In seconds, it buried him to his shoulders, then surged over his head, pouring into his ears and eyes, down his throat. For a few more seconds, he could hear the bulldozers, and then the roar faded to a dull beat pounding through the earth. The dirt continued to pack in around him with suffocating force. At once his cells adapted to the drastic drop in oxygen, cutting back on function, shunting what remained to his brain. The throbbing of the bulldozers faded completely, leaving him in total silence. He could not move, could not see or hear, could not even squeeze a sound from his lungs.

Time crawled by. Sometimes the terror would exhaust itself for awhile and he could summon the ghostly, unstable images of memory. But then the tons of dirt would press even the imaginary light from his brain and the horror would surge again. He began to feel the hemophagic leukemia inching back into his cells. It became his clock, hinting with its sickening progress at the passage of time. From the pain in his joints, he knew he must have been down here for a year or more. He longed for the disease to hurry and finish him, but knew it could not hurry—he had fed far too many times for a swift death.

He began to scream inside his mind. He could not stand this another second. He *must* move. Mustering all his strength, he bulled his shoulders against the packed earth, trying desperately to twist his head even a fraction. . . .

He saw a trace of light on his eyelids. Hope swelled in him. He strained against the tons of dirt, struggling to open his eyes—

—and awoke with a gasp.

Morning sunlight streamed through the hotel curtains. Zane drank it in hungrily, laughing out loud. His heart pounded against his rib cage. Sitting up in bed, he gazed around. What an elegant bright room, with its tall windows and sweeping drapes of red velvet. The elaborate wood moldings around the ceiling seemed the most beautiful he had ever seen. Kicking free of the covers tangled around his feet, he revelled in the easy movement of his legs. Car horns honked sweetly on the street outside, luring him out of bed to the window. He gazed hungrily down at the street. People walked along, heading for work, or turning into the coffee shop across Lafayette Square. They did not know about him. He had made no mistakes. It was only the nightmare.

Zane realized he was soaking wet and his relief soured. He picked his damp pajamas away from his body, revolted by the flood of sweat. Just another curse, along with the aches and pains of this old body he was carrying around. He was sick of it. If he could just feed . . .

Soon, Zane thought. As soon as I've learned enough about Father.

Turning from the window, Zane headed for the shower. The bed's brass head rail caught his eye. The thick metal was twisted out of shape. He must have grabbed it in the throes of his nightmare, when he thought he was struggling in the net. Vexed, he sat on the bed and worked on straightening the head rail. It took more effort than he had expected, but he persevered. It was just the sort of stupid detail that could trip him up if the wrong person saw it. No normal man, old or otherwise, could bend brass that thick with his bare hands.

When the rail was straight again except for a few dimples in the brass that refused to come out, Zane stripped off the soaked pajamas and stepped into the shower. As the soothing, warm water pounded him, he let his thoughts return to the nightmare. It was his worst fear—that he would be found out and buried. But why did it plague his dreams, too, whenever blood depletion forced him to sleep? Was it punishment for his betrayal?

Suddenly the water did not feel warm enough. Zane twisted the hot water tap until the shower began to fill with steam. Still the chill clung to him. So long ago, but he would never forget it—that first hemophage he'd seen Father hunt, the one from the north that liked to prey on children. He could see it in his mind as if it were yesterday: Father digging a deep pit in the woods, then ambushing the phage with a heavy net. The phage had been much younger than Father and not nearly so powerful. He struggled all the way, Zane thought, but we were much stronger than he was. We put him into the pit and buried him.

We. Guilt pierced Zane. Helping bury that phage was the worst thing he had ever done. How long had it survived in the dark, earthen grave? Even now, five hundred years later, the memory shamed him. If the nightmare was his punishment, maybe he deserved it. Except that I had no choice, Zane thought. What could I do? Only eighteen, and suddenly my own father terrified me. If I'd tried to beg off, he'd have known I was starting to rebel against him. He might have thrown me into the same grave.

With an effort, Zane shook off the memory. Forget the nightmare. Once he'd fed, he'd need no sleep and the nightmare would be shut out.

Stepping from the shower, Zane toweled off and went over his plans for the day. First, he needed money to keep paying the hotel bill. He would try the bank he had cased yesterday. Then, tonight, he would pick up on Merrick again. It was time to see how much his doctor friend meant to him. Zane studied the array of clothes in the closet. He must make himself look as different as possible from yesterday. His neck prickled as he remembered the near disaster in that last hotel. Father looked right at me, Zane thought, thanks to that stupid kid. If he'd recognized me, he'd have leapt on me before I could get out the door. I shouldn't have been following him so closely. And today I need a different look.

After some deliberation, Zane chose soft Pierre Cardin trousers, a green silk shirt, and a rust-colored Joseph Aboud jacket that restored an illusion of bulk to his dwindling shoulders. A glance in the mirror satisfied him that Merrick wouldn't connect him to the old man he'd seen yesterday unless they passed very close. And there would be little chance of that until tonight.

As Zane walked the four blocks to Capitol Security Bank, he thought about what he should do to the doctor. If he wanted to remain unrecognizable to his father, it would be best to avoid blood. But there were many other ways to cause her pain.

Zane entered the bank through the spotless glass door and scanned the lobby, reaching ahead mentally. No one looked his way except the uniformed guard. With a light touch he removed himself from the man's retinas. The guard blinked and then returned his attention to the people lined up at the teller windows.

Bypassing the windows, Zane strolled across to the door of the security room. One or another of the bank's cameras had probably photographed him by now, but there was nothing to be done about that and it shouldn't matter. Turning the knob gently, Zane slipped into the security room. A guard sat with his back to the door, watching the rows of monitors, his head bobbing to music from his Walkman. The tinny buzz leaking from his earphones sounded like Ice Cube, which made Zane glad his hearing had deteriorated.

Standing right behind the man, he studied the layout. Each monitor screen had its own VCR, taping the live feed on the screen. The sight of them filled him with resentment. Robbing banks used to be so easy, with only a few sets of human eyes to fool. Now all U.S. banks of any size had these damned machines, immune to Influence. Even though they had been invented by puny normals, they had to be respected, even feared, and he hated that.

Zane found the two VCRs he was interested in—the one taping the entrance to the bank's vault and the one taping the vault's interior. Someone was in the vault right now—an older woman in a blue suit. Zane watched her take packets of bills from much bigger stacks arrayed neatly by denomination in trays along the money counter. She handled it with the ingrained reverence of someone who could not have all she wanted whenever she wanted.

He waited until the woman left the vault, then noted the numbers on the tape counters of the two monitors. Now if the vault would just stay empty for awhile . . .

He watched the screens, glancing at his watch. Once twenty minutes had passed without anyone else approaching or entering the vault, he was satisfied. Maintaining his Influence on the guard's eyes, he reached over the man's shoulder and pushed Stop on both machines. The cameras continued to feed the live image of the vault entrance and interior to the monitors. Trusting the loud music in the guard's earphones to cover the sound, Zane rewound both tapes to the numbers from twenty minutes ago.

When he was done, he reached mentally into the guard's brain stem—just a light squeeze. As the man's eyes glazed over and the lids fluttered, Zane pushed Play on both machines. The monitors covering the vault entrance and interior flickered, then the tapes of the past twenty minutes began to roll. He withdrew his Influence and the guard blinked, shook his head, and pulled himself up straight in his chair. Zane backed toward the door, pleased with himself. They trusted their bloodless, mechanical eyes, and he had defeated them, too. For the next twenty minutes, even if the Radio City Rockettes crammed themselves into the vault, the entrance and inside would both appear empty on these screens.

But he still needed luck.

Zane slipped from the security room and walked up a flight of stairs, following a narrow hall to the vault. Another hall crossed in front of the huge door. Two women were approaching down that hall. Screening himself from their eyes, he took up position beside the door. It looked as though he was going to get the luck he needed—

No, both women walked past and disappeared down the hall-way.

Disappointed, Zane settled in to wait. The minutes seemed to speed by; he started to get anxious. At the fifteen-minute mark, he groaned. All his careful preparation—scouting the bank, memorizing the layout, and his efforts in the guard room today—were about to go to waste. One more minute and he'd have to give it up—

Zane heard the click of high heels approaching. A woman emerged from the hall and spun the dial on the vault door. His heart accelerated. She was young, with dark hair cut into a pageboy. Though it was barely April, freckles dusted her nose and cheeks. She was smartly dressed in a plaid skirt and wine red jacket. He caught an alluring flash of white teeth as she put her body into pushing the massive door open. Hunger welled up in him.

He hurried into the vault behind her. Her perfume—Poison—swept through his head in a dizzying wave, a sweet counterpoint to the bruised strawberry smell of her blood. Zane opened his mouth to blunt the smell. Concentrate, he thought sternly. You only have a minute left.

The woman took some bills off the stack and pulled the tally book over. As she recorded her transaction, Zane picked up five packets of fifty-dollar bills and four of twenties. The woman put the pen down. He snatched a couple of packets of hundreds and hurried out behind her, slipping through just before she swung the huge door shut again.

Instead of walking directly out of the bank, he found himself tailing the woman. As she settled behind one of the teller windows, he read the nameplate in front: Susan Zarelli. A look in the phone book under Z and he'd have her address. He mustn't kill her. But she could be useful in another way.

When Susan Zarelli approached her apartment door, Zane was there waiting. An hour of listening at the door had satisfied him no one else was already inside. As he watched her walk down the hall toward him, he promised himself again that he would not kill her—at least not today. He would just practice on her, then leave.

Susan unlocked her door. He stepped in behind her, evading as she turned to close the door. He followed her around the apartment, watching her kick off her shoes, peel away her pantyhose, and change into slacks and a sweatshirt. His head swam with the precious scent of her blood. Blood was so wonderful. No two people ever had quite the same blood. Texture, taste, and smell differed from person to person, endless variations on an intoxicating theme. He wanted very much to drink hers—but he would not. His plan for drawing Merrick out tonight was more important.

Susan went to the kitchen and got a Coke. Flipping on the radio, she hummed along with a Dolly Parton song. Zane was a bit disappointed—Susan didn't seem the country and western type.

He started constricting the blood to her brain stem. Her singing trailed off. She yawned and blinked, starting to sag. *Careful, too fast.* He eased off and she straightened again, wandering back toward her bedroom. Following, he compressed her vital arteries again. She sat on her bed. Her shoulders slumped and her head began to nod, and then she sagged over on her side. The old sense of power flooded him. How wonderful his strength, even now in this wrinkled body. How fortunate that the thrill of absolute control never faded. The life of this woman was in his hands—

No, stop it!

Zane shook the dangerous thought off. It was himself he

must control now, and that would not be so easy. He made himself focus on her beauty until a protective surge of lust for her eased his other hunger. Picking her feet up, he put them on the bed. Gently, he rolled her onto her side, then sat on the floor, adjusting her face on one of her pillows so he could see it easily.

He allowed the blood flow to her brain to increase slightly. She sighed and made a small sound in the back of her throat. Watching her face, he let his mind float, extending his Influence away from the brain stem, searching for the place of memories. At first he was lost, then he found the posterior cerebral artery and followed it into the temporal lobe.

He watched Susan's face. Her eyes slid halfway open. He made sure she did not see him. Her unfocused eyes told him she was drifting between sleep and wakefulness, just where he wanted her. He shifted his Influence a few millimeters and saw her face brighten with wonder and delight. A sense of triumph filled him. I'm there! he thought. She's inside one of her memories. She's reliving it now. Something nice, judging by her expression.

Zane wished he could know what it was—what a marvelous weapon actual telepathy would be. But that was out of his reach. He could send the blood to the neurons of memory, stimulate them, run a movie in Susan's head, but he could not see that movie himself.

It did not matter. This was all the weapon he needed.

Zane shifted his Influence across her capillaries. She sighed and her eyes focused on a new internal vista. Her face registered sorrow.

Zane's sense of triumph deepened. This was going better than he'd dared hope. It would be harder with Merrick, but he could do it, he felt sure. What about *your* memories, Father? Are they all good? Can you be trapped in them and fight me at the same time?

Zane eased Susan down into a light sleep. He found himself staring at her throat, where her carotid artery pulsed with a slow, light beat. He was so very hungry. It filled his mind, tingled in his throat and stomach—

No! Get out, *now!*

Zane's legs refused to obey the order. Dimly, he was aware of tearing his clothes off so he wouldn't get blood on them. *STOP!* he commanded himself, but he could not stop. He felt his mouth catching her throat, his teeth plunging into the pale flesh. Her blood welled into his mouth, and he went wild.

A distant part of him felt everything, the blood flowing down his throat, the lurch of her body, and then he cut all blood to her brain and she was limp as a rag doll as his exertions at her throat tossed her around on the bed. Bright lights pinwheeled inside his eyes. He could feel his body pumping up, strength flowing into every muscle like jags of lightning. He wanted to shout. He stood back and capered around her bedroom, smearing the blood all over his face and chest, then fell on her again, finding the pumping wounds.

The world rushed in to fill his head. He smelled the teak of her jewelry chest, heard the distant clank of elevator cables in the apartment building.

He sat back from her at last and took deep breaths, one after another. He felt grand, euphoric. He knew he should be disappointed at his weakness, but the firestorm of ecstacy in his bloodstream permitted no negative feelings.

After all, how much must he do to prove he was strong? Go without blood until he withered and died? How smart would that be? Because of what he had just done, he would not be able to get close to his father again without being recognized, but he had learned most of what he needed to know—where Father lived and worked, and where one of his acquaintances lived.

Besides, look how easily he had controlled Susan's memories. Mentally, he was strong enough. So why not regain his physical strength? Within hours, he would have most of it back. Another feeding or two would bring him to full strength. Then he could go after Father, and to hell with all this cautious preparation.

Zane looked at Susan and felt a twinge of sadness. He should have tried to play with her instead of feeding on her. It probably would have saved her, and it might have been nice.

His regret surprised him. What did it matter? Sex and blood—that's all normals were good for. Why couldn't Father understand that? Instead of sex, he "fell in love." As for blood, he sneaked it like a jackal, without making the kill. What must that be like, making only a tiny puncture? How did he feel when he slipped the needle in? He had the gene; the urge to kill must scream through in every fiber of his nerve and blood. And yet he resisted, decade after decade, century after century. Why? Did he really think he could become one of them?

Zane shook off the questions. What did he care about Merrick? He hated him, and that was all.

Zane looked at the torn body again, this time without regret. What was done, was done. The only decision left was how to make it count for something. He glanced at the bedroom window. Dark now—good. He wrapped the body up in the bedspread. Stepping into her shower, he rinsed all her blood off and dried himself. As he dressed, he laid his plans. He had started with a church, why not stay with that motif? With Susan, he could show the religious of Washington the power of preying.

Of course, the important thing was what he would show Merrick. I hid the last one, Father, so it would be just between you and me. This time everyone is going to know. I'll terrify your city. They'll hound you to find me. The heat will be on—just one more hurdle for you to jump.

And when I'm done at the church, I should still have time to visit your doctor friend again. What is she to you, Father? If I hurt her, will you feel the pain?

TEN

KATIE TRIED NOT to feel discouraged as she hand-carried the latest blood sample from Rebecca Trent's room down to labs. Almost 8:00 P.M.—a long day, one crisis after another. The most frustrating thing was that she'd had no chance to run further tests on the strange RBCs. Her patients had to come first, but the cells were important, too. A vicious killer was out there somewhere. If his blood hid some clue to his identity, the sooner she found it, the sooner Merrick could hunt him down and stop him.

The elevator doors crawled apart—empty, thank goodness. She did not feel up to even the minimal social demands of an occupied elevator. Leaning back into a rear corner, she eased some of the weight off her feet. She hated to think how she must look, hair frizzled, white coat speckled with blood, that gaping run in her pantyhose where she'd snagged it on the cart during the exertions of a marrow extraction. I am so damn tired, she thought. I should put an hour in on the killer's blood now, but my brain is shot, too.

She thought of the samples the pharmaceutical rep had left in her office this morning. The twelve capsules of Desoxyn had stood out from the rest, winking invitingly through the plastic bubbles on their perforated sheet, and her pulse had raised an instant, soft drumbeat of desire at her temples. She'd thrown them away as soon as the rep was gone, but they were probably still in the wastebasket under her desk.

Katie's hairline prickled. Why hadn't she flushed the amphetamines? Usually she threw anything like that straight into her office toilet.

An ache started up at the base of her throat. It's just that I've got so much more to do all of a sudden, she thought. My patients, my research with Rebecca, and now the killer's blood. I'm moving too slowly on that, letting Merrick down. . . .

Stop it!

With an effort, she put the amphetamine samples out of her mind. She would deliver Rebecca's blood to the lab and go straight home to bed. Tomorrow, she would be ready to go again. She'd find a way to squeeze in some work on the killer's blood.

To distract herself, she held up the sample she'd taken from Rebecca. Fraction Eight. In the elevator's grim flourescent light the blood looked almost blue. How bravely Rebecca faced the needle, as if she really were the stoic old lady her body falsely portrayed. Finding a good vein in her wrinkled, atrophic skin seemed to get harder every day. Blue and purple bruises still flared around needle sites from as long as a month ago. Accelerated aging meant slow healing, but it was hard not to feel rebuked by those lingering bruises. Each one marked a moment of fear and pain for Rebecca. She never complained at being stuck, even if it took three or four tries, but it had to upset her. Inside that old lady's body was a kid too emotionally unseasoned not to hate and fear needles.

Katie saw herself suddenly in the silvery walls of the elevator, a blurred face that snapped into focus beyond the upraised test tube. Her expression looked so utterly bleak that she knew she must either smile or burst into tears. She stuck out her tongue at the shimmery face, then reeled it back in quickly as the elevator doors rumbled open. Luckily, no one was waiting outside to catch her mugging. She walked the short section of basement corridor to the lab, where she left the sample with the night technician.

Back on Three East, one of the nurses hailed her as she tried to slip past the station. Resigned, Katie turned; the nurse took a second look at her and said, "Never mind."

"No, it's all right. What?"

"Jenny seems down tonight. I tried talking to her, but she clammed right up. I don't know if it's pain or what."

With a mental effort, Katie rolled back some of her weariness. "I'll look in on her."

"Thanks." The nurse helped her on with the scrubs and mask. Jenny lay on her side, her eyes wide open. Her face was white, beyond the paleness of leukemia.

Katie hurried to her side. "Jenny, what's wrong?"

For a moment, Jenny did not respond. "Nothing," she whispered at last. Katie touched her forehead. Jenny flinched away, but not before Katie felt the fever through the back of her glove. Taking the chart from the foot of Jenny's bed, Katie scribbled an order to increase the dose of acetaminophen. She also requested a stat CBC screening.

"Getting any sleep?" Katie asked.

"I sleep all the time." Instead of looking at her, Jenny gazed at the Barbie doll on her bed table. Katie's uneasiness deepened. Even when Jenny was feeling very bad, she was usually more communicative. There seemed to be a subtle barrier between them tonight. Depression? God knows Jenny had reason to be depressed. And I do, too, Katie thought. She's dying and I can't seem to do anything about it. Have I been withdrawing from her? Is that why she's acting this way now?

A terrible sense of helplessness swept Katie. "Jenny, I'm so sorry you're feeling bad. I'm trying to help, but I wish I could do better."

Jenny's eyes really focused on her for the first time. "Don't say that, Doctor O'Keefe. You're doing all you can."

"If you could tell me what's bothering you? . . ."

"I . . . keep having this . . . dream."

"Tell me about it," Katie said gently.

"A boy comes into my room. . . . He's pretty big and he's dressed in white and he wears a mask and cap, just like everyone does. . . ."

"Do you know him?"

She shook her head.

"Then what happens?"

Jenny swallowed hard. "He . . . touches me."

A sudden foreboding swept Katie. She kept her voice casual. "Where does he touch you?"

Jenny shook her head. She was very pale now.

Katie picked up the doll. "Can you show me on Barbie where the man in your dream touches you?"

Jenny stared at the doll. After a minute, she pointed to the breasts. Then her finger slid down to between the doll's legs. Katie's teeth clenched; she reminded herself that it was just a dream. Or was it?

Hiding the tension that gripped her, she set the doll down. "Jenny, are you sure you don't recognize the man in your dream?"

She shook her head. "I can't see his face because of the mask and cap."

"Sometimes you have nightmares about Doctor Giggles. Could it be Doctor Giggles?"

Jenny's eyes focused beyond Katie for a moment. "Maybe. Maybe it *is* him." For the first time that night, she smiled. "Silly, isn't it."

"No. It's scary." But Katie felt a small relief. Dr. Giggles was clearly a nightmare, and if Jenny could not tell him from the boy, the boy was probably a dream, too. Dreams were about the only semblance of life Jenny had now. While she was sleeping more and more, her pain would keep her in the light stages where most dreams occurred. Throw in hallucinations because of her fever, and you had a very confused little girl. To dream of being touched by a boy was quite natural for a girl just entering adolescence. How sad that the touches in her dream were not pleasant but frightening. Katie felt a hopeless anger at the cruelty of it. Jenny would probably never hold a lover in her arms. And now, the fear and despair of her illness were distorting the experience even in her dreams.

Still . . .

"Jenny, when you dream of this person touching you, are you here in this room in your bed?"

"Uh-huh. Just like with Doctor Giggles."

"Next time you dream about the boy, do you think you could reach for your buzzer and call for the nurses?"

"I don't know. I'm so scared I can hardly move."

"Try it, will you?"

"If I can remember. But what good will it do, since I'm only dreaming?"

"Dream nurses can chase dream boys away," Katie said. *And real nurses can catch him if he's really there.*

Jenny gave her a weak smile. "I get it. Thanks, Doctor O'Keefe. It's a good idea."

When Katie patted her shoulder very lightly, Jenny didn't flinch, but the fear still lingered in her eyes. Back at the nurses station, Katie told them about Jenny's troubling dream and asked them to keep an even closer watch on her room. She got none of the dark looks that might have met the same request for another patient. Nurses on Three East were as overworked as everywhere else, but they always seemed able to find something extra for Jenny.

As Katie was leaving the station, the phone rang.

"Doctor O'Keefe?"

Katie turned around, resigned, and took the phone. "O'Keefe."

"This is John Byner, Doctor O'Keefe. I'm at the First Baptist Church, at Fourth and New York Avenue." He hesitated. "There's been another murder."

Katie's heart sank. "Damn it!"

"Yes. I think I've found some more of the killer's blood. Can you come?"

A surge of anger burned through her weariness. *I'm going to help them catch you, you bastard.* "I'll be right there." As she put all thoughts of an early bedtime from her mind, she thought once again of the amphetamines in her office wastebasket. But she made herself walk straight down to her car.

Zane watched the older woman watch TV. She was the same one who'd come up to investigate the sound he'd made in the den, the first time he'd entered the house. Was she the doctor's housekeeper or a relative? He circled the couch quietly, viewing the woman from different angles. A rather handsome lady, in her long peach-colored robe of expensive silk. Her nose was grand and Gallic compared to the doctor's slim, straight model, but the intelligent eyes bore a strong resemblance. Even sitting on the couch, the woman had an aristocratic bearing that refused to yield to the soft cushions. And she was not eating anything. Surely, if she were a mere live-in domestic, she would be stuffing potato chips or something into her mouth.

On the other hand, her taste in TV shows was decidedly plebeian.

As Zane circled behind the woman to look over her shoulder, the cloaked and tuxedoed figure of Count Dracula swept grandly across the TV screen. The prancing poseur filled Zane with an odd mixture of amusement and chagrin. What rubbish. Stakes through the heart, shrinking away from crosses, flying around like a bat. With such melodramatic trappings who would believe? And yet this woman seemed quite rapt.

Zane watched as Dracula passed by a mirror. The camera lingered over the shot, driving home the point that he cast no reflection. That part of the myth was actually quite interesting. The makers of the movie didn't have it exactly right, but they knew invisibility was a feature of the thing they feared. Interesting, how normals could glimpse some realities only through the distorting lens of myth. They didn't know that hemophages existed, and yet their invention of vampires was not entirely accidental. What normals knew, and what they were *aware* of knowing, seemed to be two different things. Vampires, incubi, succubi—all were considered unreal, and all reflected different facets of hemophages.

Zane turned away from the TV, embarrassed that he had actually been watching the ridiculous spectacle. He felt a surge of impatience. Where was Father's doctor friend? Probably working late at the hospital, one of those dedicated types.

Zane realized the movie was heading for its climax. As the enraged mob, brandishing torches, climbed the hill toward Dracula's castle, Zane reached for the remote, then caught himself, clamping his hands over his ears instead. But the clamor of the crowd still leaked through. The sickening feeling from his nightmare—tons of dirt pressing in around his head and shoulders—swept over him. In desperation, he choked down the flow of blood to the woman's brain stem. She let out a long bubbling sigh and slumped over on the couch, deeply asleep. Snatching up the remote, he flipped to the next channel. Basketball players ran up and down the court while the announcer babbled in excitement. Zane watched for a minute, until he had purged the ugly mob scene from his mind.

Restless and annoyed, he stalked out of the living room, up the stairs. He should have done it in the first place—put the woman to sleep and reconnoitered, so when the doctor got home he would be ready. Tonight, he would start the pressure. He patted the ski mask and snub-nosed .38 in his pocket. The butt of the gun would make a good club, but he mustn't hit too hard. He was a lot stronger today than yesterday. And he must be careful not to draw blood—he did not want to slip out of control. Just rough her up a little, frighten her, then see who she called. If

Father came running, it would tell him everything he needed to know.

Standing at the top of the steps, Zane looked around. What was in the rooms past the bathroom? He started down to see. But as he passed the bathroom, he caught sight of the mirror on the cabinet door, which someone had left open. Detouring, he studied himself in the glass. Though not totally young again, his face was much improved. Most of the wrinkles had already faded in the few hours since he'd fed. His hair was still white, of course. Its natural brown color would have to grow out from the roots. Or maybe he would dye it. In any ease, he looked a lot younger—forty-five, perhaps.

Zane tipped his head back to see what had happened to the wattles under his chin. Instead, he noticed a crimson spot inside one nostril. Uneasy, he tore off a tiny piece of toilet paper, rolled it up, and probed the nostril. When he pulled it out, the tip was wet with fresh blood. His uneasiness deepened into alarm. He'd had a nosebleed! With growing horror, he stared at the glistening spot of blood. After months of blood deprivation, had the leukemia started to come back?

When had his nose bled?

With awful certainty, he knew the answer—during the kill. The excitement, the frenzy had caused a capillary to burst—

Which meant he had probably bled on the corpse.

Desperately, Zane tried to think of some other explanation, but he could not. While Susan Zarelli's blood was still fresh, he would not have been able to see his own blood mixed in with it. But when her blood dried and his did not, it would stand out like a beacon. What if the police found his blood, fresh blood that would not deteriorate? His nightmare flashed back again—the net falling over him, the pit, the bulldozers. He felt a cold surge of panic. I only left the body a couple of hours ago, he thought. Maybe no one has discovered it yet. I'll go back to the church.

Hurrying downstairs and out the back door, he ran through the darkness toward his car.

A uniformed cop guarded the rear entry to the sanctuary. Katie showed him her ID and he waved her in. Something in his face warned her and she steeled herself. She could see Merrick and some other people standing around the pulpit at the other end of the sanctuary. She was struck by what a plain, almost stark place it was—two banks of wooden pews divided by a central aisle that ended at the pulpit—

The pulpit—no, don't look!

Katie swallowed hard. A row of straight-backed wooden chairs for the elders sat along the front of a small choir loft. The National Cathedral it was not.

Why had the killer chosen it?

Let the psychologists worry about that, Katie thought. You're here for his blood.

"Katie!"

Merrick had turned away from the pulpit and was looking at her. Jumping from the platform, he hurried down the aisle and stopped her with a hand on her shoulder. "It's not good. Are you sure you want to do this?"

"I'm sure I do not," she said. "But I'm going to. Stick close to me the first minute, all right?"

He squeezed her shoulder. She reached up and patted his hand. "Okay. Let's go."

He followed her back up the aisle. Dr. Byner stood in the front of the choir loft, watching a couple of his evidence technicians dust for prints. Katie managed to get past the pulpit without looking at the body. While Byner introduced her to the two technicians, she let the corpse ease into her peripheral vision. It looked like a mannequin in a sporty white and red blouse. She made herself look squarely at the body and saw that the red spots were blood. A spotlight high in the rafters threw a blazing circle of light down on the woman, as though God himself were mourning her. She was lying on her back across the pulpit, head dangling over the front rim, feet toward the choir loft. With her arms spread out to the side, she took on the shape of a cross. Katie took a deep breath and moved up to the pulpit to see her face, *oh God, her throat. . . .*

The sanctuary dimmed around Katie. She was vaguely aware of Merrick's hands catching both elbows. *No, I will not faint!* She straightened and gulped air and her head cleared. Merrick let her go. If Byner had noticed anything, he gave no sign of it.

Steeling herself, Katie looked again. The throat had been chewed on both sides. The skin was flayed back around the woman's jaws. Flensing, the pathologist would call it. Stepping closer, she saw a tiny wet smear on the crusted blood under the woman's chin.

And something else. On her forehead, a Z was drawn in dried blood.

"Was this on the last victim?" she asked, pointing.

"No." Merrick's voice sounded hoarse with pain, or perhaps anger. The mark *was* offensive, an arrogant touch, the killer signing his work as if he were an artist.

"Did you turn the spotlight on her or did he?" she asked.

"He did." Merrick bit the words off.

Katie wished she had not asked. Before, the light had looked warm to her, almost a benediction; now it seemed cold and mocking. She continued her inspection. Crusted blood matted the woman's dark hair in back so thoroughly that it did not hang down but clung instead to the back of the neck. There was no blood on the floor. Clearly, she had been killed somewhere else, then brought here. There might be more of the killer's blood wherever the murder actually took place.

"What was her name?" Katie asked.

"Susan Zarelli," Merrick said.

"So that's why the killer put a Z on her forehead."

"So it would appear."

"Do you know where she was killed?"

"Her apartment, near George Washington University. Her boyfriend found her bed covered with blood and called us. Doctor Byner and I were working that scene when the church custodian found the body and called the police."

"Do you see the fresh blood, Doctor?" Byner asked.

"Under her chin."

"Right. Since you'll be analyzing it, I decided to wait and let you take the slide, if you would please. My kit is on the floor there."

"Fine."

A uniformed cop stepped up onto the platform. "We found out how he got in," he said to Merrick. "There's a broken basement window behind some bushes."

Byner motioned to the technicians. "Let's take a look. Maybe he left some blood there, too. You coming, Lieutenant?"

Merrick looked reluctant, but he nodded.

When they were gone, Katie felt horribly alone, though the uniformed cop still guarded the entry at the far end of the sanctuary. She stepped around the pulpit, because she had not yet really seen the woman's face and for some reason she needed to. The woman's eyes were slightly open. Her features were relaxed, almost tranquil, as though she'd never felt what happened to her. Katie hoped that was true, but it was hard to imagine a killer who had done that to her throat having any mercy in him.

Katie applied herself to getting a slide of the wet blood. There didn't seem to be more than four or five drops at most—enough for a single slide. She took one from Byner's case and eased it against the glistening smear. The surface tension of the fresh blood made it rise to the glass. She swiped the slide gently away and the droplets came up without disturbing the darker, dried blood beneath.

She heard a whisper of sound behind her. She looked around, expecting to see Byner or Merrick, but the platform was empty. Still, she had the creepy feeling of being watched. Standing very still, listening, she heard what sounded like a soft sigh. Goose bumps stood up on her arms. She peered around again, but the platform remained empty except for her and the corpse. At the far end of the sanctuary, the cop leaned on the doorjamb, studying his notebook. He did not look as if he had seen or heard anything, but he was so far away that it failed to reassure her.

Katie had the sudden horrid thought that it might be the killer, still in here somewhere, hiding. There was nowhere to hide. . . .

Except in the choir loft.

Her fingers trembled as she set the slide on a corner of the pulpit. Gathering her nerve, she walked up the side aisle of the loft and looked down each row of seats. When she got to the third row, the floorboards creaked at the opposite end of the aisle, startling her, but no one was there. She took a hurried look along the last row. The loft was empty. Of course it was—you're spooking yourself, she thought. You're not used to bloody corpses, that's all.

Returning to the pulpit, she reached for the slide.

It was gone.

Something brushed her back. She whirled in alarm; no one was there—and yet she could sense him, an evil presence very close to her. And then she felt his breath on her neck and she screamed.

ELEVEN

MERRICK TRIED TO hide the fury that simmered in him as he watched Byner and the evidence technicians sniff around the basement floor below the broken window. The tear-streaked face of Susan Zarelli's boyfriend burned in his mind. The man had felt ashamed for sobbing in front of the police.

Where was the phage's shame?

Merrick's jaw clenched. *You vicious bastard, I'm going to stop you.*

He made himself think about the more immediate task— getting some kind of control over this new evidence. He suppressed a groan. At the victim's apartment, he'd been able to check for possible phage blood before Byner arrived. But he'd had no chance here at the church—not with Byner tagging along from the apartment. There could be no acceptable reason for asking the chief medical examiner to wait while he took the first look at the corpse. So, of course Byner had trooped out onto the platform with him and they had both spotted the fresh blood under the victim's chin at the same moment.

At least the custodian who'd found Susan's body didn't see the wet blood—or didn't realize it was significant. So the damage was still confined to Byner and Katie.

Merrick had the uneasy feeling he had missed something, made a wrong assumption somewhere. The bloody Z on the victim's forehead could stand either for Zane or the victim—Zarelli. Clearly, it was phage blood under the victim's chin. But the only reason a hemophage would have a nosebleed during the frenzy of killing was that he'd gone too long without feeding. A fine explanation for the blood on the first victim but, once the phage had fed on that first victim, he would no longer be deprived. So why had he bled on the second victim, too?

Unless he *hadn't* fed on the first victim.

Pathology had definitely found teeth marks in the torn skin. No one could tear a throat with his teeth without blood touching his lips, and at that point, how could any phage resist drinking? I wouldn't be that strong, Merrick thought. Neither would Sandeman. Zane certainly couldn't be so disciplined. . . .

Unless he *didn't* use his teeth.

Merrick's confusion deepened, even as he saw how it could be done—a set of false teeth gripped in the hand. If the phage had looked somewhere else while the blood was spurting, he might have been able to keep from drinking it.

But *why?*

Merrick heard a faint, muffled scream from above him. *Katie!* he thought with alarm. Byner and the technicians kept on with their work, and Merrick realized the solid construction of the old church had kept the sound below their threshold of hearing. Backing away from them, he hurried upstairs, along the back hall and through the pastor's study. Flinging open the door to the platform, he stared, unable for a second to make sense of what he saw. The uniformed cop and Katie stood at the pulpit. The cop looked baffled; Katie's face was white. She was talking to the cop—something about a missing slide. Behind her, mostly hidden by her, was another man. Katie bent down suddenly, revealing the man's face.

Zane!

Merrick felt a cold shock in his veins, and then a staggering flood of emotion—alarm for Katie, incredulity, fury at Zane, and then a contrary longing so deep it shocked him all over again. He had the insane urge to run to Zane and embrace him. *My son!* he thought. *I haven't been this close to you in five hundred years! Even when I was hunting you twelve years ago, I only got within a hundred yards at the end. All the other times, never more than a distant glimpse. You're so handsome! You have your mother's eyes.*

But why is your hair white?

And then Merrick remembered the old man at the café—the hotel, too—and everything fell together in a stunning instant. Zane looked old because he had, in fact, not been taking blood. *He did it so he could follow me around.*

Zane, why?

You know why.

Zane's eyes burned back at him with a hatred so strong that Merrick felt a tremor of fear and anguish.

And then his paralysis broke. *Get him—*

NO!

Merrick felt another cold shockwave as he realized how close he'd come to lunging at Zane. He saw that Katie was giving him an odd look. He should have said something right away, instead of standing paralyzed, staring over her head with his jaw hanging open. He tried to find his voice. "I heard a scream," he rasped. "Are you all right?"

"I don't *know*." She stood again. This time Zane did not crouch behind her; his head, with the startling white mane, seemed to sit, leering, on top of hers.

"Was that you just now?" Katie asked.

"What do you mean?"

"I was sure I heard someone in here. Then something touched me. Did you come in and go out again when my back was turned?"

Zane raised a hand in mocking salute, then pointed at Katie's neck and drew a finger across his own throat.

With an effort, Merrick kept his face impassive. He must not let Zane know how very frightened he was for Katie. "I did step in for a second," he said. "You looked busy so I decided not to disturb you."

Her shoulders sagged. "I thought I was coming unravelled."

Merrick was conscious suddenly of the uniformed cop, an added complication. "Everything's all right, here," Merrick told the cop. "Go to the basement and see if you can help Dr. Byner."

With a touch to the bill of his cap, the man hurried away.

"Merrick, did you pick up the slide when you came in?" Katie asked.

Behind her, Zane held up a glass slide smeared with his blood. Merrick realized he was staring over Katie's head again and made himself look at her.

"I didn't take any slide," he said. "Maybe you misplaced it."

Katie frowned. She got down on her hands and knees again, searching the floor around the pulpit. Merrick's mind raced. Was there any way he could capture Zane here? The possible scenarios flashed through his mind. In all of them, Katie learned about hemophages. If her terror was not too great—if she loved him enough, he might be able to persuade her to keep the secret. But there was another danger—that she would die, here and now. If he attacked Zane, Zane could in the same instant strike the blood supply to Katie's brain. A massive stroke, a gushing aneurysm— so simple to kill her. He must despise me for protecting normals, Merrick thought. Just for that, he would strike her down if I attack him. I can't do anything until we're both away from her.

Zane smiled insolently, obviously aware it was a stalemate. The smile infuriated Merrick, but at the same time he felt a grudging respect for this new and stronger Zane—if he had gained enough discipline that he could refuse to feed after killing, maybe he could even manage to stop killing. . . .

But he did not want to stop, did he? In the past week he had viciously murdered two people.

Fear, anger, and despair swept Merrick as he appraised his son. I should never have given you blood, he thought. I fathered you twice—an innocent baby and then, because I couldn't let you die, a monster. Look at you, standing there, so smug, so unmoved by the sight of your victim. From blood I made you, and you've made it run like a river. It's on my hands, too. Not only did I make you, I'm the only one who could stop you. Instead, I've always let you slip away—Sandeman saw that. But it ends here.

Merrick's eyes burned suddenly. There was only one way to end it, and that was to put Zane in the vault.

I have to kill you, my own son. . . .

Fiercely, Merrick fought down his pain. He must be strong now. Still holding Zane's gaze, he inclined his head toward the door to the study. From there, they could go outside, find a place away from everyone. *Let's finish it.*

Zane's insolent smile faded. He nodded slowly. Merrick's heart banged in agony, like a funeral drum.

Katie rose from behind the pulpit. "It's just not here," she said. "I can't find it anywhere."

With an effort, Merrick focused on her again; at that moment Zane started backing away from her toward the other end of the platform. Another two steps down to the main sanctuary and he could slip out the side door. *He'll get away!* Anxiety shot through Merrick. He started after Zane, rounding the pulpit, but Katie caught his arm. "Where are you going?"

"I need something from my car."

"You look upset."

In his peripheral vision, Merrick saw Zane ease the push-bar of the door down. A second later he slipped out. In an agony of impatience, Merrick pulled free. He softened it by patting her shoulder as he brushed past her. "I'm all right," he said. "I'll be back in a minute. Why don't you take another slide."

"There isn't enough blood—"

And then he was out the door, closing it behind him, praying she would not follow. He looked around the parking lot but could not see Zane. Desperately he scanned the bushes beside the church, the cars parked on the street, the surrounding buildings. Zane had escaped. Merrick felt a surge of frustration—*twenty feet away from me, and I lost him.*

Merrick realized that he felt relief, too, and he must not allow that in himself. Zane must die.

At least he took his blood with him, Merrick thought. No more evidence for Katie and Byner. That must be why he came back. After this killing he must have somehow realized he'd bled.

Merrick heard the door open behind him. Turning, he saw Katie standing in the doorway, gazing at him with a frightened expression. "Merrick, you've got to listen to me. Please don't look away and don't walk off. I did make that slide and now it's gone. And whatever touched my back couldn't have been you. I turned around the second it happened and the platform was empty." She stared at him, as if she hoped he would contradict her.

He stepped to her, took her hands. "This is the first time you've seen a murder victim. It's a very frightening experience— even more frightening than you realize. Your mind can play tricks on you."

She shook her head. "Maybe I could imagine someone touching me, but physical objects don't just vanish."

"It'll turn up. We'll have the technicians look for it." Maybe

I can fake finding it, Merrick thought. I could crush a slide and claim the cop stepped on it when he ran up on the platform after she screamed. I could say I found the fragments down in the sanctuary somewhere and there's no blood on them because it stuck to his boot. . . . Merrick realized it sounded far-fetched, even to him.

She blew out a breath. "I *am* scared."

"I know." He pulled her into a hug. As he caressed her back, he felt all his old love for her, intense as ever. Behind him, he heard a car drive into the church parking lot, a white van with the words *Washington Times* on the side. His heart sank. He would not be able to keep this killing quiet. Gently, he released Katie and she pulled away.

"Did you get what you wanted from your car?" Katie asked.

"I lied. I needed some air."

"You're scared, too?"

"Of course."

For the first time that night, she smiled. He tried to smile back, but he was too frightened—for her. Why had Zane mimed cutting her throat? Just a casual threat to the nearest normal, or more? He saw us together at the outdoor café, Merrick thought. But we were arguing then about whether Katie should be on the case. And now that he's seen her here, won't he decide she's just a part of Byner's forensic team?

It seemed logical, and he wanted to believe it, but to do so would be to take a big chance. After the outdoor café, he had dropped Katie off at home, with Zane no doubt following behind. He knew where she lived.

I must keep away from her from now on, Merrick thought.

And then, with a sharp dismay, he remembered that he had not just argued with Katie in the café, he had held her hand. And then, at her door, he had kissed her good-bye. Zane had to have seen it, which meant he must at least suspect how much Katie meant to him. She's already in danger, Merrick thought miserably. I have to protect her.

From the corner of his eye, Merrick saw a woman in a trench coat get out of the news van and head toward him.

"Uh-oh," Katie said.

Quickly, he said, "Katie, after we're through here I'd like to go home with you. I'd like to spend the night."

She looked at him for a long moment. "Okay," she said.

* * *

"Merrick, what a pleasant surprise." Katie's mother opened the front door, smiling cordially, not overdoing it, but he could tell she was pleased.

"Hello, Audrey." He was happy to see her, too. Actually, in recent months he'd seen her more often than he'd seen Katie—every time he visited Gregory. He appreciated her friendliness and found it uncommonly open-minded. Not only did she not hold his breakup with her daughter against him, he could tell she wished he and Katie would get back together, though she was too tactful ever to say so. If he stayed the night, he would raise her hopes, but it couldn't be helped. He had to know Katie was safe from Zane.

"I'll be right back," Katie said. "I'm just going to look in on Gregory for a minute."

"I'll go with you," Merrick said.

Katie looked surprised, then pleased. She nodded. As he climbed the stairs behind her, he heard Audrey humming while she bustled around in the kitchen.

What am I doing?

Just this one night, he thought.

Gregory was sleeping on his stomach, his cheek pressed into the mattress. He had kicked his blankets aside. Four of his favorite stuffed animals stood an easy watch around him. The sight of his small back rising and falling in the sweet, primal rhythms of sleep went straight to Merrick's heart. He longed to pick him up, hug him. A sudden image of Zane at this age came to him, Zane lying in a very different crib but looking very much like this. He remembered Zane as a child, sunny, always laughing; Zane at twelve, dying of hemophagic leukemia. *How naive I was,* Merrick thought. *I gave him the blood without even thinking about it. I was so confident I could also give him the wisdom and strength he needed to fight what he had become.*

Where did I go wrong? I tried to be an example to him, show him it could be done. No one did that for me, and yet I'm able to resist the gene.

He thought of his own father, a kind, warm-hearted man, a normal who could have had no conception what his son would become. A fragment of memory broke loose inside him, of the cathedral in south Wessex. A murky place, torches guttering on the walls, straw on the floor, livestock wandering in, the continual echoing racket. He would stand there between his parents, holding their hands while the priest chanted the mass; just a boy, wanting nothing more than to become a village healer like his father.

Somehow, his parents, even though they had no idea of the dark thing that slept inside him, had given him the strength to fight it when it awoke.

And somehow, he had failed to pass that same strength on to Zane. *Didn't I love him enough?* Merrick wondered. *That can't be. I loved him with all my heart. Did his mother dying have something to do with it? Erlina was wonderful . . . but Zane had eleven good years with her—almost as many as I had with my mother.*

As Merrick looked down at Gregory, a spasm of fear clutched his heart. *What if Gregory has the gene? Could I let him die? Or would I risk giving the world a second Zane?* His fear sharpened, stabbing down into his stomach.

He felt Katie's touch. He gripped her hand and squeezed, closing his eyes, gulping a deep breath, then managed a smile for her. Gregory stirred and rolled over, pushing aside his stuffed companions to clutch at the balled-up blanket.

Katie tiptoed out and Merrick followed her down the hall to her bedroom. Inside, she pulled him to her again. He held her a moment, savoring the wonderful feel of her along his body. He could smell the shampoo in her hair, a tangy, apricot scent. Backing away with a smile, she walked to her dresser and began to take her clothes off, chatting with him in the casual way he remembered so well. He knew she was struggling, after the dreadful scene in the church, to find some sense of normalcy. He needed it, too, even with Zane out there, still on the loose—needed it *because* Zane was out there. *He came back to challenge me,* Merrick thought, *and yet he ran away from the church. He must still be afraid of me. But he's dangerous, too—stronger, maybe, than he realizes.*

He killed and didn't drink.

A very sobering thought. Merrick still had trouble believing it, even though he knew it must be so. He wondered again whether he should have come here to Katie's tonight. He'd made sure they weren't followed from the church, but that didn't mean Katie was in the clear—not if Zane had followed them earlier.

Still in her bra and slip, Katie turned to face him. "So are you going to get undressed or what?"

Beneath the joking tone, he could sense her fear, her uncertainty. What were they doing? No matter how familiar this felt, the reasons they had ended it had not changed. Those first months apart had been like walking over broken glass; if they did this now, they would have to tread that same lacerating ground again.

"Can't we hide in the past," Katie asked, as if reading his mind, "just for tonight?" Her eyes were luminous. Desire for her welled up in him. He removed the Glock from his shoulder holster and the smaller .38 caliber revolver from his ankle holster. With a pang, he saw that she still kept the drawer in her bed table clear for the two guns.

He undressed as she watched.

"You look good," she murmured, her voice under control again.

He felt himself springing into instant hardness. How he had missed her. She could not know how much she meant to him, how when he was with her he felt more human, less an animal, than at any other time.

He went to her and she leaned into him, gripping him between her legs as they kissed. Her tongue found its way into his mouth and he met it eagerly. She pushed against his chest to steer him backward to the bed. He spread his knees to sit, gasping as he slid down between her legs. With an urgent sound, she pushed him back and straddled him. "Oh, Merrick, I've missed you so much. Let's go back now. It's three years ago, before the trouble. Just for tonight."

"Just for tonight." He reached up for her breasts. They were so soft and perfect, small and round against his palms. He pulled her hips around the tip of him, easing her way down, already wet inside.

His hands still on her hips, he stilled them, stopping her, lifting her away. Without a word, she backed off him, and went to her dresser. As she looked for a condom, he remembered the night she'd asked why, if he was so determined not to be a father, he didn't get a vasectomy. How typically male his hemming and hawing must have seemed to her. If only a vasectomy were possible. But his remarkable, cursed cells would repair each cut in front of an astonished surgeon's eyes. His days of passing for normal would be over. And he'd still be as able as ever to father children.

Katie returned with a condom. He reached for it, but she warded his hand off. Taking her time, she put it on him, stroking him in a way that sent waves of pleasure soaring through him. Before, she had always given it to him and looked away while he put it on. Was she trying to tell him it could be different if they tried again?

We can't, Katie.

I should stop this now, he thought, but I can't.

She slid down on him again, bending forward, her nipples hard against his chest. He could have come that instant, but he didn't, keeping himself from the brink while she moved gently around on top of him.

"Ah!" Merrick gasped.

"It's before," she whispered, "and we're in love. Just for tonight, just for tonight."

"I love you, Katie."

Tears sprang into her eyes, but she arched her head back above him, her teeth gleaming in the soft light. Her hair swung around her shoulders as she began to moan softly. Realizing she was coming, he let himself feel her fully again. He came at once, rocking up into her over and over as she uttered a soft string of cries.

She collapsed over him, hugging his shoulders, planting quick kisses all over his face. Even with the dampness on her face, it felt so wonderful to touch her again. He held her tightly until she groaned and rolled away.

"I'm so warm," she said. "You burn like a furnace." Her voice was ragged, but he knew she did not want him to notice.

"Cops eat a lot of chili and peppers," he said.

"I don't think that's it."

"What do you think it is?"

"I think it's 1992 and you love me."

He smiled. "You're right."

As she lay beside him, gazing into his eyes, he felt himself sliding over an emotional cliff, hanging on by his nails. A desperate frustration filled him. Oh, yes, I love you and I love my son so very much, but it's 1995 and I can't have you, and you can't have me, because of what I am.

She buried her head against his shoulder. In minutes he heard her breathing even out. He felt a powerful longing to be truthful with her, to rouse her now and tell her everything, to let her understand why they and Gregory could never be a family. But what would he say? That he had fathered too many children already, his body staying young, theirs aging until he was forced to leave or be unmasked? That he had seen too many of his beloved grow old and die, and that the pain was worse each time.

He remembered the last ones—Alexandra and young George, the seaside house outside San Francisco. That balmy summer morning, the smell of hyacinth sweet in the air. It was only a few months after he had capsized his boat to make it appear he'd drowned: Alexandra and George sat at the kitchen table, their breakfasts untouched. He stood on the patio outside, watching them through the screen. How he longed to let them see him. He listened as they spoke of him with love and sadness. Alexandra began to cry. George held his mother, trying to be brave. The tears had started to flow down his own cheeks and he had fled in agony—

Katie prodded him from the wrenching memory with a kiss and he realized she had not quite been asleep.

"What are you thinking?" she asked.

"About breakfast."

She laughed and poked him in the stomach, then turned her back against him, nestling into the familiar perfect fit. Again, she dozed. It would be nice to sleep with her, but he was still too flush with the hotel manager's blood to sleep. He contented himself with holding her, guarding her sleep as the stuffed animals guarded Gregory's. Stroking her shoulder, he was overwhelmed with tenderness for her. The thought of telling her clung. Maybe their love could carry her through the shock and horror. And then what?

Within the year, they'd have to move. When Zane had lured him here with the killings twelve years ago, he'd had no time to set up a new identity the way he usually did. At that point he'd only been Merrick Chapman for a few years and he'd decided to use his credentials as a San Francisco homicide detective to get on the Washington force right away. After Zane ran, he probably should have started over someplace else. But the total disruption of his life was just what Zane had wanted all along and, hating to give it to him, he'd stayed on. Now he had been Merrick Chapman almost twenty years, and there was no longer any option. If Katie was to be with him, she'd have to uproot her life, leave all her friends and her medical career to start over someplace where neither of them were known. Then, in a few more years, she would have to do it again. Over and over, she would be forced to suffer the upheaval of his forced migrations. Could she manage year after year to make no slip that would expose him? Maybe she could.

And Gregory? Sooner or later, he'd have to be told. I've already failed once to win the loyalty of a son, Merrick thought bitterly.

But it was Katie that concerned him the most. As she uprooted herself again and again, the woman she saw in the mirror would, over the years, change. Katie would come to hate that aging image in the mirror as no other woman could, to fear that her young-looking husband no longer found her attractive, to mourn that she could not stay young with and for him. There could be no way out for her. He'd been able to give the others escape when he saw they needed it. Because they did not know what he was, for them he could "die." He could go fight the Normans or the Vikings or Napoleon and not come back, or, during times of peace, go hunting in the wilds and fail to return. Later came the empty Pierce Arrow floating downriver from the broken rail in the bridge, the overturned boat in the ocean.

Merrick felt a sharp longing. If he could grow old and die with Katie, he would be the happiest man alive. But he could not, and so he should not have let it start. After the pain of leaving Alexandra and George, he'd vowed never to fall in love again—and most especially to avoid women who wanted children. While Alexandra still lived, he'd had no trouble keeping that vow. Then, a few years after Alexandra died, he'd met Katie. . . .

With an effort, Merrick pulled himself from the past. Nothing in it could be changed. What mattered now was that Zane was on the offensive. Tonight's murder would make the papers, intensifying the pressure. Captain Rourke would be breathing down his neck first thing tomorrow.

If he could just find Zane's home base . . .

I'll see Sandeman again, Merrick decided. He might have some good theories about where Zane would stay—

Merrick heard a sound at the back window of the bedroom, very faint but eerily familiar: a sandy trickle of crushed mortar. The hairs stood up on his neck and his heart began to pound. How many times had he made that same sound himself? The window was two stories up; there was nothing outside for a man—a *normal* man—to cling to.

Merrick eased away from Katie and slid out of bed, making every movement relaxed and natural. He stretched, then glanced at the window. Through the crack in the drapes, he saw an eye peering in. In the next instant, the eye vanished, followed by a faint thump below.

Furious, Merrick hurried to the window. By the time he pulled the drape aside to look out, Zane was gone.

Merrick stared into the night, his fury turning inward, searing him. I've been stupid, he thought. I knew Zane might follow us here. I had to come to make sure Katie was safe, but did I have to let Zane see us making love?

Merrick's anger faded into fear. Now that Zane knows we're

lovers, what will he do? Should I warn her? But what would I tell her—watch out for an invisible man?

And there is no way she can defend herself anyway.

Merrick let the curtain fall closed again. Turning, he gazed at the woman he adored—and now had put in terrible danger. With a fierce effort, he forced himself to calmness. A savage resolve filled him. There was only one sure way to protect Katie. Catch Zane.

TWELVE

MERRICK HELD KATIE in his arms, watching her sleep. She was very warm where their bodies touched. A faint, animal scent rose from her, the musk of their lovemaking and the oil of her skin, which reminded him of how Gregory had smelled as a baby. As he breathed through her hair, it caressed his face like the soft grass of some exotic savannah.

He wished he could hold her forever.

When the darkness began to thin and her alarm rang, he kissed her awake, dressed, and said good-bye. He even drove away in case she was watching. Circling the block, he parked again half a block from her house and watched the first light turn the budding leaves of the maples a deep rose hue. Moments later, Katie bustled out the front door and into her sporty red Cutlass. The car zipped down the driveway and sped away toward the hospital with a soft growl of dual exhausts. Merrick gazed after it until it turned the corner two blocks down. As he lost sight of Katie, the dejection he had been trying to suppress welled up. Despite the shock of Zane's eye at the window, last night had been wonderful. But it must never happen again. His future could never mesh with Katie's. Like the others, she was a flower that would only wilt faster if he tried to hold it.

But he could not make a clean break with her either, as he had last time—not as long as Zane was free. Somehow, he must stay physically close to but emotionally distant from the woman he loved, until he could bury his son. Then he must give her up entirely. A harsh laugh escaped Merrick. If I weren't depressed, he thought, there'd be something wrong with me.

He started his car. If Zane meant to come after Katie, he'd find it easiest at night. She should be relatively safe in the bright lights and bustle of the hospital. *But I must be here when she gets home tonight.*

Pulling from the curb, Merrick sped across town toward the precinct, conscious of how much he had to do. Zane had been out-thinking him. He must turn that around, go on the attack. Sandeman could help him do that, but he could not go to the vault—not yet. First he must give Captain Rourke his pound of flesh for the new murder. If he did not face Rourke right away, the captain might start grilling people like the chief medical examiner instead.

Merrick gripped the wheel in frustration. Over the long haul, DC Homicide was a magnet for the kind of information he needed. If he weren't with the police, he would not have known until this morning's paper that a hemophage was in town. He liked Rourke and the detectives and was grateful for their company most of the time. But now he needed to be free of them, and he could not be, and it was galling.

Merrick parked behind the precinct building and ran up the four flights to homicide, trying to burn off some of his tension. As he entered the squad room, the noise level faded for a second, then started up again, setting off alarms in his mind. Rumors were common as heartburn in here; clearly, these men had heard one about him.

He stopped at Desmond White's desk. White suddenly became deeply engrossed in something on his own shirt. "New suspenders?" Merrick asked.

White looked up with a pained expression. "Suspenders are for firemen. These are braces, man." Merrick knew Des was only pretending to be aggrieved, that he appreciated having his clothes noticed. The man took a lot of care with his wardrobe, perhaps to compensate for his homeliness. This morning he sported a silk shirt and tie and dark pleated pants from a Saville Row suit. The braces—black, red, and green, with a subtle motif Merrick recognized as seventeenth-century Masai—had probably set him back two Cs. Fortunately, White took as much care with his work as he did his clothes, which meant he kept up with all squad room rumors.

"Are you going to make me ask?" Merrick said.

White glanced at the captain's office. Merrick saw that the door was closed. "Okay, so who's in there?"

"Detective Emerson Cooke, senior homicide lieutenant in this precinct." White chewed each word.

"Mmhmm." At once, Merrick saw the situation.

"Yeyas," Des said. "Now that your killer has made the papers, Cooke is no doubt kissing up to the captain in the hope he can steal your case. I, personally, am praying he doesn't. Last time I had to work for Cooke, the son of a bitch put me on winter stakeout eight nights running. Told me I was harder to see in the dark."

"So stop wearing dark clothes."

"I think he was, in his charming way, referring to my African-American-ness. I'm telling you, Merrick, if I pull Cooke again, I'll have to kill him. They'll put my ass in jail."

Merrick forced a smile. "Don't worry about it. This is my case."

White looked dubious.

Merrick glanced around and caught Reggie Didier and Don Roach peering his way. "My office," he called out. "As soon as I'm done with the captain. And I hope for your sakes you found me a car that didn't belong around that church."

The two swung to their computer screens and picked up their phones. White gave him an admiring look. "They teach you that in lieutenant's school?"

"There isn't any lieutenant's school, Desmond."

"No shit. If there were, they'd have flunked Cooke's ass out." White glanced at the captain's door again. "You sure you want to go in there, man? Rourke burned in here with the *Post* and the *Times* clamped under his armpits and a face that could flag down bulls. We didn't find any cars around the church and we barely started working the neighborhood, so we don't have squat to tell you. If Reggie or Don have anything new I can patch it through to you. Might be better this morning if you just slip on back out the way you came. I'll tell Rourke you already briefed us and hit the street. You getting out there ahead of your own men might impress him, make a nice contrast from Cooke's pucker.'' White made loud kissing noises.

"Thanks for the advice," Merrick said.

"But you're not going to take it. That's the trouble with free advice. I'm going to have to start charging."

The captain's door opened and Cooke inched out backward, still talking to Rourke. Merrick made sure he was right behind him when he turned. A look that might have been guilt crossed Cooke's narrow face and then he smiled.

"Chapman. Tough luck about the new murder."

"It's not luck. It's what he does."

"Yeah. This is some kind of a pervert we got here."

Merrick noted the "we" without comment. Thinking himself the oldest detective in Homicide, Cooke liked to act like he owned a piece of every case and was entitled to offer advice whenever he liked. With his gray hair slicked straight back and his pinched, acne-scarred face, he looked like a mafia enforcer; he was mean enough, but nowhere near as tough. Merrick had seen his type many times since 1880, when he had joined the Metropolitan Police in London, forerunner of all modern police departments. On every force since, in Moscow, Paris, Berlin, Stockholm, Lisbon, Melbourne, and half a dozen smaller cities, he'd encountered men who thrived by mastering squad politics, exploiting their peers, and manipulating the press. Here in Washington, Cooke had managed enough good ink over the years to gain powerful friends above Rourke in the chain of command. Where he blundered was in caring nothing for the people below him, who also could have made him look good. Most of the detectives felt the way Desmond did about him.

"Listen, Merrick," Cooke said, "I know the press can be brutal; I can help. You young guys don't realize—"

"I realize," Merrick said. "What you'd better realize is that this is my case and it's going to stay my case."

This time Cooke's smile was cold. "We don't make those decisions, the captain does. And I must say he's not too happy with you today. Two very nasty killings and you're clueless. If I were you, I wouldn't go in there right now."

"Fortunately for me, you're not me."

Rourke bellied up to the door and stared at both of them. "You guys want to chat, do it later. Merrick, inside." He jerked a thumb.

Cooke's smile widened.

Merrick pulled the door shut softly. Rourke eased into his swivel chair, wringing a chorus of squeaks from the springs. His face was redder than usual and, though the office was cool, sweat had already stained his collar and the underarms of his white shirt. Copies of the *Post* and *Times* lay open on his desk.

"The *Washington Post*," he said, "is being our friend this morning: TWO DEAD, BLOOD MISSING—not bad, all things considered. And it's in the Metro section. Our friends at the *Washington Times* are not so merciful." He held up the front page. Large headlines screamed, POLICE SLOW TO REPORT "VAMPIRE" KILLINGS.

Merrick said, "The custodian at the church called a reporter. I knew once the second killing hit the papers, the ambassador would call them up about the first one and they'd really sting us."

"So *you* told the press about the first killing."

"Better than looking like we got caught."

"That what you decided in your infinite wisdom?" Rourke glared at him. Merrick gazed back impassively until the captain's gaze faltered and fell. Merrick realized he had let Rourke see something in his eyes that should not be there in a man who looked thirty-five. *Careful.*

"Ah, hell," Rourke muttered. "You're probably right."

"Probably."

"Any leads?"

"No."

Rourke groaned. "Come on, Merrick, can't you make something up? I've got the chief and the ambassador on my neck. How about the lab?"

Merrick slipped himself back into the persona of subordinate. "Still looking for prints. No obvious ones on the body. A lot of blood on her bed, but some does appear to be missing." *More than a quart.* "Her throat was so torn up there are no good dental impressions. No sign of forced entry at her apartment. At the church, he got in through a basement window. It'll be a day or two before we can sort out prints there. There were no strange cars reported in the area. We're canvassing the neighborhood, but so far, nothing. Captain, we're dealing with a psycho, and you know what that means. Nothing's going to drop into our laps. He probably didn't know his victims—"

"Then how come he didn't have to break in?"

Because he walked right in with her and she didn't even see him. "Maybe he caught her when she was coming home from work. He may be very presentable, a man in a suit coming down the hall toward her, still early evening, good neighborhood, he just pushes in behind her. Give the lab time to do their work and I'll have more for you.''

Rourke gave the *Times* a rough shake and threw it down. "I'm assigning Stokes and Wycznowski to the case and bumping this up to 'task force' level. Lieutenant Cooke thinks he should be the one to lead it.''

"What do *you* think?"

"Come on, Merrick, you know how this works. We got two murders now, a vicious serial killer. Any more victims—or if this drags on—I'll have to shake things up. And Cooke *is* senior to you.''

Merrick's teeth clenched in exasperation. When Cooke was a rookie, he thought, I'd been with the police a hundred years. But try telling that to Rourke. Merrick imagined Cooke taking charge, ordering Byner to brief him, then humping straight to the press: *"We've recovered blood from the killer, and it is not like human blood. . . ."*

"This is my case, Captain. Stand behind me and I'll find the killer. Bring Cooke in and all you'll get is more headlines.''

Rourke blew out a harsh breath. "Damn it, Merrick, you think I don't know that? The chief likes him.''

"I'm sure you can handle the chief.''

Rourke gave a disbelieving laugh. "You've got a week— and that's if there are no more killings. This sicko seems to be on a very short kill cycle. If you don't find him fast we'll be bagging his next one.''

"I'll find him," Merrick said.

Rourke eyed him. "You got a hunch?"

And at that moment, Merrick did get a hunch. The victim's boyfriend had said she worked at Capitol Security Bank. *Why didn't I think of that before?* "I don't need hunches, Captain. I've got the strength of ten because my heart is pure.''

Rourke groaned. "Get the hell out of here.''

At the door, Merrick turned. "Any luck with getting an extra sergeant's billet for Des?"

"I'm trying, but you know how tight the budget people are.''

"He's a damned good man.''

"Sure. And he probably thinks you should be a captain, but that don't pop the nickels loose.''

Merrick headed for Robbery on the third floor, feeling oddly charged up by his encounter with Rourke. Even after hundreds of years of it, he was still not sure why running with normals invigorated him so. They knew little and had experienced even less, but their very naivete kept them open to experience. Being with them helped him notice and feel things more fully—the way they prized their houses and cars, relished their food, laughed at old jokes, got worked up over politics, chased after romance and sex even when it messed them up or killed them. He found a sort of grandeur in their short lives as they struggled to live as much and as well as they could before they died. Even the ones like Cooke were, beneath their cynical shells, trying to embrace life.

Walking into Robbery, Merrick was struck by the genteel hush. Unlike Homicide, they'd partitioned the space with blue dividers, so the detectives had to stand up if they wanted to talk to each other. Making his way through the maze of partitions, Merrick found Detective Wade Bavarro in his corner cubicle, staring at his computer screen. His bald head glistened with sweat and his fringe of black hair stood out as though the computer had just fired a shock through his fingers. Bavarro was a little long in the tooth to be fluent with computers, but he'd seen the light when he'd realized it could keep his flat feet off the street. Now he sat at his screen most of the day, running down leads among the flickering orbits of electrons.

Merrick waited for him to look up. Finally, the detective sat back, rubbing gently at his lids. Merrick cleared his throat and Bavarro jumped.

"Merrick! How long you been standing there?"

"I just walked up. Did you have a robbery yesterday—Capitol Security Bank?"

Bavarro eyed him. "Good guess. In fact, I just got off the phone with your man Reggie. You've got the murdered teller."

Merrick felt his pulse pick up.

"Susan Zarelli," Bavarro said and crossed himself. "A nice Italian girl."

To Bavarro, all Italian girls were nice. "Too nice for what happened to her," Merrick agreed. "Can you give me a quick rundown on the robbery?"

"Sure. Capitol Security reported five grand missing in twenties, fifties, and hundreds. Bank thinks it was an inside job. Seems their video system mysteriously froze on taped frames of the entry and interior of the safe."

Yes! Merrick thought.

"During the twenty-five minutes before the 'glitch' was detected, another employee saw Zarelli heading toward the safe. We been grilling the security guard that watches the monitors and he says he don't know how the hell it could have happened. Likely story. We've already booked him. As for Zarelli, she filled out the log in the safe, which makes no sense if she's the thief, and Reggie says you guys didn't find any missing money in her apartment.''

"That's right. But maybe she hid it somewhere else."

"Could be, and then an accomplice offed her and tried to make it look like a psycho thing. Or maybe Norman Bates has come back to life."

"How about the rest of their security monitors?"

"They were working okay. I told 'em last night to cull out shots of anybody who came in the bank about the time of the robbery. They're gonna send 'em over via modem. That's what I'm waiting for right now." Bavarro's computer beeped and a message appeared on his screen. "This is it."

Still photos of bank customers began flashing on the screen, a new one every few seconds. Merrick's throat felt dry. He leaned forward and watched, hoping. Three older women, four young executive types, a couple of laborers—and there Zane was, coming through the front entrance!

Containing his excitement, Merrick waited until the transmission was complete. Forty-one images had been sent. He kept his voice calm. "Wade, could you get me prints of those?"

"See anyone you know?" Bavarro asked shrewdly.

"No, but when we run them past our mug shots, who knows?"

"Yeah. We'll be doing the same." Bavarro hesitated. "The robbery is Rupright's case and you know how he is about anyone getting ahead of him."

"She was murdered, Wade. A nice Italian girl."

"I guess I could print 'em out for you right now. Just remember to act surprised and grateful when Rupright gets them over to you in a few hours."

"Thanks. Soave, right?"

"You don't have to do that."

"Would a case of Bolla be about right?"

Bavarro smiled. "Merrick, you may be a young man, but you know all the old ways. My blessings upon you."

Merrick patted his shoulder. I may be a young man, he thought. And then again, I may not. Walking away with the printouts, he felt Bavarro's eyes on his back and resisted the urge to sort through the pictures. Only one mattered, but no one else must know that. Zane still looked old when the shot was taken, but that was all right, even preferable. If he was staying at a hotel, that's how the check-in clerk would remember him. And some clerk out there *would* recognize the photo, Merrick felt sure of it.

The trick now was to find that clerk. Zane's ease at getting around—and moving bodies—suggested he had a car, which meant he could be staying as far away as the Maryland or Virginia suburbs. How many hundred hotels was that, how many thousand desk clerks, with only himself to cover them—and, if Rourke had meant what he'd said, only one week, at most, to do it?

Even if he found Zane, it would be far from over. He must then make the capture and transport Zane to the vault—and do it so quietly, so unnoticeably, that no normal got a hint of the existence of phages.

If I succeed, Merrick thought, the murders stop and the heat slowly fades. I get Byner to seal Katie's report and everything ends up gathering dust in the files. If I don't find Zane, he kills again and Cooke takes over.

The thought chilled Merrick. The photo was a good start, but he must find some way to narrow down the list of hotels.

It was time to talk to Sandeman.

THIRTEEN

MERRICK EDGED BETWEEN the cots of the dying hemophages, trying not to see them. The indigo light, shimmering off their withered bodies into the edges of his vision, made his spine crawl. What a hateful place this was.

And yet he must put his own son here.

His heart compressed with a sudden, sharp anguish. *Why did you come back, Zane? I didn't know where you were. As long as you kept away, you were safe. . . .*

With an effort, Merrick choked off the flood of regret. Zane was a vicious murderer as bad as any of the withered hemophages around him now. He did not have the option a normal father would have, of turning a murderous son over to the police. Only he could stop Zane. If he did not, that son would keep on killing the children—the innocent children—of other men. If the killers lying on these cots around him were his gift to humanity, Zane was his obligation. He must put his feelings aside and fulfill that obligation as quickly as possible—

Merrick's leg nudged a cot out of line, causing a brief screech of metal on concrete. Wincing, he listened, thinking for a second it would be all right, and then one of the steel doors at the side of the commons rang with a blow. A scream penetrated the thick metal, raising goose bumps on his arms. He stood, paralyzed, praying for the scream to stop. After a few seconds, it did, cutting off abruptly as though someone had clapped a hand over the screamer's mouth.

Shaken, Merrick hurried to Sandeman's door and unlocked it. Sandeman lay sideways across his cot, his back against the wall. His head dropped forward, his chin resting on his chest. His eyes were open but the prominent ridge of bone above them hid all but two crescents of white at the bottom. Bending down, Merrick saw the pupils peering up toward him, but Sandeman was so utterly still it was not clear the eyes were actually seeing him.

"You sure know how to cause a ruckus," Sandeman said.

Merrick grinned. "Sorry. I was in a hurry."

"It upsets them if they hear you. The ones that can still hear."

"I know."

Sandeman struggled feebly and managed to sit up straighter on the rumpled bed. Merrick noticed a smear of dried blood on his upper lip. His heart sank. That the blood would dry meant Sandeman's RBCs were breaking down. He would not be able to move much longer.

Even so, it might be another year before he could die.

Depressed, Merrick settled into the chair.

"What brings you back so soon?" Sandeman asked. "Or does it only seem soon?"

"It's soon." Merrick took the old-man photo of Zane and held it up for Sandeman to see.

Sandeman peered at it for a second. His eyes widened. "*Bazhba!* He gave up feeding. I barely recognized him."

"I *didn't*. He fooled me completely. He was able to follow me around, I'm not sure for how long. But now he has fed."

"When he murdered that woman at the cathedral?"

"No, this photo was taken after that. He killed another woman last night, which must be when he drank. His hair is still white, of course, but he looks much younger again."

Sandeman let out a rasping sigh. "To not feed . . . he has

grown strong, Merrick. Much stronger than I could have imagined.''

"Have you thought of anything since I was here last time—especially where he might hide out?"

Sandeman stared off into space with a meditative expression. "To guess where Zane would go, we must think like Zane. Not just me, old friend. You. He is your son."

"True, but I don't know him."

Sandeman eyed him. "Why are you afraid to be inside his mind? Do you think it will infect you?"

Merrick felt a stab of impatience, but kept his voice even. "I'm telling you, it's been too long since we were together. He's not the boy who ran away from me so long ago."

Sandeman returned his gaze to some distant but inner vista, staring at the wall behind Merrick as though it were a thousand yards away. "Do you remember that party given by the Marquis de Lucientes?"

Merrick felt a surge of impatience. What was Sandeman trying to do? . . .

He made himself ask the question again, in earnest. He's here all alone, Merrick thought. No one to talk to. And I come pushing in, demanding his help. He isn't asking much, just a little courtesy from me.

Thinking back and back, Merrick found the memory Sandeman referred to: The Marquis de Lucientes, yes. The castle in Spain. Though it had been at least five hundred years ago, he could still visualize it. The curving stone corridors, flickering candlelight, ten hemophages from six kingdoms of Europe, coming together for a fortnight to savor each other's company in seclusion. The marquis was the youngest of us, Merrick recalled—only a hundred and twenty. Sandeman was the oldest. I was four hundred. Zane wouldn't be born for ten years.

"I remember," he said.

"Remember the paintings?" Sandeman asked.

Merrick nodded, caught up in the memory despite himself. A phage named Cloce had brought along a collection of his work. The canvases were remarkable. If they had been displayed in a museum, they surely would have made Cloce so famous—or perhaps infamous—that he'd have had trouble taking up a new identity, as all hemophages periodically must. In essence, Cloce had invented abstract art centuries before it would ignite controversy in the world of normal humans.

"You know, of course," Sandeman said, "that Cloce influenced Cezanne."

"Really."

"He had to wait nearly three hundred years, and he kept himself totally in the background, but Cloce finally had the satisfaction, if not the credit, of seeing his ideas put before the world. And do you remember the organist who played for us at the castle?"

Merrick said nothing. He was beginning to see where Sandeman was going with this, and he did not like it.

"A true maestro," Sandeman went on. "Note perfect, every nuance of sound the stops could muster. I could never listen to a normal play after that. A hundred and fifty years later, he taught Buxtehude and later still, introduced Bach to the Margrave of Brandenburg."

"And how many did he kill?"

"Too many, I'm sure," Sandeman said. "But we *have* made contributions, haven't we? We have given a lot for what we have taken."

"The price is too high."

"I wonder if the normals who have been saved by blood transfusions would agree."

"They would have come up with that without my help."

"Maybe," Sandeman said. "But if it didn't happen until after World War II, how many would have died in the interim?"

"Probably fewer than I killed before I discovered it could be done." Hearing the self-loathing in his own voice, Merrick felt a surge of resentment at Sandeman for uncovering it. "If you believe the killing can be justified, why did you put yourself in here?"

"*I* don't believe it can be justified. But you aren't here about me, you're here about Zane. It wouldn't even occur to Zane to justify killing a normal, anymore than the average normal would think he had to justify eating a hamburger at McDonald's. That's all normals are to Zane—cattle."

"He's wrong."

Sandeman gazed at Merrick. "Is he? Or are you judging the predator by the rules of the prey?"

Merrick's anger sharpened. "Predators, prey—are you forgetting we are all humans? And if we can't judge, then what becomes of justice?"

Sandeman sighed. "Justice, yes. What an idealist you are, Merrick. Still, I must confess part of me has always admired that.

I remember you did not drink the blood the marquis served at dinner, because you didn't know its provenance. The rest of the guests thought your habit of drinking only from thugs and killers quaint, but they humored you. I think I knew, even then, where you were headed. I tried to brush it off, but it haunted me. And the rest of us haunted you, didn't we? You wouldn't drink with us, but you kept joining us—Spain, Prussia, Gascony, all the other places—because you hated the loneliness.

"Then you fathered a phage. After that, you never came to another retreat. When your own son ran from you, you felt rejected by all of your own kind. The die was cast. Free to punish in us what you so despise in yourself, you became the scourge of men like the marquis."

Merrick forced himself to take a deep breath, ease it out. "This is not about all hemophages, Sandeman. This is, as you said, about Zane and me. And it's not about punishment, either. If he would stop killing, even now . . . but he won't. And I am responsible."

"*He* is responsible."

"He is my son. I gave him blood."

"Exactly. He *is* your son."

Merrick's throat felt so tight he could barely force the words out. "What do you want from me? To say I am a hemophage, too? Don't you think I know that? I walk down the street and I notice the vein in a man's throat, and suddenly I long to kill him. Merrick Chapman, homicide detective, looks down at a body with a bloody, torn throat and he feels the thrill of the kill. He *thirsts*. Bloody hell, Sandeman, every day of my life, I struggle to feel like a man, not a beast. In my heart, I am a vicious killer. Is that good enough for you? But I don't do it, do you hear me? I don't *do* it."

Sandeman's expression softened. "Poor Merrick, the lion who lies down with the lambs."

Merrick swallowed, trying to get control of himself, but the resentment still burned in him. "You question me—you of all phages, who are giving up your life for them. If you're so ambivalent, why did *you* stop killing them?"

Sandeman closed his eyes. For a long moment, he said nothing. "Because they look like us," he whispered at last. "We're the only predator on earth who looks just like its prey. Nature gave us the perfect camouflage, Merrick. Maybe in the end, it disguised us too well and fooled not just my prey, but me."

"You weren't fooled. They are our brothers."

"I don't know. Our differences are very real, too." Sandeman shook his head slowly. "I wish I could bond with them the way you do—maybe I wouldn't need to be in here."

"You've never loved one?" Merrick asked, intrigued.

A faraway look came into Sandeman's eyes, then abruptly vanished, as though extinguished by an act of will. "There have been normals here and there I might have loved," he said brusquely. "But I knew if I did, I wouldn't be able to stand the pain. That I would have to run from them before they grew old and died. How can you bear that, Merrick? What do you get from them that could be worth such torment?"

"The memory of what it is to be young."

Sandeman cocked his head. "Isn't that painful, too?"

"They make me laugh, Sandeman. They help me *feel*. If it sometimes hurts like hell, so be it. Has your way brought you less pain?"

Sandeman gazed around his small room. "This isn't *my* way. For me, it's the only way." He gestured at his teetering stacks of books. "My link to them is here."

"The part of them that doesn't die," Merrick said.

Sandeman gave him a defiant look. "That's right."

Merrick's earlier resentment melted, replaced by a deep sadness for his friend. "I wish I could take you out of here."

"And when I killed again?"

Merrick shrugged hopelessly, unable to answer.

Sandeman's gaze bored into him. "Tell me something. If I asked you to let me out, would you?"

The question startled Merrick. "You told me never to release you."

"Maybe I've changed my mind."

"You said even if you changed your mind, not to let you out, not even if you begged me."

"So your answer is no?"

Merrick felt a deep unease. *"Are* you asking?"

Sandeman looked at him for a long moment. "No. But thank you for taking me seriously."

Merrick had a sudden powerful sense of the other phage's terrible isolation, so much worse than his own. It must, in fact, be causing him tremendous emotional pain, perhaps worse than the physical pain of his deteriorating condition. How courageous Sandeman was. He had chosen death to keep from killing. And not a quick death, either—for a phage, there was no such thing.

Merrick wondered again what he had so many times: *If I could not control myself, would I be as brave?*

"I'm not sure I can help you find your son," Sandeman said.

Merrick felt a sharp dismay. "Not sure you can, or not sure you want to?"

"I choose to be here," Sandeman said. "The others . . . in the beginning, they scream for weeks."

"Their victims would have screamed, too, if they had been allowed."

"For *weeks*, Merrick."

Merrick felt again the oppressive weight of walking through the vault commons. Did Sandeman think he was immune to that horror? "If I could make it quick," he said, "I would. There is no mercy for us."

"Too true." A stubborn note remained in Sandeman's voice.

Merrick leaned toward him, willing him to understand, to unbend. "I must stop Zane."

For a moment, Sandeman would not meet his eyes. Then he sighed. "I suppose it has come to that. If you don't get him, he'll get you."

"If he can."

Sandeman gave him a hard look. "Don't be too sure he can't, my friend. He is much stronger now. That first victim at the cathedral—if blood touched your lips, could you refrain from drinking?"

"I don't think blood touched his lips. I think he used dental plates to rip her neck, then collected the blood in a basin, probably without ever looking at it."

"Still, he must have smelled it. He must have wanted it terribly, but he didn't take it. He's stronger now, Merrick. And don't forget, he may have learned a new form of Influence."

Merrick felt uncomfortable. "That is only a theory—"

"It's more than a theory. I . . . have reason to believe that Zane will try to enter your mind."

Merrick felt a pulse of fear in his gut. "What reason?"

"A few months ago, when one of your other 'guests' down the hall began screaming, I decided to try and do something about it. I reached out, hoping he might let me Influence his brain stem, give him sleep. Instead, I felt myself to be in an entirely different place. The tissue was lush with blood vessels. I could sense the aura of neurons, more dense even than in the retinas. His screaming stopped abruptly."

Merrick felt a jolt of recognition. "You did it when I came in, just now. You stopped him from screaming."

"Yes. I did it the last time you were here, too, and a number of times before and since. The screaming, and then I reach out and it stops. Merrick, I believe I am entering their brains. Not the stem, the brain proper. I have no sense of their thoughts—it isn't mind reading. But I can get in there—and it has an effect on them. It seems to tranquilize them. Hemophages, but they have shown no ability to resist."

Merrick stared at Sandeman, stunned. Zane, able to enter minds—it was frightening. He did not want to believe it, but Sandeman wasn't just theorizing, not if he could do it, too. "When you're in their minds, can you tell which part?"

"No. It might be their memories, but I can't be sure. If I could see their faces, I might know. But I don't want to see their faces." Sandeman's eyes closed. The white lashes quivered together.

Merrick felt cold. "If Zane *can* enter minds," he said, "it's all the more vital that I stop him. My best chance is to find him and surprise him, attack instead of defend—"

"Does he know about you and the doctor?"

Merrick's stomach clenched. "Yes. I have to go after Zane, but I plan to guard her as much as I can, especially at night."

"I presume you're keeping fed?"

Merrick nodded. "Maybe he won't bother with Katie."

Sandeman looked grim. "He will bother with her, you can be sure. She's the chink in your armor, my friend. Zane will try to hurt you through her, I'm certain of it. He might not intend to kill her—at least not right away. But his appetite *is* for women of breeding age. Even if he intends only to toy with your Katie, when one of us draws blood, it is hard to stop. . . ."

Sandeman looked away and Merrick realized he was ashamed. It hurt him to see it. Sandeman had no reason for shame. He had tried his best to feed through transfusion equipment, planning to take just a pint or two in the little bags. He'd always ended up cutting their throats. But he had cast off all shame when he had put himself in here.

Sandeman's bony hands doubled into fists. "I wanted so much to hold back," he said in a low, hoarse voice. "But nature put killing in our genes, Merrick, stronger even than the thirst. We were made to thin the herd, not just milk it. Goddamn nature to hell!"

"Yes."

Sandeman pulled a deep, ragged breath. His eyes narrowed in concentration. "Once, in Singapore, I ran into Zane in the lobby of Raffles. In the 1940s, I met him several times at the Ritz for drinks, and, six years ago, at the Balzac in Paris. What's the classiest old hotel in town?"

"The Jefferson," Merrick said, "or maybe the Hay Adams."

"Those will be a good start. Show that photo to the desk clerk. . . ." Sandeman grunted. "Listen to me. You know that. Concentrate on suites and penthouses. Don't go tonight—do it in the morning. Tonight, you must guard your Katie. . . ." He slumped back. "I've got to rest. I'm sorry. I'm just so . . . weak."

"You are the strongest man I have ever known." Merrick eased Sandeman down on the cot and covered him with a blanket. As he hurried from the vault, his mind turned back to Katie, and he was more afraid than he had ever been in his life.

FOURTEEN

PEERING DOWN THROUGH the dark leaves at the lights in the doctor's back windows, Zane burned with impatience. He needed to get in there, start to work on her, but he didn't quite feel safe yet. He could not be sure he was strong enough to take Merrick on directly tonight. He should feed at least once more before he tried that. Which meant that, before he moved against the doctor, he must make sure Merrick was not around.

He won't be in the house again tonight, Zane thought. If he means to ambush me, he'll do it out here, so she won't see it, won't discover what we are.

The wind rose a little, making the treetop sway. Zane tightened his grip, wishing he could have used one of the taller oaks instead, but it was still too early in the spring for them to have leaves. The maples were ahead, as always; the new foliage in this one hid him quite well. It felt odd to worry about being seen; he did not like the feeling at all.

Zane felt his teeth clench in chagrin at how he'd let Merrick spot him last night. Up until that moment it had been so perfect. Watching them, knowing he'd guessed right and found a vulnerable spot. Then the mortar had crumbled under his fingers, a bare whisper of sound. Clever, the way Merrick had pretended not to hear it, lying in bed that extra few minutes, stretching so casually.

He must have fed recently, Zane thought, to have such wolfish hearing. I should have dropped down the minute I made the sound—or better yet, left quietly the minute I saw what they were doing. When she undressed with him, I knew everything I needed to know. And Father would not have realized it—would not be guarding the house now. I'd be able to stroll up the front sidewalk tonight.

Remembering his father and the doctor locked together in sex, Zane felt a tremor of disgust. It had made him almost sick to watch them last night. Father had let her climb on top of him, given her equal status, let her be the aggressor, even. How could a phage even pretend to surrender power? It was dangerous.

Zane felt a mixture of anger and resentment at the doctor. She, and a long line of female normals before her, had made it easier, so much easier, for Father to betray his own kind. The other women were beyond reach, but the doctor was not. Through her, Father could be punished. I can't hurt him the way he's hurt me, Zane thought. He rejected me from the start. He thinks I left him, but he left me, by refusing to accept what I am. And then he hunted me. He wants to destroy me, his own son. For five hundred years I've lived in fear of him. He'll have to fear me only for a few weeks. But I'll make him suffer as much as I can.

Zane imagined the pain in Father's face each time the doctor screamed. He'd have to harden himself to those cries, he knew. Torturing women was not his thing. He loved the rush he got when he took their lives, the feeling of absolute, godlike *control*, when they went limp and surrendered their essence to him. But hurting them had never been a part of it. He always shunted blood from their brains first, making sure they felt no pain.

But for you, dear Father, I'll make an exception. The more you love the doctor, the greater will be your pain. You'll watch your lover die, then I'll bury you, and you can die the long, blind, suffocating death you wanted for me.

A silhouette appeared in a bedroom window. Zane's eyes

adapted at once, penetrating the shadows on the doctor's face. Her expression was wistful as she gazed out at the night. Was she thinking about Merrick, wishing he were with her? Oh, yes, he loves you, Zane thought bitterly. Meanwhile, he despises me. I'll try not to kill you tonight. I want to draw it out as long as I can. I hope you are brave.

Keeping his eyes on the house, he started down the tree. A shadow shifted along the back of the house. Zane froze; holding his breath, he focused in on the shadow.

Father!

Zane felt a cold rush of fear. *How long has he been there? He must have just walked around from the front. I didn't even hear him. I almost gave myself away.*

He clung to the trunk of the maple, not daring to move. If Merrick looked his way now, he'd see his leg dangling down below the cover of leaves. Dare he pull it up? No, the movement would attract Merrick for sure.

Zane felt his heart pounding against the trunk. He watched, petrified, as Merrick strolled along the back of the house. He was staying in the shadows. He's just making rounds, Zane told himself. If I wait, he'll walk back around to the front.

Or I could try to get into his memories.

Sudden anxiety made Zane's nails dig into the bark of the tree. Go ahead, he urged himself. You can do it!

But what if he failed? What if all it did was put Father on alert? The distance was too far, he was too vulnerable up here in the tree, he wasn't mentally ready.

Zane stared at Merrick, anger mixing with his fear. *Move on, damn you!* The window opened with a crisp sliding sound. Merrick looked up as the doctor leaned on the sill and eased her face into the cool night breeze. For a moment, he gazed up at her as if mesmerized, then he backed around the corner of the house, a movement so fluid and stealthy that Zane felt a grudging admiration.

As soon as Merrick disappeared, Zane slipped down the trunk, blocking himself from the doctor's vision. He hurried out between the houses that backed onto hers, slid into his car and started it. Using a light touch on the accelerator, he rolled slowly down the street. As he drove away up the long hillside of Georgetown's residential district, his fear faded into frustration. He'd had a chance to test his new powers and he'd held back out of fear. And now he was running. He hated running.

One more feeding, he told himself, and I'll never have to run again.

He began to feel calmer. It was not so bad, the way things had worked out tonight. Merrick was afraid now, or he would not have been there standing watch. It's *good* that he saw me last night, Zane thought. Knowing I'm aware of her, he'll have to be afraid all the time, whenever he's away from her. The punishment has started already.

After a moment, the night air began to chill Katie and she closed the window. Downstairs, she could hear Mom watching Letterman—an energetic babble of words, then laughter from the audience. The sound warmed her, drawing her downstairs to the living room.

Mom was grinning at the TV. She glanced over the top of her glasses at Katie. "I thought you went to bed."

"Couldn't sleep," Katie said.

Picking up the remote, Mom muted the TV and patted the sofa beside her. Katie went over and sat down. "I don't want to interrupt your show."

"Don't be silly. I was about to fall asleep anyway."

Katie squirmed on the couch, trying to get comfortable. "Listen, about last night, Merrick and I . . ."

"That's all right, it's none of my business." Mom eyed her. "Of course, if you want to talk about it. . . ."

"I know you like him. I don't want you to get the wrong idea. We're not getting back together."

"I see."

Katie realized she did want to talk about it. "Merrick and I have worked hard," she explained, "to change what we had before into simple friendship. It can't be more than that. Last night we were just acting like it was the past, happier times, and all that."

"Is it so wrong to act?"

"Not wrong, no. But I want something real, Mom. And the longer I pretend I can have it with Merrick, the more likely I am to miss out entirely. I should be looking for someone else. Gregory needs a father."

Mom cleared her throat and plucked a piece of lint from the elbow of her sweater. She looked as if she wanted to say something but wasn't sure she should.

"What?"

"I was just thinking how much like me you sound—you know, after your father died. I loved him very much and I grieved for quite awhile, though I tried not to be obvious about it. Eventually, I began to plan how I would find a nice decent man and marry him."

Katie was fascinated. She remembered little of the years Mom was talking about. She had been too young to feel her father's death fully, or her mother's grief. "The whole time I was growing up, I never realized you might be thinking of getting remarried."

"Oh, yes."

"Were you lonely?"

"Actually, no. I had my work and I had you. But I just felt you needed a father. I started sizing up eligible men. Fortunately, I kept an eye on you, too, and that finally wised me up."

"What are you trying to say? That Gregory doesn't need a father?"

"Did you?"

Katie hesitated. What a loaded question. Yes implied her mother had failed her, and in no sense was that remotely true, but saying no demeaned the importance a father could have had for her. "I wished my father were around," she said. "I still do. But, no, I didn't feel the need of a substitute."

"Exactly."

Katie thought about it. She wasn't ready to say that Gregory wouldn't benefit from a father figure, but it was nice to get an alternate point of view, one that said she and Gregory were all right the way they were.

"You meet quite a few men in your job," Mom said. "Do any of them appeal to you?"

"Some of them as friends." Katie thought about Art and laughed. "I think my resident has a crush on me, and he's a gorgeous young man, too. But even if I were free to fall in love with him, he doesn't . . ."

"Begin to compare with Merrick," Mom finished.

Katie sighed in exasperation. "Once I'd been with Merrick, all other men seemed . . . I don't know, like children. There is something very special about Merrick that I can't quite put my finger on. You get a sense of great mental and physical strength paired with restraint. For a man who sees such brutality, he is very gentle. It hasn't hardened him, only made him strong. I *admire* him, do you know what I mean?" Katie threw up her hands. "I need to get over these feelings."

"Katie, you feel the way you feel. When you don't feel that way anymore, you'll be over it. I'm still in love with your father. No other man began to compare with him. Maybe I wouldn't let them compare, and maybe I should have, but I didn't, so here we are."

Katie felt a wave of affection. "Yes, here we are."

The phone rang. Katie had a sinking feeling. When a call came late at night, it was usually the hospital—and bad news. "Let the answering machine take it," she said. "If it's anything serious I'll pick up."

The phone rang three more times and there was a pause as her taped message played silently. Please don't let it be about Jenny, she thought. The machine beeped, signalling the caller to record his message. No voice came from the machine. Neither did the three beeps that would signal the caller had hung up. As the silence grew, she began to feel uneasy. If the caller didn't want to leave a message, why didn't he hang up?

Because he knows we're here.

Mom frowned a question at her. Katie just shook her head, struck by an irrational feeling that if she said anything the caller would hear her.

Beep-beep-beep.

Relief flooded Katie. The soulless computerized voice of the answering machine said, "Twelve-oh-three, A.M." The tape whirred as the blank section rewound.

"Strange," Mom said.

"Probably a wrong number." Katie wished she could believe it, but somehow she didn't.

Mom got up and tugged the curtain behind the couch together, closing the slight crack in the middle. Settling on the couch again, she said, "I read in the *Post* about that terrible murder last night. Merrick was quoted. Then it dawned on me that you and he came here just after he must have been at the scene."

Katie hesitated. She hadn't wanted to say anything, but there was no way around it. "I'm helping out on the case."

Mom looked excited and a little worried at the same time. "I knew something was wrong the minute you came in. You were rather pale."

"It was appalling."

Mom looked sympathetic. "I understand that a good deal of blood was missing. Is that why you were called in?"

"Yes." It wasn't entirely untrue.

Mom said, "You've been on this case since the first victim, haven't you—the one found at the cathedral."

"What makes you think that?"

"Something's been bothering you. You've cried out in your sleep a few times. And you're biting your nails."

"Am not." Katie looked at her right thumbnail and was surprised to see ragged indentations.

"Seeing those bodies must be awful. Is there more?"

Katie started to bite the thumbnail. Mom slapped playfully at her hand. I do need to talk about it, Katie thought. I can do that without breaking my promise to Merrick if I say nothing about the blood. "You have to promise to keep this strictly to yourself."

Mom nodded.

Katie told her about last night—losing the slide, feeling the touch on her back, even though no one was there. She shivered. "I know, it sounds impossible."

"You told Merrick?"

"He said my mind was playing tricks on me because I was afraid. Maybe he was right."

"But you don't think so."

It was not the reaction Katie had expected. She felt uneasy all over again.

Mom crossed her arms and hugged them against her, as if trying to protect herself from something. For a moment, her eyes were far away. "Your Grandma Guillemin once told me a story about being caught alone in her skiff in the bayous after nightfall one evening. Right about the same time there had been some local killings where the throats were slashed. Blood was missing. Mother was out harvesting her crayfish traps and lost track of time. When she realized the sun was setting, she started rowing for home. The killings were very much on her mind and she was really putting her back into it. Suddenly she saw a dark form walking along the shore, keeping pace with her. She couldn't see who it was but she hailed him anyway. He didn't answer. She picked her shotgun up from the gunwale and, in that instant, the man vanished."

"You mean he ducked behind a tree?"

"She said he vanished. One second he was there, the next he wasn't."

Katie gazed at Mom, wondering why she wasn't smiling in disbelief. A week ago, she would have. Not now. But she couldn't quite buy it, either. "You say it was a man—"

"It looked like one to your grandma."

"Well, I just don't see how a person could make himself invisible," Katie said. "If someone is there, light will bounce off him. It's a law of physics."

"That's been my attitude, too, more or less. Trouble is, that wasn't the only strange thing I was told about or saw for myself growing up in the bayous. I could tell you other things. . . ." The faraway look crossed Mom's face again. She gave her head a slight shake. "But let's just stick to this. First my mother, then my daughter—there's got to be some explanation."

Katie thought about it. "Well, vision happens in the brain, so it *is* subjective, not objective. There's such a thing as hysterical blindness. And there are built-in flaws in the eyes, too. The main one is at the back of each eye where all the visual neurons gather into a bundle and exit to the brain. It's called the blind spot. You aren't aware of it because of differences in perspective between the eyes and because the brain seems able to fill in with what it would expect to see based on surrounding context."

Mom sat forward. "Blind spots. That's very interesting. I didn't know that."

"But last night I was searching, moving my head—and eyes—in every direction. If someone was there, his image would have been sliding all around on my retinas, not just hitting my blind spots."

"Maybe this thing can create other blind spots on your eyes, bigger ones that move on your retinas when it moves."

"It?" Katie said skeptically, but she felt a chill.

"All right, him. Whatever."

"Mom, if he can do that, he's got abilities beyond anything I can explain."

"That doesn't mean it's impossible. Katie, I'm not a scientist, but I don't believe in magic either, any more than you do. I do believe there is a lot about the universe we don't know. I'm old enough to remember a time without television. I like to think I was a fairly intelligent girl, even when I was growing up in the bayous, but if you had told me when I was ten that a person could step out on the moon and, because of invisible rays broadcast through the air, we could all see him do it in a little box with a glass screen, I'd have told you you were crazy."

"Sure, but—"

"But nothing. We think we know what's impossible but we don't. Let's try looking at this another way: Someone had to take that slide. Have you thought about who had a reason?"

"The killer." The cold fear Katie had tried to bury last night spread through her again. This possibility had nagged at her, but putting it into words and having someone take her seriously made it so much more real. The killer had the best of all conceivable reasons to steal that slide: because it could prove he was not a normal man.

"If you're right," Mom said, "it means he knows about you now—"

"Stop it!" Katie shuddered.

Mom leaned toward her and took her hands. "I'm sorry. I know you're scared, and I certainly don't want to make it worse. I'm a bit scared myself. Scared is all right. It's just your brain's way of telling you you'd better do something, take precautions." Mom hesitated, looking like she wanted to say something more.

"What?"

"Remember that *Post* article, about Neddie Merrill?"

"Sure," Katie said.

"Would you mind if I asked her to come up and stay with us awhile?"

"Oh, Mom—I don't think a psychic is going to do us any good."

"No, no. It's just that I've been thinking how nice it would be to see her again. And with you gone during the days . . ."

She's more afraid than she's letting on, Katie realized. She gave her mother's hands a squeeze. "Of course you can have Neddie for a visit. This is your home, too. Call her tonight if you like."

"Thank you, dear." Mom looked relieved.

"Can Neddie shoot?" Katie asked, attempting to joke.

Mom managed only the barest of smiles. "One thing *has* always intrigued me," she said, "about that story of your grandma's. Why did the man vanish when she picked up her shotgun?"

"I don't know, unless he didn't want to get shot."

"Exactly. Just because Mother could no longer see him didn't mean he wasn't still standing right there. He wasn't a ghost. He could stop a bullet. That was the part that made Mother's account stick, that scared me the worst, because it said he had substance—he was real." Mom glanced around the room. "You know, it mightn't hurt to take a few precautions around the house. The ironworks that put in our front railing also makes those fancy ornamental bars to protect your windows. Maybe we should have them do that for us. It can't hurt just on general principles, living in the city."

"I don't know, Mom. Even the fancy ones look so—"

The phone rang again. Katie jumped, startled. Sliding to the end of the couch, she snatched up the receiver. "Hello."

"Someone is watching your house right now."

The voice was deep and powerful, very clear, and yet Katie was not sure she'd heard him right. "Excuse me?"

The line stayed silent. Katie's scalp prickled. "Who *is* this?"

The connection broke and, after a few seconds, the dial tone buzzed in her ear. The phone rattled as she replaced it in its cradle. "It was a man. He said someone is watching our house right now."

Mom's shoulders twitched in an involuntary shudder. "Did you recognize his voice?"

"No." Katie went to the front window, her heart pounding with alarm. Parting the drapes, she looked out front. The streetlight cast dancing shadows of maple leaves on the lawn and sidewalk. She could see no one. She headed toward the rear of the house, through the dining room to peek out through the curtains over the kitchen sink. The backyard was much darker than the front but there was still enough light to see. She searched the tree trunks, the hedge of holly in the back. For a second, she thought she saw a shadow slipping along the hedge, but it melted away as she centered on it. As she stepped to the back door and fumbled the porch light on, her mother stood behind her, gripping her shoulder. The sixty-watt bulb spilled a dim light across the yard. She stared at the spot where the shadow had moved. The low hedge was still. No one was there.

Or no one she could see.

Katie felt a deep chill. She thought of Gregory upstairs in his bed. "We'll call the ironworks," she said, "first thing tomorrow."

FIFTEEN

ZANE HUNG UP the phone and strode down M Street toward the parking place he'd found four blocks away. Frustration gnawed at him. A phone call fell far short of what he'd planned for tonight. Still, it had been effective, he could tell from the fear in the doctor's voice. Let her worry, Zane thought. Let her tell Merrick about the call. Let him realize I saw him but he did not see me.

Zane opened his jacket, hoping the cool breeze would soothe him. Though traffic had thinned some after midnight, cars still rolled up and down Georgetown's main drag. A gang of skinheads in their funky black clothes swaggered along the sidewalk toward him, probably on the way to one of their dim, raucous watering holes. The big fellow in the lead stared aggressively at Zane; obviously, he thought he looked ferocious. Zane knew he ought to humor the imbecile and move aside but he didn't feel like it. When he continued at full stride, the skinhead turned and parted his retinue with mocking sweeps of his arms.

"It's my hairdresser," he cried. "Let her through, let her through."

Zane ignored him, but as he stepped past, the skinhead bumped him hard.

"Oops. Sorry, Sylvia."

Keeping his hands in his pockets, Zane directed a mental pinch to the blood vessels in one optic nerve. The skinhead gasped as he lost his sight in that eye and staggered, blinking, against the wall of a liquor store. The others gathered around him and Zane left them behind, shutting out their concerned babble. In a moment, the brainless twit would get his vision back. It might worry him for a few hours afterward, but probably not.

As he walked on, Zane debated whether to feed again now. He would need at least one more to bring himself back to full strength and the youthful appearance he liked. But his body had not yet finished processing last night's blood. If he drank again so soon, his system would start in on the new blood and some of the old would be wasted. No harm in that, but there was another consideration—to make each killing cause the maximum trouble for Father. Right now, Zane thought, he's sneaking around alone waiting for me to attack his lover. I'll give his anxiety time to work on him. Let him spend all night out there waiting. Every drain I put on his nerves will make him weaker in the clinch.

Zane slid into his car and drove slowly down M Street, checking out the people on the sidewalks. A young couple stepped out of J. Paul's and headed toward Wisconsin Avenue. The woman wore a long leather coat. Her blonde hair hung down along the back, fine and straight. The man with her was dressed like a lawyer or broker, a couple of young professionals out spending their money on the latest trendy drinks. Zane slowed his car and pulled to the curb lane to get a better look at the woman. She was rather pretty. In fact, she reminded him of Ann Hrluska.

Zane felt a sudden desire for the woman. She glanced at him and he smiled at her. The man saw him, too, and frowned. Zane ignored him, thinking of Ann. Was she still in the area? Just thinking of her brought a surge of lust. He'd not been finished with Ann when Merrick had run him out of Washington. Would she still be attractive after twelve years? Probably—she'd been young then and couldn't be much more than thirty now. I'll pay her a visit, Zane thought. Give her some more erotic dreams.

He imagined it: making love to Ann, then letting her wake

up as he left. She'd sit up in bed, her body flushed with passion. Would she remember that she'd had the same vivid dream twelve years ago, three nights in a row? Could it have been her husband? No, he's so deeply asleep it couldn't have been him.

Zane felt a strong pulse of excitement. He remembered the softness of Ann's pale thighs under his palms, their inviting lack of resistance as he had rolled them apart and entered her. Her eyes, half-slitted, had not seen him but had instead tracked some incubal dream lover. Her mouth, soft and accepting in sleep, had tasted of hazelnut coffee.

Did she still live in the same house after twelve years?

One way to find out. After all, he had nothing else to do—except go back to his hotel. He had fed, but he was still depleted enough that he might fall asleep. And dream.

Twelve years ago, Ann had lived on Mason Lane in a new development in Fairfax County—a bedroom community forty minutes from Washington. Zane turned into her street and pulled his rental car onto an undeveloped lot. A dirt drive left by surveyors still led into some trees that hid the car from the roadway. Shutting off the engine, Zane grabbed his briefcase from the backseat and removed the suction cup and glass cutter, slipping them into his coat pocket.

As he stepped out of his car, he became aware of the moon, nearly full, shedding a strong, milky glow over everything. He'd have preferred overcast, but it didn't really matter. He would be careful, as always.

He stood a moment, studying the housing development. This far into the country, the houses were spaced far apart on large lots. The windows were dark in all but the house Ann Hrluska had lived in twelve years ago. The left front windows of that house glimmered, indicating that the light was probably coming from a rear room—the kitchen, if he remembered right.

Still mindful of the bright moon, he trotted across Mason Lane toward Ann's house, scanning the blackened windows of the other houses, alert to any touch in his mind that would indicate someone starting to look his way. He registered nothing.

As Zane walked up the drive, he heard the rattle of a chain in the backyard. A dog appeared between the slats of a low gate. Just as it barked, he squeezed down on its carotids and it plopped over, unconscious. At the same instant a man's voice from the rear of the house said, "Quiet, Snapple." The sound was slightly muffled, as if it had come from an open window. Perfect!

Zane pushed the sleeping dog back with the gate and took a moment to arrange it in a curled up sleeping position, nose over paws. Then he walked along the back of the house toward the light that spilled from the kitchen's bay windows. He felt tense, springy with excitement. Stopping at the center of the window, he gazed in.

And there she was! Ann and her husband James sat at a table. James looked up toward him—a common previsual response—then down at his hands again. The man had grown a paunch and lost a lot of hair in the last twelve years. Ann had lost almost nothing. The fine-featured beauty of her early twenties still graced her face, betrayed only by a few faint lines at the corners of her eyes. Zane gazed hungrily at her. Her breasts swelled nicely under her blue sweater. A strand of the straight blonde hair he remembered so well hung down across her forehead, giving her an air of vulnerability. She looked weary and . . . sad?

"I don't know," James said, shaking his lowered head from side to side like a man who had been punched. His voice was low and the window was only open an inch, but Zane was recharged enough with blood to hear him clearly.

Ann gazed at her husband with a fierce, agonized concentration. "We have to give it time. The doctor said she might get worse before she gets better."

"How could she get any worse?" James mumbled. "I don't see how she could, without . . ."

"Don't say it," Ann pleaded, and he didn't.

Zane wondered who was sick. Ann's mother? Or James's, perhaps. No matter. Clearly, the still-lovely Ann needed rest, sweet dreams. Lucky I'm here, Zane thought with a smile.

James looked up at his wife. His eyes were rimmed in red and Zane realized with distaste that he had been crying. "So what do we do, Ann?"

"We pray, just like we have been."

"I still think another doctor might—"

"Please don't start that again. Doctor O'Keefe has the best reputation of anyone in the Washington area."

Surprised, Zane stepped closer to the window. Had he heard right? Dr. O'Keefe—Mary Katherine O'Keefe? What kind of bizarre coincidence could connect him to both Ann twelve years ago and Merrick's lover now?

Ann covered her husband's hand with her own. "When

Jenny got sick, Doctor Prestowitz recommended Doctor O'Keefe straight off. And the two experts you've called since both said the same thing. She's the best around for treating childhood leukemia.''

Jolted, Zane leaned into the window, seeing the two people in a sharp new focus that burned on his retinas. *Childhood leukemia! Might it be hemophagic?* Go on, he thought. Let me hear more!

"All I know," James said, "is she's been in the hospital for months and she hasn't done anything but get steadily worse. That's not supposed to happen. They can treat kids with leukemia nowadays."

When Ann looked straight up at him, Zane realized he'd pressed a palm against the glass and it had almost cracked. Ann blinked, then looked at her husband again. The storm of feeling in Zane's mind blew her words away. He felt his heart pounding against his backbone. *How old was this girl with childhood leukemia who was not responding to treatment?*

Zane went to the back door. It was locked. With a soft growl of impatience, he studied the end of the house. An oak overhung the roof, but the drainpipe would be quicker—and quieter, since he wouldn't have to jump down. Fortunately, the pipe was copper, not aluminum, and wouldn't be as likely to bend under his weight. He grabbed the drainpipe and pulled himself hand over hand to the roof. Spreading his weight between his hands and feet, he worked his way along the steep pitch to the first dormer window. Locked, damn it. Removing the glass cutting tools from his pocket he pressed the suction cup into the glass and circled it with the blade. The glass popped out without a sound. Reaching an arm through, he unlocked the window and inched the sash up until he had room to slide through.

Zane found himself in a child's bedroom. The moon cast a chill, bluish light through the room, revealing bookcases, a white dresser, and a small canopied bed. Stuffed tigers and lions and a giraffe sat in a neat row at the head of the bed, gazing at him with black button eyes. The bed was made with crisp perfection but he could smell dust in the spread. Posters of teenaged actors covered one wall. Printed on each photo was a scrawled signature meant to look personal—"Love ya, Corey; Love always, Jason," and so on. For some reason the harmless fraud offended Zane. He imagined the girl who lived in this room—Jenny—gazing alone at the pictures and wishing the signatures were real. He looked for a photo of her, and saw a picture on her night stand, but when he picked it up, he saw it was only another juvenile TV star.

Zane searched the low bookcase for photo albums, finding instead romantic fiction about secret gardens and the daughters of princes. On Jenny's dresser sat stacks of comic books whose neatness proclaimed a mother's hand.

Maybe Ann would keep a photo of Jenny in her bedroom.

Zane stepped into the long hall and oriented himself, moving quickly down to the master bedroom. Photos of a young girl on the verge of adolescence were enshrined on both bed tables. Zane picked one up and stared at it, fascinated. She looks like me! he thought. She has Ann's straight, blond hair, but she has my eyes, my mouth!

A wave of dizziness swept over him and he sat down on the bed. His chest felt full of air and the blood sang in his ears. Was it really possible? The timing would be about right. He had last been in Washington a little over twelve years ago. When he'd checked into his hotel, he'd seen Ann working the front desk and had later followed her home. He'd come to her in her big bed three different nights, sinking her husband into unconsciousness and rolling him out of the way. Each night he'd passed the small bedroom that now contained Jenny's things. It had been empty back then. And Ann certainly had not appeared pregnant.

But sometime after Merrick had chased him out of the area, Ann had had a daughter. And now that daughter was dying of a leukemia that resisted all treatment!

Zane had a wild urge to run back downstairs, let James and Ann see him, ask them if Jenny had any strange hungers. But they'd probably be too startled and terrified to answer, and then, having let them see him, he'd have to kill them without learning anything.

Zane heard footsteps coming up the stairs, a man's tread, making clumsy attempts at stealth. Zane suppressed a groan. Did I make a sound? he wondered. He couldn't remember. He got up, restored the picture to its place, and waited, facing the doorway.

James appeared in the hallway, one hand braced on the wall, his eyes wide. "Who's there?" he muttered, entering the bedroom with slow, cautious steps. Zane felt a prickle along his neck each time the man's eyes centered on him, even though he knew James could not see him. Come on, get moving, he thought impatiently. As James crept around the side of the bed, Zane stepped out of his path. With exaggerated, almost comic stealth, the man opened his closet door and peered inside.

Hurry up, damn you!

Finally, James relaxed. He plodded out of the bedroom and back downstairs. Zane could hear him reassuring Ann. When they found the hole in the glass in Jenny's window, they'd feel a little less sanguine. Maybe he should do something about that.

Zane gazed at the picture one last time, wishing he could take it with him. Back on the roof, he stopped to inspect the oak tree. One of its budding branches overhung Jenny's window. Zane checked the bed of jonquils that ran along the base of the house. Sure enough, several twigs and a bigger piece of branch lay among the flowers, knocked down by the recent winds. And it was still quite breezy.

Though he burned with impatience, Zane climbed down the drainpipe, grabbed the largest piece of deadwood, and scaled the pipe again. Taking no care about the noise, he bashed out the pane where he'd removed the glass, destroying the smooth, circular edge left by the cutter. Leaving the branch half through the window, he jumped to the ground. As he hurried away, the dog roused itself enough to bark, and he could hear the frightened voices of Ann and her husband through the kitchen window. When they discovered the branch, they would be relieved; if he wanted to come back later, they would not be on the alert.

Zane felt a surge of exhilaration. Right now, what mattered was the hospital—Dr. O'Keefe's hospital in Georgetown. He would go there now, pay this Jenny Hrluska a visit. If she had the strange hunger, then it was not coincidence that connected him to both the beautiful Ann and, twelve years later, the best blood doctor in town. The connection would be Jenny—a new hemophage, *my daughter!*

SIXTEEN

AT THE SECOND luxury hotel of the morning, Merrick hit pay dirt. He knew it the instant the manager of the Hay Adams took the photo of Zane from him—the involuntary rise of the eyebrows, the slight widening of the eyes.

"I'm not sure. This is rather grainy."

"But you do have an idea."

"Well, it could be Mr. Gray."

Merrick felt his heart accelerate, but he kept his face impassive. "What room would that be, Mr. Eaton?"

Instead of answering, Eaton continued to study the picture. He was a handsome, white-haired man in his mid fifties, with the kind of ingrained, wary courtesy Merrick had seen before in veteran hoteliers. Eaton wore a sweater vest under his suit coat, even though his office was quite warm. On his desk, this morning's *Post* and *Times* flanked a steaming cup of Red Rose tea. Clearly, the man loved information—and he was sure to want more about Zane.

Eaton handed the photo back. "This seems to be from a security camera. Is Mr. Gray in trouble, Detective?"

Translation: Does "Mr. Gray" *mean* trouble for the Hay Adams's well-heeled guests? If the answer didn't satisfy Eaton, he'd have his security force nose around Zane. The thought made Merrick's neck prickle. He said, "The picture *is* from a security camera, but only because Mr. Gray happened to be in the Capitol Security Bank two days ago about the time it was robbed. We've been trying to talk to all patrons who were there, in case anyone saw something significant without knowing it. If you could get me Mr. Gray's room number? . . ."

Eaton gave an apologetic wince. "I'm afraid that's a problem, Detective. I'm foursquare for helping the police as much as I can, but you say Mr. Gray's not a suspect in a crime and you don't even know if he was a witness to anything, so he's entitled to the privacy any reputable hotel would give him. Of course, that's no problem for you, since you can just call him through our switchboard."

Merrick battled frustration. Eaton was doing his job the way it should be done, but time was wasting. And the last thing he could do was call Zane's room. He said, "I find people are less nervous if I've had a chance to shake hands and act harmless before they learn I'm a cop."

"I can understand that." Eaton eyed him. "I *am* curious about something, though. If Mr. Gray was doing business at the bank, why weren't they able to give you his name?"

"Mr. Gray didn't quite get as far as doing business. Apparently he stopped in to make a deposit, then discovered he'd forgotten his money. The teller remembered him because he was a nice old man and fairly chatty, but if he gave her his name, she didn't recall it."

Eaton leaned forward and tapped a command into his desk computer and Merrick realized, with relief, that he was satisfied.

Now, if I could just get a look at his computer screen.

"Come to think of it," Eaton said, "I don't recall seeing Mr. Gray the last couple of days. I hope after all your trouble he hasn't checked out."

What he has done, Merrick thought, is dropped about thirty years off his age. And if he doesn't want you to see him, you won't.

"Mr. Gray is still with us," Eaton said.

A fierce joy swept Merrick. *Got you!*

The manager picked up his phone and punched in a number. With an effort, Merrick kept himself from lunging forward and snatching it away. Damn the man!

After a moment, Eaton hung up. "Apparently, he's gone out already this morning."

Merrick wanted to strangle Eaton. If Zane *had* been in, he'd now be racing down the rear fire escape.

"I wasn't going to mention police, of course," Eaton added. "Just tell him it was the manager, and ask if everything was satisfactory."

Merrick nodded, calming himself. No harm done, he thought, and it's good to know Zane is out. Now I can set up an ambush. He said, "I'll give Mr. Gray a call later. Good day, Mr. Eaton, and thanks for your help."

"Not at all."

Back in the lobby, Merrick waited until a guest standing at the small, elegant check-in counter finished his business and walked away. Then he slipped over the counter and crept up beside the lone clerk, editing himself from the periphery of her vision. She stood at her computer for a minute, then turned away and busied herself with the cash drawer. He stepped to the screen and scrolled quickly through the guest census. Fortunately, he had done this before, but it had never been so important—

There, Mr. Edward Gray, Suite 12-A—the *penthouse!*

Bless you, Sandeman, Merrick thought fervently. His heart pounded with exultation. Turning to the bank of room boxes, he removed the plastic key tab from 12-A and substituted a spare from another box.

He made sure he placed it exactly as the other had been.

Then he slipped back over the counter and hurried out to his car to get the chains.

Katie reached into the small basket cage, caught a mouse by the tail and lifted it out.

"I thought you were afraid of mice," Meggan said.

"Not anymore," Katie said. *What I'm afraid of now is a killer I might not be able to see.* The thought that it could be standing there now, invisible, a few feet away from her and Meggan, raised a rash of goose bumps on her arms. This was crazy. Why was she spooking herself?

Katie eased the dangling mouse to the treatment board and

pulled it gently backward by the tail as, with her other hand, she trapped it inside the mortar. The small, round bowl had thick sides for grinding up coarse chemical compounds, but the clear glass models like this one turned out to be ideal for holding mice still for an injection. Keeping hold of the mouse's tail, Katie positioned the mortar's pouring lip over the base of the tail.

"You're sure I'm not distracting you?"

"Don't be silly. I'm glad to see you. Aren't you usually in surgery by now, though?"

"My first case was a partial laryngectomy that went faster than I'd planned. I had a few minutes free, and your gorgeous resident told me I'd find you down here."

Katie glanced at her, impressed at how good she looked, even with her blonde hair pinned up. Her surgical cap had left a faint red line across her forehead, but her lipstick had not yet been smeared by the mask. Wrinkling her nose, Meggan glanced around at the rolling carts of rat and mouse cages. "I'd forgotten how gamey it smelled in here."

"That's the feed. Once you get used to it, it's not bad—kind of malty."

"So what are you doing?"

"That experiment I told you about—the girl with progeria. I've been injecting fractions of her blood. This is the eighth."

"I thought you were using rats."

"I have been—over there on cart two, the first eight cages. I decided to switch to mice because they metabolize faster." Katie picked up her loaded syringe, drew the mouse's tail straight, and lined up the 26-gauge needle with the central vein that ran down the tail. Aware suddenly of a slight tremor in her hand, she took a deep breath to help steady up and fed the hair-fine needle straight into the vein, first try. She eased the plunger down, then lifted the mortar and deposited the mouse in a new cage. "You get your own private room now," she said to it, sliding the door shut. "But your friends are right over here through the mesh in the next cage."

"Not only aren't you afraid of mice," Meggan observed, "you are talking to them."

"You talk to your cat."

"Cats have brains. Have you decided whether you're coming to our housewarming party?"

"I'd like to," Katie said, "but I'm not sure yet." Parties, she thought. How long since I've been to a party? Turning from the mouse cages, she found Meggan studying her.

"Are you all right?"

"Sort of," Katie said.

"Bad day already?"

"Bad day, bad week, this study is going nowhere fast, you name it."

Meggan nodded. "If you decide you want to talk about it, just let me know."

"Thanks." Katie gave her a quick hug and began to feel a little better. She peeled off her rubber gloves. "I'm off to rounds."

"Any interesting cases?"

"A twelve-year-old girl with leukemia that won't respond to treatment."

There must have been something in her voice, because Meggan gave her a long look, then said, "I'll walk you up."

Katie said good-bye to Meggan at Jenny's door. When she walked into the child's room, she was struck at once by a vague uneasiness. Actually, Jenny looked a bit better today. She had abandoned the tortured elbows-and-knees posture and was lying on her back. Hints of color marked her cheeks. Her eyes, half open, looked almost eerily tranquil. So why this sense that something wasn't right? "How are you feeling?" she asked.

"A little better," Jenny said.

Katie noticed a red stain on one of her front teeth. Her uneasiness sharpened. "Did you have another nosebleed last night?"

"I don't think so. I slept all night. I didn't dream about Doctor Giggles or . . . the other. I dreamed I had gotten wet in the rain and had to lick the water off me. I was really thirsty and it tasted good."

Katie felt relieved. Good dreams, for once. So what was that red stuff on Jenny's tooth—?

Someone rapped on the door. Turning, Katie saw Art, and behind him the residents and medical students he was leading on rounds. "You ready?" she asked Jenny.

"Sure."

Katie waved the group in. They had turned in their white coats for surgical scrubs for this stop on the tour. Katie wondered what it must be like for Jenny to have to look at everyone in masks and caps, to see only their eyes, feel only their gloves when they touched her.

Art started his presentation. After a smooth start, he got a bit flustered, forgetting to turn to Jenny, throw her a comment so she would feel like a participant rather than a specimen. His forehead above the mask seemed a little pale, as though he might be sick to his stomach. Katie noticed that the R-1s and medical students also seemed ill at ease, glancing around the room as Art talked. They feel it, too, Katie thought. What is it?

She remembered other young patients she had lost to leukemia. Sometimes, right before they died, they seemed to rally. Doctors even had a term for it—"the glow before you go." Was that why Jenny looked a little better, because death was mocking them?

"Any ideas about Jenny's constant hunger?" Art asked, looking mainly at the residents.

A woman medical student said, "How about pica?"

"Go on."

"It's a metabolic disorder where people have a craving to eat dirt."

"Eeeeuuww," Jenny said.

If anyone smiled, the masks hid it. Art added a few brief remarks about pica, noting that Jenny had tested negative for the mineral deficiencies typical of the disorder. He asked for other suggestions. No one had any. He sped on with his presentation, summarizing the course of Jenny's treatment to date in a few terse sentences.

What's wrong with all of us? Katie wondered. She found herself looking anxiously around the room, but there was no skeletal figure in cowl and dark robes holding a sickle.

When Art glanced at her, she realized he had finished. She nodded and he led the medical students out. She wanted very much to follow him; instead, she made herself settle beside Jenny's bed. Jenny rolled her head to the side, peering into a corner of the room, then gazing restlessly all around. "Were you in here last night, Doctor O'Keefe?"

"No. But the nurses come in to check on you every half hour. Sometimes they don't turn on the lights because they don't want to wake you."

"No, it wasn't the nurses. . . ." Jenny bit at her lip and Katie saw the red fleck again. At the same instant, she felt a rude nudge on the shoulder. She turned in her chair, thinking maybe Art or one of the residents had come back in, but no one was there. The hairs bristled on her arms. *It's here!* she thought. The terror she had felt at the church returned in a rush and she fled into the hall. She did not stop running until she reached the nurses station.

* * *

Zane kept his teeth bared until Katie was out of the room. Who was this doctor to bring in a horde of masked strangers to torment Jenny? They had treated her like a piece of meat. It was outrageous and he had taken all he could stand. He had not relaxed his control completely, just let a subliminal flash of his face through to her brain. The way she'd panicked, he must have looked as enraged as he'd felt.

Zane returned his attention to Jenny. His anger faded and an incredible feeling of possessiveness swept him. His daughter—there could no longer be any doubt! The one good thing about the barbaric spectacle he had just witnessed was that it confirmed Jenny was a hemophage. Until all their babble about strange hungers he had not been sure. It wasn't as if he could wake Jenny up and ask her. She'd taken the tiny portions of blood he'd managed to squeeze from her wrists, but that proved nothing, since he'd had to keep her asleep. Even if he'd been certain she was a phage and his daughter, it was much too soon to expose her to the truth about herself—or him.

He wished he had been able to do more for her during the night, but each time he'd cut his wrist, it had started to heal almost before he could get it to her lips. She'd gotten only a few drops each time. She was still near death, he could tell. She needed at least a pint, as fast as she could get it. He could try the blood bank again. The cooler door was massive, with a combination lock, but by now the morning crew of technicians would probably have started arriving. He could make one of them open the cooler—but that would cause a real uproar. Even if the cooler were open and he could slip in undetected, the only fresh whole blood would be a few packs people had donated for their own upcoming surgeries. A single unit of that would be instantly missed and cause too much fuss.

Better to go out and find a fresh source of his own.

Zane took out the transfusion packs he had stolen from the blood bank and studied them. A square plastic pack, a dangling tube, and a needle. How hard could it be? The packs looked small, so he'd stolen five of them. Even if they were missed it would cause no great alarm. They would have to be the answer until he could get his daughter out of here and teach her to hunt for herself.

Zane leaned over Jenny, as close as he dared, keeping back a few inches so she would not feel his breath on her face. Her eyes gazed unseeingly up into his. They were a beautiful, liquid blue. Even though terribly wasted from leukemia, she clearly resembled him—the way her lips were shaped, the strong, clean line of her jaw. You're mine, he thought ecstatically. Mine, mine!

I'll save you, he thought. I'll help you through the shock and panic. I'll kill for you, then teach you to hunt for yourself. My father tried to make me loathe myself, but I'll teach you to love what you are. You will never run from me in fear. We will be together, always.

Zane left Jenny's room, his heart soaring. He would find someone now to kill so his daughter would live.

Katie leaned on the counter at the nurses station, her hands pressed into her face. She felt a tap on her shoulder.

"Are you all right, Doctor?" Rosa, the charge nurse, asked.

Katie looked up at her, but could not find her voice.

Rosa's pencil-fine eyebrows arched in concern. "You're white as a sheet!"

Katie could still feel the cold flush of terror in her veins. Something was in that room with Jenny.

And I ran like a coward, leaving her alone with it.

I've got to go back, she thought. But I can't, I just can't go back in there alone. Maybe I could ask Rosa—no, it might hurt her, too—

Rosa took her firmly by the shoulders. "Doctor O'Keefe, tell me what's wrong."

Before Katie could answer, a buzzer went off behind Rosa— one of the call buttons, bleating urgently over and over. Rosa gave Katie a look of alarm. "That's Jenny's room!"

"Oh, God!" Katie turned and ran back down the hall. She heard Rosa's footsteps pounding behind her and knew she should warn her—but what would she say?

God help us both, she prayed.

SEVENTEEN

KATIE GOT TO Jenny's room first. For a second, she froze in shock. Jenny was lying on her side, the buzzer still pressed in her hand, the sheet all around her face soaked with blood. Blood poured from both nostrils. Her eyes were open but glazed.

Rosa's feet slapped the tile behind her, breaking her from her paralysis. "Call the station," Katie said, "and get us a gurney down here, stat. Then call surgery, then the blood bank—O negative, three units, straight to OR. Platelets, too."

Rosa nodded, taking one quick look at Jenny as she ran to the phone on the bed table. Katie pulled open the drawer of the table and grabbed a roll of gauze she'd stored there when Jenny's nosebleeds had first started. Cutting two large strips, she fashioned them into plugs and forced them up Jenny's nostrils, then applied pressure. The blood soaked through at once, as she'd expected. This was no ordinary bleed from the nose itself but a massive hemorrhage from somewhere farther back in the naso-pharynx. The thrombocytopenia from Jenny's leukemia may have caused it and had certainly made it worse. Even in an otherwise healthy person, a hemorrhage this major would be a serious prob-lem; with Jenny, if the surgeon had trouble locating the source, she could be dead in minutes.

Rosa slapped the phone down. "All set."

An instant later, a rumbling squeak swelled in the hallway. On the run, a nurse and an orderly barreled a gurney into Jenny's room and lifted her onto it. Katie kept one hand on the blood packs as she ran alongside, gripping Jenny's hand with her other. "Hang on, sweetie, we're going to get this stopped. You're going to be all right." Katie watched for any sign that Jenny was as-pirating blood. The hemorrhage was undoubtedly pouring down her throat; at any second, she could either choke or vomit.

"Stop at the station," Katie said. "I'm going to intubate her."

Rosa ran ahead and handed the endotracheal tube to Katie as the gurney drew even with the station. Praying that the touch she had developed as a resident would come back to her, Katie slipped the tube into Jenny's throat, wiggled it a little and popped it down.

"Good job," Rosa said, boosting the gurney forward again. Katie felt a spark of pain as her hip slammed into a wheelchair, sending it banging into the wall. She pressed fresh gauze into place and kept talking to Jenny even though the child's eyes had now rolled up in her head. The OR elevator was waiting when they got there and the ride down took only seconds, but by the time they reached the main floor, Katie's hand was again drenched with blood. She stayed with the gurney as it banged through the double doors into the surgery suite. From the corner of her eye, Katie saw Meggan Shields scrubbing at one of the big sinks. She had only a second to be glad before an OR nurse grabbed her arm, showing her a wad of gauze. "I'll repack her, doctor. We'll take it from here."

"Good." Katie hurried over to Meggan.

"Posterior nosebleed?" Meggan asked over her shoulder.

"Yes. This was the girl I mentioned in the biolab this morn-ing. She's already critical with end stage leukemia."

"Okay. We'll need at least three units."

"On their way, along with platelets."

"Good. Wanna scrub in?" Meggan jerked her head toward the next sink and yelled for another nurse.

Katie pulled off her bloody scrubs and started lathering up. As her hands performed the ritual, her mind raced over the procedure. Anesthesia would be a major problem, because Meggan would be working in the area where the inhalation mask was usually fixed. The anesthetist would have to give Jenny a heavy dose of Pentothal and keep her under with a drip. But Jenny's tolerance for barbiturates would be very low—

Katie jerked as a face flickered in her mind, glaring eyes, bared teeth, there only for a second and then gone. She stared down into the streaming water, shocked. It was what she had sensed in Jenny's room just before the nosebleed. Briefer than a flicker of lightning, but terrifying.

Katie stood upright for a second at the sink, feeling a new kind of terror. *Am I going crazy?*

Bending over again, she scrubbed viciously at her hands, trying to force her way through the fear.

What bumped you?

"Nothing!" Katie realized she'd spoken aloud. She glanced to the side, embarrassed, but Meggan was already gone.

"Doctor?"

Turning, she saw an OR nurse waiting behind her with a cart of sterile towels, scrubs, mask, and gloves. Katie felt her face turning red, but she said nothing and held out her arms. The nurse avoided her gaze as she dried her hands and arms, helped her on with the scrubs and gloves, and tied her mask and cap in place. I'm probably not the first doctor she's heard talking to herself, Katie thought.

In OR, Katie circled the gurney, standing across from Meggan so she wouldn't be in the way of the instrument nurse. Jenny's arm stretched out to the side, taped on a support, pentothal dripping through the IV line. Beside the pentothal drip hung a plastic pack of O negative blood, draining into another line. The anesthetist had laid strips of thin tape over Jenny's eyelids to help keep them from rolling open and drying the eyes. Meggan had already cut an incision through Jenny's upper gum line and was threading a fiberoptic scope through the cut, over the palate.

"Ah, Katie, hold that right there, would you?"

Katie pinched the thin shaft of the fiberscope, steadying her hand against Jenny's teeth. Meggan fitted the eyepiece of the scope to her eyes and twisted the dial on the side, advancing the inner filament higher inside Jenny's skull. "Can't see it. Hold on." Meggan's voice was very tense.

A nurse sponged up some of the blood that was still pouring

from Jenny's nostrils. Katie could not take her eyes from Jenny's face. It was white as chalk. *Please, God, don't let her die, I'll do anything you want. . . .*

She stopped when she suddenly realized what she was asking: that the miserable, awful life of a young girl who was certainly dying anyway be prolonged.

"There it is!" Meggan exclaimed, and in spite of everything Katie felt a surge of hope.

"Holy shit, two of them, big ones. Hold it right where it is, Katie, I'm going to run the cauterizer up. Bad veins. Bad, bad veins!"

Katie felt herself grinning under the mask.

And then she saw Jenny's eyes flutter. Straining against the tape, her lids pulled free and popped open. Incredibly, impossibly, her head started to turn.

"Hold her!" Meggan cried.

Katie grabbed her jaw with her other hand, immobilizing her head.

"More pentothal," Meggan snapped at the anesthetist.

"I've given her all she can handle."

"Well, damn it, she's moving!"

"She can't be!"

From the corner of her eye, Katie saw the anesthetist stand up, stare at his gauges. Suddenly, she could smell his sweat. "This can't be," the man said in a strained voice. "With what I've given her, she shouldn't be able to twitch."

Jenny's eyes rolled to the side. It could only be an involuntary response—had to be—but it seemed as if she were trying to see something above Meggan's shoulder. Still holding her jaw and the fiberscope, Katie glanced up to where Jenny's eyes were staring, but all she could see were the pentothal drip and a fresh bag of O negative the nurse was hanging up.

"Got it!" Meggan said. "The last one."

Almost at once, the torrent of blood from Jenny's nose stopped. Her eyes stared at the blood a moment longer, then slipped shut again. Katie felt a cold flutter of dread in the pit of her stomach, and then it passed, driven out by her joy that Jenny was alive. Jenny still had a chance.

The key to Suite 12-A did not work. Baffled, Merrick stood a moment looking down at the plastic tab in his hand, as if he might find the answer in its pattern of perforations. He pictured Zane switching the extra room key in his box with one from another box. In spite of himself, Merrick smiled. *Clever devil.*

He set down the suitcase. The chain and short-handled sledge hammer inside, wrapped in layers of mover's padding, made no sound. He retraced his steps down the long, hushed hallway to the open door he had passed. The housekeeper was still on her knees in the bathroom, cleaning the tub. The tab of the computerized master key peeked at Merrick from a baggy pocket of her apron. The danger was not that she'd see him, but that she might hear him or feel him slip the key out.

She did not.

When Merrick returned with the key, the housekeeper was circling in the bedroom, patting her pockets and looking worried. Quietly, he laid the key on the bathroom floor and hurried back to Zane's suite. Pulling the suitcase out of the doorway, he entered the suite and stood a moment, gripped by a fierce tension. He'd done it, gotten into Zane's lair. It would take Zane at least twenty seconds from the ding of the elevator to reach here—plenty of warning. The stairwell door was almost as far away, and its squeak was louder than the elevator bell.

Merrick stationed the suitcase around a corner from the door. Raising the lid, he folded back the padding to expose the sledge hammer, chain, and padlock. Each time he heard the elevator or stairwell door, he'd take up position here. When Zane passed the corner, he'd strike simultaneously with the hammer and Influence. *All I need,* Merrick thought, *is to stun him for a few seconds—long enough to bind him in the chain. Then I carry him down the back fire escape and drive to the vault, and it's all over.*

Don't underestimate him. Remembering Sandeman's warning, Merrick felt a sharp foreboding. What if Zane *could* enter minds?

What if he is stronger than I am?

Then he will bury me.

Merrick tried to put his fear aside. Fear might make you run faster, but he could not run. What he needed was anger, *outrage.* Zane had killed thousands of people. He was a vicious murderer—

My son.

Merrick made himself focus on the horrible image of Sheila Forrester lying bloodied under the bushes—

The elevator pinged. As he moved into position, the air seemed to thicken around him, dragging at his legs. Lifting the hammer from the suitcase took all of his will. A door opened and closed down the hall and relief flooded him.

Reprieved, he prowled around the suite, too agitated to stand still. It was a beautiful place, Persian rugs and polished parquet, Louis XIV chairs and high windows hung in velvet. Sandeman had been right about Zane's taste for luxury. In the bathroom wastebasket, Merrick found a couple of empty packets that had contained brown hair dye—evidently Zane had got tired of having white hair. An electric razor, a toothbrush, and paste sat on the marble vanity.

In the suite's spacious bedroom, the brass head rail on the king-size bed caught Merrick's eye. It seemed dented in several places. Inspecting the metal, he saw that the heavy rail had been twisted out of its shape, then imperfectly restraightened. Rage? Anguish? Was Zane even capable of anguish?

Merrick went to the beautiful mahogany desk in the sitting room. Easing the top drawer open, he found an artist's sketchbook. No surprise here—in their long lives, most phages tried their hand in the arts sooner or later. He had even done it himself.

Opening the pad, he *was* surprised at what Zane had drawn—a woman's face, beautifully done. He's better than I ever was, Merrick thought with a strange, uneasy pride. The next three pages revealed three more women's faces. No lolling tongues, no torn throats; all of them had been drawn radiantly alive.

The next page stopped Merrick short, a pretty, oval face framed in straight, light hair. He had seen this woman before, and not that long ago. He tried to think where, but could not. He had seen a number of Zane's victims. Might this be one of them? He imagined the face lax in death, then stopped as he felt the dark, involuntary call of the kill. No, this was not one of Zane's victims, he felt sure. At least not yet.

Merrick paged ahead until he recognized another face. This one he could put a name to—Sheila Forrester, the dead woman at the cathedral. Her head was done at a slight angle from full face, her eyes peering into the distance, a soft smile on her lips. The sketch book seemed suddenly to burn against Merrick's fingers as he realized that his instinct was right and this was a gallery of Zane's victims. He drew them before he killed them, part of the thrill of the hunt for him.

Repulsed, Merrick almost put the pad back in the desk; instead, he looked at the last drawing. It was not finished, but it took him only a second to recognize the eyes. *Katie!* Alarm jolted him. Even with her hair barely blocked in, the mouth only a line,

Zane had captured her. Furious, Merrick ripped the drawing from the pad and tore it to shreds. You can't have her, he thought—not even on paper. When you walk through that door, your killing days are over.

Shoving the pad back in the drawer, Merrick stalked to the position he had chosen. This time when he picked up the hammer, it felt light. *Now* he was ready. He had been looking for his son here. His son was dead, had been dead almost five hundred years, and he did not want to know any more about the thing that had replaced him.

EIGHTEEN

ZANE INCHED THROUGH rush hour traffic, looking for a good place to make the kill. He realized he was grinning and tried to stop, but could not. He had not known it was possible to feel such elation; it swelled inside him, made him seem new and strange and wonderful to himself. In Jenny's room this morning, realizing she was, beyond all doubt, his daughter, he had felt himself step out of the old shell that used to be Zane.

I'm a new man, Zane thought. I'm a father!

He gazed out at the sidewalks of Pennsylvania Avenue. Look at all those juicy normals, rising like prairie dogs from the subway or climbing down from the buses, toting their briefcases in a joyless stampede to work. . . .

A stampede that, in just a few minutes, would dwindle away. He'd better find a good place soon. His daughter needed blood. As a father, he had certain responsibilities.

Of course, after all the women he'd played incubus to, he must have been a father before, many times. But he had never *known* it before.

Zane's head gave an involuntary shake. How strange it felt to examine his life, but suddenly it intrigued him. He had never killed a woman after mating with her, but neither had he ever gone back years later, as he had with Ann. From time to time, the thought of children might have entered his mind, but since the genetic odds made it unlikely even for a phage to father a phage, why care?

I did it, though! Jenny is not only mine, she's my own kind.

Zane's reverie broke as he saw a little tree-lined plaza tucked against the complex of buildings. It looked like a good kill zone. He parked in an alley across the street. When he got across the street, he realized the plaza was even better than he'd hoped. A brick path formed a diagonal shortcut across the block, right through a grove of photinia. The tall bushes provided a screened space in the middle of the plaza where he could snatch a woman while she was hidden from view instead of making her seem to vanish into thin air.

Zane positioned himself beside the densest photinia bush. Almost at once, he heard footsteps. Leaning forward, he saw a man coming and, about twenty feet behind him, a woman. Beyond her, there was no one. The woman was in her twenties, smartly dressed. She toted a large portfolio case that swung with each confident stride. The spacing was right—the man far enough ahead that he wouldn't hear even if she managed to make a noise.

Zane stepped back as the man passed him by. He focused on the clip-clip-clip of the woman's heels. Ordinarily, he loved that sound, but he felt no excitement now, only a strange anxiety. The breeze blew her perfume to him, lilies of the valley, and he knew that, after he'd drawn blood for Jenny, he would taste it on her skin. Even that brought only the dullest anticipation. *Don't worry about it. You've never killed under such pressure before. Just get it over with.*

When the woman was about ten feet away, he stepped into her path, blinding her to him. She was not beautiful, but she had wonderful, pale skin, flawless as porcelain. He felt himself backing up again. Paralyzed, he gazed at her face, her white throat, and then she was past him, her heels tapping on the brick. Shaken, Zane watched her go.

What happened?

She reminded me of Jenny. Not her features, but that pale skin, the air of innocence.

Zane cursed silently. When he taught Jenny to hunt, he'd have to do better than this. Feeling confused and cheated, he watched his prey walk away. Traffic had thinned now, allowing the woman an easy jaywalk across the street. As she passed the mouth of the alley where he'd parked his car, he saw a man step from its shadows, clamp an arm across her throat, and drag her backward out of sight.

For a second, Zane stared in shock, unsure he'd really seen it. Then he found himself running toward the spot where she'd disappeared, dodging in front of a car, dimly hearing its horn blare as he sprinted into the alley mouth. *What am I doing?*

He plunged deeper into the shadows of the alley. There was no sign of the woman, but he heard muffled cries ahead. As he dashed into a loading area, he saw a pale leg kicking over the concrete sill of a truck dock. Leaping onto the dock, he grabbed the rapist by the shoulders and lifted him off the woman.

She rolled away, scrambled off the platform and ran away screaming. Filled with a strange, wild fury, Zane spun the man around, grabbed his throat, and lifted him high again. Thrusting his face into the terrified face of the rapist, he felt a flurry of panicked kicks against his shins. He wanted to snap the man's neck; with effort, he held back.

"We need your blood," he said. "My daughter and I."

The rapist's throat bulged with a choked-off scream, and then his eyes rolled up and he went limp. Zane looked for the woman. She was out of sight now, but he could still hear her frenzied screams. Someone would respond; time to get out of here.

Slinging the rapist over one shoulder, Zane ran to his car and threw the limp body into the backseat. He started the car and drove from the alley, his hands trembling on the wheel. He had no idea why he had done what he had just done, could make no sense of it.

A groan came from the backseat. Zane constricted the flow of blood to the rapist's brain and the sounds stopped. He drove for awhile, somehow steering, even though nothing really registered. Was this how normals saw when a phage interfered with their vision?

I've got to pull myself together, he thought.

Looking around, he saw that he had driven down near the waterfront on Maine Avenue. He pulled into a parking place behind the wooden shanties where the seafood wholesalers would open up in a few hours. This early, the docks were still deserted. Zane carried the rapist down to the ribbon of shore under the closest pier, out of sight of anyone who might come along. The air stank of spoiled fish people had thrown under the pier. Propping the unconscious man up against a wood piling, Zane fumbled a transfusion pack from his pocket. He jabbed the needle into the man's throat, but his trembling hands made him miss the vein. Cursing softly, he constricted a jugular at the base of the man's neck until the blood piled up and swelled the vein. This time the needle slipped in easily. As the dark red blood streamed down the tube into the pack, Zane's head hammered with a sudden, uncontrollable rage to kill. He fell on the man's neck with his teeth—

No, JENNY! Remember Jenny.

Zane rolled to the side and scrambled to his knees, facing away from the man, struggling for control. He must not tear the throat. Not until he had enough for Jenny.

He waited as long as he could, then turned. The needle was still in place. The bag sat, full and bulging, on the man's lap. Zane prepared another bag. This time, after he had centered the point of the needle on the vein, he looked away as he slipped it in. Still, he could almost feel the man's flesh against his teeth. He swallowed hard, trying to still the clamor in his throat. Only a little longer, a little longer—

He tore the needle out, took off his coat, and lunged into the body, dimly hearing the man's head crack against the post, and then his teeth broke the skin and the warm flood of blood gushed down his throat. The body kicked once under him. He drank until the heart stopped pumping, then sucked at the ragged wounds his teeth had made. Finally, he sat back, satisfied.

The dead rapist stared at him with dusty, accusing eyes.

"Sadist," Zane murmured. "You got what you deserved."

Turning away from the dead man, he washed himself in the silty backwaters of the Potomac. He dropped his bloody shirt into the water and watched it sink out of sight. As he got up to leave, he realized he was not finished. He must make this kill count against Father, too. Hidden away here, the body might not be discovered for days, especially with the smells of rotting fish to cover up the odor. . . .

Suddenly Zane realized that delayed discovery was just what he wanted. It would allow him to control just when the body was found, to make it happen at the worst possible moment for Father. He wedged the body up into the dark crevice where the rising bank met the underside of the pier. No one would see it there. Slipping the bulging blood packs inside his coat, he put it back on, got out from under the pier, and strode up the bank to his car.

As he drove to the hospital, he felt uneasy, a little depressed. His mind kept going back to the way he had let that woman go. She had been perfect, just the sort of kill he craved, but today he'd had absolutely no appetite for her. What if it persisted, happened each time he lined up a victim? The thought oppressed Zane. Killing was the purest of thrills. It provided the peaks in his life. If he were to permanently lose those flashes of rapture, what could replace them? He would have lost everything that gave his life meaning.

He would become like Father.

Zane shuddered. If he became like Father, then Father would have won, would have gotten what he had wanted from the very beginning. *Be like me or I will kill you.* Had Father ever understood what he was asking? Merrick, the Puritan—before there were Puritans. In the centuries before needles and transfusions, a wound that would bleed enough to feed a phage would go on bleeding until the victim died, so Father, too, had been a killer many times. Each time he had no doubt wallowed in guilt, even though he killed only those he felt most deserved to die—enemy soldiers, nobles who enslaved their subjects, abusive landowners, murderers, violent thieves. . . .

It had felt good in a weird way, to kill that rapist.

Zane groaned. This was insane. He was not turning into his father. I backed off that woman because she reminded me of Jenny, he thought. And that's why I wouldn't let that filthy normal rape her. As for killing him, I did that because I needed blood fast, that's all. I love to kill and I always will. It will come back to me.

The important thing now is to make my daughter truly mine.

At the hospital, Zane found a supply room and pulled on the surgical scrubs, cap, and mask he'd seen the others wear in Jenny's room. He'd avoid the hospital staff, but Jenny would see him, and he needed to start her off with what she was used to. Her first impression of him would be a good one—a doctor coming in to help her.

Zane found his way to a supply cupboard and took a large plastic foam cup from it. He poured the blood into the cup and took it to Jenny. Her appearance shocked him. She was pale as death—much worse than when he'd left her only a few hours ago. He knew with sudden and absolute conviction that without blood she would be dead before nightfall. What if she was too far gone to drink?

Fear clamped Zane's heart. Bending over her, he murmured her name. Her eyelids fluttered, then closed again. Tenderly, he slipped a hand behind her shoulders, appalled at their thinness— he could feel each bone of her spine. A faint, sweet odor of sweat rose from her gown. As he sat her up, she groaned.

"I know," he murmured. "It hurts." And he did know. He remembered.

Jenny's eyelids fluttered again, then opened part way. She licked her lips and gazed dully at him.

"I've brought you a drink," he murmured. He held the cup to her lips. At first nothing happened, then he saw her nostrils flare as she picked up the scent of the blood.

"It's tomato juice," he said. "Drink it and you'll feel better." He tipped the cup against her lips.

At first, she only wet her tongue. Her throat convulsed as she swallowed. The second swallow came more easily. She took a deep, trembling breath and leaned into the cup. He tipped it back, watching her drink, watching the trace of color swim into her cheeks, and it was the best feeling he had ever had in his life.

When the cup was empty, he eased her back down in her bed again. She gazed up at him sleepily. "Who are you?"

He longed to tell her he was her father, but knew it was too soon. He smoothed her brow with his hand. It felt awkward, but wonderful.

"You're not wearing gloves," she whispered.

"No. Sleep now, and I'll come back later. Sleep as long as you can. You're going to feel much better when you wake up, I promise." She nodded and her eyes slipped shut.

Bending over, he pulled his mask down and kissed her forehead. "Jenny, my Jenny."

Detouring to the linen room, he discarded the scrub pants and strode out of the hospital to his car. He felt like a god. His daughter would live. And she has a father, Zane thought, as I did not. One who loves and accepts her as she is.

You think you're so good, Merrick, but the only right thing you ever did was give me blood.

Zane opened the gym bag in the backseat, pulled off the scrub top, and put on a fresh shirt. Starting the car, he headed for his hotel. It would be good to be in a safe place for a few hours.

He had a lot to think about, plans to make. He had come back to bury Father, to repay agony with agony, and nothing would deflect him from that, but now he had a new mission, too—to make his daughter splendid, strong, invincible.

And proud of what she was.

NINETEEN

MERRICK STOOD AGAINST the wall of the hotel room, listening to the hallway outside. Only two sounds in the world mattered: the ding of the elevator or the squeak of the stairwell door. Dozens of times in the past three hours he had heard one or the other, but Zane had not come. Merrick checked his watch and the unease that had been building in him the last few hours sharpened. Soon he would have to leave. Katie would be coming home from the hospital, and he dare not leave her unprotected. While he sat here in Zane's lair, Zane might already be keeping a similar watch in Katie's house.

He sketched her in his book.

I'll wait thirty more minutes, Merrick decided. Come on, Zane, come *on.*

* * *

As he passed the main desk, Zane noted the position of the key in his box. It looked unchanged. Surely it would be all right to go straight up. . . .

Remember who is hunting you.

He waited until there were no guests at the desk. Silently swinging over the counter, he slipped the plastic key from his box and studied the pattern of perforations. His scalp prickled. For a second, fear drained the strength from his legs, and then a vast resentment filled him. *You bastard! How did you find me?*

Once again, Merrick heard the distant ding of the elevator. Lifting the hammer, he counted off the seconds.

Footsteps whispered closer along the hall carpet. He flattened himself against the wall, filled with a sudden, fierce tension. Drawing a deep breath, he held it, willing himself to total stillness.

Someone knocked at the door.

Merrick frowned, incredulous. What was this?

"Bellman," said a voice on the other side of the door, and the knocking came again. For a moment, there was a silence, then Merrick heard the hiss of paper sliding across the marble sill. The steps receded down the hall. When the elevator had dinged again, and the doors slid closed, Merrick peered around the corner at the sill. The envelope had made it all the way through, with no part left in the hall. Careful to make no sound, Merrick retrieved it. It was not sealed. The note read:

> Dear Dad,
>   Let's meet for drinks at O'Keefe's.

Zane had signed it with a Z, drawn in red ink. In his mind, Merrick saw the Z Zane had drawn in blood on Susan Zarelli's forehead. His heart stuttered with fear. He ran from the suite.

Fear still echoed through Merrick as he sat in Katie's living room, sipping coffee with her and Audrey. Ten o'clock, and still no sign of Zane, but he might be out there right now, watching the house, waiting.

How the hell had he sniffed out the trap?

And that note, brazen, taunting. That was not the Zane of twelve years ago.

I have to spend the night again, Merrick thought.

He tried to catch Katie's eye, but she was deep in conversation with her mother. All evening, her gaze had been friendly but opaque, giving him no signals, accepting none. Was she sorry about the other night? Of course, she must be. No matter how they'd both pretended it was a momentary flight to the refuge of their pasts, it had not been the past, it had been now, and it had opened up the wounds all over again.

I'll stay outside, Merrick thought.

At least he knew the inside of the house was clear. During the evening he'd managed to stick his head into every room. Now that dinner was over, he could excuse himself and pretend to drive off, then take up his watch in the bushes outside.

He should do it now.

"More coffee?" Audrey asked.

"Yes, thank you."

Katie walked to the front window, parted the drape and looked out, then quickly turned away. "Those bars," she said. "I wonder if I'll ever get used to them."

"I think they look good," Merrick said, "very New Orleans."

"They're still bars, though."

"It's a good idea, living in the city."

"Yes, that's what Mom and I decided."

Merrick knew it was more—the invisible touch Katie had felt in the church, the missing slide. At the same time, she seemed a little sheepish about the bars, which meant she wasn't sure her fears were real. His job was to keep them from becoming any more real—for his own sake as well as hers.

But he was glad for the bars. She'd gone all out, covering every window, even upstairs. The iron was thick and strong. He'd prefer a foot of cured, reinforced concrete like the walls of the vault, but it might be enough to keep Zane out. In fact, unless the note had been a bluff, it could well be why Zane had not gotten inside. Merrick took some heart at the thought. It was possible that the note *was* a bluff. Despite its bravado, Zane had to be scared, after being tracked down to his hotel. And if he had really meant to come here, why would he advertise it?

But I'm still going to keep watch tonight, Merrick thought.

Audrey came back with the coffee pot, poured him another cup, then gave a stagy yawn. "I think it's time I tottered off to bed. You two young people don't get into any mischief down here."

Katie gave her a complicated smile.

After Audrey had gone up, Merrick said, "I thought your mother stayed up late."

"She does. She just wants us to be alone."

"That might not be such a good idea."

Katie looked at him. "No."

He knew he should get up then, get out. Instead, he said, "Any progress with the blood cells?"

Katie sighed and leaned back into the couch. "I tried to rerun the hemoglobin tests on the original sample. No go. Those cells are just as fresh as the day you brought them in. That strange barrier—I'm not sure it's really a wall—is impervious to the acid normally used to break blood down for analysis. I'm considering other possible reagents that might work. We'll see what happens tomorrow."

"How about your resident—Art?"

"He's been scouring the literature in his spare time—which is rare—but he's come up with zilch, so far." Katie leaned her head back on the couch. Merrick could feel a change in her now that her mother was out of the room. He realized she had been keeping up a cheerful front, that she was, in reality, depressed about something.

"Want to talk about it?"

She rolled her head toward him. "It's Jenny Hrluska. She suffered a severe hemorrhage and had to go into surgery. Meggan Shields got the bleeders very fast and saved her life—for the moment—but I don't think she can last much longer." Katie's voice was heavy with dejection.

I could still save her. Thrusting the thought from his mind, Merrick slid across to Katie and put a hand on her shoulder. "I know this must be very hard for you."

"She's such a wonderful child. And I did nothing for her. Nothing."

"You've done all you could." Merrick tipped his head back and stared at the ceiling, feeling miserable. Just one unit of blood. *And then Jenny becomes one of us, a killer.*

Katie yawned, a huge, jaw-cracking yawn that was not in the least stagy.

"I should go," Merrick said.

"I'm sorry," she said, remaining on the couch as he got up. "I'm just so damn tired."

"You haven't exactly had an idle day."

"No. But I ought to have more energy than this."

The rasp of longing in her voice roused a sudden uneasiness

in him. Was she ill? "Maybe you ought to take a day off."

She gave a short, harsh laugh. "Right." Her throat convulsed in a hard swallow, and his uneasiness turned to concern. Her eyes seemed focused slightly beyond him, full of a yearning he could not quite identify. But for some reason, it made him think of himself, when he needed to feed.

"Are you sleeping?" he asked softly.

"Like a baby." She focused on him again, and he could see the effort it took, her expression sealing over in a smile. Her phone rang and she snatched up the receiver with a sudden, tense energy. "Hello?" Her shoulders slumped in apparent relief. "Yes, he's here."

He took the phone. "Merrick."

"Yo, Lieutenant, this is Des. I'm down at the Washington Marina, off Maine Avenue. I think you'd better get down here. Our psycho has struck again."

Merrick's heart sank.

"At least I think it's our killer," Desmond said.

"What do you mean?"

"Well, the stiff is a man this time. His neck has been pretty roundly chewed though, just like the two women. God, I hate this fucking animal."

Merrick cursed silently. He had to go, no choice. He'd just have to bring Katie with him.

"The body was hid pretty good under a pier," Des said. "We might not have found it for a week, but someone called it in—anonymously, of course."

"I'll be right there," Merrick said and hung up the phone.

"Another killing?" Katie's eyes were wide.

"Yes. I might need you to look at the blood."

"Doctor Byner will be there, right? If there's any blood, he could take a slide for me."

"Yes," Merrick admitted.

"I . . . I'd rather not be around another murder victim, Merrick. Even if I don't see the body, I'll imagine it."

He nodded, stymied. How perverse—now that he wanted her at a crime scene, she was begging off.

Would the bars on her windows be enough?

Maine Avenue was about forty minutes round trip. An hour at the scene, with luck, he could be back in under two. If he did not go, Rourke would have all the reason he needed to turn the case over to Cooke.

Merrick took Katie's hand. "Good night. Thanks for dinner."

"You're welcome." Hanging onto his hand, she pulled herself up from the couch. She glanced at his mouth, but did not lean over for a kiss.

Before getting in his car, he took a turn around the house, searching in the trees, behind the hedges. There was no sign of Zane.

Still, Merrick's neck prickled with foreboding as he drove off toward Maine Avenue.

TWENTY

WITH SAVAGE PLEASURE Zane watched Merrick's car pull away from Katie's house. He waited a few minutes to make sure Merrick was not circling back, then lifted the briefcase from the backseat and removed his glass cutter and a bowie knife he'd taken from a man in Tennessee back in the eighteen hundreds. He hefted the knife, savoring its weight and exquisite balance, brushing his thumb across the razor-sharp blade. *This is for your lover, Father. And for what you wanted to do to me today.*

Zane realized he had brought the blade of the knife against his other hand; he was so furious at Merrick he had almost cut himself. He pulled the blade away, but his fury remained. He'd managed to retrieve his sketchbook and some of his clothes earlier, when it became clear Merrick meant to stick with the doctor all night, but that was the last time he could go near the hotel. Worse, he had no idea how Father had found him there—which meant he must avoid all hotels now, even if he had to stay in his car.

Give that round to Father, Zane thought, but only a half a point, because he didn't get me.

Now it's my turn.

The rage and resentment boiled up in Zane again. He had planned to catch Father first, chain him, and force him to watch while he made his precious normal scream. But this would be better. Merrick would go mad thinking of how he had left her to be tortured and killed. He would blame himself for her suffering.

And this way I won't have to actually hurt her, Zane thought. Just kill her.

He watched the house a moment longer. The downstairs lights were out now, leaving only the one in the doctor's bedroom. Then it went out, too. He studied the fancy bars that protected each window. *We shall see, blood doctor.*

Slipping from his car, he ran to the rear of her house. The upper windows in back were barred, too. He felt a grudging respect for her judgment. Most people only barred the lower ones, but the doctor was taking no chances.

Zane chose a first floor window at the corner of the house to minimize the chance of sounds drifting up the central stairwell. Gripping the bars, he tested them; they resisted firmly. They were good wrought iron, an inch in diameter, spaced four inches apart. It would be easier to tear their bolts from the mortar than to bend them—but that would make too much noise.

Setting his feet apart, Zane gripped the two bars nearest the center of the window and pulled at them. They moved an inch. Gritting his teeth, he increased the pressure and they bent a few inches more. His muscles began to burn with the effort. Rage swelled in him. *Damn you! I'm coming in and you can't stop me—*

Zane let go of the bars and stood back with a gasp. His fury had turned the tide, opening a fifteen-inch gap in the bars—a tight squeeze, but good enough. He attached the suction cup to the window, ran the cutter around it, and slipped the circle of glass out through the bars. Unlatching the window, he eased it up, then grabbed the bars and wormed through the gap into a small pantry.

The house was silent. Tucking the glass cutter back inside his jacket, he hurried through the dark kitchen to the foot of the stairs and stood, listening again. It was quiet up there, and totally dark, but the doctor could not have been in bed more than a few minutes. If she'd been tired enough, she might be asleep, but he could take no chances.

Zane leaned forward and planted his palms on the outside edges of a step. Spreading his weight between his feet and palms, he crept up the stairs, avoiding the stress points in the wood. Halfway up, he miscalculated and a board creaked softly. He froze, but there was no answering sound upstairs. He finished the climb without another sound.

Keeping to the wall, where the floorboards were less springy, he headed toward the doctor's bedroom—and stopped as a high, babyish voice murmured briefly behind him. He turned, intrigued. What was that?

A half-open door near the bathroom spilled the soft glow of a night-light into the hall. Zane crept back down the hall until he stood in the doorway. A young child sat in its crib gazing tranquilly out the door. On impulse, Zane lifted his Influence and the child blinked, then smiled shrewdly and pointed at him.

It had Merrick's eyes.

Zane felt a curious mixture of amusement and pain. Father, Father, he thought. You just don't learn, do you? And Dr. O'Keefe, keeping a little secret from me. Is this my half brother?

"Hello," the child said in a soft, tentative voice.

Zane waved a finger at him.

The child started to say something else and Zane mentally touched his brain stem, just enough to make him plop onto his side. Sleepily, the kid stuck his thumb in his mouth. A moment later his eyes slid shut.

What's your story, kid? Zane wondered. Do you have the gene? I know—we can't tell yet. But wouldn't it be something if, under that sweet baby fat, you're really a man-eater? Right now, I've got business with your mother. But after she's gone, you can be my new weapon against our Father. So I will see you later . . . *alligator?*

Zane glided back down the hall toward the doctor's door. It was open, no doubt so she could keep an ear on her kid. Zane went straight to her bed. She lay on her side, facing away from him toward the front window. The slow, even rhythm of her breath told him she was asleep, but not very deeply. He watched her for a minute, then drew the bowie knife from its sheath. He moved around to the other side of her bed so he could get at her neck more easily. Moonlight slanting through her front window cast a creamy glow on her throat and face.

She must be alive while he made the small cuts all over her

body, so she would bleed properly for the pathologist. But he would put her far under, make sure she felt nothing. There was no need for her to suffer—only for Father to believe she had suffered. Then, one clean, deep stroke to the throat, and he would drink his fill. Her blood should not be wasted, and best of all, it would enrage Father.

Zane bent close, readying himself to compress the brain stem and plunge the doctor into deep unconsciousness.

The phone beside her bed rang, making him jump. He almost sent her deep, then realized the phone would wake up the older woman, perhaps bring her in here, and then he would have to kill her. He had no quarrel with her, and it was an unnecessary complication.

He stepped back. On the third ring, the doctor groaned and reached for the phone, bringing it to her ear without opening her eyes. "O'Keefe," she mumbled.

"Oh, Doctor, this is Rosa on Three East. I'm sorry if I woke you."

"It's all right. I had to get up to answer the phone anyway."

A tinny crackle of laughter on the other end of the line. "I don't think you'll mind waking up for this one. There's been a dramatic change in Jenny. She's awake and stronger than she's been in weeks."

The doctor's eyes popped open and she sat up in bed, her face suddenly transformed with joy. Zane felt a sudden, strange ache in his throat.

"Her color is better," said the nurse, "and she asked for something to eat."

"That's wonderful."

"Do you think we should call her folks?"

"Let's wait until morning. They haven't been getting much rest lately, and if this pans out as a remission, the news will be just as good then."

"Right. Again, sorry for the late call, but I just wanted to congratulate you. If it weren't for you and Doctor Shields acting so fast today when Jenny began to hemorrhage, she might not have lived to turn the corner."

"You were right in there slugging, too, Rosa."

"True," the woman said and laughed.

Dr. O'Keefe hung up the phone and gazed happily at the ceiling. Zane stared at her, unable to move, a shocked breath locked in his lungs. Jenny had hemorrhaged? Suddenly he remembered how much worse she'd looked when he came back with the blood—so ashen. He'd been afraid she might be too weak to drink. Had Dr. O'Keefe really saved her life? A chill passed through Zane, a delayed shock as he realized that he might have been too late with the blood if it weren't for this woman.

Footsteps creaked up the hallway toward them. Still frozen in place, Zane watched as the older woman he'd seen the other night tiptoed in. "Katie, are you all right?"

People call her Katie, Zane thought.

She swung her legs out of bed and grinned at the woman. "It was the hospital. Mom, it's Jenny. I think she's going into remission!"

"Wonderful!"

Katie got up and swung her mother around in a clumsy dance, until their slippers came off and they sat down on the bed, laughing.

Zane felt a peculiar burn in the center of his chest. Slipping past them, he crept down the stairs and wormed through the gap in the twisted bars. He walked across the backyard and kept going, jumping fences, silencing the occasional yapping dog with automatic twitches of his mind.

At last he stopped and, kneeing against a tree, pressed his forehead into the rough bark. What had happened to him back there?

She saved my daughter's life.

No, Zane thought. She just prolonged it a bit longer. *I* saved Jenny. If it had been left to this doctor, she would die.

He rose and gave his head a violent shake, trying to clear it. Where had these feelings come from? If he started permitting feelings for normals, who knew where it would end? He would find some reason not to kill anyone, and then he would die.

I have to be strong now, Zane thought. Father wants to destroy me. For five hundred years I have never drawn a safe breath. He's hurt me, over and over, made me suffer. Now he has to suffer, too. I have to kill the doctor, kill her now.

Merrick was almost to Maine Avenue before he registered what his detective had said: *an anonymous caller.*

Cold horror rose in him. Starting his siren, he screeched through a U-turn and headed back toward Katie's house, praying that the bars were strong enough. As he neared her house, he switched off his siren. Anxiety burned in his chest like a trapped breath. He parked in front of the next house and sprang from the car to stare up at Katie's front windows. They were intact, the bars straight. Hoping, he ran to the back of the house.

The bars at the pantry window were bent. His heart skipped a beat. Dread welled up in him. *Please, no.*

An instant later, he stood in the pantry with no memory of squirming through the window. The air smelled of coffee and the breaded catfish Audrey had served for dinner. There was no scent of blood. Zane had been here, might still be here, but he had not cut her—not yet.

Drawing the nine-millimeter automatic from his shoulder holster, Merrick crept up the stairs. He made almost no sound— but enough for Zane to hear if he was still around. The gun comforted him only a little. Bullets could not kill Zane or even wound him in any serious way. Still, a shot in the brain could stun and disorient him for a few moments—enough to get him back out to the car where the thick chain would do the rest.

Merrick crept down the hall to Katie's room. She sat on the edge of her bed gazing out the window. She did not seem upset. As he watched, she sighed and lay back, gazing up at the ceiling with a happy smile.

What the hell?

Merrick crept around the room, checking the bathroom, under the bed. Maybe I scared him off, he thought.

Backing out of Katie's room, he checked the nursery. Gregory lay on his side, his eyes open, sucking his thumb.

Why was he awake?

Letting his son see him, Merrick held a warning finger to his lips as Gregory smiled and sat up. "We have to be very careful," Merrick whispered, "or we'll wake Mommy and I'll have to go. Okay?"

Gregory nodded happily.

"Did you see something a little while ago?"

"I saw you, silly."

"Before?"

"Uh-huh. I was asleep and you came and then I was asleep again and you came back now. Kiss Ralphie." Gregory picked up one of his teddy bears and held it out.

Merrick felt a chill. Zane and I look a lot alike, he thought. He was up here, roaming around inside the house. But he didn't hurt Gregory or Katie. Why?

"Play with me!"

Merrick winced at the loudness of Gregory's voice. He heard the floor creak in Audrey's room. Waving at Gregory, he stepped across the hall, flattening himself against the wall as Audrey passed him and turned into Gregory's room. A moment later, Katie emerged from her bedroom. She walked down, passing so close he could smell a hint of toothpaste on her breath, and joined her mother. The two women fussed over Gregory, telling him to lie down and go to sleep.

"Uncle Merrick was here," Gregory announced.

"I know," Katie said. "He had dinner with us, didn't he?"

"He was here now."

Merrick saw Katie and Audrey exchange a glance. No doubt they were thinking: *Poor boy; he needs a father.*

And I need my son, Merrick thought bitterly. But I can't have him.

Katie bent over her son, covered him tenderly with his blanket, and nestled his teddy bears against him. She kissed his forehead. Over her shoulder, Audrey blew Gregory a kiss, too. Then the two women headed back to their bedrooms. Merrick followed Audrey, checking her bedroom, then the hall bath, then heading downstairs. He covered the lower floor and the basement, checking every room.

Zane was not in the house.

But he had been here—and had harmed no one.

Relieved and mystified, Merrick returned to the pantry and squeezed out through the bars. He lowered the sash, then worked on bending the bars back straight, cleaning up after Zane as well as he could. There was nothing he could do about the neat round hole in the glass, but at least it was something that could have been done by a normal man.

Merrick searched the backyard, then circled the house, satisfying himself that Zane was really gone. He stood in the yard, baffled. Zane *did* call in the murder, Merrick thought. And it worked—I was gone more than half an hour. If he'd wanted to kill them tonight, they'd be dead.

So what *did* he want?

To scare Katie—and me? It would explain why he left the bars spread apart, because he knew Katie would find them tomorrow morning and tell me. Maybe he's telling her—and me—that he can take her any time he wants.

All right, Zane, message received.

I can go to the crime scene after all, Merrick realized. If Zane was going to hurt Katie tonight, he'd have done it. I'll radio Des, tell him I was delayed. If I get over there fast, maybe I can still hang onto the case when Rourke hits the ceiling tomorrow.

Hurrying back to his car, Merrick hoped it was not already too late to salvage things. This third "vampire" murder would put immense pressure on Captain Rourke, and the quickest fix would be to take the task force away and give it to Lieutenant Cooke.

And the irony is, I wouldn't give a damn, except that Byner will have to tell Cooke about the blood.

They'll find out what you really are.

The ancient fear rose in Merrick, so familiar, yet never losing its raw power over him. His stomach churned as he drove back toward Maine Avenue again.

You could take care of Cooke.

He tried to push the thought aside, but it clung. It would be so easy, so impossible to detect. A few pushes of Influence, nothing lethal, just something to take Cooke out of action for awhile.

Why not? Merrick thought defiantly. You use Influence on someone each time you feed.

But feeding was different, he knew. About that he had absolutely no choice. And when a person was asleep in his bed, the gentle dilation of his jugulars to keep him that way was a mercy, done for his benefit. It left no trace on his heart or mind the next morning.

Merrick remembered what he had said to Sandeman in the vault. It's what we do that counts, not what we "are." If he was going to live with normals, work with them, accept their trust, he couldn't start using Influence on them when he thought they might threaten him—not even the ones he didn't like.

Especially the ones he didn't like.

If I do, Merrick thought, then I will always be a hemophage and I will never be a man.

TWENTY-ONE

WHEN MERRICK WALKED into Captain Rourke's office the next morning, Detective Lieutenant Emerson Cooke was already there. Cooke did not bother to stand, offer his hand, or even nod. He gave Merrick the smug smile gray-haired men reserve for young upstarts they have beaten. Merrick supposed he ought to be offended, and if he were merely older than Cooke, he might be; instead, he felt a brief, cold amusement. What would this pup do if he knew Lieutenant Merrick Chapman, aka Martin Trenhaille, Alex Green, Edward Fitzhugh, Trevor Smith, Aidan Killeen, and too many other names to remember, was born in 1068, not 1960?

The same thing he's going to do if he gets this case and learns about the blood.

All amusement fled as Merrick thought of life on the run— his face on warning posters wherever he went, the constant hiding, never again being able to feel, even for a moment, that he could belong.

"'Morning," Rourke said. "Sit down."

"Thanks, but I'm still on my first wind." Merrick glanced at Cooke, who sprawled in his chair as if he'd just finished a long day.

Cooke's narrow, pocked face reddened. "Brains are what count, kid, not wind. Someone out there has killed three citizens and you don't have a clue who it is."

Oh, but I do.

"Shut up, the both of you," Rourke growled. To his credit, he looked miserable. A muscle twitched in his jaw, and he seemed unable to look directly at either of them. This is it, Merrick thought grimly. He's going to give the case to Cooke.

"Will you sit down a minute, damn it?" Rourke pleaded.

Merrick pulled up the chair next to Cooke. This close, he could feel the man's pulse, sense the looping patterns of his blood flow. The network of veins and capillaries in Cooke's throat and brain stem glowed on Merrick's awareness. *No, I can't, I must not.*

"You're probably wondering why I called you both here," Rourke said.

Cooke chuckled appreciatively.

Merrick said, "Captain, this isn't right and you know it. No one catches a serial killer the first week unless he kills in front of somebody. There's nothing anyone else can do that I haven't done already. I've been living with this case from day one. No reflection on Cooke, but he'll be starting over, cold—"

Rourke raised a hand. "Yeah, yeah, all right. I can't argue, but it's been decided. What you don't understand is the kind of heat I get. This particular serial killer has a very short cycle. That means everything happens on fast forward. You better digest that, too, Cooke. A couple more killings without a perp and you can fade into the wings with Merrick and the rest of us because we'll be carrying coffee for the FBI. All they got to do is say he took a victim across a state line. I'm surprised that hasn't happened already. Last time I looked, Maryland and Virginia were a few blocks from here.

"I'll catch him," Cooke said confidently.

Not in a million years, Merrick thought. And if you do, you're dead.

"Bottom line," Rourke said. "Merrick, can you work with Lieutenant Cooke, or do I have to take you off the task force?"

A small push, enough to knock Cooke out. Just this one time.
"I can work with him," Merrick said.

"Yeah, but can you work *for* me?" Cooke asked. "Because that's the way it's going to be."

Rourke looked pained but said nothing.

"As long as I'm your exec," Merrick said, "I can work for you."

"I don't know," Cooke said thoughtfully. The bastard was enjoying this.

Merrick looked at Rourke. "I'm the other lieutenant on the case. Unless you plan to demote me."

"No," Rourke said. "Hell, no. He's your XO, Cooke. You try and get along with him, too."

"Sure," Cooke said. "As long as he does what I say without beefing."

"Okay," Rourke said, "effective immediately, I—"

Merrick gave the brain stem a mental squeeze and Cooke pitched forward out of his chair. Merrick caught him before he could hit the corner of Rourke's desk and eased him to the floor.

"What the hell?" Rourke said. On hands and knees, Merrick pressed his ear against Cooke's heart, listening desperately for a heartbeat. The captain stamped around his desk, sending vibrations through Merrick's palms . . . there! A steady, even beat. Merrick felt a small relief.

Rourke bent over them. "What'd he do, faint? The excitement must have been too much for the son of a bitch."

"Wh-What?" Cooke said. He pushed Merrick off his chest and sat up, looking groggy but unharmed. "What happened?"

Rourke eyed him. "You passed out. You been drinking?"

"Hell no," Cooke said. "Smell my breath if you want."

Rourke looked revolted. "I don't want."

Cooke clambered back into his chair and pulled at his collar, loosening his tie. "I'll be all right. Just give me a minute."

Rourke circled back behind his desk, sat down. "I don't know. Maybe we ought to have you checked out by a doc."

"I'm telling you, I feel fine." Cooke glared defensively at Merrick. "I missed breakfast, that's all. I just need to get my blood sugar up."

Rourke looked as if he couldn't believe anyone would miss breakfast, but he said, "All right then. As of now, I'm putting you—what the *hell?*"

This time Cooke stayed on the floor. Merrick bent over him again, sick with guilt, terrified that he'd gone too far. Cooke's pulse was rapid and erratic. Froth bubbled from his mouth.

"Call an ambulance," Merrick shouted. "Now!"

Good cheer filled Katie as she studied the blood values in Jenny's chart. Art sat on the other side of her desk, legs crossed, one foot bouncing with manic pleasure. Everyone on Three East was happy this morning. Katie was happy, too; so happy that for the first time in days she didn't feel bone weary—so happy it would be easy to just accept the great numbers and not try to figure out why they had happened.

She handed the printouts across to Art. "Feast your eyes."

Art scanned the blood values and shook his head. "It's great, Katie. Yesterday she looked like she couldn't last another day—and that was *before* you rushed her off for emergency surgery. All I can say is Jenny must have one hell of a doctor."

Katie eyed Art, unsure how to take the compliment. "I'd love to take credit, but you know good and well we didn't do this. I've never seen a leukocyte count drop so far so fast. This is a miracle, pure and simple."

"For your next one, can you turn my Jeep into a Jaguar?"

"Cut it out, Art. I want us to learn something from this."

He studied the printouts again, shaking his head. "Sudden remissions do happen. I could believe these numbers over a couple of weeks, but this is virtually overnight." He looked up at her. "Do they serve champagne down in the caf?"

Katie smiled. "Somehow, I doubt it."

"Want to go down for a cup of coffee, then? There's something else I'd like to talk with you about."

Though his voice was casual, his wide-open eyes told her he was anxious. She had the sudden premonition that he was going to ask her out.

Someone rapped on the door. Katie turned, grateful for the reprieve. Sharmane, her chief tech from Hematology, stood in the doorway, holding another printout with both hands, as though it were a sacred scroll. Katie waved her in.

Sharmane nodded at Art and said, "Doctor O'Keefe, I thought you should see this." Instead of handing the printout over, she gazed at it.

"What is it?" Katie said.

"That screening you ordered for GI bleeding."

Katie remembered scribbling the order in the chart a day ago, as Jenny's thrombocytopenia had continued to worsen. "Yes?"

"When we came to get the sample," Sharmane said, "the patient had been taken to surgery for a severe posterior nosebleed. So we didn't get the stool sample until nearly midnight last night."

"Okay, and?"

"And there's no occult blood."

"What?" Katie said. "Let me see that." Sharmane handed her the printout. The value for occult blood read 0.0. Mystified, Katie handed the printout to Art.

He looked at it and frowned. "Impossible. Jenny had to have swallowed a lot of that blood, at least some of which would have passed through the intestine."

"Any chance of a mix-up in samples?" Katie asked.

The tech's face screwed up in an offended frown. Katie reminded herself that, since Sharmane had become chief lab tech six months ago, there had not been one sample mix-up, the longest errorless streak since Katie had joined the staff at Georgetown.

"All right," Katie said. "Thanks."

Instead of leaving, Sharmane said, "Have you looked at this patient's blood lately?"

"Not for a few days."

"Could you come down a minute and take a look at it?"

"Is something wrong?"

"I'm not sure. I think it's better if you look at it without me saying anything else."

Curious and a bit uneasy, Katie motioned Art to come along. In the lab, Sharmane led them to one of the light microscopes. Katie bent over and twiddled with the controls until Jenny's red blood cells firmed into sharp focus. She saw nothing unusual about them. They were fresh cells, healthy and plump, about the right size, with flushed centers. And then she saw the membrane.

Jenny's blood looked like the killer's.

A slow chill percolated through Katie, crawling up her spine, spreading down her arms. The membrane was very faint, just as it had been in the killer's cells under Dr. Byner's microscope that first night. How could this be? She did not *want* it to be.

She waved Art to the scope. He bent over it, then straightened a little too quickly. When he looked at her, his face was impassive.

"Y'all see what I mean?" Sharmane asked.

"A slight thickening in some of the cell membranes," Katie said.

"Right."

Katie remembered what Merrick had said about keeping the murderer's blood a secret. But this was not a murderer's blood. This was the blood of an innocent little girl. Still . . .

"Don't worry about it," she told Sharmane. "It's a rare side effect of chemotherapy. It seems to coincide with rapid remissions of leukemia. It's not in any of the textbooks that I know of, but I've seen it before, once or twice. It's harmless." From the corner of her eye, she saw Art giving her a strange look; she ignored him.

"Well, that's all right then," Sharmane said. "If you're happy, I'm happy." She sounded relieved—this was not anything she'd studied in lab school.

"You did right pointing it out to me," Katie said. "I'd rather see something that's not important than miss something that is."

Sharmane looked pleased. One of the new techs came up with a question and she moved off to help him. Katie slipped the slide out of the microscope. "Get the rest of the sample," she told Art, "and meet me at the electron scope."

By the time he came in with the ten cc tube drawn from Jenny this morning, Katie had the slide staged in the electron scope. She bowed her head into the greenish flow from the screen. Under the immense magnification of the electron scope, the dark wall around the cells was impossible to miss. Katie's heart sank; she had hoped the electron scope would show up differences between Jenny's blood and the killer's. Instead, it confirmed the similarity. The membrane on Jenny's cells might be a bit thinner, but otherwise it looked identical. She stood back for Art.

He looked, straightened. "What does this mean?"

"I don't know. Art, in the past week we have found previously undiscovered structures on the RBCs of two *very* different people. Could it be some weird kind of infection? I've been running tests on the killer's blood while I've been treating Jenny. She's vulnerable to infection—"

"Come on," Art protested. "You've worn scrubs, gloves, and a mask every time you've been in her room, right? Not totally sterile, I'll grant you, but not an easy barrier for an infection to cross either. Even if you touched the killer's blood directly and didn't wash your hands . . ." He shook his head helplessly.

"There's another possibility," Katie said. "That the killer suffered the same type of leukemia as Jenny, then had a remission just like she's having."

"Okay," Art said slowly, "but how likely is that when Jenny's 'type' of leukemia, as you put it, is so rare that we've never seen a course of symptoms like hers before?''

"Not very, you're right. Jenny's leukemia *has* been strange from the start—in my experience, unique. I found only one other similar case in the literature, and there was no mention in that article of any RBC abnormalities—but no remission was reported either.'' Katie felt a rising excitement. "Look, it seems a very long shot that we have two nearly unique cases fall into our laps like this, but if it's true, it's the best possible news for Merrick.''

"Detective Chapman.'' Art's voice was oddly flat.

"Yes. If the killer had leukemia, he'll be in hospital records somewhere, and if his symptoms were as rare and resistant to treatment as Jenny's, his doctor would probably remember him. Even if it happened years ago, there's a decent chance his case can be tracked down.''

"A chance,'' Art agreed. "But we've got to remember that, until fairly recently, three out of four childhood leukemias were treatment-resistant—which is to say most of the kids died.''

"But how many of them had the strange hunger?''

"True. Detective Chapman could search on that. He'd probably get further talking to doctors than sifting through records. Termination files might or might not mention a bizarre symptom like 'a strange hunger.' What doesn't fit often gets put aside.''

"Good point. We'll tell Merrick when he contacts hospitals to ask for whichever doctor or nurse has been around the longest on Hematology.''

Art nodded. He bent back over the electron microscope screen.

Katie said, "Of course, we still don't know a damned thing about that membrane. How does it resist powerful reagents designed to break blood down? Even massive bombardment by electrons doesn't destroy it—''

"Uh . . . yes it does—in Jenny's case, anyway.'' Art stood back, motioned her to the screen. The membrane was gone. Jenny's blood cells were shriveling under the electron stream.

Katie felt a small relief. "It's *not* the same.''

"Apparently not—not quite. But it held up longer than any normal RBCs would have.''

"Maybe these cells have a milder, intermediate case of whatever causes the membrane. Is the blood in the test tube still fresh?''

Art held the ten cc test tube up and swirled it. "Appears to be.''

"Put a few drops on a slide for me, will you?''

"You want to see if they stay fresh just exposed to air?"

"Right."

After he'd prepared the slide, Katie carried it to the lab bench beside the electron microscope and slid it onto the stage of a conventional microscope. "Let's see how it does sitting under just regular light." She turned the scope on and peered down through it for more than a minute.

"Watched blood never dries," Art quipped.

She smiled but continued to stare at the blood cells, charged with anxiety, hoping fervently that Jenny's blood would break down under normal light, too. It wasn't a very scientific attitude: Blood was only blood; it did not determine personality or behavior, but she really did not want the blood of a wonderful, innocent child to be like the blood of a killer who tore throats with his teeth.

"Let's go to the caf, "Art suggested, "get that cup of coffee and come back. If the blood dries while we're gone, we can make another smear and you can stare continuously at it."

"I don't feel like a coffee."

Art cleared his throat. "Uh, Katie, I *do* need to talk to you. And when I do, I'd like to be looking at your face, not the back of your head. Come on, ten minutes."

Katie remembered her earlier feeling that Art was going to ask her out. I'm not ready for this, she thought.

But, if he is determined to do it sooner or later, maybe sooner is a better time to deal with it than later. "All right," she said. "Let's go."

Zane squeezed through the crowded basement hallway of Georgetown hospital toward Hematology. The jostling horde around him filled him with distaste. He did not like people touching him. A change of shifts must be in progress, great for losing oneself in a crowd but terrible for getting Katie alone.

If he could ever find her in the first place.

She was not in her office, not on Jenny's floor, so she must be down in her lab. Risky, coming here to kill her, but he wasn't having much luck at her house. Zane's scalp prickled as he remembered running back to Katie's last night only to find Merrick's unmarked cruiser sitting out front. How had the old bastard gotten back so fast?

Zane swallowed a growl of frustration. Father seemed psychic, tracking him to the hotel, guarding Katie at all the right moments. It was almost scary. . . .

With an effort, Zane got hold of himself. It *was* scary, but fear was the last thing he needed. Fear had driven him away last night when he should have gone into Katie's house and taken her and Merrick both. Instead, he had run without thinking. When he'd decided to go after Father, he'd known the fear would be there, but not this bad. Even when he wasn't aware of it, there it was, hiding in his nerves and muscles, stronger than a reflex. Five hundred years, he'd lived with it, and it had burrowed in deep.

But he must conquer it. And the first step was to avoid giving Father too much credit. The old bastard was *not* psychic, he was simply smart. He must have guessed who had made the anonymous call about the murder victim.

So I try again today, Zane thought.

Ahead, he spotted the door marked HEMATOLOGY. Almost at the same moment, it opened and Katie stepped out, followed by a handsome young man in a medical coat. Keeping people between them, Zane waited until Katie and the other doctor passed him, then fell in at a distance behind them. Maybe she's headed for her office upstairs, he thought, encouraged. Then, if the man goes somewhere else, she'll be alone. I can kill her there and have plenty of time to get out of the hospital before she's discovered.

Zane patted the handle of the bowie knife hidden under his sport coat. He could feel his breath coming faster, driven by a sense of urgency. There could be no saving Katie for later, keeping her alive to torment Father at the end—his dangerous lapse into sentiment last night proved that. He must kill her quickly, get her out of Merrick's way before she could poison his judgment as she had Merrick's. When he was ready to bury Father, her son could fill in for her at the graveside.

She did not save my daughter, I did.

Through the crowd, he noticed how close the young doctor, if that's what he was, kept to Katie—closer than necessary. And she was not moving away. Interesting.

Instead of taking the elevator, they ducked into the stairwell. Zane followed them up, staying one landing behind, treading lightly and letting their footsteps cover his. Katie and the man exited at the first floor. Zane followed them down a wide hall and into the cafeteria. Keeping well back as they poured coffees and paid, he found a table near theirs and sat with his back to them. A bank of windows looked out on a central courtyard; Zane watched in the reflection as the young man pulled out a chair for Katie. When was the last time I saw that? he wondered.

Are they involved romantically?

Zane smiled. Wouldn't it be nice if Katie were running around with this guy while she pretended to love Merrick? I could tell that to him, before I bury him. Give him a movie to run in his head, help him while away all that time before he dies.

Zane sucked a deep breath, scalded by his own hatred. His eyes burned with a strange, hot anguish as he imagined being Father, lying trapped under the earth, unable to move, to get blood. *The only way we can die. He wants to do it to me, but I will do it to him. And then the fear will go away at last.*

TWENTY-TWO

As Art put sugar in his coffee, Katie tried to prepare herself. Though she couldn't be sure Art was about to ask her out, just the idea was making her nervous—she actually had butterflies in her stomach. She couldn't become romantically involved with her own resident. If that's what this was about, she'd have to choose her words very carefully, hurt him as little as possible.

Art looked up at her. "Katie, I'm falling in love with you."

She felt her heartbeat pick up. "Art—"

"Please hear me out. I know this is the wrong place to say it, sitting at a sticky Formica table, coffee and goulash in the air instead of wine and roses, clacking trays and beeping pagers instead of Debussy in the background. But what can I do? Clinical supervisors aren't supposed to date their residents. I can't start out waving two tickets to the Kennedy Center and work my way up. I can't even take your hand now, no matter how much I want to. Our roles are a wall between us. Here in the caf, that wall is thinnest. I hope you can hear me through it now.'' A slight huskiness betrayed the calm of his voice. Under that handsome and composed exterior a fire was burning; she could feel its dangerous heat almost as if Art *had* reached across and caressed her hand. *Careful!*

Katie chose her words carefully. ''Art, I'm flattered and honored. It's not some rule against dating I care about, it's the fact that it really is a very bad idea for people in our position. There are just too many pitfalls, too many other people who can get hurt. I'm not sorry you told me, and I won't forget it, but I think for a lot of reasons we shouldn't go on with this conversation.''

''That depends on how *you* feel about *me.*''

How *do* I feel? Katie wondered. Or how would I if I let myself? ''Art, I can't even let that enter my mind.''

He gave her a pained smile. ''At least you're not saying you *don't* love me—or that you couldn't.''

She struggled for the right words. ''You know how much I like and respect you, but once I let romance get a toe in the door, I'm compromised. You're a great resident. I haven't yet had to say a harsh word to you. Tomorrow I might, and you need to believe I will.''

''I understand the problems,'' Art said, ''believe me. I also know we could avoid them. Here at the hospital, I wouldn't touch you, look funny at you, no secret jokes or signals, nothing I wouldn't have said or done before. And we'd make sure no one ever saw us together outside the hospital.''

Katie felt her pulse rising. He makes it sound possible, she thought. . . .

No, we shouldn't even be discussing this. She took a sip of coffee and glanced around. No one seemed to be paying the slightest attention to them, and yet she had the strange feeling they were being watched, listened to. The four people at the nearest table were talking so loudly they couldn't have overheard anyone else. Beyond them, a big man sat, gazing out the windows. He had his back to them and his stillness indicated he was lost in some sort of reverie.

Katie told herself she was just being paranoid. Focusing on Art again, she saw the hope and fear in his eyes and her heart went out to him. How hard it must be, putting his feelings on the line when he knew she had to reject them. It made her see him not as a student or a trainee but as an equal. Surprised, she realized she had never once let herself think of him that way.

And she must not now.

"If you weren't my clinical supervisor," Art asked, "could you fall in love with me?"

"I can't just step out of character that way. I *am* your supervisor."

Art chewed at his lip. "Don't get me wrong. The last thing I want is to throw away that relationship. You have done so much for me. You are helping me become the kind of doctor I want to be. You're a superb teacher—not just words but example. I watch you all the time. I admire your strength. Working with leukemic kids isn't for the weak. And your compassion. Not just the sick kids—you'd have to have a heart of stone *not* to have compassion for them—but the rest of us, too, the people who work with you. The way you made me look good in front of my father the other day . . ." Art held his hands up, dropped them to the table again, groping for words. "You can't imagine what that meant to me. I've always admired Dad and wanted more than anything for him to be proud of me. If he is, he gives very little sign of it, so I've learned not to let my feelings show either. But you gave me a chance to see how Dad really feels about me. I was crazy about you before that, but that was when I knew I had to tell you.

"My God, Katie, how could I help but fall in love with you? If all you've ever meant was to be kind, then thanks. I won't bring this up again. But if you feel anything more for me, don't say no, because we can find a way."

Looking into his eyes, Katie felt the current flowing through her again, the dangerous heat. Art was a handsome and desirable man. She wondered for just a second what it might be like to kiss him, to call him into her office, lock the door, fall into his arms. . . .

She felt a rush of heat to her face. What was she thinking? That wasn't even love, that was lust.

But maybe it could be love, too.

I've been telling myself over and over that I must find someone else, forget Merrick. . . .

But with Art I would just be jumping from one impossible situation to another. It's so frustrating. Are the only men I can want men I can't have?

Art leaned forward. "Katie, can I ask . . . is there someone else? I overheard some nurses talking about you and Lieutenant Chapman. I gathered that was a couple of years ago and there's been nobody since."

"This is another thing we shouldn't be discussing."

"Okay, sorry." He folded his hands on the table. "Katie, I couldn't feel the way I do about you and not tell you. Whether something comes of it or not, I will now go back to being your resident again. If that relationship is the only one we can have, I prize it and am still committed to it. You will see that I can love you and no one here will guess it. The next move, if any, is up to you."

Katie nodded, struggling for words. No matter how she felt or came to feel about Art, there could be no romance, in or outside the hospital, while she was his supervisor. "Art, I appreciate everything you've said, but—"

"No 'buts'—*please*. If the time comes when you want to do something, it's your move. Can't we leave it at that?" His voice was low, almost desperate.

"Yes, we can."

Art let out a deep breath. Hooking an arm over the back of his chair, he made a show of gazing around the dining area. "So," he said brightly. "You mentioned you've been doing tests on the killer's blood. Want to bring me up to date?"

Katie heard a chair scrape close by, a sudden, harsh sound. The table with the noisy foursome had departed, she saw, and the man beyond was still gazing out the cafeteria windows. Beyond him, a busboy was clearing off trash. The sound must have carried from there. No one seemed close enough to overhear, but her paranoia welled up again, a light buzz of unease. She bent toward Art and spoke in a low voice. "I haven't been able to get past the membrane," she said. "It's still resisting all reagents. I've never seen anything like it. How about your research?"

Art shook his head. "If anyone has ever seen blood like this before, either I haven't found it yet or they didn't write it down. I'll keep plugging."

"Good." She checked her watch. "Ready to go back?"

"Ah . . . if you need me, sure. I've got a ton of charting to catch up with, but I could get that done later tonight. . . ."

Katie was puzzled for a second; every resident always had a ton of charting to catch up with. Then she realized that, despite his casual front, he must be stinging inside. He could use a little time off somewhere by himself right now. And the last thing he would want was any hint of sympathy.

"Okay," she said breezily. "See you later."

When she got back to Hematology, she let herself in through her office door and picked up a fresh logbook. It would be a good idea to start taking notes on Jenny's blood right from the start.

As she started into the lab to see if Jenny's blood had dried on the slide, the phone on her desk rang. She snatched it up. "O'Keefe."

"Katie?"

Her mother's voice was so tense Katie almost didn't recognize it. Her hand tightened on the phone. Mom rarely called her at the hospital—and never for idle chitchat. Was Gregory sick? "What is it, what's wrong?"

"I'm not sure. I heard a noise in the pantry and found a bird flying around in there. Someone cut a piece of glass out of the window, leaving this perfectly round hole—"

Katie felt suddenly cold. "Is Gregory—"

"He's fine. The bars look straight. I don't see how anyone could have gotten in. It's very strange. . . ."

"I'm coming home. I'll be right there." Katie hung up and started for the hall, then stopped, trying to decide if she should call Merrick—

And then the room went gray and faded away. . . .

She heard a strange rushing noise in her ears, *wuh-wuh-wuh*. Her throat was very dry. As she tried to swallow, she realized her neck was arched, that her head was hanging over the back of a chair. The rhythmic rushing noise faded, becoming a steady pulse of blood against her eardrums. Opening her eyes, she gazed up at a pattern of acoustic tile.

"Sit up," a deep voice said.

She brought her head forward with an effort and pulled in her dangling arms. She realized she was sprawled in her desk chair. I must have passed out, she thought. I got the call from Mom and I was leaving and? . . .

Feeling a dull alarm, she started to get up; a hand on her shoulder pushed her down again. She turned in her chair, but she could see no one behind her.

"Doctor, I want the blood cells."

She could hear where the voice was coming from—a spot behind her, high up on her bookshelf. Her heart leapt and began to pound. It's *him!* she realized, the same man I heard on the phone—the one who told me someone was watching my house.

"The blood cells, doctor."

"I . . . I don't understand. I can't see you. Where are you?"

"You *do* understand. I heard you in the cafeteria just now, talking about the blood cells with your resident. Don't say you don't understand again or I'll hurt you.''

''Why do you want the cells?'' She could not believe she was being so bold.

''The less you know, the better, believe me. Now, where is the blood? I want you to show me.''

Katie got up and took a step. A hand closed on her arm—by the feel of it, a large hand. Her head swam. This couldn't be happening.

''Let's go, Katie.'' The voice was warmer, now, encouraging. She went into the research lab where she'd been doing all the work on the killer's blood cells. On *his* blood cells, she thought. A sudden image seared her brain—the woman draped over the pulpit, the tattered throat. Katie's knees buckled. A hand grabbed her other arm, holding her upright.

''I'm scared,'' she said.

''I know, but you can do it.''

She led him to the safe where she kept the slide and the tube of blood Dr. Byner had given her after the first murder. Her fingers felt stiff as she dialed the combination. The unseen hands kept their grip on her arms, firm but not painful. She jerked on the door. It would not open.

''Try again.''

She did, and the safe opened. As she took out the slide and test tube, her fingers trembled so badly she almost dropped them. The hands released her. The slide and test tube vanished, plucked from her grasp.

''Is this all of it?'' the voice asked.

''Yes.''

''You wouldn't lie to me, would you, Katie?''

She felt a blade press against her throat, pulling her back against him. She froze, too terrified to move or cry out. ''No. God, no,'' she finally managed.

''Where did you get this blood?''

''It was on a murder victim at the National Cathedral.''

''Ah.'' The knife loosened for a second, then tightened on her throat again. ''Who else knows about the blood?''

''I don't know.''

''Come on. Who called you in on the case?''

''The medical examiner. He found the blood.''

''Is he the only one who knows?''

''I have no idea. How could I?'' It was the truth—she

couldn't be sure Byner hadn't told someone else. And she wasn't going to mention Merrick or Art to this creature.

"Have you made your report to him yet?"

"No. I haven't been able to learn much. That membrane—can you tell me—"

"No," the voice said. "Now we will go back in there to your office and call this medical examiner. You will tell him the blood sample deteriorated just like normal blood—that there is nothing unusual about it after all."

"But it stayed fresh for days. It has a strange extra membrane that shields the cells—they *know* that."

"They?"

"The pathologist, whoever."

The creature was silent a moment, the pressure of the blade steady now. "You just convince him the blood is normal now. Tell him there's no point doing any more analysis. You don't have any more time to put in on the case. Understand?"

Katie tried to think. "He'll ask me for the blood back."

"Fine. Put the same amount of normal blood on a slide and in a test tube. Let it dry out. If he asks, give him that."

"Who are you? *What* are you?"

"Put that out of your mind. There's really no point thinking about it. If you tell the police an invisible man took the blood, they will be sure you have gone insane. They'll have nothing more to do with you. But I will. I'll kill you and your son and drink your blood."

Gregory—he knows about Gregory! Katie shuddered against the knife.

"If you try to cross me in any way, now or later, I will kill you. I can get to you any time I like. I go wherever I want, do whatever I want. No one can stop me. You must understand that. Do you?"

She needed to swallow but was afraid the blade would cut into her throat if she did. "Yes."

"Good. Let's go. Back to your office."

As the knife left her throat, he grabbed her hair and held it tightly, making her head jerk with each step. Back in her office, he eased her down into her chair. She fumbled through her Rolodex, her mind blank with fear. Byner, Byner—here it was.

At that instant, someone knocked on the door. "Katie?" Art's voice called.

"Come on in." She gasped as the hand still entwined in her hair jerked her head back. The blade pressed her throat again.

"That was very stupid."

"It's my resident," she whispered. "He has a key. He'd be in in a second anyway."

"Then he'll die, too."

"That isn't necessary. Please, I'll do what you want. I'll do it today. I know you can get to me any time. I'll do it, I swear."

The key turned in the lock.

"Remember your son," the voice grated. The blade left her throat and the hand released her hair.

The door opened. "Hi," Art said. "I decided the charting could wait."

"Good." Her voice came out in a croak. *Act natural, you must act natural.* As she stood, her knees wobbled and she leaned forward to prop her hands on the desk.

"Katie, what's wrong?"

"Bit dizzy."

Art started toward her. *No! Keep him near the door!* She made herself hurry around the desk to him. He caught her arm and she kept going, pulling him along into the hall. A couple of techs were horsing around outside Hematology, squirting each other with saline squeeze bottles. They stopped guiltily as soon as they saw her. When she smiled at them, they glanced at each other in surprise. How could they know how happy she was to see them right now?

"Are you sure you're all right?" Art asked.

"I think so," she said. "But walk me up to the nurses station, will you?"

"Sure."

The elevator doors opened on an empty cage; Katie almost balked at getting on, but the stairwell would be just as empty and her legs still felt too shaky to walk up. Backing into a rear corner, she scanned the elevator around Art. Had the creature gotten on with them? Her spine crawled as the cage rose, but nothing happened. On Three East, only one nurse sat behind the station, and the waiting area across from it was empty of visitors. Katie's heart sank—lots of people around, that's what she wanted.

"Feeling better?" Art asked.

"A little," Katie lied, "but maybe I'd better take the rest of the day off."

"Good idea."

"If anything comes up, give me a ring at home."

He gave her a searching look and she managed a smile for him. A nurse coming up the hall saw her and stopped to ask a question. Katie didn't understand a word. Art, bless him, saw she wasn't tracking and took over for her, walking off with the nurse, casting a worried look back over his shoulder. Katie waved, trying to project reassurance. She stared beyond him down the corridor. A hysterical urge to laugh bubbled up her throat. What was the use of looking for the thing? If it didn't want her to see it, she wouldn't.

Turning back to the nurses station, she picked up the phone. The nape of her neck prickled; she turned, searching the empty waiting area. For a second, the air seemed to shimmer right in front of her. She fought down a gasp; the creature was there, she was sure of it. *Don't react. Act like you aren't aware of it, and maybe it will leave you alone.*

With trembling fingers, she dialed the phone.

Merrick sat at his desk, thinking about what he had done to Cooke. He did not feel guilty. A few hundred years ago, he would have. But then he'd come to understand what guilt was. A way of letting yourself off the hook.

I did it, but I didn't enjoy it.

I violated everything I believe in. I used my power against a man with no defense against it, the way a bully puts his hand in the face of a younger, weaker kid and pushes him to the ground, but if I'm sorry, that will balance things out.

No.

Guilt was for people who intended to go on sinning, a self-administered punishment, ten Hail Marys, and then you were forgiven and could feel better—until the next time. No guilt, no, but what he had done made him feel heavy, miserable, disheartened. Because there were two Merricks—the hemophage and the man, and today he had been the one he hated, and if he was going to be that, there was no reason to go on living.

Pushing up from his chair, Merrick went to his window. The street below the district headquarters was quiet now, the ambulance long gone. Cooke had been conscious by the time the paramedics had arrived. They'd put him in the back of the wagon, groggily protesting as he saw his moment of triumph slipping away. Rourke had assured him it was just for a day or two, let the hospital run some tests and when you're back on your feet, we'll talk about it.

Closing his eyes, Merrick concentrated on the way Cooke's face had looked as they put him on the stretcher—scared, hurt, unable to understand what had happened to him, but still wanting to get back up, to outdo the young stud Merrick, grab one more chance to prove himself before the retirement board told him his time was up. *I will remember his face*, Merrick thought. *I will not do it to anyone again.*

His phone rang. It seemed to come from far away, from another life that had lost its importance. But it persisted, so he went back to his desk. "Third District Homicide, Lieutenant Merrick."

"It's Katie. I'm at the hospital." She was speaking very softly, as if afraid of being overheard. "I need you, Merrick. Can you pick me up?"

Recognizing the fear in her voice, he felt his heart miss a beat, then stutter to life. "Of course."

"Do . . . do you expect to be on duty tonight?" Her voice quavered.

Has Zane done something to her? Merrick's grip on the phone tightened. "Katie, what is it, what's wrong?"

"I can't talk now," she said, "but I need you to stay with me tonight—all night. Can you do that?"

"Yes."

"Good." Her voice held only a small relief. "I'll wait for you at the nurses station on Three East. Please hurry."

"The nurses station? . . ." *Why didn't she just meet him in the parking lot?*

"Merrick? . . ."

"I'm on my way."

Ten blocks from the hospital, Zane stopped his car and threw the blood and the slide down a sewer. He got back into the car and sat, his mind spinning. He thought of the dream, all those people blindly grabbing him in the net, carrying him to the pit—

Damn Katie!

An intense frustration gripped him. He needed to kill her, get her out of the way, but finding out she had his blood had saved her life—for a few hours. If he had just taken the cells, then killed her, it would have caused the opposite of what he must achieve. He could imagine the screaming headlines now— BLOOD EXPERT SLAIN, STRANGE CELLS STOLEN. It would be even worse if he tried to find and kill everyone who might know about the blood. Who knows how many people Katie or the pathologist told and swore to secrecy? No, the only solution now was to confuse the information they'd gained, diminish its importance as much as possible. That process had to start with a benign report from the chief expert.

Despite himself, Zane had to admire Katie's nerve. She had been clever—and very brave—to call his bluff like that. She'd outmaneuvered him for the moment, but it didn't really matter, as long as she made the call to Dr. Byner.

And I will see that she does.

Zane shook his head, still half in shock about the blood. Katie'd had the cells since the first killing. So why hadn't it hit the papers? Blood that couldn't be destroyed is found on a murder victim—could a whole police department keep a secret like that?

No. Merrick's hand was obvious in this. He must have gotten the pathologist to restrict the information. Clearly, Merrick hadn't found the blood himself, or no one would have known, but he must have been there when the police pathologist noticed it, and limited the damage. Good for him, Zane thought, then gave a bitter laugh. Keeping normals from discovering them was probably the only thing he and Father agreed on.

When Katie phoned him, Zane thought, Father promised to stay with her tonight. *That will be perfect. I'll slip up on the house and blind him with his memories before he even knows I'm there. I'll tie him with a chain and keep the others asleep. In the morning, I'll make Katie call in her report to the pathologist. I'll hold a knife to her son's throat if I have to. Then I'll use her car to drive her and Father into the country. I'll make Father watch while I kill her, and then I'll bury him.*

Zane closed his eyes, willing confidence into himself. *It will work,* he thought, *as long as I make sure Katie's death doesn't look suspicious. That wouldn't do at all, not so soon after she's given the pathologist her report. After I've buried Father, I'll put Katie's body in her car and drive into a tree. No one will know she didn't die of an accident.*

Except Father.

TWENTY-THREE

MERRICK SAT WITH Katie on her living room couch, holding her in his arms. He felt a helpless fury at Zane for terrorizing her—and a cold dread every time he thought about how much worse it might have been. Zane had held a *knife* to her throat. If he had slipped, if he'd drawn blood . . .

Katie glanced at her mother, who sat rigidly on the edge of a wing-backed chair, and then at Merrick. The fear in her eyes tore at his heart. "You do believe me, don't you?" she asked. "I mean, that the man—or whatever it is—was invisible?"

Even though she had told him everything in the car on the way to her house, hearing the question staggered Merrick all over again. I should try to convince her she imagined it, he thought. But if by some remote chance I succeed, what then? She'd believe she is going insane.

"I believe you," he said, "but that's because I believe *in* you. I know that no matter how impossible something sounds, if you said it happened, it happened."

She took his hand and squeezed very hard.

"But Katie, you must not, under any circumstances, tell this to anyone else."

"He's right." Audrey found her voice at last. "We've got to keep absolutely quiet about it."

"I know, I *know.*" Katie's voice shook. "He warned me if I told the police, he'd kill Gregory." She gave Merrick another frightened look. "My God, you *are* the police, but I had to tell you."

Audrey said, "Katie, I'm still not clear why this . . . creature threatened you. What did it want?"

Instead of answering, Katie looked questioningly at Merrick, as if asking permission. He realized she hadn't even told her own mother about the blood. The strict way she'd kept her promise gratified him, but now that Audrey knew Zane—this *"creature"*—could hide itself from someone's eyes, it hardly mattered if she also learned it had strange blood. Merrick nodded and Katie turned back to her mother, quickly filling her in.

"I see," Audrey said. "I'd been wondering exactly why the police called you in. So this creature wanted its blood back."

"Yes. Remember how it bumped me in the church after the second murder? It must have realized I was taking a sample of *its* blood rather than the victim's, so it nudged me to distract me, then stole the slide. Later, it must have started worrying that it might have bled during the first killing, too, so it shadowed me at the hospital and overheard me in the caf today, talking to Art about the blood."

Merrick was surprised to find himself wishing they would stop calling Zane "it." But how else should they refer to someone so monstrous?

"When are you going to call the medical examiner?" Audrey asked Katie.

"I really don't want to do that," Katie said.

"You have no choice," Audrey said. "Just tell him the blood is completely normal now. Tell him you'll send him a full report and it's been nice working with him."

"And let this creature that's killed three people just walk away and go on with its monstrous life?"

"What can you do to stop it? You've got to think about Gregory."

"Hold on, Audrey," Merrick said. "He's my son, too. The

minute Katie talks to Doctor Byner, the killer will have no further use for her.''

''And then he'll kill me and Gregory anyway.'' Katie dropped back onto the couch. Her hands trembled as she pressed them against her cheeks.

Merrick squeezed her shoulder. ''I'm sorry to frighten you, but we have to be sure we do the right thing here.'' He felt a fresh wave of fury at Zane. This was insane, impossible. He would do anything to have Byner believe the blood was normal. Anything but put Katie's life in danger.

Audrey shook her head. ''I don't know. Merrick, if this creature does keep a close watch on her, won't it be enraged if she defies it? It can hide itself at will. It could be in this room right now, watching us.''

Katie shuddered.

Quickly, Merrick said, ''I'll get a police guard posted here on the house. I can tell my captain the killer tried to break in and has made calls threatening your life. We'll show them the hole in the window.''

''But you'll still stay tonight, too, won't you?'' Katie's voice was sharp with fear.

''Yes. Unless there's another murder, and then I'll get back as quickly as I can. Either way, I'll make sure you have a police guard outside at all times. I'll have you wired and get my own receiver, Katie, so I can monitor you even when you're at the hospital. Audrey, we'll put a wire on you, too, for when Katie isn't home. The guys in the patrol car will know at once if anything starts to go wrong, and they can run in.''

''What are you going to tell them?'' Katie asked. ''To watch out for invisible men?''

Merrick did not smile. ''Don't even joke about that, Katie. I know cops. Any hint of the paranormal and they'll stop taking you seriously.''

''Oh, dear,'' Audrey said.

Katie turned to her. ''What's the matter?''

''Speaking of the paranormal, Neddie Merrill is due this afternoon. She's taking a cab from the airport and will be here in an hour or so.''

''That's all right,'' Katie said. ''As long as she doesn't take out a crystal ball in front of the cops.''

''Oh, no—Neddie's not like that at all.''

''Who is Neddie Merrill?''

Katie looked faintly embarrassed. ''She's a . . . clairvoyant woman Mom used to know who's been working with the New Orleans police, helping them track down killers.'' She gave an exasperated smile, but Merrick did not return it. A few very rare normals seemed able to instantly sense hemophages even when they couldn't see them. He'd never run into one himself, but he'd heard Sandeman talk about it. Normally he wouldn't want to be around such a person, but Katie and Audrey already knew something "unnatural" was out there. Any extra warning they could get that Zane was around would be all to the good. And anything this woman cared to say about it to the press would matter only to people who already believed in psychics.

Audrey gave Merrick a worried look. "Neddie Merrill aside—and whether we talk about the paranormal or not—if the police are guarding this house, they may discover for themselves what this thing is like.''

"They may. But let's hope having a patrol car out there will deter the killer and keep everything nice and quiet.'' Merrick put a reassurance into his voice that he did not feel.

The two women were silent a moment and then Katie said, "Merrick, what in God's name *is* this thing? It kills and takes the blood. Why? And don't tell me it's a damned vampire.''

Audrey paled. Before she could say anything, the phone rang. She held the receiver to her ear cautiously, as though it might explode. "O'Keefe's residence.''

Picking up the whisper of sound from the receiver, Merrick recognized the voice of Art Stratton, Katie's resident. "Is Katie okay?'' Stratton asked Audrey. "I was with her a little while ago at the hospital and she seemed, well, pretty shaky.''

"She's right here, Doctor Stratton,'' Audrey said. "Shall I put her on?''

"If you would, please.''

"Hold on.'' Audrey handed the phone to Katie. Stratton asked Katie how she was doing. Merrick could not hear the tone of his voice well enough to be sure, but the words revealed a concern beyond that of a coworker trying to be polite. Did Stratton have a romantic interest in Katie? The thought panged Merrick. He knew his jealousy was unworthy. If he could not have Katie, why should she be denied the love, the normal life, she needed?

But first I have to make sure she lives through this.

"Katie,'' Stratton said, "Ann Hrluska is here and she'd like a few words with you.''

"Hi, Mrs. Hrluska.'' Katie seemed suddenly to perk up.

Some color returned to her face, along with a genuine smile. Strange, Merrick thought, with Jenny dying.

"I just wanted to tell you how overjoyed we are," said the faint voice on the other end of the line.

"Yes," Katie said, "isn't it wonderful?"

Merrick wondered what the hell they could be talking about.

"When can we take her home?" Mrs. Hrluska asked.

"I need to run a few more tests," Katie said. "But if she continues to improve at her present rate, it won't be long at all, I promise you."

Merrick kept his face calm, but his mind reeled with shock and foreboding. Jenny doing better? It would be wonderful, except that there was only one way it could have happened.

"It's just that she looks so good now," Mrs. Hrluska said. "Her father and I are very anxious to have her back with us."

"I understand. And I'll do my best to hurry things along."

"Thank you, doctor. I can't tell you how much this means to us. We had almost lost hope, and then you brought her around. You're terrific!"

"Thank you," Katie said, "but I don't think it was me. Actually, the only word I can think of to describe it is *miracle*."

No, Merrick thought. Not a miracle. Someone gave Jenny blood. Only a hemophage would know to do that. And Zane is the only other phage around. If Zane has been tracking Katie, he could have seen Jenny, but why feed her? Zane is no Samaritan, even for other hemophages. Does he have some connection to Jenny?

Suddenly Merrick remembered the sketchbook he saw in Zane's hotel room—the face he had recognized but couldn't identify. It had been Jenny's mother—Ann Hrluska. She'd come in once or twice when he was visiting Jenny. A pretty woman, and the sketch proved Zane had, at some point or the other, become quite familiar with her face.

But if the sketchbook was of people he had killed or meant to kill, why wasn't Ann Hrluska dead now?

"Testing, one two three," Katie said.

Merrick gave Katie an encouraging smile, glad to hear the strength in her voice. She was starting to fight now, to claw her way back emotionally from what had been a horrifying experience.

"That's it, doctor," said the uniformed cop as he exchanged

signals out the front window with his partner in the patrol car. "He's reading you fine, but please don't hold the watch up to your mouth. It'll pick you up just as well at your side, and you don't want an intruder to guess you're wired."

Katie nodded sheepishly.

Why would Zane give Jenny blood?

"Now you, Mrs. O'Keefe."

" 'Suddenly . . . there came a tapping,' " Audrey intoned, " 'as of someone gently rapping, rapping at my chamber door.' " She sounded calm and professorial, but she was still shaken, Merrick could tell.

The patrolman checked with his partner outside again. "Okay, he heard you five by five. That's cop poetry for real good."

Audrey smiled.

And why would he have drawn Jenny's mother in his sketchbook?

The technician said, "There's no need to take your watches off, even in the shower. They're waterproof to two hundred feet. You turn the transmitter off by pulling the stem out, but I recommend you both leave them on as much as possible. If someone jumps you, it might be too late to turn your wire back on."

"We understand," Katie said. "Thank you."

Merrick said, "Did you put a receiver in my car, too?"

"Yes, sir," the technician said. "You'll be able to pick her up within a hundred yards."

"Good. Thanks."

When Audrey had closed the door on the cop and technician, Merrick turned to Katie. "I think I should check things out in your office and lab, where the killer grabbed you." *And take a look at Jenny.* "Would you feel all right about me leaving?"

"You'll be back before dark?"

"Definitely."

"Go ahead. Mom and I will be fine—the Mounties are right outside." Katie covered her mouth, and he knew the real significance of the wire had dawned on her: The two men in the patrol car were going to hear everything she said.

"Do be careful," Merrick murmured, cupping a hand over his ear.

She nodded, sobered.

He wanted to kiss her, so he did. Audrey pretended not to see, but she looked pleased.

Driving to the hospital, Merrick was free at last to focus on

Jenny. She'd gotten blood from Zane, no question—no one else would have known to do it. Clearly, there was some attraction there, and to Jenny's mother, too, but what could it be?

Whatever it was, it might create a chance to catch Zane. Logic said he would be making contact with Jenny again, at least several times. It would take more than one feeding to bring Jenny back to health and make her into a powerful phage; there would be no point to giving her one feeding and walking away. I can try to catch him with her, Merrick thought. His hands gripped the wheel with sudden, strangling force. *You threatened Katie and my son. I'm going to take you out.*

And what about Jenny?

Merrick began to see the full enormity of what Zane had done. Jenny was going home soon. If he did bury Zane, she'd have no one to feed her and would have to feed herself. Did she know that drinking blood was what had saved her? If so, she'd see no choice for herself but to begin killing.

And then I will have to hunt her, put her in the vault.

Merrick groaned, sickened. Everything in him rebelled at the thought of catching the young girl he had come to love, carrying her, screaming, into the dark woods. If he had to seal her behind one of the steel doors, it would break his heart.

I'll help her, he thought desperately; teach her that she doesn't have to kill.

Like you taught Zane?

A terrible, trapped feeling gripped him. *Damn you, Zane.*

Parking in the hospital lot, Merrick hurried up the stairs toward Three East. As he walked down the Hematology wing toward Jenny's room, he tried to clear his mind of fear about Jenny's future. He would face that when the time came. At Jenny's door, Merrick froze as he saw Zane standing behind Jenny's parents. Zane's eyes widened in shock and surprise.

He stepped up close behind James Hrluska.

Merrick nodded to show he understood the threat.

Zane pointed at Merrick and jabbed a finger toward the door. *Get out.*

Merrick's heart sank. His intuition had been right. Zane wanted much more than just to give Jenny first blood. He wanted Jenny. But why?

Suddenly, the vehemence of Zane's gesture struck Merrick, the fierce, protective look in his eyes.

Could Jenny be *his?*

Stunned, Merrick looked from Jenny's face to Zane's. See

her eyes, the line of her jaw. She *could* be his daughter! *He was here twelve years ago, and Jenny just turned twelve.* Staggered, Merrick stared at Zane. Was that why Ann Hrluska, so beautifully drawn in his sketchbook, was still alive?

No! Zane kills women, he doesn't make love to them.

Merrick felt thunderstruck, unable to move. He had never given much thought to his son's sexual habits. But he did know that none of Zane's victims he had seen had been molested. Zane was a vicious predator, but he was not a sexual psychopath.

Which meant he must find some other outlet for his urges.

Jenny *was* his daughter—Merrick knew it with a sudden, dread certainty.

And my granddaughter!

Feeling a sudden, choking pressure in his throat, he stared at his son. There was so much to say, but neither of them could speak without revealing themselves to Jenny and her parents. *So here we stand, like Gabriel and Lucifer in some biblical play, unseen angels of light and darkness, contending over the lives of three mortals.*

No—two mortals and a newly minted immortal.

Merrick knew he should not take his eyes off Zane but he couldn't help himself. Gazing down at Jenny, he felt his heart soar. *Mine!* he thought. She looked wonderful. She was sitting up in bed—something she had been unable to do for weeks—talking happily with her parents. Her voice was strong, her animated face flushed and healthy-looking. Even knowing why, Merrick could not suppress his joy. She would live—the awful decision had been taken out of his hands. . . .

By Zane—the angel, not of light, but of darkness.

Merrick looked up from Jenny to find Zane staring at him with an intense, savage concentration. Merrick's scalp prickled. Suddenly the room faded and he was looking down from his horse at Ancelin. She caught his boot playfully and said, "I don't see why you won't take me hunting with you."

Merrick felt as if his heart would break. She was so beautiful, even now, at nearly forty. Most people her age had begun to wither and hunch, but the lines in Ancelin's face only made her more lovely, forming a smile even when she was not smiling. He longed to pull her up with him for a last kiss, but he knew it was better to do nothing unusual today, nothing that would make her wonder later, when he didn't come back.

"You don't want to hunt," he said. "It's cold at night in the woods. I can just see you sleeping on the wet ground."

"But I miss you. The children are grown. I have nothing to do."

"You could rethatch the roof," Merrick suggested, looking past her to the bungalow on the Gascon hillside where he had spent so many happy years with her.

"Thatching is your job," Ancelin replied.

"So is hunting. You would probably shoot an arrow right through me."

"You do resemble a wild pig," she said, pretending to pout. A gust of wind blew her graying hair out to the side in a still-thick banner. Merrick felt a lump rising in his throat. "How did I ever marry a Frenchwoman?" he asked.

"Because I decided to make an exception."

Unable to stop himself, he leaned down from the horse's back, curling an arm around her shoulders and pulling her up for a kiss, a last kiss. She squealed as her feet dangled off the ground. Her lips tasted like the mulberries they'd had at breakfast—

Merrick blinked, disoriented. Ancelin was gone, and he was ... where? A hospital room, Jenny, *Zane!*

But Zane was gone, too.

For a second Merrick stared at the empty space where Zane had stood, too stunned to move. *What happened to me?*

Go after him!

Merrick slipped into the corridor. Zane was nowhere in sight. Merrick took one step toward the elevators—*no, he'd take the stairs.* Reversing course, Merrick hurried to the stairwell and yanked the door open. The whisper of feet stopped a few landings above, leaving a faint aftershock on his eardrums. He leaned into the space in the center of the stairwell and peered up through the protective screens. He could see no one—whoever it was had either left the stairwell or was keeping back against the wall. It's you, isn't it? Merrick thought. You went up hoping to fool me.

He ran up the stairs, hearing a scramble of feet through the sound of his own footsteps. On the sixth floor, he stopped, listening again. Nothing ...

Except for the chortle of a pigeon—

Merrick ran up another flight and saw the open window. He stuck his head out and saw Zane rolling on the grass, seven stories down. Before Merrick could get a leg out the window, Zane was up and running through the parking lot. Merrick hesitated. If he jumped, too, his legs would be too shocked and bruised to pursue Zane for at least a minute—and by then Zane would be gone. Frustrated, he felt a touch of awe at Zane's daring. After a leap like that, he should still be lying in the grass or at least limping. Apparently being four centuries younger held some physical advantages even for a five hundred-year-old man.

As Zane reached the street, he turned and looked back. His gaze centered on the window and he flung a defiant fist in the air. Merrick started to climb out and Zane scrambled across the street, narrowly evading two cars. He disappeared into an alley without looking back.

Burning with frustration, Merrick pulled himself back inside. He sat down on the steps and tried to think. What would Zane do now? He knows I know about Jenny, Merrick thought. He'll want to get her away from me. Will he kidnap her?

Not yet. Jenny doesn't yet know what she is, or she wouldn't have been talking happily with her parents. In her own mind, she is still Jenny the normal girl. Even Zane must realize that if he tries to wrest her away from her parents by force, she'll hate him. First he must show her what she is—but he must be careful with that, too. If he shocks her too severely, she'll hate him for that, too, and run from him.

Merrick remembered his own horror at first blood, that day so long ago on when he'd found himself drinking from a dying man's throat. His whole world had collapsed around him. He'd felt unspeakably monstrous. He'd run from his family that day and never seen them again.

Zane knew the danger. Clearly—and wisely—he'd given blood to her without letting her know what it was. He'd probably keep feeding her for awhile, gradually letting her understand what it was, indoctrinating her, easing her into the shock of knowing she must drink blood to live. If he meant to win her loyalty, it would take skill and patience, and most of all, time.

Which means I will have time, too, Merrick realized, to see that he doesn't succeed. Still, he was horrified at the thought of Zane playing father to Jenny, dominating her, teaching her to hunt and kill, encouraging her instincts until she was as monstrous as he was.

How do I stop him? Merrick wondered. I can't kidnap her— she'd hate me as surely as she would Zane, and I'd lose all chance to help her. No, she must stay in the hospital for now. Both Zane and I will have to approach her here.

Until one of us buries the other.

Merrick felt a stab of foreboding as he remembered the vision of Ancelin. A memory, but more than a memory—so vivid it seemed entirely real. It had smothered him like a mental straitjacket, wiping the hospital room, Jenny, and Zane from his consciousness. His subconscious mind must have maintained Influence, or the normals would have seen him. But he had been at Zane's mercy. How could his mind have strayed so far back at such a critical moment. . . .

With a shock, Merrick realized that Zane had done it to him. Sandeman had warned that he might be able to enter minds, and Sandeman was right. Neuroscientists could evoke memories during brain surgery by touching the temporal lobes with tiny electrodes. When this happened, the patient did not just remember, he relived whatever was evoked. Clearly, Zane could do much the same thing without electrodes, without opening the skull, by directing blood flow.

He is stronger than me.

Terror struck Merrick like a physical blow, a fear greater than any he had ever experienced. Suddenly he understood—now that it was over—what it had meant to be invulnerable, stronger than everyone, stronger even than the most savage phage he had ever hunted. For nine centuries, what he had thought of as fear was not fear at all. *This* was fear, knowing that Zane could beat him. That he might actually end up under the ground, trapped under tons of dirt, dying a slow and painful death, while Zane roamed the world free and unchecked.

Merrick's terror spilled into near panic, clamping his chest, making it hard to breathe. He fought the suffocating dread, trying to find an anchor, a ray of hope.

If Zane is stronger, why did he run?

And then Merrick realized that Zane might not have been running; that he might have been seizing an opportunity.

Katie!

Horrified, Merrick ran down to the parking lot and his car, praying he would get to her first, feeling another wave of dread as he realized that, even if he did, he might not be able to save her.

TWENTY-FOUR

MERRICK SAT IN his car outside Katie's house, waiting for the fear to recede, trying to get his breathing back to normal. Zane wasn't here after all. Katie, making small talk with her mother and their newly arrived house guest, sounded fine, if guarded. And who wouldn't be, knowing her every word was being heard by two strangers out in the street?

Or maybe the skeptical scientist in Katie made her feel ill at ease around someone who claimed to be a psychic.

Merrick turned up the sound on his own receiver. The small speaker made Katie's voice sound a little tinny, but he found himself listening avidly to her. Knowing he could lose her—truly lose her—and that there might be nothing he could do, made him painfully conscious of how much he loved her. His heart started to pound with fear again, and he made himself sit back in the seat, roll his head from side to side to loosen the rigid muscles.

As long as he was alive, there was still a chance.

Zane ran, he thought, but not to attack Katie. Why, then? Was he, in fact, afraid of me—even after what he showed he could do to me? No, it makes no sense.

Maybe he was trying to draw me away from Jenny.

But why? Does he think I'd hurt her?

You *were* letting her die.

Merrick felt a sudden ache in his chest, as though a giant hand had squeezed down on his heart. I didn't realize she was my own flesh and blood. . . .

And if you had, would you have saved her?

Merrick pressed his hands against his face, fingers digging into his eyelids so hard that stars exploded on his darkened retinas. It had seemed so clear before. If he saved Jenny, she would almost certainly become a killer—that was just as true today as it had been a week ago. Did she suddenly deserve to survive as a phage just because his blood flowed in her veins? If so, he had learned nothing from Zane.

If I'd known she was my granddaughter, Merrick thought, I would have given her blood.

I *have* learned nothing from Zane.

He groaned. But, damn it, she's my *granddaughter*. I don't care, I have to help her. I'll do better than I did with Zane. This time, I'll do it right!

But first I'll have to find a way to take out Zane—

Merrick's car phone rang. He stared at it, annoyed at the interruption, still thinking of Zane as he snatched it up. "What?"

"Mr. Chapman?"

Merrick pulled a deep breath, eased it out. "Yes."

"Uh, this is Rudy Frank, out in California? Hope I'm not disturbing you."

The watchman. "No problem. What's up, Rudy?"

"Well, I wanted to tell you there was a guy came by your house. I was pruning the hedges and he walks up the front walk. I keep people away like you said, but sometimes if they look nice and harmless I make a little conversation and run them off real gentle. That works better, you know?"

"I understand."

"Well, this guy really loves your house. He said he wasn't a Realtor, but he'd like to buy it. I told him it wasn't for sale. But he started talking big money, like a million-two. I ran him off, nice and gentle, but money like that, I thought I ought to let you know."

Merrick's teeth clenched. He reminded himself that the watchman could not possibly fathom how much the place meant to him. Alexandra and George, the last people he'd loved before Katie. The pain of losing them still clung. But someday, when the memories enshrined in that house gave more pleasure than pain, he planned to return there to live.

If I survive Zane.

"The house is not for sale," Merrick said, "under any circumstances, at any price."

"Well, I told him that."

"Good. You were right to call me. If he comes back, let me know right away."

"Will do, Mr. Chapman."

As Merrick hung up the phone, the nape of his neck prickled. Was someone checking up on him? The first few years after Alexandra died and the house had stood empty, calls like this had been common. Then the area Realtors finally had got it through their heads that the cozy place by the sea was not going on the market, not today, not next month, not next year. Occasionally, a new freelancer not connected to a real estate agency came by. But this man had not claimed to be a Realtor—

"Merrick?"

Katie's voice reached him through the receiver. Turning, he saw her at the front window, peering out at him. He waved.

"What are you doing, sitting out there?" she asked. "Come on in and meet Neddie."

Merrick waved again, but stayed where he was. If this Neddie was one of those rare people Sandeman knew of who had a sensitivity to phages, going inside would not be a good idea. What if she shook his hand, then fainted dead away, or started screaming?

"You promised to spend the night," Katie reminded him. "If you'll clean the catfish, we might even let you eat dinner with us."

Seeing no way to avoid it, Merrick got out of the car and started up the front walk. He had bigger worries than a strange woman from the bayous pointing a finger at him. Before the night was over, Zane might bury him, leaving Katie and Gregory at the mercy of a creature with none to give. And after them, an entire city would lie at the feet of that creature, a killer more powerful and vicious than its citizens could imagine, a drinker of blood, who now had two mouths to feed. . . .

* * *

Zane sat beside Jenny's bed, listening to the late-evening silence of the hospital gather around him. The pit of his stomach throbbed steadily, and he felt a nervous ache in the palms of his hands. In a few minutes he would go to Katie's house, finish what he had come to do. Merrick had promised Katie he would stay with her all night, and whatever else the old bastard might be, he was a man of his word.

I've got you now, Zane thought.

But, still, a sense of triumph eluded him. He ought to be ecstatic. Today, he had proved he could Influence Father, could freeze him inside his memories. . . .

But did it really mean he was stronger?

When he had left the room, there had been no cry of surprise from Jenny's parents, which meant Father had somehow maintained his Influence on their vision even while he'd been lost in memory. Most phages were so skilled at the trick they could almost do it in their sleep, but still, it did not bode well. What will happen when I put my hands on him tonight to chain him? Zane wondered. What if the physical contact breaks the mental one and frees him to fight?

The pulse in his stomach sharpened. Even now, he was not completely over his fear of Father. Maybe that wasn't so bad— it would keep him from overconfidence.

Gazing down at his sleeping daughter, Zane found the resolve he needed, the extra edge. Here before him lay a second reason to bury Father, almost as strong as the first. There could be only one reason Merrick had shown up at Jenny's room. He already knew about her, Zane thought. He knew she was dying of hemophagic leukemia and was keeping track of her to make sure she died—that she didn't get blood. Katie must have told him about Jenny's sudden and startling recovery. He knew I was the only one who could have given her blood. So he came here, hoping to find me with her.

Did he guess she's mine?

Even the thought of it chilled Zane, rousing a fierce, protective urge in him. Whether Father had guessed or not, she would be in danger from him, oh yes, just for being what she was. The vicious old hunter would want to destroy her, like he'd destroyed every phage he could catch for five hundred years.

But he won't get the chance, Zane thought. Tonight, he's guarding his lover and their son. I'll take them, all together, just as I planned. And then I won't have to worry about Jenny anymore. . . .

Hearing soft footsteps approaching down the hall, Zane turned to watch the door. A moment later, a man leaned in, a big fellow, hardly more than a boy, dressed as an orderly in white pants and short white jacket with snaps at the shoulders. He gazed at Jenny, his expression oddly intent. Probably curious about the hospital's "miracle" girl.

Annoyed, Zane stood and moved silently to Jenny's bedside. *My daughter is not on display for you sheep.* For an instant, he relaxed his Influence, giving the boy a subliminal flash of him. The orderly blinked and backed out the doorway. Zane heard his steps recede as he scurried away down the hall. As if she had sensed something, Jenny groaned softly in her sleep. Her face was pale now, and a slight frown marred her smooth forehead.

Gasping a breath, she opened her eyes. She peered around the room with an anxious expression, and then her shoulders relaxed. A radiant smile transformed her face, warming Zane. Hello, daughter, he thought. You're feeling much better, aren't you? You're alive—and you're going to stay that way; I promise you.

Easing into the chair again, he watched as Jenny turned on the light on her headboard then took her doll from her bed table. She fiddled with the doll's clothes and smoothed her long blonde hair, glancing at the door, as if afraid someone would come in and catch her at it. Apparently she thought she was too grown up for this sort of thing. She did not yet know that she was, in another sense, a newborn, about to discover a new world. His job was to remove the fright and terror of that new world and show her its exhilaration.

Zane watched with growing fascination as Jenny's finger moved from the doll's hair to its throat. She stroked it, her face transformed by a sudden intense concentration. Then her eyes clouded and she set the doll back on the bed table. Fascinating! Zane thought. Maybe she will be drawn to young women, too, just like me. But I won't try and sway her. I'll let her follow her nature. And I'll teach her to love it.

But first I have to save her from Father.

Tonight, *now.*

Zane got up silently and walked out.

TWENTY-FIVE

At DINNER, KATIE noticed that Neddie Merrill kept stealing glances at Merrick when he wasn't looking at her. Maybe she, too, had picked up his tension. Though he looked physically relaxed, his eyes had a crackling intensity Katie could not decipher. Something had changed in him since he'd gone off to the hospital. Maybe after Mom and Neddie went off to bed, he would tell her about it.

"I'll clear off the dishes," Merrick said.

"No you won't," Mom said. "Not after all your good work on the catfish."

"You could have been born in the bayous," Neddie agreed, "the way you handled that filleting knife."

Asking Neddie up for a visit had been a good idea, Katie decided. The woman was a surprise, she had to admit. She wasn't sure what she'd expected—flamboyant gypsy clothes maybe, and lots of melodramatic pronouncements. But Neddie was very down to earth, a tall, slender woman with a good smile and a soft Cajun accent who dressed in the kind of conservative, tasteful dresses you might find in a small-town business office. At dinner, when she wasn't casting furtive glances at Merrick, she had drawn him out on big city police work. She'd shown a real interest in Katie's life as a doctor, too, and she had yet to volunteer a word about herself or anything psychic.

"I'll help with the dishes, then," Merrick offered, but Katie caught him glancing into the living room.

"Go play with Gregory," she said.

Smiling, he left them and went to his son. It gave her a warm feeling to hear their voices, Merrick's smooth bass and Gregory's piping soprano. As she carried a stack of fragrantly messy plates into the kitchen, the phone on the wall rang. Setting the dishes down, she answered it. "Katie O'Keefe."

"Doctor, this is Desmond White. Is Lieutenant Chapman there?"

Something in his voice sent a tremor of foreboding through her. "Yes, hold on."

Watching Merrick's face, hearing his voice go flat and hard, she knew it was something bad. The happy banter at the sink behind her faded to stillness. He has to go, she thought, and all the warmth of the evening fled.

When he hung up, his expression was stark.

"There's been another murder," she said.

He nodded. "A church again. A young woman, left on the pulpit, like before."

"Oh, no," Mom whispered behind her.

Katie looked at him, stricken. "And the police were guarding me. I wish they'd been with her, whoever she was."

Merrick took her shoulders. "He would just have killed someone else. . . ." He left it unfinished, but she knew what he was thinking—*not someone else, Katie—you.*

With an effort, she made her voice firm. "You have to go, Merrick. We agreed to that when I asked you to stay. We'll be all right here. We've got the bars, and the new alarm system."

"I'll be back as quickly as I can."

Kissing his cheek, Katie felt the rigid muscles beneath the skin. With a nod to Mom and Neddie, Merrick hurried out. She watched from the front window until his car disappeared down the street. One of the men in the patrol car gave her a wave and she felt a small reassurance. Merrick would hurry back, and she was far from alone.

Letting the curtain fall back, she trailed a finger down the wire tucked along the edge of the window. Her mother had shelled out an extra hundred to have the alarm system installed immediately. With both doors and every window in the circuit, it added an extra layer of protection to the bars. Now, if an intruder broke or cut glass as someone had done the other night, or jimmied a window or door, a loud alarm would sound. . . .

But when will this be over?

Katie's knees sagged and she leaned against the window, afraid, and yet tired, so very tired. She could almost feel the burn of spent adrenaline in the small of her back. Too many shocks lately, pushing her up to peaks of frantic energy, then letting her down again—too low, into dark valleys of weariness. She could not afford to be let down. Something was out there, and it wanted to hurt her and Gregory. She needed to stay sharp every minute now.

I need something. Some Dex or Ritalin—

Katie cut the thought off, shocked by its power. How could she want it so much when the physical dependency was dead, broken years ago? It's all in your mind now, she thought, because you're under stress. So stop thinking about it.

She heard Gregory whimpering in the living room. She turned from the window in a rush of anxiety, and then Gregory's whines turned to enthusiastic growls and she realized he was only playing. Moving to the edge of the living room doorway, she watched him. He was making two of his teddy bears fight each other, thumping them together and supplying high-pitched growls and whimpering cries as needed. She wondered if it was his way of registering the shadowy fears that had invaded his house. He often expressed his mood through his toys. A bunch of them surrounded him now—more stuffed animals, mixed-up pieces from several wooden puzzles, a learning board complexly cratered to accept different shapes, plastic cows and pigs from his farm set, four or five foam balls in Day-Glo colors.

Gregory ended the fight with one bear sitting on the other. "Go away. Be good," he growled.

"No, no," the other bear squeaked.

Gregory made the top bear bite the other's throat.

Chilled, Katie stepped into the room. Amazing, what children picked up on. He must have overheard Merrick taking the call about the new murder. Looking up, Gregory announced, "My bears had a fight."

"I can see that. Who won?"

"The *good* bear."

"Why were they fighting?"

"The bad bear wanted to eat the good bear, but Uncle Merrick wouldn't let him."

Katie knelt beside him. "Is the good bear safe now?"

"I think so."

She pulled him into a hug. "You'll always be safe with Mommy." She wished she could be as sure as she sounded. "Help me put your toys in the box and we'll take them upstairs to bed."

"Can I play with my cards?"

"Sure."

Upstairs, Katie put the toy box in Gregory's closet and gave him his collection of picture postcards. He got under his blanket and started sorting through them, his favorite bedtime activity. Sometimes he told her stories about the colorful cards, but tonight he seemed content just to study them, one by one. Katie saw that she'd left the closet door open. Closing it, she noticed the full-size Louisville slugger Merrick had brought his son a few visits ago.

"Uncle" Merrick, she thought with a pang.

It would be another two years before Gregory was as tall as the bat, let alone able to swing it. For most fathers, a gift like that was an impatient down payment on future family ball games. But she had the feeling Merrick had given a teenage gift to a two-year-old because he knew that, when Gregory was big enough to swing the bat, he would no longer be around.

Katie saw that Gregory had finished with his cards. He lay back, pulling a teddy bear to each cheek. His eyelids were heavy with sleep. "Good night, sweetie," Katie said.

"Good night, sweetie," Gregory murmured.

Katie kissed him on the forehead and headed back downstairs, her heart full. Mom and Neddie were in the living room, sitting on the couch sipping coffee. Katie poured herself a brimming cup and took a chair across from them. Mom said, "We were just talking about this awful new murder."

That's because you don't have teddy bears anymore, Katie thought. "It is terrible," she agreed.

"Neddie thinks it may be a copycat killing."

"Really? Why?"

Neddie shrugged. "Just a guess, from working with the police on some serial killer cases. From what I've heard about the first three killings here, the murderer was careful to 'stage' each one differently. Why would he suddenly copy himself almost exactly? It makes more sense to me that someone else—an admirer, as awful as that sounds—copied him."

Katie realized that it did make sense. It also made her uneasy. The call to Merrick had appalled her, yes, but she'd felt some relief, too, knowing that tonight the killer had struck somewhere else. But maybe the creature she feared had not struck tonight—not yet.

Excusing herself, Katie went to the hall closet, unlocked the gun box in the top, and took out the .357 magnum Merrick had given her. She made sure it was loaded, then took it back into the living room and set it on the table beside her chair. Neither Mom nor Neddie said anything. Katie thought of her promise to Merrick to brush up on her shooting at the police range. She hadn't done it—no time and lots of excuses. She despised guns, hated the greasy feel of one in her hands, the kick, the deafening noise, the whole idea of shooting anyone. Ironically, despite all that, when she'd let Merrick teach her to shoot, she'd been quite accurate. *I might be rusty now,* she thought, *but I can still hit anything the size of a man at twenty paces.*

If it's visible.

Mom cleared her throat. "What happens, Neddie, when you work with the police?"

Neddie sighed. "Usually, they bring me things—an article of the victim's clothing or maybe a match or candy wrapper the killer left behind. When I touch them, I sometimes get impressions about the people connected to them."

"Like that article in the *Post*," Mom said, "where you found the killer by touching a bullet taken from the man he shot."

"Yes."

Mom gave Katie a hopeful look and Katie realized what she was thinking: Let Neddie touch the bars at the pantry window. Katie's first impulse was to shake her head, but then she felt a twinge of guilt. Neddie was good enough to fly up here, she thought, and I've been ignoring one of the central elements of her life just because I don't believe in it. Katie pointed to her watch. With a nod, Mom pulled the stem up to turn the wire inside off. Katie did the same and felt an instant relief. With the burglar alarm in place, they'd have enough warning to turn the wretched things back on.

She said, "Neddie, Mom thinks the creature that threatened me in my lab may have gotten into the house by bending the bars over the pantry window. . . ."

Neddie rubbed her mouth. "I could try," she said softly.

She did not seem at all eager, and Katie had second thoughts about bringing it up. "If you'd rather not—"

"No, no."

Katie led the way, turning on the light in the pantry, lifting the window so that Neddie could get at the bars freely. A cool breeze, laced with the ripe smell of mulch from the yard outside, blew in. A half moon silvered the tips of the grass and the tops of the bushes. Neddie gazed at the bars a moment, then grabbed the middle two at the bottom and began to slide her hands up. Closing her eyes, she gave a little gasp.

"Neddie?" Mom said.

"Yes. It came in here."

The hairs stood up on Katie's forearms. Could the creature really be strong enough to have bent those bars?

"He is very lonely," Neddie murmured, "and . . . obsessed." She opened her eyes and drew her hands back, rubbing them on her skirt. She looked searchingly at Katie.

"What?" Katie said.

"Would you mind if I looked upstairs in your bedroom?"

Katie felt the prickle of goose bumps again, crawling along her neck. "Come on." She led the way upstairs. Too late to back out now. She would just let Neddie do her thing, respond courteously, and try to forget about it.

Neddie drifted around the room like a sleepwalker, over to the wing-backed chair, pausing at the window that looked out on the backyard, then homing on the bedside. There she knelt with the slow care of a seventy-year-old. She stared at Katie's pillow, her eyes wide. Her shoulders jerked in a sudden shudder. If she was acting, she was very convincing—Katie could almost see the thing kneeling where Neddie was kneeling, staring at her sleeping face.

Abruptly, Neddie stood. "Could we go back downstairs?"

"Of course," Katie said.

Back in the living room, Neddie gripped her coffee cup as if she were seeking its warmth. Mom brought in the pot from the kitchen and freshened everyone's cup. Katie took a deep gulp, savoring its hot strength in her throat, the small kick in her veins.

Neddie gazed down at her cup. "I don't want to frighten

either of you needlessly. Sometimes I'm wrong about these things. I don't always see clearly."

Katie forced a smile. "It's all right. I don't think I could be any more scared of this thing than I am, anyway."

Neddie nodded. "It was in your room. More than once, I think."

Mom pressed a fist to her mouth. "But it didn't harm her."

"It is full of conflicting emotions," Neddie said. "Very powerful feelings. Hate, loneliness, and an intense black . . . desire. It's odd, but I think I may have sensed a creature like it before, a long time ago. When I was a girl, I was visiting Mrs. Gaillard—you remember her, Audrey, she lived about a mile down from you. I heard the dock that led to her porch creaking and I looked out the window, but I couldn't see anyone. It terrified me. I ran to Mrs. Gaillard's front door and threw the bolt. She saw me and said, 'Whatever are you doing, child?'—no one locked their doors in those days. Mrs. Gaillard went to unlock the door, but before she could, the handle turned very slowly, just once, and the door moved a little. Then the dock creaked again, and after a few minutes, I didn't sense it anymore. The next morning, down the bayou about a mile, Clyde Lelonge went missing and never was found. His pillow was soaked with blood."

Katie found herself listening with a dread fascination. This story seemed connected to Mom's story about Grandma Guillemin in her skiff—the man who vanished when she picked up her shotgun. Could another thing like the one in the hospital yesterday have stalked the bayou fifty years ago?

"Do you have any sense of what this thing looks like?" Mom asked.

"A man," Neddie said at once. "But I don't have to tell you it has powers greater than any man's. It looks young, I think, but it is very old." Neddie glanced toward the dining room. "It's odd," she said, "but when we were all having dinner, I kept thinking I sensed something. I'd try to focus on it, but it would fade. When it was in the house, the thing might have passed through there and left traces, except that . . ." Neddie shook her head. "I don't know how to explain it exactly. The feeling I got in the dining room was similar to the one I just got in your bedroom, but not the same."

Katie felt confused. "Are you saying there might be *two* of these things around?"

"Either that or two very different personalities in the same one," Neddie mused. She started to sip her coffee, then set her cup back on the saucer. She cocked her head for a moment, then turned and peeked through the curtains behind the couch. Katie glanced inquiringly at Mom, who shrugged.

"Oh, dear," Neddie whispered. "I think it may be out there."

Katie felt suddenly cold, as if an icy wind had blown through the room.

"Neddie, are you sure?" Mom whispered, getting up.

"Yes."

"Where is it?" Katie asked.

Neddie did not answer. Her gaze darted around the room. Katie felt her heart pounding in her throat. She thought of Gregory, asleep upstairs. "Neddie, tell me where it is," she demanded.

"I can't tell exactly." Neddie's voice was suddenly hoarse with alarm. "But it's here."

Katie hurried into the foyer and checked the street. The patrol car was still in place. The window was intact, the door locked. Her fear eased a little. The alarms would ring if anything tried to get inside.

She heard a sound behind her and whirled, but it was only Mom, heading for the stairs. "I'm going to Gregory," she said, and hurried up the steps.

Katie turned back to the window. "You, in the patrol car," she said. "I think we may have a problem. Can one of you come in please."

The patrol car remained as it was. Neither door opened. Katie felt a rush of fear. She tapped at the watch. Wasn't the wire working?

I turned it off!

Frantically, Katie fumbled at the stem, pushing it in again. "Hello?" she said. "Patrol car, we need your help."

The car remained still. She could see no movement in the dark interior.

"It's inside!" Neddie cried from the living room.

Katie's scalp prickled. She ran into Neddie. "Where? Where is it?"

But Neddie started shaking her head. "Oh, no," she said. "I can't, it's too much." She hurried toward the front door; Katie called out but she didn't seem to hear. Before she could stop her, Neddie threw the bolt and ran outside.

Katie ran after her. "Come back!"

Neddie either didn't hear her or ignored her, running away down the street in a jerky, panicked gait.

Katie slammed the door and relocked it. "You cops out there—we need you!" She stared through the window at the patrol car. After a moment she could make out silhouettes inside. The heads of both men lolled back on the seats. Katie's blood ran cold. "Mom!" she cried.

No answer.

Panicking, Katie dashed upstairs to Gregory's room. Mom sat on the floor. Her lips moved, but no words came out. Seeing Katie, she gasped and pointed at the crib. Gregory was gazing at them both with wide, frightened eyes. Katie scooped him up and he wiggled in her arms. He did not seem hurt.

"Mommy," he said, "the man touched my back."

She pulled up his shirt. Drawn on his back, in what looked like blood, was a broad Z.

Katie felt an explosion of fear and fury. Putting Gregory down, she shouted, "Show yourself!"

For just a second, she saw him, over in the corner, a big, dark shape, and then he vanished again. The gun—where was the gun? *Downstairs!* She lunged into Gregory's closet and grabbed the baseball bat. Swinging it back and forth, she waded into the corner of the room where she'd seen the shape, only dimly aware of what she was doing. A terrible rage filled her, squeezing her vision down to a red-tinged tunnel. She lashed the bat around again and felt it connect solidly, though she could see nothing. A whiff of air fanned her face, then Mom lurched to the side as though someone had bumped her. The boards in the hall creaked. Katie ran into the hall, flailing with the bat, but all she could find was empty air.

The stairs creaked and she ran down them, probing with the bat. It brushed something ahead of her. She screamed and lunged forward, but the creature was beyond reach again. She saw the front door open and close. She tore it open and ran down the walk to the patrol car, yanking on the handle, yelling. The door popped open. Inside, one of the cops raised his head and opened his eyes. He yawned deeply.

Katie started smashing the car with the baseball bat.

Zane's panic eased slowly as he gazed down at his daughter, safely asleep in her hospital bed. A vast confusion filled him. *Where was Father?*

His usual car wasn't out front, Zane thought, but I assumed

he'd decided to ride in the patrol car. He promised Katie he'd be there all night. What happened?

Half dazed, he settled in the chair by Jenny's bed. What a fiasco! All that preparation—peeling a hole in the roof, marking the kid to terrorize Katie into calling the medical examiner—and then everything had blown up in his face. Damn it, how had the women known he was there? He hadn't made a sound, he was sure. They'd shocked the hell out of him, dashing upstairs suddenly like that. With Katie swinging her bat and screaming at him, he'd known Father must be right behind her, but when he'd run out of the kid's room to take Merrick on, no sign of him!

The next part was a blur; rushing back here, terrified he'd find Jenny's bed empty. But here she was, safe. Father wasn't at Katie's and he wasn't here either.

Not yet.

A chill passed through Zane. Getting up, he slipped to the door and searched the corridor in each direction. Empty. Despite the light that spilled from the nurses station, the whole hospital seemed asleep.

But Merrick could be creeping up the stairs right now.

Retreating to the chair, Zane sank into it, galled and frustrated. We've each got a hand on the other's throat, he thought. Father wants to bury Jenny, but to do it he must risk that I won't get Katie while he's gone. If I go after Katie and him, I'll leave Jenny unprotected. So now it's a war of nerves. One of us will have to take a chance and attack.

The question is, who has the most to lose?

TWENTY-SIX

KATIE DREAMED SHE heard a rooster, then it crowed again and she realized it was real. A rooster in Georgetown? She opened her eyes, her mind still thick with sleep. The ceiling was too far away, rosy with sunrise. Where—?

The creature broke in last night. It went after Gregory!

Katie felt a cold surge of fear. Rolling to her side, she looked at her son beside her in bed. He was gazing up at her, his thumb in his mouth. Just looking at him made her feel better. She hugged him and tousled his hair. The rooster crowed again.

"Do you know what that was?" she asked.

"Rooster goes cock-a-doodle-doo," he answered, reciting from one of his books. She kissed him and sat up, yawning. After last night, she could not believe she'd been able to fall asleep.

"Where are we, Mommy?"

"Auntie Meggan's, out in the country. Remember? Uncle

Merrick drove you and me and Grandma out here last night.''

''Are you scared?''

''No, sweetie. We're safe here.'' She hugged him again, distressed at the fear in his voice. We *are* safe, she thought. We might not have seen it following us, but we would have heard it. She called up the reassuring memory: They'd pulled off the road and sat there, hidden by the bend in the road. The cool night air pouring in the open windows had been windless and still, no sound of a car behind them for almost two minutes. Then they'd heard the distant growl of an engine and, in another minute, a Porsche had flashed by, a young couple inside. There *is* a chink in its armor, Katie thought. It can keep us from seeing it, but last night in the house, even though I couldn't see it, I could *hear* it.

She tried to feel encouraged, but it was a very small chink. A car engine made noise, but on foot the thing was eerily quiet. She'd heard it in the hallway outside Gregory's room and again on the creaky steps, when she was only a few feet away. But it had managed to open a four-foot hole in the roof and climb down from the attic so stealthily that they wouldn't have known it was in the house, if it hadn't been for Neddie.

Poor Neddie. She'd sounded so scared when she'd called. *I'm sorry for running, Katie, but I can't be around this thing—it fills my brain with panic. I'm just not strong enough.*

That's all right, Katie thought now, it's not your fight, it's mine. Her anger, still smoldering from last night, flared up again. This thing was terrorizing her and her family. It kept coming after them, and it wasn't going to stop—not until she called Dr. Byner about its blood. That was what the *Z* on Gregory's back had been about, a reminder of its warning. But if she called Byner, it would be finished with her, and it would kill her.

We're safe right now, she thought, but how long until it finds us? Even if it doesn't, I can't just stop going to work. Sick people depend on me. Without me, some of them might die.

I have to go on the attack.

But how?

She thought about the gun last night, sitting uselessly on the end table in the living room. If only she'd had the gun . . . What? Would she have dared shoot it in Gregory's room? Maybe next time, she'd have a chance to use it. But only if the creature let her see it, and why would it do that? It wasn't going to just stand out there at twenty paces waiting for her to put a bullet in its chest. No, it would grab her out of thin air, like it had at the hospital. Even if she could hide a .357 magnum inside her medical coat, she would have no chance to pull the gun out once the killer had grabbed her.

A knife—

No. Stabbing someone required even more movement than shooting them. Even if her arms were loose, it wouldn't let her stab it.

A *syringe!* she thought. All you need to move is your thumb! A syringe full of sodium pentothal. Hell, a syringe full of arsenic or potassium cyanide! If I'd had one when it grabbed me in the lab, I could have injected it right through the pocket of my lab coat. It doesn't seem to feel pain—I really connected that one time with the bat last night and it didn't even grunt. . . .

But what about its blood?

Katie's excitement faded. For poison to be effective, the bloodstream had to pick it up and carry it around the body. The membrane on the killer's cells so far had been impenetrable. Were its body cells also invulnerable? If so, no poison would work.

But if she found something that would break up the membrane on the blood cells, it ought to work on tissue cells, too. She already knew potassium cyanide wouldn't work, because the CBC Analyzer had bathed the killer's red blood cells in it trying to get a hemoglobin reading. Not only hadn't the cells broken up, they had shed the lysing agent completely. The blood had also resisted all other reagents she'd tried, not to mention a thousand-kilovolt stream in the electron microscope.

Katie felt a mix of fear and frustration. How could you fight a being that could knock two cops unconscious without touching them, that could scale a brick wall without leaving any marks of a ladder in the dirt, then peel shingles, wood slats, and insulation up like tissue paper?

Katie pushed her fear aside. Surely this thing was not completely invulnerable, or it wouldn't have been so anxious to get its blood back. The creature's blood was the key, she felt certain of it.

I don't have its blood anymore, she thought, but I have Jenny's. Though it's not exactly the same as the killer's, hers *does* have a membrane strong enough to resist electron irradiation for more than a minute. Smeared on a slide, it stays wet and fresh for hours. I'll go in today and get Art to cover for me on the ward. I'll hammer that membrane with everything I can think of. . . .

Suddenly, Katie remembered that she'd promised Merrick

she'd call in sick today and stay at Meggan's where she was safe. He wasn't going to like her going in.

But she couldn't just sit here. She had to do something, fight back.

She kissed the top of Gregory's head, got out of bed, and went to the window. The slanting morning light sparkled off the dew of the estate's long front lawn. At the end of the driveway, Merrick stood beside his car, sipping from a mug. It worried her that he was still here. With a new murder on his hands, he should be back in the city, running the investigation, not here trying to protect her. She'd tried to get him to go back last night, but he'd insisted on waiting until morning, just to make sure.

I'll go down now, she thought, and send him on his way.

Instead, she watched him a moment longer. He looked so tall and strong in the morning light. But this was tearing him up inside, she knew. When he'd seen Gregory's back last night, he'd held his son close with great gentleness, but she had felt his rage. How strange that horror and death had thrown her and Merrick back together. His company had been almost the only good thing about the past week. She'd felt his arms around her again, seen the old love in his eyes. That same love had been there the day they'd parted; it had not been enough to keep them together then, but maybe what they were going through now would change things. Maybe we can try once more, she thought.

If we survive this.

Katie dug out the robe she'd tossed into her suitcase last night and put it on over her nightgown. Slipping into her sandals, she walked down through the kitchen. On the big oak breakfast table lay an envelope addressed to her. When she picked it up, a set of car keys, wrapped in a note, fell out:

Dear Katie,

I beat you into work this morning, nyah, nyah, nyah. Cereal over the fridge, muffins in the microwave. In case Merrick has to strand you, use the Riviera—the tank's full. Tonight we'll have our first cookout of the year—chicken weenies, yum, yum. See you later.

Love, Meggan

P.S. Don't even think about going back to your house until they catch that burglar.

Gratefully, Katie pocketed the keys. As she walked down the driveway toward Merrick, she checked the armada of cars parked in front of the garage. The Jeep Meggan's husband drove was gone, too—Josh must have got an early start to one of his construction sites. Katie felt like a sluggard. How long since she'd slept past sunrise? Last night must have taken more out of her than she'd realized. She still felt tired and, if she could get past Merrick to her lab, she'd be facing the most challenging day of her life.

I could try to get some dexedrine at the hospital—

No.

Merrick walked a few steps to meet her, his feet crunching on the gravel drive. "Good morning."

She gave him a quick kiss. "How was the couch?"

"Very couchlike."

"Poor baby. Anything new on the murder?"

"I radioed Des a few minutes ago. He thinks he might have a couple of leads."

"Neddie thought it was a copycat killing."

Merrick raised an eyebrow. "Interesting. I think so, too."

"You need to get going."

He eyed her. "Are you sure you'll be all right?"

"Absolutely. Good luck on that hospital records search. I'm sorry I didn't tell you sooner about Jenny's blood, but . . ."

"You've had a lot on your mind." He gave her a grim smile.

"Maybe you'll get lucky," she said, "and find a doctor or nurse who remembers a case like Jenny's. Make sure whoever you assign to do the calling remembers to ask about all three key factors: one, strange appetite, two, failure to respond to standard treatment, and three, rapid remission."

Merrick nodded, looking uncomfortable. "What do you think this means for Jenny?"

Katie knew what he was really asking—she'd been expecting the question before now. "Don't worry," she said. "Blood doesn't determine personality. She has the membrane now, but my best guess is it's related to her remission—and nothing else. She and the killer *may* have an atypical course of leukemia in common, but that's all."

He seemed only slightly relieved. She wished she could feel as sure as she'd just sounded. Scientifically, everything she'd said was correct. But they were in unknown territory here.

"How about you?" Merrick asked. "Are you all squared away at the hospital?"

She hesitated, knowing he wouldn't like what she was going to say. "Merrick, I've got to go in—no, wait, just hear me out. You have to go after this thing. So do I."

He looked at her intently. "Katie, how?"

"By finding a way to attack its blood."

"I thought he took it all."

"I'll use Jenny's blood. It isn't the same, but anything that breaks her membrane down may work in stronger doses on the killer's cells. I'm releasing her this morning—that's another reason I have to go in—but I'll take a final blood sample first."

"You're sending her home so soon?" He sounded alarmed, and she realized again how much he cared for Jenny.

"I'd like to keep her, but she's doing too well to justify it. Her parents want her home. I can't blame them. No one knows how long this remission will last."

Merrick took her hands. "Katie, you're safe here. We know the hospital is part of the territory he's staked out. If you go in, there's a good chance he'll see you and either kill you straight out or follow you back here so he can get Gregory, too. Before you take a risk like that, you've got to give me a chance to catch him."

"How?"

Merrick looked pained and she realized that it had sounded like a challenge. "I'm sorry," she said. "But we have to face facts."

"Katie, promise me you'll stay here."

She hesitated, hearing the plea in his voice. If I don't promise, she thought, he'll stay with me today, even though it means risking his career. I can't let him do that. He has to go back, run his investigation. He won't do that until he feels sure I'm safe.

"All right," she said. "Art can take Jenny's blood and sign the release."

Merrick looked tremendously relieved. "Thank you, Katie."

She kissed him, meaning to make it a quick peck, then throwing her arms around his neck and drawing his head down. At last, needing a breath, she pulled back.

"What was that for?" he asked with a grin.

"For caring so much."

He hopped into his car. Watching him drive away, Katie felt terrible. It was the first time she had lied to him. But this creature had put its filthy hands on her son. She could not hide from it forever. Merrick could go after it with a gun; she would hunt it with her microscope.

I know more about you than anyone, she thought. I'm going to stop you, whoever, whatever, you are.

"Just what the hell do you think you are doing?"

"Running a murder investigation." Merrick faced Captain Rourke with fatalistic calm. Rourke leaned on his desk, palms flat, the weight of his massive chest and belly swelling the veins over the backs of his hands. His fury did not surprise Merrick but he could not suppress a certain disappointment. Why must normals always be so fiercely protective of their precious rules and procedures?

Because they could control so little.

"Damn it, Merrick, how do you expect to conduct a murder investigation over your goddamn radio? And don't ask me which one of your detectives ratted you out, because none of the loyal bastards did. I went to the church myself and you weren't there."

"I thought it would be better if I went where the killer was."

"Not only were you—what? What the hell are you talking about?"

"Remember the patrol car we put at Doctor O'Keefe's house? When I was on my way to the church, I tried to raise it on the radio and couldn't. So I left Des in charge and went over there. The killer was in her house."

Rourke sat down heavily, suddenly deflated. "Christ, you're telling me he tried to do two women in one night?"

"I think the church was a copycat. There was no Z on the victim—a detail we kept out of the papers." *And they found too much blood.* "Doctor O'Keefe's house was the real thing. Fortunately, we made him miss."

Rourke stared at him. "You say he was in the house. How the hell did he get past the stakeout?"

Merrick told Rourke about the two patrolmen being knocked out, the hole in Katie's roof, the bloody mark on Gregory's back.

Rourke stared at him, pop-eyed. "You're saying there *was* a Z on the kid?"

"Just like the one on the second murder victim. I'll have the report on your desk by noon."

"Well, Jesus, did the kid get a look at him?"

"No—and besides, he's only two." Merrick tried not to sound defensive, but he was not going to have police grilling his son. "No one saw the killer," he said emphatically. "Doctor O'Keefe went to check on her son and found him sitting there with the bloody brand on him. She heard the killer creeping around in another part of the house and tried to raise the patrol car over her wire, but they were busy staring at the insides of their eyelids. He must have used some kind of gas because there wasn't a mark on them. Fortunately, I was trying to call them, too. The killer must have run when he heard my siren." Merrick hoped Rourke wouldn't check with the neighbors. There had been no siren. When he'd arrived, Zane was already gone and Katie was bashing the police car with Gregory's baseball bat.

Rourke stared at him. "Why didn't you send one of your men?"

"They were all busier than I was at the moment. Come on, Captain, if it weren't for the budget, Desmond would have made sergeant a year ago. You know how good he is—"

"Did you call for backup?"

"I couldn't be sure the two patrolmen weren't inside having hot chocolate with the doctor. I tried phoning her, but the line was busy." Another lie, but hard to check.

Rourke glared at him.

"Okay, so I took a chance."

"What the hell were you doing the rest of the night?"

"I called in a forensics team to go over the doctor's place, then got her and her family away to a safe house."

Rourke pulled his collar open. He looked like someone who had just won the thirteen-inch TV instead of the Lincoln Town Car. "You put her where the killer can't find her?"

"That's right."

"Well, okay, good. But really, Merrick, this might be the break we've been waiting for, don't you think? If this killer's got a thing for the doctor, why don't we put her back in her house, beef up the stakeout, and nail him when he tries again?"

Merrick began to feel a little angry. "Nail him? Is that before or after he cuts a Z on the doctor's throat? Captain, he put two cops out without them ever seeing him, then bypassed barred windows and a state-of-the-art burglar alarm. Doctor O'Keefe is a citizen, not a cop trained and paid to act as bait."

"Well, let's at least find a cop who looks like the doctor," Rourke growled. "Let her walk back and forth in the house and hope this bastard is dumber than you think."

"Fine." It was not fine, but it was good procedure and there was no way he could talk Rourke out of it. He just had to hope Zane didn't go in and kill the policewoman out of spite.

Rourke looked out his window. "Merrick, wherever the doctor is now, I want you to put a team on her to protect her in case this nut finds her.''

"I'll take care of that."

"Meaning you'll assign a squad to stake her out?"

"Meaning I'll take care of it."

Rourke sighed. "I seem to remember you dating a lady doctor. In fact, it seems her name was O'Keefe. This her?"

"That was a couple of years ago."

Rourke eyed him. "Uh-huh. Don't you think maybe you've lost your objectivity here?"

"No."

"Good. That means you'll put the team on her."

"No."

"No," Rourke echoed. "I think I'm beginning to see why you didn't call for backup. Who do you think you are, the Lone Ranger? We got a whole police department here for protecting citizens. What are you afraid of, that someone in the department will leak where she is and the killer will go get her?"

"Stranger things have happened. Besides, those two in the car last night were no help."

Rourke rubbed his chin. "You got a point. But you've also got a problem. They discharged Cooke last night. The doctors ordered him to take a day off before he came back. But he's due in tomorrow, and then it's his show."

Merrick battled a sense of frustration. He had expected this, but that didn't make it easier.

"Tomorrow," Rourke said, "you and I and Doc Byner are going to sit down with Cooke and you're going to brief him on all this. There's a good chance he'll want to question Doctor O'Keefe and her kid himself—"

"I took full statements."

"I know, I know. But what matters is what the guy running the task force wants. All you'll have to do is make sure the doc and her kid get in to see him here."

"After which he'll have her followed so he can stake her out."

Rourke gave him a strange look. "Would that really be so bad? She could use the protection, seems to me."

There is no protection, Merrick thought. Except Zane not knowing where she is. But how do I tell Rourke that?

"Anyway," Rourke said, "if Cooke tells you to bring her in for further questioning, you can't refuse. If you do, you'll be off the case. And maybe that sergeant's billet will open up for Desmond after all.''

The blood rushed to Merrick's face. You gutless sheep, he thought. ''Captain, I've done my best for you. If you put Cooke on this case, it's because you won't stand up for your own men to your superiors, and every cop in this precinct is going to know it.''

''Don't tell me how to do my job,'' Rourke growled.

Suddenly, the idiocy of it, the sheer unfairness of this callow normal with no inkling what he was doing, became too much for Merrick. He stood and stared into Rourke's eyes. He could sense the blood straining past the plaque in the captain's carotid arteries. He was dangerously close to a stroke. For a second, Merrick found himself reaching out mentally, starting to squeeze the arteries. He broke off, repulsed at himself. Had he really come to this, an inch away from killing a man? He'd do it to save Katie, but Katie *was* safe—as long as he didn't give her location away. He might even do it to save himself—if it would work. But he couldn't save himself by destroying everything inside himself that made him a man instead of an animal.

''If you're going to take a swing at me, do it, before the suspense kills me.'' Rourke was trying to joke, but there was real fear in his eyes, and Merrick realized he had leaned forward on the desk.

He straightened. ''Is that all, Captain?''

Rourke sighed. ''You're a good man. You're a hell of a lot smarter and wiser than Cooke. Sometimes its hard for me to believe he's the one with the gray hair. But I am going to catch this maniac if I have to sell my soul to Satan.''

''Is that all?''

''Yes, that's all. Have your report on my desk by noon. If you catch the killer before seven o'clock tomorrow morning, no one will be happier than I will. Otherwise, be here tomorrow at seven sharp so you and Doctor Byner can brief Lieutenant Cooke.''

A bitter sense of futility filled Merrick. He thought, I know right where your killer is, Captain—with his daughter. But I'm not stronger than him anymore. When I go up against him, if I lose, you won't see me at seven sharp tomorrow, or ever again. And you won't have just one ''vampire'' out there, you'll have two. Your fatal accidents and missing persons count will go up, the blood will flow like a river, and no one will hear the screams.

TWENTY-SEVEN

DESPITE HER ANXIETY at being at the hospital, where the creature could get at her, Katie felt a sense of wonder as she examined Jenny. The leukemia appeared to be in total remission. Amazingly, the rashlike stippling of her skin caused by broken capillaries was gone. Even with a total remission, it should have taken days for the capillaries to heal and the rash to fade as the body broke down and then carried away the tiny pinpoints of clotted blood. Instead, it had taken hours. Jenny's skin was flushed and firm.

Mystified, Katie continued the exam, conscious of Ann Hrluska's eager gaze, the sound of Jenny's father pacing in the hall outside. Despite their comforting nearness, Katie could not shake the fear buzzing along her nerves. Part of it, she knew, was being in this particular room, where she had felt the killer's presence just before Jenny's nosebleed. When she'd walked in today, she'd managed to kick a toe into the corners, trying to make it look like absentminded pacing. But the creature could have evaded her easily; she could not shake the creepy feeling that it might be in here now.

She checked Jenny's gums and palpated the lymph nodes under her arms. No swelling—remarkable.

"Want to arm wrestle?" Katie asked.

Jenny gave her a "you're weird" smile, then saw she was serious. "Sure!"

Katie sat down on the other side of the bed table and Jenny leaned forward, planting her elbow and offering her hand. Katie took it, noting its healthy warmth, then gasped as Jenny jacked her arm over flat on the table.

"Oh," Jenny said. "I'm sorry, did I hurt you?"

Katie gazed at her astonished. "Have you been practicing that?"

"No."

Her mother stepped forward. "Are you all right, Doctor?"

"Oh, yes. Just surprised."

Ann gave Jenny a mock stern look. "Don't do that to any boy," she teased.

"Let's try it once more," Katie said. "Give me a second to get set." She braced her arm. Jenny started pushing and she could feel her forearm bending back despite everything she could do. Then, abruptly, Jenny's strength seemed to fade.

"You're too strong, Doctor O'Keefe," she said with a smile.

Katie wondered if she had held back on purpose.

"That's it for the exam," she said. "I'll just take one last sample of your blood—"

"Eeeee!" Jenny grimaced.

"Now you do what the doctor says," Ann said. "She saved your life."

"That's right," Katie said, "so don't give me none of your lip." She fitted a needle to a dry ten cc vacuum tube, found the vein at the crook of Jenny's elbow, and swabbed it with alcohol. The vein was nice and fat, pumped up from the arm wrestling. Despite her protest, Jenny watched with apparent fascination as the needle slipped in and the dark venous blood streamed into the tube. Katie taped a piece of gauze over the puncture. "Keep some pressure on that for a minute, while I talk to your mom and dad, okay?"

Out in the hall, Katie spoke in a low voice to the Hrluskas. "Jenny seems fine. I've never seen such a rapid recovery—in fact, it's so unusual that I think we should continue to keep a close eye on her.''

James Hrluska's happy expression faded a little. ''You think she might relapse?''

''There's no evidence of that, and I certainly don't want you to worry. Right now, she is in perfect health, with no sign of leukemia. I guess it's just my nature as a scientist to wonder how such a miracle could have happened. If I could understand it, maybe I could work it on some of my other patients.''

Ann took her hand. ''We'll watch her like a hawk. Doctor . . . thank you.'' Impulsively, Ann pulled her into a hug. Katie returned the hug, then felt Jenny's arms snaking around her, hugging her and her mom from the side.

''Hey, you were supposed to keep pressure on!''

''It stopped bleeding. I checked.''

Katie repositioned her arm to include Jenny in the three-way hug. It felt awkward but very nice. ''Thank you for everything, Doctor O'Keefe,'' Jenny said in a small voice.

Katie felt a lump rising to her throat. She pulled Jenny close in her own private hug, thinking, I love this kid so much. Giving her a final squeeze, Katie said, ''You'd better go, before I decide to keep you around to coach me on my arm wrestling.''

She watched Jenny and her parents until they stepped on the elevator. At the last moment, Jenny turned and gave her a little wave. Katie waved back, waiting until Jenny was gone to rub her shoulder. Jenny's surprising strength made her uneasy. What had she been doing, pumping iron in her room when no one was looking? She wasn't just fully recovered, she was stronger than she should be.

And the question was, what did the membrane on her blood cells have to do with that?

No, Katie thought. Jenny is fine. Her parents will watch her. The question is, can I find an agent that will break down the membrane on these blood cells? If I can, maybe the next time the killer comes around, I'll have a nasty surprise for him. For a second, she let herself imagine it—the killer grabbing her from nowhere, and then she would pull the loaded syringe from her pocket and plunge it into him, and turn his blood to sludge. The image gave her a fierce satisfaction.

But she was a long way from accomplishing it.

Katie took the sample of blood down to her lab. As she entered the room where the killer had held a knife to her throat, her fear surged again. The slide she'd taken yesterday shortly before the creature had attacked her still sat on the stage of the light microscope. One look through the eyepiece told her that the blood had dried out. There was no longer any sign of the membrane. A pink Post-it note stuck to the tabletop beside the microscope bore a cryptic message from Art: "via after 4 hr., cren at 5." So yesterday's sample had remained fresh between four and five hours. That meant she should have at least a couple of hours to try and break down the membrane on the new sample before it began to deteriorate on its own.

With a silent thank you to Art for following up, Katie took the new sample into the small chamber that housed the electron microscopes. After she closed the door and put the blood on the workbench, she picked up a mop she kept in the corner for spills, held the handle in front of her, and walked around the small room, probing and listening. She poked the mop handle under the work bench and into the cabinets, thrust it into the corners and used it to sweep the tops of a bank of files. Finally, satisfied she was alone, she locked the door and put the mop back.

Quickly she prepared a slide from the new sample of Jenny's blood. Step one was to verify that the membrane was present. It would wilt under the flow of electrons, but she had plenty more blood in the test tube. Katie powered up the scope, placed the slide, and looked into the viewing screen.

The membrane was there all right. She gazed at it, waiting for it to break down. Maybe seeing it happen would give her a clue about how to attack the blood. She watched for five minutes. The membrane remained. Under the electron scope yesterday, hadn't it disintegrated after less than two minutes? With growing uneasiness, she continued to watch. At fifteen minutes, the membrane still showed no sign of breaking up.

Something had changed Jenny's blood once again.

Katie felt a sharp foreboding touched with awe. Though she'd seen it once already with the killer's blood, it was impossible not to feel impressed all over again. A thousand kilovolts, she thought.

She sat back from the scope, trying to understand. Jenny's blood was no longer merely similar to the killer's, it was the same. Why?

A soft rap on the door made her jump. "Who is it?"

"Art."

The voice was muffled by the steel door. She had to be sure. "What does GVH stand for?" she asked.

"Graft versus host disease. And the Detroit Tigers won the

1968 World Series. Come on, Katie, open up—I've got something important to tell you.''

She unlocked the door and managed a sheepish smile for him.

Instead of smiling back, he looked worried. "Are you all right?"

"Sure. Before I released Jenny this morning, I took a new sample from her. Want a peek?"

He glanced into the viewer. She was glad to see him, even if he was interrupting. "Our friend the membrane," he said.

"Art, it's been in there for fifteen—make that seventeen—minutes."

He frowned. "What the hell?"

"Exactly."

"And you released her?"

"Had to. Hospitals are for sick people, in case you haven't noticed. What did you want to tell me?"

"Not tell, show."

Katie glanced at the tube of Jenny's blood. The membrane was now impervious. She no longer had to race the clock to break it down before it dissolved on its own. But time was still against her, as long as she had no weapon against the killer.

"Ten minutes," Art promised.

With a chill, she remembered what had happened the last time he had promised that. But she said, "All right."

She walked with him through the steam tunnel that led, under a sidewalk, from the hospital to the biolab annex. When it sank into her where they were going, she began to feel a low excitement. In the lab, Art walked straight to the cage of the mouse she'd injected two days ago with Fraction Eight. Carefully, he lifted the mouse from its cage. She stared at it, hardly daring to believe what she saw. The mouse was hunched and grizzled. In just under twenty-four hours, the pink skin of its nose had turned dry and brittle. Two days ago, the mouse had been young. Today it was old.

"Hallelujah!" Katie shouted.

Half an hour later, after she'd learned all she was going to from an external exam of the mouse, Katie sat with Art in the tiny canteen just off the biolab. She was still thrilled about Fraction Eight, but the membrane on Jenny's red blood cells was already dragging her back down like a huge counterweight. If she didn't find a way to fight back against the killer, she might not be around to see if Fraction Eight really panned out.

"This is a fine place," Art said, "for a future Nobel prize winner to be celebrating—surrounded by brooding vending machines."

"Art, people don't get Nobels for curing extremely rare diseases. And let's not get ahead of ourselves. This is great, fantastic. It suggests that something in Rebecca's blood *is* contributing to her rapid aging—"

"Suggests?"

"We have to look at the mouse's cells to verify aging. Maybe Fraction Eight just made the mouse sick."

"Come on, Katie, that mouse went from young to old in forty-eight hours. You know the difference between a toxified rat and an old one. We'll do a cell biopsy, of course, but that mouse is now a senior citizen, I'm telling you."

"What if it turns out to be a nonfilterable virus—something we can't detect with any known methods and can't remove from Rebecca's blood through dialysis?"

"We take more fractions and treat them until they don't cause aging in mice. We don't necessarily have to identify or even filter the agent, Katie, just neutralize it. And, Jesus Christ, none of that matters right now. That comes tomorrow and next week. Right now you should be the happiest woman on earth!"

She smiled, feeling just a little of it. "I should, shouldn't I?"

Art sighed. "What's wrong, Katie?"

She longed to tell him. More than anything, she did not want to go back to her lab alone. But if she told Art everything she knew about the creature, she might be sealing Art's death warrant. The creature had already shown that it considered the facts about its blood dangerous. The less Art knew beyond that, the better. She said, "I'm happy about Fraction Eight, really I am. But we've had so many failures. I just want to be sure, okay?"

"If you say so."

She took a sip of her Dr Pepper, lingering, not wanting this moment to fade, though she felt the pressure of time passing. Even if something happens to me, she thought, Art can see Fraction Eight through from here.

But I want to be around to see Rebecca stop aging.

"We'll start tomorrow," she said. "I need to finish up with Jenny's cells today. While I'm working, I'll think about our next steps with Fraction Eight. You do the same. We'll compare notes in the morning.'' Reluctantly, Katie started to get up.

Art leaned forward. ''Katie, before you go, there's something else I need to tell you. I was on my way to do that when I got sidetracked by the mouse.''

She settled back again, glad for a moment more of his company. He glanced down at his hands, looking suddenly uncomfortable. ''Did you know Merrick Chapman used to live in San Francisco?''

''Sure. Why?''

''Well, you know I'm from out that way. I have a buddy in the area who's in the NIS—Naval Investigative Service. I asked him to do some checking for me—''

Katie felt a rush of indignation. ''Damn it, Art, that was out of line.'' She stood again but he caught her arm.

''I *know* it was,'' he said urgently. ''I'm sorry. But you've got to listen to me now. It's very important.''

She stayed standing, wanting to walk out, but not quite able to.

''Merrick still owns a house out there,'' Art said quickly. ''The first time my buddy approached to check the place, a caretaker ran him off. He came back later and was able to get inside. No one was home, but it was fully furnished and looked lived in. There were photos of a woman and young boy on an end table. My buddy pulled the woman's photo out of the frame to see if he could find a photographer's stamp. He found another photo sandwiched inside, between the one that was showing and the backing of the frame. It was of Merrick and the same woman.''

Katie shrugged off a pang of jealousy. So what if Merrick had been with another woman out there? That was twelve years ago. What did Art think he was proving?

''Before my friend could get any further,'' Art went on, ''he heard someone coming and had to hurry out, but he took the second photo with him. He faxed a copy of it to me.''

Art took two pieces of paper from the pocket of his lab coat and slid one across the table. It showed Merrick and a good-looking woman with dark hair. Their heads were very close together and they were smiling. Katie's heart sank. The woman's hairstyle was a bit old-fashioned, but there was nothing old about her—she looked around twenty-five. More importantly, Merrick didn't look a day younger than he had this morning.

This photo wasn't from twelve years ago, not from Merrick's past. It was from his present.

''This was on the back of the photo,'' Art said in a low

voice, sliding the second piece of paper across the small round table.

At first Katie saw nothing on it. Then she noticed the writing down in one corner. The fax transmission had degraded it, but not so much that she couldn't read it: *To my dear Alexandra on our fourth anniversary, Love, Merrick.*

Katie sank into her chair, staring at the words "fourth anniversary," impossibly, damnably, in Merrick's own hand. The scrawled message of love for another woman battered at her, crumbling her sense of reality; showing her a new and darker one. No, she thought. No. But the words only sank their teeth deeper into her. *Merrick, married.*

She looked up at Art, aching, furious. "Why did you do this? Did you think it would win me over?"

"No." Art looked miserable. "I could tell in the cafeteria the other day that wasn't going to happen, because you still love Merrick. You may not believe this, but I liked him myself. I only wanted to be sure, before I bowed out, that you wouldn't end up hurt by him. I wish to God this photo didn't exist, Katie. But it does. It looks like Merrick has a wife and kid in California."

"I don't believe it."

Art reached a hand toward her, drew it back. "I'm sorry. I'm so sorry."

Katie felt a dim pain in her fingers and realized she was gripping the sharp edge of the table with desperate force. She couldn't seem to let go.

Would Art have faked the photo? No, never.

There must be some other explanation. Merrick had never tried to hide the fact that he'd lived in California before he came to Washington. Maybe this woman and the boy had died in an accident, and it was too painful for Merrick to talk about. It would explain his ambivalence about Gregory. . . .

No. Merrick had been on the Washington police force for twelve years and his face in the picture was not twelve years younger. Katie felt ill. Was the whole universe going to turn on its head? So much all at once, she couldn't deal with it, she wouldn't—

"I'm going to resign my residency," Art said.

Katie stared at him, not sure she'd heard. "What?"

"I'll find a new position. If I have to repeat a year, so be it."

Katie took a deep breath, tried to concentrate. She was furious at Art, but she could not let him resign. "You don't realize what you're saying. What hospital will want you if they know you walked out on a residency?''

"I'll tell them I fell in love with you."

Katie stared at him. "Yes, and? . . .''

"And you either didn't love me or wouldn't let yourself because I was your resident, and that either way, the best thing for me to do was remove myself from the situation.''

"If you think any residency committee will think that's an adequate reason for quitting, you're crazy—just plain nuts!''

"You're angry with me right now. I understand.''

"I'm mad as hell at you, but I won't let you do something so *stupid!*''

"It's my decision, not yours.''

"Shit!'' Katie yelled.

Art gave her a little smile. "I believe that's the first time I ever heard you swear.''

"Don't tempt me!'' she shouted. "And don't even think about resigning.'' *Merrick Chapman has a wife and kid in California.* Katie's face felt hot with humiliation. How could Merrick have deceived her so thoroughly? He'd played her for a world-class fool. He hadn't wanted to be a family with her and Gregory, because he already had a family. He must be flying to the coast on his days off. What was he telling this other woman and son? That he was FBI or CIA? A traveling salesman?

What did it matter? Merrick was lost to her, and she was about to lose the only other man she cared about.

And, somehow, she had to find the strength to go back to her lab and get to work.

Katie thought of the drug cabinet at the nurses station.

TWENTY-EIGHT

STANDING BELOW THE Hrluskas' bedroom window, Zane reached up mentally to Ann and her husband. Their slow, metronomic pulses told him both were asleep. Only ten-thirty, but they'd had a big day, hadn't they? *Taking my daughter home with them.*

The sly stab of jealousy surprised Zane. For twelve years, Jenny had been a normal, and he could hardly begrudge the Hrluskas that time with her. But now she had been born again. Thank you very much, Ann and James, but I'm Jenny's father now, and it's time she started getting to know me.

Projecting Influence into the bedroom above, Zane constricted the carotid arteries and brain stems of the two sleeping adults, plunging them into a deeper unconsciousness that would not wear off before morning. They and the dog could sleep in tomorrow but he had work to do—wonderful work!

Zane turned his attention to Jenny's window. The glass he'd

broken last time had been repaired; though the night was cool, the window was open a couple of inches. She's like me, he thought, pleased—she doesn't like to feel cooped up. He shinnied up the drainpipe. On the roof, he lay still, tuning himself to his daughter's blood flow. She was awake, he could tell. Her pulse had the quick, fluttery rhythms of sudden alarm. Though he had been very quiet, she must have heard him. This further evidence of her sharpening instincts pleased him even more. ·

Reaching mentally into the rich network of blood vessels in her brain stem, he soothed them, shunting blood away until she had drifted into a dreamlike stupor. He held her there as he walked across the roof to a spot above her window. Slipping his legs over the edge, he dropped from the roof, caught her sill, and chinned himself so he could look in at her. She lay on her bed, facing him, her eyes half closed. They opened wide for a second when she saw him, but he adjusted the blood flow and the alarm faded from her face. She gazed at him with a vague interest. Keeping hold of the sill with one hand, he eased her window up and slipped inside.

Jenny sat up slowly and dangled her legs from the edge of her high bed. "Detective Chapman," she said drowsily. "What are you doing here?"

Zane controlled his irritation. He *did* look like Father, whom Jenny must have seen many times as he checked to make sure she was dying. And her brain was muddled right now.

"I'm not Detective Chapman, Jenny dear," he said. "But I know him." Gently, he took her hands. He longed to hug her to him, but she was just at the level of consciousness he needed right now. Too much physical stimulation might wake her.

And he must not move too fast emotionally, either.

"Who are you?" Jenny mumbled, gazing sleepily at him.

"I'm someone like you. I understand everything you've been through."

"You had leukemia, too?"

"Not just leukemia, the same special kind you had. I was hungry all the time, and no one could help me. Then someone did and I got better very fast, just as you have done."

Jenny smiled. "Is that why you always came to see me?"

"I'm not—" Zane suppressed his annoyance a second time. "Jenny, I am not Detective Chapman. I look like him because he and I are related. And you are related to me."

Her jaw dropped open. "I am?"

"Yes."

"Are you my uncle?"

An overwhelming impulse swept Zane. "I am your father." At once, he saw it was a mistake.

Jenny's brow furrowed. "No. My father is in there." She pointed to her parents' bedroom. "Why are you lying to me?"

Feeling her blood starting to race, he clamped down on her— too hard, catching her as she sagged over. Flustered, he sat with her, working her slowly back to the awake but dreamy state he needed. Her eyes opened and she peered at him with a dull suspicion. He tried desperately to think. He must not stumble again, or tonight's opportunity would be lost. He could affect her levels of perception and consciousness indirectly through her blood flow. He could ease an adrenaline rush of alarm that way, but her thoughts and convictions were beyond his reach. If she decided he was dangerous, that judgment might stick even in the morning, when she woke up thinking all this had been a dream.

How can I *reach* her?

He looked around her room for inspiration and found it in her bookcase. "You sure have a lot of books."

"I like to read."

He pulled out the well-worn book he'd seen last time. It had a regal-looking king on the cover, holding the hand of a young girl dressed as a princess. He held the book up to her. "Remember this story?"

Her expression softened. "Sure. It's my favorite."

"I could tell." He ran his finger along the worn binding and she smiled. "How many times have you read it?"

"Oh, seven or eight."

"What's it about?"

"It's about this girl in an orphanage who was stolen away from her real parents when she was a baby, and she goes through all this grief and then she finds out her father is really a king. He finds her and takes her home and she becomes a princess."

Zane felt as though the heavens had opened up and smiled on him. Probably a common theme in fantasies for young girls, but tonight it seemed fated. He touched his daughter's hand. "Jenny, you are like that princess. Deep inside, you've always felt that, haven't you?"

She gave a slight nod, but he saw the fascination in her eyes and knew he was on the right track now. She's thought about it, he realized. On some unconscious level, she knows that paunchy bald man in the other room is *not* her father.

He said, "I am like the king in this book. I am very powerful and wealthy. After you were conceived, but before you were born, I was forced to flee from here or be killed. It is still dangerous for me here, but I have come back for you. You don't have to do anything yet. Just let me help you. I'll come and visit you at night in your dreams, like tonight. Sometimes I'll bring the special wine for you to drink, like I did at the hospital. Soon, I'll explain about the wine. I'll explain everything and when you feel ready you can decide. You *are* a princess, Jenny. When you join me, there will be nothing you can't have—diamonds, money, a fine place of your own. You'll never be sick or afraid again. I will protect you always. . . ."

Jenny looked at him with wonder, and then a shadow of unease crossed her face. "I dream I'm killing people. It's scary."

"I know," he said, "but your dreams are normal. They are good. Don't be afraid of them. Soon, I'll show you what they mean."

"There's this one person I dream I'm killing," she said. "And I *want* to do it."

Wonderful! he thought. "Tell me about that."

She hesitated.

"Jenny, you can say *anything* to me. You can never be bad in my eyes. Please tell me."

She looked down at her hands. "When I was in the hospital, I dreamed that this man came into my room and . . . touched me. He told me he'd kill me if I told anyone. I dream I'm killing him. And it's . . . fun."

Zane felt a touch of foreboding. "Describe this man."

"He wore white. He was kind of big and he had short hair. He had this funny jacket, with snaps along here, like my dentist's."

Zane realized with a shock that she was describing the orderly who'd started to come into her room early that morning a few days ago. It was not a dream. The swine had molested her, then threatened her! Rage burned through Zane. A filthy normal, preying on his magnificent daughter. You are a dead man, he thought. You will find out how "helpless" my daughter is, as soon as I can make her ready.

He took Jenny's hands. "You are becoming something strong and wonderful now. No one will ever be able to hurt you again. I will help you punish the man in your dream. You must trust me. . . ."

He felt her waking up. Worried, he intensified his Influence, and for a second her veins constricted, then they dilated again. A cold alarm rushed through him. Was she this strong already? No, it couldn't be. But it was—he was having trouble now, keeping her in the hypnotic state; if she woke up fully, she'd be terrified. *Get out!*

He sprang to her window and dived through, landing on the grass below. Looking back, he saw Jenny at the window, her eyes wide with fear. Using all his power, he blanked himself from her eyes. Then he glimpsed movement above her on the roof.

Father!

With a flash of rage, he understood. Jenny was not resisting him, Merrick had interfered, had projected his own Influence into Jenny's arteries to awaken her.

Zane ran to the drainpipe, scaling it in seconds. When he gained the roof again, he saw Merrick edging away at the opposite end. He struck out mentally, reaching for the memories, but Merrick leapt down from the roof. Zane found Jenny again and squeezed down carefully on her brain stem, enough to put her to sleep. She would awaken later, slumped at the window, thinking she'd walked in her sleep.

Enraged, he ran across the peak of the roof to the other side. Merrick had run over the front lawn and across the road. Zane leapt down, rolled, and sprang up running, trying to catch up. As Merrick disappeared into the woods, Zane put on an extra burst of speed, determined not to let him get away. Entering the woods, he was slowed by the uneven forest floor, treacherous with rocks and fallen branches. He could see Merrick up ahead through the trees, running with greater sureness. He must have staked out his route, studied the ground in advance. Zane slipped on a wet spot and went down; he sprang up at once, but he had lost ground. He could still hear his father ahead, but could no longer see him. As he tried to pick up the direction of the sound, it faded entirely.

Zane wanted to scream with frustration. *Don't ever come near my daughter again. I'll kill you, I swear I'll bury you. I'll cut your woman. I wasn't going to let her feel it, but now I will— I'll make her scream, and I'll make you watch.*

Zane heard the growl of a car engine starting up. He turned and ran out of the woods to his own car, parked in the undeveloped lot across from Jenny's house. Gunning the engine, he sped to the nearest corner and turned, skirting the patch of woods, hoping to cut Merrick off on the other side. As he neared the intersection, Merrick's car sped across in front of him, heading back toward Washington. Zane restrained an impulse to floor the accelerator—Merrick was driving a high-powered police cruiser;

there was no chance of overtaking him in this rental car.

Turning through the intersection, Zane pulled off the road and watched Merrick's taillights until the car vanished over the next rise. Is he trying to draw me off from Jenny, Zane wondered, so he can come back and take her?

No. He's running. He's scared of me.

Zane felt a savage grin break his rigid mask of fury.

But if he's so scared, why did he try to take Jenny while I was with her?

Zane's smile faded in confusion. I almost caught him tonight, he thought. If I hadn't been so preoccupied with Jenny, I might have heard him on the roof and taken him before he even got to her. What did he hope to gain that would justify such a risk?

Why would he care about waking up Jenny and making her afraid of me if all he wants is to grab her and bury her?

Maybe he doesn't want to bury her.

Stunned, Zane stared at the dark country road: Why didn't I see this before? He wants to take Jenny away so he can raise her himself. He couldn't make his son over in his own image, so now he wants to try it with his granddaughter. What a snake! When he didn't know Jenny was my daughter, he was happy to let her die. But once he understood who she was, he saw a chance to refight the battle he lost five hundred years ago. He thinks he can use her to vindicate himself—and punish me.

Zane did not know whether to be furious or relieved. With savage exultation, he realized what a huge miscalculation Father had made. To win Jenny over would take time, and time was the one thing Father wasn't going to have. He'll have to leave her with her parents for now, Zane thought, just as I'm doing. He would need to make a number of careful approaches to her, just as I must. I missed him tonight, but if he keeps coming, I'll catch him and bury him before he can get anywhere with Jenny.

And the stalemate is over! I can go after him and Katie tonight without worrying. Even if he doubles back on Jenny, he can't win her over in a night.

Zane pulled onto the road and headed back toward Washington, savoring his victory. The balance had shifted his way. Even better, Father had run from him! How good that felt. For almost nine centuries Merrick had been the alpha phage, more powerful than any other. Now he knew what it was to be afraid.

Turning onto Katie's street, Zane stopped the car and peered up the block toward her house. A slight movement in the bushes in front caught his eye. There—two shadowy figures crouching down behind the raggedy hedge. A couple of cops. Zane smiled contemptuously. No doubt they thought the darkness was hiding them. Clouds covered the moon, and it *was* quite dark, but only if you had the frail eyesight of a normal.

One of the figures shifted and Zane glimpsed the bulky outline of a high-powered rifle. It sobered him a little. A gun like that could definitely slow him down—but first the fool had to get him in his sights, and that wasn't going to happen.

But what were all these police doing here? Surely Father knew they would be ineffective.

And where was Father? His car was not out front.

Curious, Zane slipped from the car and trotted down the street, staying in the shadows, alert for the ripple of nerve that would signal someone had spotted him. He circled into the backyard, moving soundlessly, seeing more men crouched behind the hedge that bordered the rear of Katie's property. Peering up at the roof, he saw that the shingles had been repaired where he went in last night. Someone was no doubt watching the roof tonight—

Movement caught his eye—Katie stepping into the lighted square of her bedroom window. . . .

No, not Katie.

Zane almost laughed out loud. He had to give them credit. She did resemble Katie somewhat—a little chunkier, in her bulletproof vest.

He slipped back down the street to his car. Driving past her house, he counted four more men in unmarked cars. Have fun, you silly sheep, he thought.

His amusement faded as he turned back down toward M Street. He should have guessed that, after his raid last night, Katie would no longer be at home. If she were, Father would have been there with the normals, knowing he couldn't trust them to keep her safe. No, he'd bundled her and her kid off somewhere he thought was out of danger.

Which was why he'd felt free to come visit Jenny.

Not very sporting, Zane thought. You know where Jenny is, but I don't know where Katie is. I don't even know where to start looking.

Annoyed and uncertain, Zane slowed the car. It was now almost midnight. Even if Katie had gone to the hospital today, surely she wouldn't still be there.

On other hand, he had no better place to look.

* * *

Too tired to be frightened, Katie sat on the narrow bed in the on-call room, looking at the five Ritalin capsules in her hand. A fierce hunger for them battled with a weariness so strong that part of her longed just to close her eyes and drop into sleep.

If only she could be sure she'd be safe here.

She glanced around the room. Nine feet long and only a few feet wider than its door, it felt smaller to her than it had during her residency. She was glad it was small—a sweep of her arm under the bed, a quick march into the corners and she could be sure she was alone.

Trouble was, there was no lock on the door—the nursing staff had made sure of that. Exhausted residents grabbing a 3:00 A.M. nap often required a good shaking to get them up, and that could not be done from the other side of a locked door. She would have to rely on the sound of the latch, and it wasn't very noisy. It wouldn't be hard for the creature to slip in without waking her.

But first it had to find her. She had asked the nursing staff to tell no one she was in here. Unless the thing approached the station and heard them talking among themselves about the chief of Hematology who'd chosen to spend the night in a lowly resident on-call room, she should be safe enough.

Katie found herself longing for the simpler times of her residency, when her worst difficulty had been the patient in 301 or a night call in Emergency.

And that "little" problem with amphetamines.

She looked at the capsules again. A sweat had sprung up on her palm, and they were starting to stick to her skin. Her residency, yes—until the past week, she had been sure those had been the most difficult years of her life.

Oh, Merrick.

Katie's eyes began to fill with tears. Desperately, she brushed them away. She could not bear to think about Merrick, must not think about him, or she would use up every reserve she had.

Carefully, Katie picked the five capsules from her sweating palm and put them on the small stand beside the bed, hiding them under a tissue. She would just lie down now, get four or five hours sleep, so she could go back to the lab. . . .

How could Merrick be so deceitful? Everything she had felt for him was based on a lie. All the times she was with him, and for the last two years, when she couldn't get back on track because of how she felt about him. All wasted—

Stop it!

Katie closed her eyes and smoothed the lids, feeling an answering burn of fatigue. Nearly midnight, almost twelve straight hours in the lab, and still no solution. Maybe her subconscious would come up with something while she slept. She had to find a way to break down that membrane—something that would go inside a syringe.

But what hadn't she tried? She'd run through every hematological reagent she had in stock, then branched out to alcohol, bleach from the hospital laundry, ammonia from Housekeeping, hydrogen peroxide, chlorine, plumbing liquids, cleaning compounds; she'd worked her way through the acids and bases from the chemistry lab at the other end of the corridor—nitric acid, hydrochloric, acetic, potassium permanganate—everything they had that was or might be caustic. Any one of the agents would have destroyed a normal blood cell and wreaked havoc if injected into the bloodstream.

None had had the slightest effect on Jenny's blood.

Katie leaned back against the metal headboard of the bed, too exhausted to think about it anymore. An image of Gregory popped into her mind. Remembering his sweet, high voice on the phone, she closed her eyes to keep the tears back. The phone on the bed table beckoned, and she reached for it, then realized Gregory would have been in bed hours ago.

She started to let her eyes close, then forced herself up and to the door. Turning the knob several times, she mentally recorded its sound. If you hear this, wake up, she told herself firmly. Back at the bed, she started to sit, and then everything blurred and dissolved into darkness. She had a dim sense of falling, and then of someone catching her. . . .

TWENTY-NINE

KATIE FELT SO sleepy she could barely think. She'd been falling, but someone had caught her and put her on her bed. She saw a blurred face above her—tanned forehead, thick brown hair. He was as beautiful as an angel.

I must be dreaming, she thought.

The creature moved above her like a giant, gorgeous moth, and she realized he was taking off his shirt, arms rising, fanning out and dropping again. Something plucked at the buttons of her lab coat. She felt it sliding away between her body and the bed, a strange, erotic sensation. She heard distant sounds—the clink of a belt buckle, the tap of her shoes falling to the floor.

So warm in here. She felt totally, gloriously relaxed. Above her, the beautiful man in her dream looked down. His dark eyes burned with a hot passion for her. She let her eyes slip shut again. A hand, large and warm, caressed her bare breast with an infinite gentleness, and she felt her nipples swell and harden under the silky touch of his fingers. Wonderful sensations flooded her, a ripple of nerve over her stomach, strong, gentle fingers sliding her thighs open across the sheets, the marvelous hands encircling her buttocks and lifting her toward him. She heard a soft gasp and realized it was her own. She opened her eyes again and saw him above her. Darkness pooled in his eyes, and for a second she was scared, then his hands enfolded hers and held them to his smooth, hard thighs and her blood surged and she felt more powerfully aroused than she had ever been in her life. She wished he would lean down to kiss her but he stayed back, tall and upright above her. She rocked her hips, wanting him to slide in, but he did not. She felt him pulling back. Focusing on his face again, she saw that his expression had gone cold.

Fear welled up in her as he backed away.

Then another tide of well-being washed through her; she could feel every cell of her sipping at it. She could no longer see the dark angel, but the wonderful sensations he had started in her had gone too far to stop. Her own blood caressed her, blood flowing into her most intimate folds, swelling them with pleasure. She gasped again as the golden silky feeling spread up through her, encircling her with warmth. Well-being passed through her like a warm ocean wave bubbling away gently around her feet. She lay still, gazing up at the sun in the molten sky, feeling the cradling sand beneath her back. For a second, the sun looked like a light recessed in the ceiling, then it became a sun again before fading away into darkness in which the pain at her throat was only a pinprick. . . .

Perched in a corner of the ceiling, arms angled out along its junction with two walls, his foot propped on the door lintel, Zane gazed down at Katie. He was still erect, engorged with blood. The thwarted urge to enter her hammered inside him. How easy it would be to drop down now and finish what he had started, take her in her sleep. How glorious to slip inside her, feel her smooth legs around him.

Could I take her and still kill her? he wondered.

No, I couldn't.

Exasperated, Zane silently cursed the invisible barrier that constrained him. What caused it? Damn it, he did not go inside women for love—it was purely physical. Surely, he felt nothing for them, nothing at all. And yet, in five hundred years, he had never been able to kill a women he'd had sex with. Taking his pleasure with Katie now was too high a price if it kept him from killing her. And die she must.

Zane stared down at her, deliberately goading himself with her loveliness. He found his gaze straying to Katie's throat and quickly looked away. Even though he'd pulled a loop of sheet around it to cover it, he was better off avoiding all thought of the twin puncture marks, the twin rivulets of blood. Gazing at her bare skin, pale as alabaster, he thought what a special beauty it had—flesh that had given up blood. He could feel the warmth of the two transfusion packs nestled between his shirt and chest. Sealed away from the spoiling touch of air, the blood would stay fresh for awhile. If he could get back to Jenny before it started to clot, they would drink together—

Stop it!

With a sigh, Katie rolled onto her back; for a second Zane was afraid the sheet would come away from her throat, but it did not. If he could cover her more fully . . . but he did not want that. It was important she wake up naked. She must be afraid, panicked, for the rest of his plan to work.

Zane glanced at the phone on her bed table, making sure he had a good view of its numbered keys. Father had tried to hide Katie and the child away, but it wasn't going to work. You'll call home, won't you, Katie? When you wake up, you'll see the marks on your throat and you'll wonder if I got to your son, too. You'll have to call, and then I'll have you both.

Katie awoke slowly, feeling a chill on her skin. Her watch, on the bed table, said 8:27 A.M. She knew she should get up, but she was still so tired. She reached for the covers, but there were no covers. As her hand brushed her bare shoulder, she realized she was naked.

Alarm flooded her and she sat up with a gasp. *Where am I?*

The on-call room, yes. Fragments of a dream clung to her, but she could not put them back together. Why was she naked? She had planned to sleep in her underwear, but she could not even remember undressing that far.

Confused and afraid, she stepped over to the tiny washbasin. In the mirror above it, she saw two scabs on her throat, round and red, each surrounded by a ring of bruise. Horror welled up in her. Doubling over, she threw up in the sink, heaving until her stomach was empty. Weak and shaken, she clung to the rim of the sink. *It found me last night. It drank my blood.*

She fumbled the faucet on, splashed water on her face, and washed her throat, careful not to break the scabs. Turning back to the bed, she snatched up her clothes and pulled them on. Though the room was warm, her teeth began to chatter.

Gregory! she thought. Did it find Mom and Gregory, too?

In an agony of fear, she reached for the phone, then hesitated. What if the thing was still in here? She grabbed the mop from the corner and hurried around the room, jabbing it into the corners, lashing the tiles under the bed, clenching her teeth with each thrust. But the mop handle swung freely, finding nothing.

She dropped the mop and punched in Meggan's number. She felt a light draft on her neck, a sudden, subtle change in the room's air, then her mother answered.

"Are you all right?" Katie asked.

"Yes, we're fine. How about you?"

Katie's racing heart subsided a little. "I'm all right. I . . . I just wanted to check."

"Are you coming back this morning?"

For a second, Katie actually considered it. No. She must get back to the lab now, find a way to break down that membrane—it was more important than ever.

"I'll call you and let you know," she said.

After she hung up the phone, she sat on the bed and pressed her hands against her face, fighting for control. Somewhere out there the thing was walking around with her blood in it. She had to fight back, but the thought of going alone to her lab now terrified her.

If she called Merrick—

No! You can't trust Merrick anymore.

Art, she thought desperately. Maybe Art would come down with me. He could help me think, give me ideas. And I wouldn't be alone. He'll be on duty this morning. . . .

Unless he really did resign his residency.

Katie started out of the on-call room, then went back for the amphetamines. As she picked them up, she felt a flash of despair at her weakness. I won't take them, she thought. Not unless I have no choice.

As Merrick approached Captain Rourke's office, he knew he should be planning for the coming confrontation with Lieutenant Cooke. Instead, all he could think of was Katie. Something was wrong there. Twice now he'd called Meggan's, and both times Katie had not answered the phone. According to Audrey, the first time she'd been out walking with Gregory, and the second she'd taken Meggan's car to a nearby country store. Possible, certainly, but there had been that strained note in Audrey's voice. She was not a good liar.

Why doesn't Katie want to talk to me? Merrick wondered. Is she angry because I pressed her to stay at Meggan's instead of going in to the hospital?

Or did she actually go in?

No, he thought. She said she wouldn't, and she has never lied to me. . . .

At the door to Captain Rourke's office, Merrick realized the squad room was dead silent behind him. His stomach knotted. In the next minute, he would have one last chance to avert disaster. He must not take it.

He opened the door and stepped through. Dr. Byner stood at one corner of the desk, tapping his fingers restlessly. Rourke sat back in his chair with a glum expression, while Cooke perched on the edge of his seat across the desk.

"Good morning," Merrick said.

Byner and Rourke said good morning; Lieutenant Cooke gave him a quick, condescending nod.

Merrick wanted to knock him down again, to kill him. It was all right to want it. But he was not going to do it. Dread raised a metallic taste in his throat, as if someone were forcing a blade down it. Byner was going to tell Cooke about the blood now. Rourke would be furious that Merrick had never told him. At first it would seem under control—an official reprimand for withholding evidence, reassignment to another case. Then it would get into the papers, because Cooke loved headlines and would like nothing better than to be the cop in charge of chasing a vampire killer with "supernatural" blood. People would want to scoff, but Cooke would have a chief pathologist and a top blood expert to back him up. And the question of why Lieutenant Merrick Chapman had tried to suppress the evidence would get played up instead of fading. Cooke might like to lead that charge himself. Inquiries into Chapman's background would reveal a faked birth certificate; someone would try to get ahold of the lieutenant's medical records and would find out those were faked, too, that he'd managed to evade ever having a blood test himself. They would demand one, and then he would be running, not just from Zane, but from everyone he'd tried to make his friend. . . .

"Chapman?" Rourke prompted.

Merrick realized that Byner and Cooke were both looking expectantly at him. He could either start briefing Cooke now or kill the man. It's him or me, Merrick thought.

No. It's his life or my *way* of life.

A strange, fatalistic calm settled over Merrick. What good would the company of normals be if he could not stand his own?

"We'll start with the first murder," he said to Cooke. He summarized his investigation up to the point where the two patrolmen guarding Katie's house had been knocked out. He covered the invasion of the house as quickly as possible.

Before he could press on, Cooke said, "So where is Doctor O'Keefe now?"

Merrick felt Rourke's hard gaze on him. "Doctor O'Keefe asked that I tell no one where she is."

"Screw that," Cooke said. "Your duty is to me and this department. If the killer finds her and cuts her throat, and we aren't protecting her even though we know he's tried it once already, how do you think it will look in the papers?"

"How will it look if I tell and someone leaks it and the killer finds her because of that?"

"That's not your decision anymore, Chapman. It's mine." Cooke glanced at Rourke. Finding no visible support there, he glared at Merrick. "Doctor O'Keefe and her kid are witnesses, Merrick. It happens that I'm not satisfied with your questioning. I want their phone number."

"I can't give you that."

Cooke slapped the arm of his chair. "I won't have you defying me and the department out of some misguided notion that you're protecting your old girlfriend. Everyone here knows you two were lovers. You're probably still screwing her—"

Oh, you foolish man, Merrick thought wearily. He did what was expected, standing and taking a step toward Cooke, who flinched back in his chair, then rocketed to his feet, too.

"Sit down you two!" Rourke snapped.

Merrick eased back into his chair and Cooke did the same.

"Let's leave the matter of where Doctor O'Keefe is hiding until the end," Rourke said.

Cooke shot him an annoyed glance. "Captain—"

"Doctor Byner needs to get back to his work," Rourke said. "Why don't we hear from him, then he can be on his way and we'll settle this other thing."

Here it comes, Merrick thought.

Byner started talking, going over his reports, obviously saving the blood until last.

"Anything else?" Cooke asked, when Byner had finished going over the information in his reports.

"Nothing," Byner said evenly.

Merrick's heart leapt. He wasn't going to tell Cooke about the blood!

But why?

"All right," Rourke said. "Thanks, Doc."

Byner nodded and walked out without a word.

Cooke turned to Merrick. "Now, are you going to tell me where I can reach Doctor O'Keefe?"

"Go to hell," Merrick said.

Cooke turned back to Rourke. "I want this bastard off the case."

Rourke sighed. "You are off the case, Merrick. I'm putting you on leave with pay, pending a disciplinary hearing for insubordination."

"Right," Merrick said. He got up and walked out, catching up with Byner in the parking lot as the pathologist was sliding into his long, black Chrysler. Merrick leaned on the roof and Byner rolled down the window. "You wanted something?"

"I appreciate your not telling Cooke about the blood," Merrick said. "But if he finds out some other way, you could lose your job."

"How's he going to find out? You? Doctor O'Keefe?"

Merrick looked at him, baffled. "But you wanted to bring in more help. You fought me on keeping it under wraps."

"Do you still think it should be kept under wraps?" Byner asked.

"Yes."

"Then that's good enough for me. Doctor O'Keefe may not find anything that will help us. If she does, I will take it to Cooke and if they want my job, they can have it. I've been thinking of getting out anyway and reading slides for some nice private partnership."

"Come on, you love your work. Why else would anyone stay in it as long as you have?"

A small smile curled the corner of Byner's mouth. "You really don't get it, do you?"

"No," Merrick said helplessly.

"You're a good, decent human being, Merrick, and a hell of a cop. You treat people with kindness and respect, you work hard and you're clean of any corruption. You don't just help out your fellow cops, you help look out for their kids. Forget that bastard Cooke. This department is full of people who respect you, like you, owe you, and would go to the ends of the earth for you. I am one of them. Now, if you wouldn't mind, I need to get back to work.''

Speechless, Merrick watched Byner's car pull out of the lot and disappear up the street. The black Chrysler was strangely blurred. Merrick felt an incredible sense of lightness and exhilaration, as if his chest were filled with helium and his feet would lift from the pavement. He put his career on the line for me, Merrick thought. *This department is full of people who would go to the ends of the earth for you.* A sense of wonder filled Merrick. He had tried to be a friend to Byner and many others, because they gave him more than they could ever know just by accepting him into their lives. But never had he imagined that they might feel such affection for him, such loyalty as Byner had just shown. After all, he was not really one of them.

But to them, I *am,* Merrick thought.

He realized he was standing in the middle of the police parking lot with tears. rimming his eyes. Blotting them away, he headed to his own car—

Could he still use the police cruiser?

Rourke had said nothing about that. Merrick slid in and pulled from the lot, wending his way through the morning rush hour, thinking about Byner and Cooke and the investigation he was no longer running. Until today, he had needed to stay in charge—or thought he had—in order to keep Byner in line. I just got a reprieve, Merrick thought. I'll drive out to Meggan's tonight and tell Katie what happened; how Rourke took me off the case and Byner risked his career to keep the blood secret. I'll ask her, for Byner's sake and for mine, to wait a little longer to report any findings, explain that I have a plan to find and defeat the killer, and if I succeed, neither Byner nor I will have to worry about the report.

Now all I need is a plan to defeat ''the killer.''

Merrick gave a harsh laugh. A reprieve, right. *Maybe I can't beat Zane, but at least I know how to find him.*

Knowing he might be going to his grave, Merrick drove out of town toward Jenny's house.

THIRTY

As MERRICK TURNED onto Jenny's road, he saw a white station wagon pull from the Hrluskas' driveway. The car turned toward him, wipers beating against the gray morning drizzle. It passed with a hiss of tires on wet pavement, and he saw Ann Hrluska at the wheel with her daughter beside her. Jenny was talking with great animation, waving her hands and bouncing on the seat. Her mother's happy smile touched and saddened Merrick. Jenny must suspect by now that she was no longer a normal girl, but her mother was still blissfully unaware that she did not really have her daughter back . . . and never would.

Using the Hrluska driveway to turn around, Merrick followed at a distance, looking for any other car that might belong to Zane. He could see none. Maybe Zane was crouching down in the backseat. But why crouch, when he could sit straight up without Ann Hrluska seeing him?

If Zane *wasn't* with Jenny right now, where was he?

Merrick had a grim premonition that Zane was out killing someone to get blood for Jenny. If true, there was nothing he could do about it. The thing now was to stick with Jenny until Zane came back to her.

Then finish it, one way or the other.

Merrick's curiosity grew as the station wagon passed up a grocery store and a shopping mall. When it turned in at a long brick building surrounded by soccer and baseball fields, Merrick realized with surprise that Jenny was going back to school. Surely she had missed too many classes to have any hope of making up the spring term, which would be over in a few more weeks. . . .

She wants to feel like a normal kid again.

Merrick's heart went out to her. She must know something's wrong, he thought, but she probably doesn't know she's drunk blood, or she'd be afraid to let herself be around her friends again. When she does understand, she'll panic. If I could just help her, show her that she can still be with people, even remain with her parents, if she wills it.

Merrick pulled into the front lot, parked a few cars away from the station wagon, and watched as Jenny got out. A little wave and she was off, hunching through the drizzle toward the entrance. As Ann Hrluska passed him on the way out of the lot, Merrick saw a sheen of tears on her cheeks that somehow went with her smile. What a wonderful feeling this moment must give her. Only a week ago she must have despaired that this day would ever come. Merrick felt a surge of good will toward her, the mother of his grandchild. If I survive, I'll do my best to save Jenny, he vowed silently.

He sat in the parking lot, watching the playing fields all morning, while the drizzle stopped, the gray clouds cleared away, and the day warmed to a balminess more typical of late May than April. At noon, hundreds of kids poured out onto the soccer and ball fields. Merrick got out and walked to the blacktopped drive that divided the playing fields from the rear of the school. After a moment, he located Jenny in the crush of kids spilling across the road. She and two other girls veered off to the bleachers of a softball field, picking at their bag lunches and watching as a group of boys and a few girls got a game going. One of the batters hit a sizzling foul tip that sheared straight toward Jenny. Reaching up reflexively, she caught it barehanded. Merrick could hear the slap it made clear across the road. The two girls with Jenny cringed, then clapped as they saw Jenny was all right. Several of the boys on the ball field stared at Jenny. Standing, she burned the ball back to the pitcher, a scorching rocket that bounced out of his glove with a loud smack. More boys stared. The two girls with Jenny pulled at her arms in delight and clapped her on the shoulder. She shrugged away from them and bent over her lunch, and Merrick knew just what she was thinking. *How did I do that?*

After a minute, she left the girls and walked along the side-line away from the crowds of playing kids. Merrick took off after her. "Hi," he said, catching up.

She turned and her glum expression vanished in a wide smile. "Detective Chapman!"

"I thought I'd drop by and see how you were doing."

She cocked her head. "Did Mom tell you I was here?"

"No."

"Then how did you know?" Her voice sounded a little wary, and he knew it was the gene, the instincts of paranoia she would need for the rest of her long life if she was to pass undetected among her prey.

"I drove by your house to see you this morning," he explained, "and you passed me on your way to school, so I decided to come over at lunchtime and see how you were doing."

"It's great to see you," she said. "Want a cookie?"

"Sure." Merrick ate it with a show of appetite, but his stomach was in knots. What were the right words? "You sure look better."

"I know," she said. "Isn't it strange? I was dying and then, just like that, I got over it." Her eyes looked troubled.

"So everything's great, huh?"

She gave a little laugh. "Right."

"Having a rough time?"

She eyed him. "What makes you say that?"

Merrick stopped walking. She stopped, too, and faced him. "I never told you this when I used to visit you," he said, "but I had leukemia, too, once. The same kind you had."

Her forehead wrinkled in a slight frown. "Weird."

"What's weird?"

"I had a dream two nights ago. A man who looked a lot like you came into my room and told me the same thing you just said. I thought he was you, but he said he wasn't."

Zane. "Have you had other dreams?"

She looked away.

"They're bad dreams, aren't they? You dream you are killing people. In your dreams, you enjoy it. Now you're starting to think about it when you're awake."

She gave a sharp little gasp, then gazed at him with a mixture of fear and wonder. "How did you know that?"

"There are two important things to remember," he said. "The first is that you are *not* a bad person because you dream or feel this, only if you *do* it. The second is that *nothing* can *make* you do it."

Her expression lightened a little, touched by hope.

"You may hear something different," Merrick said, "from the man who came to you in your dream a couple of nights ago. He might tell you to act on your dreams. You must not believe him. You are a good person, and *you* can control your own life."

"What about the medicine?" she whispered.

Merrick realized she meant blood. "You won't have to hurt anyone to get what you need."

She gazed at him. "You said you had . . . leukemia, too."

"I still do."

"But it's not really leukemia, is it?"

Merrick hesitated. "Jenny, you must not tell anyone, including your parents, what I am about to tell you. They wouldn't understand."

"I know," she said. "Tell me."

"Leukemia is just a side effect. It is caused by a gene that you were born with. You could not help it and you are not to blame. People who have the gene feel perfectly normal until around age twelve. Then they get leukemia and the strange hunger. Most of them die, but a few live . . . and change."

"Because they get the medicine."

"That's right."

"And it's not really medicine, is it?"

"What do you think it is?"

"I don't know." Her voice rose to a near wail on the last word, and he realized she was not ready to hear it yet.

"You're scared," Merrick said. "I know just how you feel. I went through it myself. At first I thought I was terrible, a monster. Then I realized I was not. I still have terrible urges just as you do. I never give in to them and you don't have to either." He took his card from his wallet and gave it to her. "My phone number is on there. You can call me any time day or night. I'll do my best to help you through this. But even if something happens and I'm not around, remember that it's not what a person feels that makes her a bad person, it's what she does."

"What do you mean, 'if something happens'?" Jenny said fearfully.

Merrick wondered if he should tell her that Zane was his enemy, that Zane wanted to kill him. It might turn her against Zane. . . .

Her own father.

Merrick realized he could not do it. She must choose. Not because he prejudiced her, but because she saw which way was right. After tonight, if he did not see her again, she must understand that he had not abandoned her willingly, or everything he had said might be wiped out in resentment. "I'm a policeman," he said. "I'm trying to catch a very dangerous killer. I think I know where he'll be tonight. I'll try to capture him but he may be too clever. He may capture me instead. If he does, you won't see me again."

Jenny's eyes teared. "Don't you have anyone to help you?"

"No."

"No other police, no friends?"

"Not for this . . ." Merrick gazed at her, stunned. Sandeman! he thought. Sandeman has learned how to do what Zane does— he got the phage in the cell to stop screaming. I could go there now, get him to show me. Maybe I could learn to block it.

But is Sandeman still strong enough?

"I *do* have a friend," he said to Jenny. "Maybe he can help. But if he can't, remember that I didn't want to leave you. And trust yourself. You're smart. You'll figure out how to get the medicine without hurting anyone. You don't have to be alone. I know you can do it."

A bell sounded from the direction of the school. Jenny turned toward it, with a look of longing that pierced Merrick. He saw her friends waiting for her. He wanted desperately to hug her, but it would leave her with too much to explain to her friends or any teacher who might be watching. "Better get going," he said. "You don't want to be late for class."

She ran to catch up with the other kids, turning once to wave at him, and Merrick, afraid he might never see her again, let the tears fill his eyes.

Sandeman appeared to be asleep on his bed. Blood trickled from both nostrils. Merrick's heart sank. Gently he wiped the blood away with his handkerchief. At his touch, one of Sandeman's eyes slid open, then the other lid trembled, rising with visible effort.

For a moment, his eyes failed to focus and then he looked at Merrick without speaking. All thought of asking for help fled as Merrick gazed at the pale, skeletal face. He knew with a terrible certainty that his old friend had passed an invisible line and was now more dead than alive.

"I would like to sit up," Sandeman whispered.

Merrick gently took the bone-thin arms and sat Sandeman up on the bed amidst the litter of his books. He was light as a husk. Sandeman's wretched condition tore at Merrick's heart. "Let me bring you blood." The words sprang from his mouth before he could stop them.

"*Nyet!*" Sandeman hissed.

Merrick squeezed his shoulder.

"Have you caught Zane?" Sandeman asked.

"No."

Sandeman studied him. "Are you sure you want to?"

"Want has nothing to do with it. Over the last five centuries, I've put hundreds of my own kind in the ground. If I shy away from Zane because he's my son, their blood will cry out to me."

"Then why haven't you caught him?"

"You were right about him," Merrick said. "He is stronger than I am."

Sandeman closed his eyes for a second and nodded, clearly not surprised. "If Zane is stronger, why hasn't he caught you?"

"Because he is preoccupied." Merrick told Sandeman about Zane and Jenny.

Sandeman grinned and his face seemed to lose its ghastly pallor for a moment. "You have a granddaughter! Congratulations!"

Merrick smiled, too, warmed by Sandeman's joy for him. "She's wonderful. I'm so afraid for her."

Sandeman gave a slight nod. "And for yourself."

"I can take whatever comes."

"Except the worst tragedy of your life, repeating itself. You once loved Zane as much as you now love your granddaughter."

Merrick shook his head, trying to answer, but he could not. A terrible grief rose in him, choking him to silence. Bowing his head, he covered his face. After a minute, he felt Sandeman's hand on his shoulder.

"How exactly is Zane stronger?" Sandeman asked softly.

"You were right about him—he's found a way to push Influence beyond the brain stem, into the mind." Merrick told Sandeman what Zane had done to him in Jenny's hospital room, how he had stood, lost in his memories, completely vulnerable. "If he can do that to me, how can I stop him from killing? How can I save Katie, Gregory, my granddaughter?"

Sandeman gave no sign of hearing. His eyes had slipped shut again and he seemed to be sleeping. As the minutes passed, Merrick felt the silence of the vault all around him, the tons of earth pressing down. "I did love Zane," he said softly.

"I know," Sandeman whispered.

Merrick's face burned.

"You'll need my help."

Merrick felt a gratitude that was also pain. "You're too weak," he protested.

"My body is weak. My mind . . . still has its moments."

"I could still save you."

"It's nothing I can't stand," Sandeman murmured. "This suffering is clean. Outside, with the constant burn of blood on my hands—that was worse."

Suddenly, Merrick was on his belly in the mud. It was night. Smoke, thick with the smell of gunpowder, hung in the air above him, blotting out the sky. All around him, men moaned and screamed for help. The sharp, salty smell of blood washed over him in intoxicating waves. He crawled to his right, finding the body of a French infantryman. The man was moaning softly. A musket ball had torn a gaping hole in his lower belly. He would be dead before morning. Merrick dilated the blood vessels in the soldier's brain stem and throat, dumping the blood away from the brain, taking the man down and down, until there was no more pain, only sweet oblivion.

Then, using his bayonet, he cut the soldier's throat and drank his blood—

And then he was back with Sandeman.

He blinked, disoriented. "Bloody hell," he said.

"Where were you?" Sandeman said.

"Waterloo."

"I'm sorry. I have no control over it. Did you have any sense that it was a memory?"

"No. I was there. It was real."

"Then we must practice. Detection is the first goal. You can't learn to resist unless you can at least guess that you have been switched from reality into memory. You must try to develop a dual consciousness. If you can be the one to attack Zane, you will be expecting his counterattack and that may help. Now, get ready."

Merrick nodded. He concentrated on Sandeman's face, on what was about to happen to him—

He sat at a table in the Boar and Dagger. Outside, in the streets, he could hear the revellers celebrating the equinox. He knew he could not get drunk, that his body would not let him, but he was trying anyway. He picked up the stone mug and drained it. He smelled a haunch of venison roasting on the tavern's fireplace. He should eat something, but he was not hungry. The innkeeper waddled up to his table. "Another for you, stranger?"

"If you please." Merrick dug a coin from his purse and flipped it to the man.

"Right away, sir, right away."

Merrick thought of Oriana. By now she would have decided he was dead, waylaid by the highwaymen around Winchester and thrown into a river. She would mourn and be done with it. What will *I* do? Merrick wondered.

Opening his eyes, he saw Sandeman gazing at him. With a wrenching feeling in his stomach, he realized he was back in the vault. Again, he had failed utterly to tell memory from reality.

"I touched you on the chest," Sandeman said. "Did you feel it?"

"No," Merrick said.

"Let's try again."

... Walking through the tall, pine-fragrant forests of Wessex. Teaching Zane to make an arrow. Sitting on a barge working its way slowly along the Thames, feeling the thin sunlight of spring on his face, trying to ignore the ripe smell of the river ...

Over and over, Merrick tried to block Sandeman. He began to feel a slight sense of unreality at the beginning of the memory, a flicker of the dual consciousness Sandeman was talking about. But it was not enough to throw Sandeman out. Maybe if they had more time ...

But they didn't.

"It's not working," Merrick said with despair.

"I don't know," Sandeman said. "I thought I felt you pushing back on the last one."

Merrick shook his head.

"We will try again."

"No. You are exhausted. You've got to rest."

Sandeman slumped back against the wall, his face gray.

A sudden suspicion struck Merrick. "Sandeman, just how long have you had this ability?"

"A couple of months."

"That long? You could have used it against me and walked out of this vault weeks ago. And yet you've chosen to remain here."

Sandeman gave him a pained smile. "Not exactly. For the past six months, I haven't been *able* to walk."

The pain in his voice chastened Merrick. "I'm sorry. I didn't realize."

"Don't be sorry. I came to you of my own accord because I couldn't stop killing. If I had decided to walk out, my soul would be lost now. One more thing—don't ever offer me blood again."

"No."

Sandeman drew a long, rasping breath. "We'll practice more tomorrow."

"No," Merrick said. "There's no more time left. Zane is killing for two now."

Sandeman winced. "Do you think you can find him to-night?"

"He'll be with Jenny."

"Then we'll go together. You'll carry me. When we get close to Zane, I'll give him a dose of his own medicine. You will bind him and I'll keep him locked in his own memories while you do whatever you must do."

Merrick felt a renewed hope, and then fear for Sandeman. "You will leave the vault? Are you sure?"

Sandeman's face lit with a mixture of terror and desire. He said, "Merrick, I want to see the sky, one more time."

Merrick took both his hands, overcome with grief for them both. "What will I do, Sandeman? If we *are* somehow able to defeat him, if I put my own son in the ground, what then?"

Sandeman gave him a look filled with sorrow. "I think you know."

"I'll be finished," Merrick said. "I will have to die." He was surprised at how little fear the words aroused in him. They were almost a relief. Had he, without recognizing it, been winding down already, even before Zane came back? Hanging onto the house in San Francisco, then staying in Washington after he broke off with Katie, fantasizing about growing old and dying with her. Yes. Long before Zane had come to challenge him, he had begun to grow careless of his life.

"If I put my son in here," he said, "I will be able to stop taking blood and die. I'll be strong enough at last."

"No," Sandeman whispered. "You will hate yourself enough at last."

THIRTY-ONE

KATIE FOUND ART sitting in the waiting room of the administrator's office. She was desperately glad to have found him, but he looked so depressed. He sat forward on the edge of the chair, elbows on his knees, head hanging down like a man about to go to the electric chair. He looked strangely diminished in jeans and blazer, without the ever-present medical coat. Her heart went out to him. He could only be here to·resign, to risk ruining his career over his feelings for her.

He looked up as she sat down next to him. "Katie!"

"I need your help."

His expression lightened, but only for a second. "I do have an appointment."

"Does the administrator know what you're here for?"

Art nodded.

"Then I'm sure he'll be happy to put it off. If you still want to do this tomorrow, I'll move heaven and earth to get you a new residency." *If I'm still around. And if I'm not, your reason for leaving will be gone.* "Please, Art."

"Katie, what's wrong? What happened?" He eyed the Band-Aid on her throat.

She glanced at the administrator's secretary, who sat behind an oak desk guarded by two tall corn plants. "I can't talk about it here."

Art went to the secretary's desk and said something to her. She smiled and nodded, looking relieved. The administrator wasn't the only one who would be sorry to see him go.

Art said nothing until she'd shut the door of the lab behind them. Then he took her arm. "Katie, what happened to your throat?"

"Art, this is going to seem very strange, but I have to do something before I can tell you anything. If you think I've lost my mind, you're free to go."

Art sat down on a lab table.

Katie took a deep breath, then marched to the electron microscope room and retrieved her mop. She poked it into every corner, along the files and under the tables, then came out and shut the door. She repeated the exercise in the larger lab, feeling Art's eyes on her. She thrust the mop handle, then listened, thrust and listened, until she had poked and prodded into every nook large enough to hide a man. She went to the lab door and locked it, turned and looked at Art. He was not smiling, and she felt a surge of gratitude.

"The killer can blind you to him," he said.

"That's right."

"Jesus Christ."

She tilted her chin up and pulled one end of the Band-Aid back. "What do you think of these?"

He peered at her throat and gave a low whistle. "Needle tracks."

She felt absurdly relieved. She had known that's what they must be, but she'd needed someone else to say it. Why had the creature tried to make the marks look like a vampire bite? Did it have a sense of humor?

Why am I not laughing?

"Judging from how pale you are," Art said, "you are either terribly frightened, or you just gave a couple of pints of blood—from your right jugular vein."

"Both," Katie said, feeling queasy. Blood had been missing

from all of the victims and now it was missing from her. . . .

But she was still alive.

"Katie, what the hell is going on?"

Now that the moment had come to tell him, Katie hesitated. He would help her because he loved her. But what if he ended up like the woman on the pulpit, his throat torn open, his promising young life drained out? "You should go," she said. "You should get out of here right now and not have anything more to do with me."

"You're probably right," Art said. "I've watched enough movies to know that women who look like their throats have been sucked by vampires are invariably trouble."

In spite of herself, Katie laughed. "It's not funny, Art, believe me."

"I believe you. Now tell me."

I can't go on alone, Katie thought. And if I stop now, how many more people might die?

She told him her theory—that the thing could hide itself by creating another blind spot on the retinas—and noted that it did not seem able to do the same with sound. She told him it could knock a victim out without touching him. "It's been up close to me a couple of times without knocking me out," Katie finished, "so I might be able to get it with a weapon that will work up close. A syringe full of poison would be ideal, but so far I haven't found anything that will dent that RBC membrane. Poison won't be effective if the creature's body cells are as well shielded as its blood, and I think we have to assume that."

"What have you tried so far?"

She went over the list of reagents and caustic liquids.

Art gave her a curious look. "Did you make up a different slide for each test?"

"Yes."

"Then there can't be much left—we didn't have that much of its blood to begin with."

"I'm using Jenny's blood."

Art looked shocked. "You're what?"

Katie told him how the creature had taken its blood back. How Jenny's blood was now the same. Art looked shaken. He sat down on a lab stool. "Jenny, Jesus," he murmured. "So her blood went on changing."

"That's right. And I'm as worried as you are, but we can't let that hang us up right now. We are trying to stop a killer and we have to stay focused on that."

Art shook his head. "All right, you've tried brute force. Let's see if we can think of another approach. You were telling me what you have figured out about this thing. Is there anything else?"

"Not that I can think of," Katie said. "Wait—it doesn't have any clotting factors."

"That's right," Art said. "It puzzled the hell out of us that first day. What use can that be to it?"

She shrugged. "I don't know. The creature should have bled to death like a hemophiliac, even if the cut was very small . . . unless the ruptured blood vessel healed quickly—extremely quickly."

"Rapid regeneration?" Art said.

"More than rapid—almost instantaneous."

He looked grim. "If you're right, and if its other tissues can heal as fast as its blood vessels, then even a deep knife or bullet wound to the heart or brain might not kill the thing, might not even hurt it that much—or not for long."

Katie thought of Merrick, out there hunting the creature with only his service revolver. It made her afraid for him, as afraid as if she still loved him—

No, don't think about that!

She said, "This just makes it all the more important that we find a way to bring it down."

"What about heat?" Art asked.

Katie looked at him, surprised. "Why didn't I think of that?"

"Because fire won't go in a syringe, but a spray bottle of gasoline and a lighter might be almost as easy to use. Why don't we try holding a lighted match to the blood?"

"It would blacken the slide, make it hard to read," Katie said.

"The autoclave," Art suggested.

"Right." She prepared a slide of Jenny's blood and put it in the pressurized steam cooker used to sterilize lab equipment. She turned the heat up to maximum and waited for twenty minutes. It took another ten for the slide to cool enough to put under the light microscope. She allowed herself a small hope as she bent over the eyepiece. The blood was unfazed. Even superheated steam under immense pressure could not touch the membrane.

"Damn it to hell!" she said.

Art took a quick look and slammed his palms down on the counter.

Katie felt a vast frustration. "How can this be?"

"The blood that wouldn't die," Art said in a *Twilight Zone* voice.

Katie looked at him. "Wait! What did you say?"

Art started to repeat it and she waved him off. "We've been focusing on the fact that these blood cells can't be destroyed. But it's also true that they don't die—or to be more accurate, don't deteriorate."

Art looked confused. "Isn't that pretty much the same thing?"

"Maybe not. What if the thing that shed these cells doesn't deteriorate either—doesn't *age?*" With a chill, Katie remembered what Neddie Merrill had said: *It looks young, I think, but it is very old.*

Art sat down, staring at her. "Fraction Eight," he said.

Katie nodded. Art went to the safe where she kept the serum fraction from Rebecca Trent's blood. She prepared a fresh slide of Jenny's blood. Art handed her a thin glass pipette. Dipping it in Fraction Eight, she picked up a single drop and deposited it on the slide. As she put the pipette down, she felt her hand trembling. *Please, let it work,* she thought. But she could not look.

Art slipped the slide into the microscope. He stood over the scope for almost a minute. "Nothing yet," he said. After another minute, he stood back from the scope and paced to the door of electron microscopy and back. He gazed at Katie, looking glum.

"Look again," she said.

He bent over the scope. A second later, he whooped, straightened, and clapped his hands above his head. "We're geniuses!"

Hope bloomed in her. Through the scope, she saw the red blood cells withering. There was no sign of the membrane. Shouting in triumph, she grabbed Art's arm and danced him around in a circle. After a few seconds, she stopped, sobered and awed by what they had discovered. Rebecca was dying much too fast and the killer much too slowly. The reason for both had just met on the microscope slide—the genetic Alpha and Omega of human blood, fitting together like lock and key. The membrane on the killer's cells could ward off massive physical and chemical battering rams, but "Fraction Eight"—a microscopic key—had opened the genetic lock with a mere touch.

But there was still something she didn't understand. "If the killer's blood is invulnerable," she said, "why is it also taking normal blood from its victims?"

Art shrugged. "A ghoulish perversion?"

"That's what I've thought. But what if it needs blood to be what it is, to survive?"

Art looked squeamish. "Are you saying it really does drink blood? Do you have any evidence for that?"

Katie felt a deepening unease. An image came to her of Jenny licking her upper lip after her nosebleed, of her eyes opening to gaze at the transfusion pack of blood, even though she was anesthetized. Jenny had been hungry for something she could not name. For blood?

Katie shuddered. "Jenny is our evidence."

Art frowned. "Katie—"

"I don't like it either. But think—after her massive nosebleed, when she swallowed a great deal of blood, her stool was negative for occult blood. What happened to it? Why didn't her body let it go through?"

"Are you saying Jenny got blood and that healed her?" Art said. "No, damn it, I refuse to believe that. We gave her endless blood transfusions and she kept getting sicker."

"Maybe the blood has to be drunk, not transfused."

Art shook his head. "That would mean her stomach or intestines were anatomically different, which would have showed up on an X ray or scan."

"Not necessarily. It could be specialized cells in the lining of her stomach or intestinal villi, soft tissue that wouldn't show up on any scans. The only way to find it would be to biopsy a sample of her stomach lining."

Art looked at her, wide eyed. "You think this specialized tissue might absorb normal human blood and transform it, adding the membrane?"

"Not exactly, but close. If the RBCs of these creatures don't wear out, then making new ones would soon clog their veins and arteries with too much blood. If I'm right, normal human blood somehow *services* the blood of these creatures. Since it's not excreted, it must be used up in the transformation process, converted to a form of energy."

"Energy," Art said in a low, amazed voice. "That would explain how the RBCs can withstand all those kilovolts under the electron scope. They're encircled with their own, more dense energy field. A high energy potential could also explain rapid regeneration." His expression became stark. "If you're right, someone *did* give Jenny blood."

"And only someone *like* her would know to do that," Katie said, "so it must have been the killer. . . ."

An awful suspicion struck her. "God, *no*," she whispered. Her knees felt suddenly weak with dread. Darkness swirled at the edges of her vision. The room tilted and then she felt Art's hands on her elbows, catching her, easing her to her knees.

"Put your head down," he said. "Come on."

She did, letting her head hang, feeling the blood slowly creep back into it. Merrick, she thought. Why did he try to get me off the case? Why was he so determined to limit knowledge of the killer's blood to just me and Byner? He didn't even want Art in on it.

And why did he always show such an interest in Jenny?

Katie got up slowly and shook free of Art's hand, feeling a desperate urge to flee, to escape what she was thinking. It can't be Merrick, she thought. I would have known before now. . . .

The way you knew about his other family out West?

Katie's dread turned to horror.

THIRTY-TWO

TRYING TO KEEP her fears about Merrick out of her face, Katie filled two syringes with Fraction Eight, fixed the plastic guards to the needles, and gave one syringe to Art. "Keep this in the pocket of your medical coat," she said. "The killer grabbed me from behind; if he stays with that tactic, even though you won't see him, you'll be able to feel him against your back."

Could it really be Merrick? *Don't think about that now!*

"If the killer grabs you," she went on, "he may also hold a knife to your throat. Don't panic. Slide your hand into your pocket and flip the guard off the needle. You may be able to inject him right through your coat. He might not even feel something as small as a needle." She told Art how she had smashed the killer hard with a baseball bat and he hadn't even grunted.

Art pocketed the syringe with a grim smile. "Here's hoping you're right."

Katie knew the confidence they were both trying to work up was false. The killer could knock them out from a distance and then cut their throats. Or he might kill them the instant they reached into their pockets. Still, Fraction Eight gave them a chance, a hope—more than they'd had before.

"Shouldn't we call the police?" Art asked.

"Not yet. All we have is theories right now. It's possible that a bullet would bring the killer down as effectively as a shot of Fraction Eight. Or that neither will work. And anyway, we don't have enough left for another syringe full. The police are going to have to do this their way and we, ours. Until we know how to fight this thing, all we'd accomplish—*if* people believed us—is a public panic."

"All right, what's next then?"

"Jenny. She's the closest thing we have to this creature, and now that I know that I need to examine her again, I'll call her parents and ask if I can come out to do a routine checkup—"

"Don't you mean 'we'?"

"No. I need you here, taking care of Three East. We have a floor full of patients who depend on us. We can't just leave them to the first-year residents and med students. I'm Jenny's doctor and her parents trust me, so I should be the one to go to her house."

Art shook his head stubbornly. "Katie, if Jenny recovered because someone gave her blood, it had to be the killer, which means he may still be hanging around her. . . ." His eyes lit with understanding. "That's what you're hoping, isn't it?"

"No." Katie put conviction into her voice, though it was, in fact, exactly what she hoped.

"I won't let you go into danger alone—"

"Art, don't go macho on me."

He looked stung, and she added, "I'm sorry, but we've got to use our heads now, not our hearts. A man doesn't stand any more chance against this thing than a woman. If there's any protection, it's in this syringe, and I can push a plunger as well as you. Besides, we know the hospital is part of the killer's turf. He's as likely to be here as at Jenny's."

Art groaned. "Call me when you get out there. Call me every chance you get."

"I will. Thanks, Art." She walked him to the door of the lab and quickly locked up behind him. Freed of the need to act calm, she felt the fear mushrooming inside her. Settling on a lab bench, she took slow, deep breaths. Merrick didn't want me working on the blood, she thought. Every step of the way he's fought that. That night in the church, he left me alone just before the killer stepped in. And later, when I chased the killer out of the house, the minute he was gone, Merrick appeared. And afterward he insisted I stay at Meggan's and not come in to work on the killer's blood. He's got Mom and Gregory—and, he thinks, me— isolated, away from police protection, in a place only he knows. . . .

Alarm surged in Katie. Hurrying to the lab phone, she dialed Meggan's house. After a few rings, her mother answered. "Katie, where are you?"

"Still at the hospital. I'm fine. So how are you guys doing?"

"Just fine," Mom said heartily, and Katie knew she was faking it, too.

"Has Merrick come by?" Katie asked.

"No."

"If he does, be very careful. Keep Gregory away from him. Under no circumstances let him take Gregory away."

"Katie!" Mom sounded shocked.

"I don't have time to explain. I think he may be . . . involved with the killer in some way. I might be wrong, but until we're sure we have to keep Gregory away from him."

"Katie, this is nonsense. Merrick loves you and he loves his son—"

"Mom, *please.* I have to go now. Promise me you won't let him take Gregory."

"I'm sure it won't even come up. But if it does, I'll do as you say."

"Thanks. I love you."

"Oh, Katie . . . I love you, too, dear."

Hanging up, Katie steeled herself for the next call she must make—to Jenny's parents. What would she find at Jenny's house? Katie's hand closed around the syringe in her pocket. What if Art was right and the killer was there?

What if it was Merrick?

I have to stop him, she thought. Whatever, whoever it is.

The sun was setting as Merrick carried Sandeman up from the vault. The dying phage was light as a bird; his legs felt stick thin and his spine was a hard, bumpy ridge. But when his face rose above the trapdoor and he saw the glorious red and gold sky above the small clearing, he smiled like a starving child gazing at a bowl of rice. His lungs rasped as he drew in the moist spring air. The balmy weather of the day had persisted—it was at least sixty-five degrees—but Sandeman had no body fat left and he began to shiver.

"I have a blanket in the trunk," Merrick said.

"No, no. I want to feel the air on my skin."

As the thin body trembled against his arms, Merrick felt a pressure building in his throat. He wanted to scream at the sky, at fate, at whatever perverse god had consigned Sandeman to this life of torment.

"It's beautiful," Sandeman whispered. "I've lived through almost half a million sunsets, but this one is the most beautiful."

Merrick nodded, not trusting himself to speak. He carried Sandeman through the darkening woods to his car. A whippoorwill warbled in a nearby treetop, a sweet cry to greet the night, and Sandeman grinned with pleasure. "He flies out to hunt now."

"Yes."

"Can you feel it, Merrick? The life all around you?"

Merrick nodded again, though he could feel nothing but anguish for his friend. He slipped Sandeman's skeletal body into the passenger seat and got behind the wheel.

"Open my window, please."

Merrick started the car and dropped Sandeman's window halfway. As the car rolled into motion, Sandeman leaned his forehead against the glass and gazed out, eyes wide, nostrils flaring. His smile widened and eased, flashing into a grin now and then, but never fading entirely. His giddy pleasure pierced Merrick. Sandeman was not ready to surrender his life. How unbearable, to love living so much and yet give it up in this prolonged and horrible way so that you would not go on taking life from others. There would never be a statue of Sandeman in any courtyard or church, his name would not go down with the heroes, the martyrs, the saints. But a better man than Sandeman had become had never lived.

Merrick parked his car along a main roadway near Jenny's, in a different place than last time. Carrying Sandeman, he walked through the woods behind Jenny's house, keeping his eyes on the faint light of her back window, visible through the budding trees. As they neared the house, the dog in the backyard started barking, and Merrick eased it into sleep. Skirting the end of the house, he settled in a line of maples and low forsythia bushes that divided Jenny's lot from the next house down the road. As Merrick set him gently on the ground, Sandeman's skeletal hands winnowed through last autumn's leaves, caressing them as a man might touch his lover.

"A good place," Sandeman whispered. "From here we can see anyone who comes in, front or back."

"Yes." He's enjoying the hunt, Merrick thought—his last. He settled beside Sandeman in the leaves; a moment later, he felt the other phage's hand clutch his wrist. "Whatever happens, Merrick, thank you for helping me."

"I've locked you away from the world," Merrick said bitterly, unable to stop himself. "I've been your jailor."

Sandeman's feeble grip tightened for an instant. " 'Those friends thou hast, and their adoption tried, Grapple them to thy soul with hoops of steel.' "

"Hamlet?"

Sandeman chuckled. "I forgot—you were English once. You probably met Shakespeare, am I right?"

"Backstage, after a performance. I forget which play. He hit me up for fifty crowns to help bankroll a new one he was writing."

"Name-dropper. Try this one: 'We are all the captives of our friends.' "

"I don't know it."

"Sandeman. Write it in your heart, my friend."

Merrick felt the burn in his throat again. Tonight, I will try to be as brave as Sandeman, he vowed silently, even if Zane carries me to my grave.

As Katie drove through the dark to Jenny's house, she fought the horrible images her imagination kept showing her—a glass of dark blood rising to Jenny's lips, the slim throat convulsing in eager swallows, a red mustache of blood on her downy upper lip. What she could not see in her mind was Jenny's eyes.

Katie shuddered and tried to relax her hands on the steering wheel. She must think of something else, or she would lose her nerve. . . .

Art. Why can't I love him back?

I like him, she thought, a lot. He's handsome, bright, and brave. He can make me laugh, too. And he does love me. She remembered the surprised pleasure on his face when she'd joined him on the ward. On the phone, Ann Hrluska had said Jenny was at school and would stay after for band practice, but to come out around six. When Art realized she hadn't changed her mind about going out to Jenny's, but had only postponed it—until after dark—he'd tried again to persuade her not to go. Fortunately, the force of habit won out once again and he'd accepted her order to keep covering the ward. She was glad, but at the same time, maybe that summed up the problem. She and Art had started out in such an uneven relationship, not just boss and employee but, in the long and grueling tradition of medical training, virtually master and slave. He had been a great resident, doing everything she'd asked, and his reward now was that she had trouble seeing him as an equal.

He understands that, too, Katie thought. That's why he's thinking of changing his residency. And he's right. If we're going to have a chance together, I'll have to let him go.

The thought of losing Art saddened her, but she could find no other feelings beyond that, no anticipation at the thought of being free to date him, no pleasure in the thought of dating anyone. The deadness inside her maddened her. Merrick had done this to her, Merrick, Merrick, making her believe he loved her while he hid his whole life from her—not just another woman, but possibly murder. Not just murder, but torn throats, missing blood, horror too ghastly to comprehend.

Shaken, Katie stopped the car on the shoulder of the road and stared out the windshield at a swarm of gnats dancing in her headlights. Confusion gripped her. Could the man who had been so loving toward her and Gregory also have held a knife to her throat and painted in blood on his own son's back? If so, what kind of terrible split must exist inside him?

A semi rumbling past threw grit against the windshield, breaking her paralysis. Katie pulled onto the road again. She could make herself crazy with theories; what counted were facts— and right now Jenny was the best available source of those. Turning onto Jenny's road, Katie tried to put all emotion aside. She must act natural and professional with Jenny and her parents while she learned the truth—or as much of it as she could.

And if the killer was with Jenny, too, and it attacked, and she could not see it? . . .

Then she must forget that it might be Merrick, forget all he had ever meant to her and plunge the needle in.

When Merrick heard the car pull into Jenny's driveway, he knew it wasn't Zane. Zane would never make such a frontal approach. The headlights didn't spill onto the tree line, so he felt safe raising his head above the forsythia bushes. The car was a Riviera, like the one Meggan owned. . . .

Merrick stared in shock as Katie got out of the car and went up to the door. He started to get up, then felt Sandeman's hand clutch his shirt. "No, Merrick."

He sank back, knowing the other phage was right. But bloody hell, what was Katie doing out here? She was supposed to be safe at Meggan's. She must have driven here to check up on Jenny. If Zane showed up while she was here and Katie became involved, it would give Zane an extra weapon.

From the bushes, Merrick watched with growing alarm as Ann Hrluska answered the door, gave Katie a big hug, and pulled her inside. Clearly she was expected. Had they asked her to dinner? This was a disaster.

And there wasn't a damned thing he could do about it.

Katie left the Hrluskas more frightened than when she'd come. This time, when she'd taken the blood sample, she'd deliberately "forgotten" to put a swab on the puncture site. It had bled one drop and then stopped. Within seconds, she could no longer see the tiny injection wound. It had healed completely, right before her eyes.

While she was close to Jenny, she'd pretended to stumble and Jenny had caught her, standing her upright again as easily as if *she* were the child. I'm six inches taller than she is, Katie thought. I outweigh her by thirty pounds. She didn't even grunt when she caught me.

And there's something different about her now. She is preoccupied, there's a . . . darkness inside her. If the killer *is* feeding her blood, maybe she's beginning to suspect. Her parents still don't see it, because they don't want to, but she's *changed,* and she knows it.

Katie shuddered, though the evening was quite balmy. Starting her car, she backed from the driveway and drove around the corner. As soon as she was out of sight of the house, she stopped the car on the shoulder, put on the jacket she'd brought with her, and crept through the woods until she was across the road from Jenny's house. Patting her pocket to make sure the syringe was still inside, she settled down to wait. The house was quite far away and half hidden by the trees, but Katie resisted the urge to move closer. If the killer came tonight, the farther away she was, the less likely he'd know she was out here and blind her.

As Katie sat in the dark woods, a sense of unreality crept over her. The killer *is* a vampire, she thought. Not like in the movies, a real one. And Jenny is, too.

She shuddered. Every impulse told her to get up and get out of there. Who did she think she was? She wasn't a cop or a soldier, she was just a doctor with a syringe in her pocket, taking on a demon—not from fantasy, but reality; a ghastly reality through which everyone else seemed to be sleeping. But if I don't try, she thought, he'll come after me again, and after Gregory. I know too much for him to let me live.

I've got to make my report to Byner, she thought, as soon as possible, in case the killer gets me. I'll go see him tomorrow, take some of Jenny's blood and tell him everything I've learned. Byner saw the membrane, too. He'll believe me and he'll make sure the hunt goes on even if something happens to me. Merrick doesn't want me to talk to Byner, but I won't tell Merrick. If he's not the killer, the worst thing that might happen is the press having a field day. And if Merrick *is* the killer, then I should have done it days ago.

Katie stared at the house; it started to burn and shimmer on her eyes. Hours passed. She moved her legs and arms periodically to keep the stiffness out. The ground cooled beneath her and she began to feel the chill creeping up into her body, despite the jacket. Something rustled through the leaves nearby—a mole, or maybe a rat. The downstairs lights in the house winked out one by one and two came on upstairs, then went dark again.

A wave of weariness swept Katie, filling her with consternation. How could she feel sleepy, when her life might depend on what happened in the next few hours? She thought of the amphetamines in her pocket, and her pulse picked up. Her throat convulsed in a dry swallow; she could almost feel the capsule sliding down. Odd, how a thing with no taste could create such hunger.

She reached for her pocket, then drew her hand away again, gritting her teeth. In another half hour, if she absolutely couldn't stay awake.

Her stomach felt hollow; a feeling of doom settled over her. If I do this once, she thought, it will be much easier the next time, and the next. How long before the monkey's on my back again and I don't think I can live without them?

You idiot, you're probably not going to live anyway.

She grinned in the darkness, even though it did not seem funny, not in the slightest. . . .

And then she saw him. Suddenly, he was there, striding across the front lawn, a tall man dressed in dark clothes. She scrambled up to her hands and knees—

The man—or whatever he was—stopped in mid-stride and cocked his head. Katie's hackles rose as she realized he had heard the soft rustle she'd made in the leaves, a hundred yards away. What chance have I got against that? she thought.

But I have to do it—for Gregory.

She slipped the syringe from her pocket and ran from the woods, across the road. The man turned to face her. His shoulders were very broad. She could not see his face in the dark, but with every step she took she grew more sure it was Merrick. She raced toward him, trapped in nightmare, barely feeling her feet touch the ground, aware only of the syringe clasped in her right fist. Jumping the culvert at the edge of Jenny's front lawn, she drove herself forward. She was only twenty yards away, but the man still waited with unearthly stillness. Terror swelled in her throat, and then all feeling left her legs. The sharp scent of grass filled her head and then everything faded away.

THIRTY-THREE

MERRICK HEARD SOMEONE slipping across the front yard beyond the Hrluska's house. It surprised him. He thought Zane was across the road, watching Jenny's house from the woods, but that must have been a raccoon or deer. Listening to the whisper of feet through the grass, Merrick knew it could only be a phage.

His stomach lifted, as though he'd just leapt off a cliff. Terror flooded him, blanking his mind for a second. This is it, he thought. He fought the rush of panic, trying to break its hold on his muscles. Sandeman touched his wrist, eyes questioning, too blood-starved to hear the stealthy approach at this distance.

Merrick mouthed, *Zane,* then rolled slowly up onto one shoulder until he could see through a break in the bush. Zane, yes, on Jenny's front yard now, gliding toward the far corner of the house—

Across the road in the woods, leaves rustled; at that moment,

Zane stopped in mid-stride and turned his head to listen. With dismay, Merrick realized it was not an animal, and then he saw Katie dash across the road and run straight at Zane. Horror seized him. What did she think she was doing? Zane would kill her!

All fear left Merrick. As he sprang from the bushes, Katie's legs lost their rhythm and she sailed head down into the grass as if she'd been shot. She lay with a terrible, deathly stillness. For a second, Merrick stood in shock, and then, exploding with rage, he charged.

Zane whirled toward him, eyes suddenly wide. Merrick saw surprise and fright on his face before Zane turned and fled toward the house. A light winked on in the Hrluskas' bedroom. No face appeared at the window, and Merrick knew Zane must have shunted the blood from their brains, leaving them unconscious. Zane ran to the rear corner of the house and flew up the copper drainpipe hand over hand, legs splayed out behind. Merrick grabbed the pipe and followed him, grabbing at his ankle. Reaching the top of the drainpipe, Merrick saw the foot striking at his face and dodged. He swung himself sideways onto the roof while Zane scrambled away up the steep pitch.

Following him, Merrick heard the squeak of bedsprings through the shingles below him. Bare feet slapped across wood. *Jenny!* he thought with alarm. He reached down mentally to put her back to sleep but felt her resist. Then he saw Zane stop at the peak of the roof and turn back toward him. Zane's expression was no longer afraid but angry. Charging up the steep pitch of the roof, Merrick slipped on a loose shingle and fell. Zane leapt down on top of him. A big knife flashed in the starlight and thudded into Merrick's chest, piercing a lung. Blood spurted from his chest and he felt a distant thread of pain as the lung collapsed, then reinflated. The knife flashed down again, but Merrick caught Zane's wrist and flipped him over and onto his back. They slid down together toward the eaves, and Merrick felt the knife again, slashing deeply through the muscles of his shoulder, then glancing off bone and skittering away across the roof. For a second, his arm was numb and then the cells sealed together, but he knew he was weakened. He lunged for the knife just as Zane did. Grabbing the knife in his left hand, Merrick slashed at Zane, but Zane rolled away and sprang up, scuttling toward the big chimney at the far end of the roof. Merrick caught up as Zane scrambled headfirst down the chimney brick. Merrick followed him, also head down, slashing at Zane's ankles. Blood sprayed up into his face, and he saw the tendon tear almost through, then reseal, but at least Zane had been taxed, too.

On the ground, Zane hobbled a few steps, then turned with bared teeth. Knife raised, Merrick charged at his son and . . .

Then he was standing beside Rowena's grave, blinded by grief. She killed herself, Merrick thought. Because she thought I was dead. He looked across at Rowena's father. The earl looked small against the gray sky; the wind whipped his ermine cloak around his legs. Tears poured down his cheeks and Merrick wished he did not have to hide himself from the old man's eyes. He longed to reveal himself and beg forgiveness from the earl for destroying his daughter's life. I should have known, Merrick thought, that she wasn't strong enough. I should never have fallen in love with her.

The wind picked up, howling through the embrasures of the castle turrets, as though Rowena's spirit was crying out from the grave. A thin mist of sleet stung Merrick's face, mingling with his tears. He could feel a steady pounding in his chest. . . .

   Zane

And knew it was his heart

   Only a memory; Zane is attacking you

his heart breaking for poor Rowena

   He is striking the blade into your heart, you must

and the castle and Rowena's father blanched gray and faded into the mist and the stars wheeled over Merrick's head and then he felt the grass against his face, wet with his own blood. The knife plunged through his back into his heart again and he felt nothing more.

Zane stood over his father, filled with a savage triumph. I did it! he thought. I brought the old bastard down! He'll be out for awhile. What's that on his belt? Chain? Zane grinned up at the black sky. He brought it to tie me up. Thank you, Father, most kind of you. You'll go to your grave wearing your own chains.

Kneeling, Zane jerked the coil of thick chain from Merrick's belt and . . .

Then he saw Father sitting at the other end of the dugout canoe. The sun gleamed off the brown water. On the shore nearby, the stilts under the Dayak longhouse cast soft ribbons of shadow across the sandy commons. Excitement filled Zane at being in this strange, new place. Was there any part of the world Father did not know? Ah, it was good to be with him, good to be a hemophage. What other English lad of only thirteen had seen such wonders? In the year since Father had fed him first blood, he'd been to France, Spain, and now this faraway, exotic land of Borneo.

If only Mother could be here, too. She would love the Dayak sun, this golden blanket of heat, so different from cold, foggy England. If they had lived here, maybe she would still *be* alive. He remembered her cough—the way it jerked her head down, the blood on her pillow those last few months. Back then, before he had gone through his own illness, blood had been so different, so terrifying. . . .

Zane glimpsed the bad thing inside himself; misery and guilt stabbed him before he could look away.

Maybe it was better Mother died when she did.

"Son?"

Looking up, he saw a question in Father's eyes. He forced a smile. Father squeezed his shoulder, giving his cheek and affectionate pat as he pulled his hand back. Clearing his throat, Father said, "Here's how you hold the spear." He grasped the long, polished pole in the center and tilted the sharp point down toward the water.

"Let me try." Zane took the spear and held it at the angle Father had demonstrated.

"The important thing to remember," Father said, "is that the fish will seem to be closer to the surface than it actually is— look out!"

Excited at the sudden glint in the water, Zane threw the spear so hard that the narrow canoe tilted and went over. At once the swift current dragged him under, filling his lungs with water. Panicked, he thrashed out blindly, tumbling against the bottom. Powerful arms encircled his chest and he relaxed. Father walked him across the bottom sand, up the sloping bank until his head broke the surface. Ashamed, he laughed, spewing a pint of water from his lungs. Still holding him, Father fell down on the sand, laughing, too. They lay there laughing together under the hot sun, while the people from the longhouse gathered around them, staring at them as if they were mad. . . .

Zane blinked as the vision vanished and he found himself in darkness again, wandering across the grassy yard. Blood dripped from the long knife in his hand. Dazed, he stared at it. The blood looked black in the weak light of the stars.

Turning, he saw Merrick crawling toward Katie's prone form

at the other side of the yard. *He got into my mind! He can do it, too!*

Zane felt a surge of fear. He knew he should run after Father, chain him while he was still weak, but what if Father attacked his mind again?

I had forgotten about Borneo, Zane thought. The memory was so vivid—the warm sand, laughing with Father. I loved him. I *idolized* him.

Bitter tears filled Zane's eyes, and then he heard a cry from the house. Turning, he saw Jenny at an upstairs window. She was pointing at Katie and Merrick. Zane's heart sank as he realized the danger he was in. She loves them both, he thought. If she thinks I've done this to them, she will hate me!

Zane reached out to dull her senses, to make her think it was only a dream. She resisted. He gazed up at her, startled and unnerved, but pleased, too, at her growing strength. He struck harder and she leaned against the corner of the window, shaking her head in a daze. God, she was so much stronger now! She might rouse again any second. He must go to her at once. Nothing— not even Father—was more important.

Leaving Merrick in the grass, Zane hurried to the house and flew up the wall to the window where she stood, barely feeling the mortar. Jenny opened the window for him and he slipped inside, into what appeared to be a guest bedroom. Jenny was fully alert now; she stared out to where Father was kneeling over Katie. "Why did you do that?" she asked in a cold voice.

"He attacked me," Zane said softly. "I had to defend myself. But you see, Detective Chapman is all right."

"What about Doctor O'Keefe?"

"She'll be all right, too. I only put her to sleep."

Zane watched with frustration as Father picked up Katie's limp form and walked away into the woods across the road. I almost had him, he thought.

But he struck back. He has the power, too.

Zane felt suddenly furious at the way fate was cheating him. He was not stronger than Father anymore. His advantage was gone. . . .

But I still have one weapon in reserve, Zane thought. I know where his son is. When I hold my knife to his son's throat, he will come crawling to me on his knees, and Katie, too.

Now I have to think about Jenny.

Zane took her shoulders, feeling the new muscle there, and

turned her toward him. "You're very brave," he said. "That would have scared most people."

"But I'm not most people, am I?"

"No. I think you know that now."

"You're the man who came to me in my dreams," she said, "but it wasn't a dream, was it?"

"No."

"You said you were my father." Her voice was guarded.

"I am. Can't you feel it?"

She shook her head. "My father is in there asleep." But there was no conviction in her voice this time.

Zane did what he had wanted to do from the moment he saw her—he pulled her into his arms, hugging her to him. He felt her shiver, but she did not push him away. "Ah, Jenny. If only you could know how much you mean to me."

"I know," she said in a small voice. "You saved me. You brought me the medicine."

"Yes. I would never have let you get so sick, if only I'd known. But I . . . didn't know where you were. When I found out, I came back here just in time to save you. You are special, Jenny, like me. You have great powers and they'll get even greater. Pretty soon you'll understand everything." He studied her face. It looked a little pale. "Are you hungry now?"

"Yes," she whispered.

"I have a place I want to take you," he said.

Merrick sat in the woods across the road, cradling Katie's head in his lap, terribly weak from his wounds, heavy with despair. Sandeman had kept Zane from chaining him, but only just. Zane had come out of the clash stronger, much stronger. What would he do now?

The front door of Jenny's house opened and Zane and Jenny, walked out together. Zane stood a moment, staring at the place where Katie had fallen. A chill ran up Merrick's spine. If Zane tracked him now, it would be all over. He was too weak to defend himself or Katie, and Sandeman was clearly not strong enough to hold Zane off in his memories for long.

Zane looked up from the grass and stared across the road. Merrick held very still, knowing the slightest movement would give him away. The back of his neck prickled as he felt Zane's gaze sweep over him.

Then Jenny tugged at Zane's hand and he turned away. They

cut across the neighbor's front yard and disappeared through the line of trees that formed a windbreak between houses. Merrick realized they were heading toward the main road, where Zane must have parked his car. Stop him! he thought, but knew he could not.

He waited until he heard the car start up and pull away. At the same time, he felt the last trickle of blood stop inside his chest as the rips in his heart finished healing. Struggling to his feet, he picked up Katie. She was a dead weight, still deeply unconscious; he could sense no torn blood vessels in her brain, but she had been hurt, concussed, as surely as if Zane had struck a physical blow to her head.

Merrick carried her across the road, glad to feel some strength returning to his legs, and veered over to the forsythia hedge. Sandeman looked up at him with wide eyes. "Thank God!"

"God has nothing to do with any of this," Merrick said. "You are the one who kept Zane from burying me."

Sandeman's expression was grim. "He's very strong. But I got in at last. Is Katie all right?"

"I think she will be. But I have to get her to the hospital. I'll just put her in the car and be right back to get you."

"No. Take her straight there. Then you can come back for me."

Merrick hesitated, torn. "What if Zane returns before I do and finds you?"

"He won't. I'm very good at not moving. And even if he does, what can he do to me?" Sandeman gave him a smile meant to look devil-may-care, but Merrick knew he was afraid of Zane. All of creation should be afraid of Zane now.

"I'll make it as fast as I can," Merrick said.

"Don't worry about me," Sandeman murmured. "Worry about Jenny. You realize what is happening."

Merrick nodded, agonized. "He's taking her out to hunt."

"That's right. And if he gets her to kill tonight, you won't be able to save her."

Zane parked the car in the lot behind the orderly's garden apartment. He looked up at the third-story bedroom window, feeling both anger and a keen anticipation. The filthy animal thought he was safe, that he could take his pleasure pawing the body of a defenseless young girl and pay no price. But he was about to pay the ultimate price.

Jenny leaned over to see where he was looking. Zane was very encouraged by her lack of fear, her interest in what was happening. She was developing more quickly than he'd dared hope. And tonight would be the critical moment.

"What's up there?" Jenny asked.

"Remember the man dressed in white, who came and touched you when you were in the hospital?"

Jenny's expression darkened. "Yes."

"That's his room up there. What he did to you was very evil. He has probably done it to other young girls, too. And he will most certainly do it again."

Jenny's jaw clenched. Her pale face showed distress, as if she saw where this was heading. Zane felt a touch of doubt, but reassured himself. She was hungry. That would make the difference.

"You and I are going to make sure he never hurts another little girl," Zane said.

Jenny's eyes widened. "Me?"

"Don't worry, I'll help you."

She looked at him with fear, but he could see a glimmer of trust there, too, and it thrilled him. "Come on."

Getting out, he led Jenny across the lot. He said, "We'll stay in the shadows as much as possible. It's late, but if someone looks our way, I'll sense it and block us out of his vision. Before long you will be able to do that, too."

"Wow. Really?"

"Yes. It will come to you in a few more days or weeks. Then it will seem like you always knew." Zane stopped at the foot of the brick wall.

"What are you doing?" Jenny asked. "Don't we have to go inside?"

"No." Zane knelt. "Climb on my back. I'm going to take you for a ride. We have to be very quiet, so don't say anything, all right?"

She nodded, her eyes alight now. Hooking her arms over Zane's shoulders from behind, she wrapped her legs around his waist. As he started up the wall, she gasped and nestled her head against his shoulder, but after a minute she pulled away again to look down. Zane's heart filled with joy. She's so brave! he thought. "You will be able to do this before long, too," he whispered.

He stopped beside the orderly's bedroom window.

"Can you feel him in there?" Zane whispered.

"No," Jenny whispered back.

"Just relax and feel him inside your mind."

"I . . . feel a little beat," she said. "It's slow."

"That's his pulse," Zane whispered. "It's slow because he's sleeping. Can you make it even slower?"

After a minute, he felt the pulse slow, even though he had done nothing. "Good!" he said. Keeping his grip on the brick with one hand, Zane forced the window open. In another moment, he and Jenny were inside. She stood, gazing down at the sleeping man. The sheets were twisted around his legs and his mouth was open. Zane wanted to leap on him at once, start tearing his throat, but he held back, watching Jenny.

A look of revulsion crossed her face. "It *is* him," she whispered.

"Yes."

"He kept touching me, and there was nothing I could do."

"I know." Zane hugged her against him. "You will never again be helpless. But other girls are not so lucky. So you must kill him."

Jenny gasped and backed away from the bed. "I can't."

"Of course you can. You were born to do it. And he deserves it."

She bit at her lip and tears started to flow down her cheeks. She shook her head, still backing up, and he saw with sharp disappointment that it was too soon after all. In two quick steps, he stood at the orderly's bedside. Pulling the bowie knife from his belt, he slashed the bared throat open. The body arched on the bed and the orderly made a bubbling sound, then fell back, limp. With a fierce effort of will, Zane turned away from the blood toward his daughter. Jenny was cringing in horror against the wall, and for a second, he thought all was lost. Then she came forward automatically, and he could see the pumping blood mirrored in her eyes in the instant before she fell on the man and began to feed.

THIRTY-FOUR

KATIE DRIFTED AWAKE. Gazing groggily at the slanting light, she wondered if it meant sunrise or sunset. A long shadow divided the light into twin shafts that blazed across the orange tile floor. She could not remember any wing of Georgetown Hospital having an orange floor, but this *was* a hospital, no question—the bed's chrome guardrail gleamed only inches from her eye and she could hear a meds cart squeaking down the hall. A sweetish whiff of rubbing alcohol pierced her nostrils and faded. I should be afraid, she thought. But I'm just too tired. Her eyes started to slip closed again—

The shadow moved.

Katie lurched up on her elbow, twisting toward the window. Her ears rang and everything went gray for a second and then the silhouette moved toward her out of the blazing light.

"Sorry," Merrick said softly, "I didn't mean to startle you."

She started to relax, then remembered: *Merrick, crossing the lawn at Jenny's house, then nothing. Is he here to kill me?*

"How are you feeling?" His voice was soft, full of concern, and Katie wondered what game he was playing. Whatever it was, in her shape she'd better play along.

"I'm very sleepy," she said. Actually, she wasn't anymore. She wanted to get up and run out of the room, but if he was here to kill her, she wouldn't get very far. "What time is it?" she asked.

"Around five-thirty. You're in George Washington University hospital. I brought you in last night. You've been asleep almost eighteen hours."

Katie stared at him, stunned. Eighteen hours! If Merrick meant to kill her, he'd had plenty of chances. *He wants to know how much I know,* she thought. *Act like you don't remember anything.*

"What happened?" she asked.

"I was hoping you could tell me," Merrick said. "I found you lying unconscious on the Hrluskas' lawn late yesterday evening. I brought you here rather than to Georgetown so the killer won't know where you are. The doctors think you had a concussion, but they can't find any head trauma. Also, your hematocrit was way down so they gave you two pints of blood."

Katie was aware suddenly of the puncture wounds on her throat. Her fear rose again. *You didn't need the doctors to tell you about my low hematocrit, did you?*

"Katie, what on earth were you doing out there?"

She hesitated, wondering how far she dared go. "I could ask you the same question."

"I wanted to make sure Jenny was all right," he said.

You wanted to feed her again. Katie shuddered, shifting her shoulders to hide it from Merrick. She wished there was someone else she could suspect. But if it wasn't Merrick who had struck her down in the darkness last night—without touching her—it was a near twin. And why do it, unless he was guilty of something terrible—of giving Jenny blood? Just the thought was horrifying. A year ago, Jenny had been a normal little girl. What must it be like for her now? How could she stand to drink it, knowing what it was?

Maybe she doesn't know, Katie thought. She trusts Merrick. He visited her a lot while she was sick. Was that why—to build up her trust so he could feed her? That must be why he was there last night, and when I tried to stop him, he struck me down. . . .

But why didn't he just kill me then? Why bring me to the hospital?

Maybe he thinks he can hide his true nature and hold onto our relationship.

A nightmarish sense of unreality swept Katie. The man she had loved and trusted, drinking blood, giving it to a child? She must be dreaming it, *please God, let it be a dream, let me wake up now.* But Merrick continued to gaze down at her, his face now masked in shadow. A cold dread swept her. The Merrick she had loved was only an artful shell. This creature standing by her bed only pretended to be that man, only pretended to care about her. He was, in fact, a vampire—not a dream or a myth, a terrifying reality.

"I thought we had agreed you would stay at Meggan's," Merrick said.

"For how long? Merrick, I have patients who depend on me. And I wanted to check on Jenny, too...." Katie swallowed, struggling to keep up her end of the charade. "How...how are you coming with your investigation?" she asked.

"I've been taken off the case." He explained—something about precinct politics—but she wondered with alarm if the police had started to suspect him, too. If so, he would be more dangerous than ever—

She realized Merrick had finished talking. "I'm sorry," she said.

His expression became more intent. "It's all right. I'm still very much in the chase."

She knew she should stay in character, ask him to be careful, but she could only nod. "Does Mom know I'm here?"

"Of course," Merrick said. "I told her you'll be fine and to stay put. Whatever is after you is still out there. As long as she and Gregory stay at Meggan's they'll be safe."

"I want to call her."

Merrick picked the phone up, dialed, and handed her the receiver. She felt a wave of frustration. How could she warn Mom that Merrick might be the killer with him standing right there? Could she ask him to step out? No, it would make him suspicious. Maybe she could slip something in, but she must be very careful. Mom came on the line; Katie reassured her that she was all right, then asked to speak to Gregory. Tears started leaking when she heard his voice, but she kept her own conversation cheery for him. When Mom came back on, Katie told her she'd be home soon and to keep a close eye on Gregory. She put a special emphasis on the last, willing her mother to remember her earlier warning not to let Merrick take him. When she hung up, Merrick put the phone back. She could read nothing in his expression.

"I need to tell Art I'm here," Katie said.

"I called him after I checked you in," Merrick said. "He's covering for you."

"Still, I should call him. I need to review patients with him—"

"He's a very competent young man," Merrick said. "I'm sure he'll do fine. Right now you need to rest." He stroked her forehead. His hand was warm, his touch, against all reason, strangely soothing. She felt her fear sinking into a bog of sleepiness. The fading golden light flowed through the window, thick as honey. Drowsily, she remembered the last time she'd had this feeling—when the dentist gave her a shot of Demerol. Merrick leaned over and kissed her forehead. "You rest now," he said, "and I'll come back later, when you're feeling better." A sluggish alarm stirred in her. He's putting me to sleep, she thought. Fight him. She tried to summon her will, but then she couldn't remember why, and the glowing room slid away under her eyelids. The last thing she heard was Merrick saying, "Sleep. . . ."

Katie awoke with a start in darkness, her heart pounding. *Where am I?*

Voices drifted in from the hall, two women, laughter bubbling away. The only light came from the hallway. It was night. Anxiety welled up in Katie. She was still in GWU hospital. Merrick made me sleep, she recalled. He can come back and get me whenever he wants. I've got to get out.

She fumbled with the bed rail, easing it down, then swinging her legs carefully out of bed. She felt weak, but clearheaded. As long as she took things slowly, she should be all right. What should she do now?

Go after Merrick.

The sense of unreality gripped her again. With an effort, she shook it off. This was real; nothing could be more dangerous than sinking back into her bed. There is a vampire, she thought—I *know* that. Everything points to Merrick, but I have to be sure. First I'll go to my house. It's the last place Merrick would expect, and if the police are still staking it out, I'll be as safe there as anywhere. When I get there, I'll call Meggan's to check on Mom and Gregory, make sure they're all right. And then? Her mind went blank for a scary moment.

The syringe, she thought. Do I still have it?

She stood and located the closet door, then a wave of dizziness forced her to grab the foot of the bed. *So weak.* She turned on the lamp on her bed table and shuffled to the room's small closet. Her knees felt rubbery; just the few steps left her lightheaded. It was maddening—just when she needed to be strong, she felt like she'd just come off a week of the flu.

Opening the closet door, Katie found her clothes hanging neatly on hangers. She checked the pocket of her jacket and was heartened to find the syringe, loaded with Fraction Eight. Maybe her luck was beginning to change. She dressed, trying to hurry, but found that she could only handle buttons and zippers by slowing way down. At least she'd been given a transfusion—without it, she probably would have fainted by now.

Suddenly, she realized just what she did need.

Searching the other pocket of her jacket, she found the five Ritalin capsules, still wrapped in a tissue. Before she could argue with herself, she popped one into her mouth and swallowed it dry. She could feel it crawling down until it dropped below the hollow of her throat.

An ugly vision flashed through her mind, of herself a month from now, swinging back and forth between fatigue and manic energy, fighting the old battle again. Or, worse, not fighting it.

A month from now might never come.

The thought was oddly soothing. Emptying her mind, she sat on the edge of her bed to wait for the surge of strength that would begin around her heart and then flow down to her legs. First there would be a smell—yes, here it came, black and slick, like damp glass in a reptile house.

And then she felt the boost. Strength welled up in her magically, from nowhere, followed by a wave of optimism. She had done the right thing, taking the Ritalin. All she had to do now was get out of here and hail a cab.

Katie peeked out her door to make sure no nurses were looking her way. The elevators here were in the usual place near the nurses station. No way could she slip past them without being seen. Heading the other way, she made it into the stairwell. In the lobby, two floors down, she hesitated at a bank of vending machines. Not hungry, no, but that was the amphetamines, and she knew she should eat something.

She bought two Snickers and forced them both down.

The clock in the lobby said nine-twenty. Two cabs idled outside the big glass doors. Ten minutes later, she paid the cabby off and walked up the front steps of her house. She could see no sign of a stakeout, but the lights were on inside. A woman about her height appeared as she opened the door.

"Doctor O'Keefe?"

"That's right," Katie said, "but you'd be convincing from a distance. My bathrobe even fits you."

The police woman gave her a slightly sheepish smile. "I'm Corporal Etta Todd."

"You have real courage to do this, Corporal. I'm grateful to you."

"No problem. Uh, we weren't expecting you to show up, Doctor."

"I hope I'm not ruining the stakeout."

"Not unless the killer's watching right now. Actually, the detective in charge of the case—Lieutenant Cooke—has been wanting to talk to you."

Katie's heart sank. Talking to a curious detective for two hours was the last thing she needed right now. "Do me a favor," she said. "I'll be happy to talk with Detective Cooke, but I need a shower and I have a little phone business to conduct. Could you wait a half hour or so to call him?"

Etta hesitated. "You *will* see Detective Cooke tonight, won't you?"

"You bet," Katie lied. "I want to talk to him, too. I just need to take care of a few things first."

"All right," Todd said.

"Thanks. And thanks again for what you're doing."

"I just hope we catch him."

"Me, too." But you won't, Katie thought. Not if it's Merrick. Only I have a chance. A cold knot formed in her stomach. She hurried upstairs to the phone in her bedroom and dialed Meggan's house. Meggan answered, sounding very tense. "Oh! Katie, I . . ."

"Meggan, what's wrong?"

"Now don't worry—everything's under control. We were going to call you if necessary, but you need to rest and I'm sure it will all work out—"

Dread swept Katie. "Meggan!"

"Gregory seems to have wandered off. He was out in the backyard around sunset, and your Mom was there, too. She turned her back for a second and when she looked again he was gone.

I'm sure he's back in the pines behind the house somewhere. We've got police searching the area—''

"Has Merrick been there?"

"What? Well, yes, your Mom said he came by in the late afternoon wanting to take Gregory for a ride, but she said no and he left—''

Katie hung up in mid-sentence. Her heart pounded with terror. Merrick took Gregory!

No, not Gregory, *please*...

Katie pressed her hand to her forehead, fighting for control. Where would Merrick take him?

His house, Katie thought.

She went to her dresser and rummaged frantically until she found the key Merrick had given her when they were dating. Then she hurried to the bathroom and took another Ritalin, washing this one down with water. Downstairs, she stopped by the closet and took down the box with the .357 magnum and shells inside—

"Ready for me to call Detective Cooke?"

Katie nearly dropped the box. Heart pounding, she turned to Etta and forced a calm smile. "Not quite," she said. "I need something from the drug store. Then I'll be back and you can call him."

Etta looked doubtful, but Katie gave her a reassuring smile. She made herself walk with slow calm to her car. Starting up the Cutlass, she drove slowly down the street until she was around the corner. Then she gunned it up Wisconsin toward Merrick's house in upper Northwest Washington. The second hit of Ritalin did a glissando up her spine, making her fingers dance nervously on the wheel. She could feel the drug feeding her agitation, but that couldn't be helped. She needed every edge she could get now.

What if Merrick didn't take him home?

Katie slowed, then hit the accelerator again. Even if Gregory wasn't there, it was her best hope of finding a sign about where Merrick might have taken him.

Merrick, *why?* she thought. If you hurt him, I'll kill you. So help me God.

She stopped in front of his house. Seeing lights on inside, she felt a rush of hope—and fear. Taking the gun from the box, she loaded it in the glow from the streetlight and checked the pocket of her medical coat to make sure the syringe was still there. She ran up the front walk and onto the porch. Passing the swing triggered an unwanted image of summer nights here with

Merrick, lulled by the soft squeak of the chain. At the door, she started to slip her key in, then froze as she heard a child cry inside.

Gregory!

In an agony of fear, she jammed her key into the lock and turned it.

THIRTY-FIVE

KATIE RUSHED THROUGH the front door, pointing the .357 magnum at the ceiling ahead of her so she wouldn't endanger Gregory. There he was, sitting on the floor! His little shoulders hunched and he let out another terrified squall. Her heart leapt with terror. What was wrong? Was he hurt?

He turned toward her and stopped crying at once. "Mommy!"

She swept him up with one arm, then heard a sound from deeper in the house. Merrick charged through the kitchen door, pulling his gun from his shoulder holster as he ran. His face was dark with fury. Terrified, she pointed her gun at him. "Drop it!" she cried.

Instead, he pointed his service revolver over her shoulder. "Put Gregory down," he said in a low voice, "and move away from him."

She started to refuse, then realized she must do it—she could not risk Gregory being hit by gunfire. Easing him to the floor, she circled three or four steps away; at once, he began to whimper. "It's all right, sweetie. Mommy wants you to go in the kitchen now. Go ahead. I'll come get you in a minute. You stay there until I do, okay?"

Gregory ran into the kitchen.

Merrick said, "Throw the gun to me, Katie."

"No. You put yours down first."

"I can't do that. There is . . . someone behind you."

"Right." I have to shoot, she thought. Before he hides himself from me. She straightened her arms in the classic shooting stance. He was looking past her again, his eyes wide with fear, his service revolver still aimed at her shoulder. She pointed the .357 magnum at his heart. Shoot! she thought.

But she could not.

And then she felt hands close over hers, squeezing down hard, forcing her finger to pull the trigger. The gun boomed in her hands, and blood spurted from the center of Merrick's chest. "No!" she screamed, and tried to pull her hands free. She watched, horrified, as Merrick pitched forward onto his face.

The unseen grip released her and she dropped the gun and rushed to Merrick. Kneeling over his body, she felt a suffocating pressure in her chest. *A nightmare, wake up, she must wake up,* but she could not. Sobs tore at her throat.

"You had to do it," said a voice behind her.

Turning, her mind numb with shock, she saw another Merrick towering over her. No, not Merrick, but close enough to be a brother. "I *didn't* do it," she said. "You *made* me."

"I had to. He's very dangerous. You had the right idea, believe me."

Gregory! she thought. Stay in the kitchen, please, God, make him stay in there.

The man knelt beside Merrick. Snatching a coil of thick cable from his belt, he bound Merrick up, starting with his ankles and working his way up until four or five loops pinned Merrick's arms tightly to his sides. Katie watched passively, a cold numbness creeping through her. She realized with alarm that she was slipping into shock; she fought it, taking slow deep breaths until her head cleared. The man brought the small loops at each end of the cable together and locked them with a padlock.

"He . . . he's not dead?" Katie asked.

"No." Getting up, the man retrieved Merrick's gun and the one she had thrown down. "Done!" he said.

She tried not even to look toward the kitchen. Gregory was keeping quiet. But had this . . . creature seen him before? *Talk to him, keep him engaged.* "Who are you?" she said.

"My name is Zane."

"I didn't see you. Are you a . . . a vampire?"

He looked pained. "Please. Vampires are fairy tales."

"You know what I mean. Are you like Merrick?"

Zane looked startled. "You know what he is?"

"Yes."

He shook his head with what seemed like admiration. "You *are* a very smart lady. The proper term for us is hemophage, from the Greek."

"Blood eater." Katie felt queasy. "Why did you make me shoot him?"

Zane stared at Merrick's prone form. He walked over and put a foot on Merrick's back, pressing down lightly for a moment. Merrick didn't move. "He has drunk the blood of thousands of human beings."

Katie looked at him, staggered. *Thousands?* "No, that can't be."

"As God is my witness."

His voice was serious, utterly convincing. Despair welled up in Katie; with a fierce effort, she held back tears. We're still in danger, she thought. Where does Zane fit into this? "Do you . . . eat blood, too?"

Zane gave her a measuring look. "I must, to survive. But I don't kill. Every few weeks, I slip into someone's house, put them deeply asleep, and take a pint or two with transfusion equipment."

"Tell her the truth," Merrick groaned.

Katie looked down, stunned. A bullet in the heart and five minutes later, he could talk? Merrick rolled to his side. A surprisingly small circle of blood soaked the center of his shirt. As she stared at it, a metallic lump appeared in its center; a second later it dropped to the floor and she realized with a shock that it was the slug from the .357 magnum. Merrick's body had pushed the bullet back out!

"Easy," Zane said, reaching out to steady her.

"Katie," Merrick said, "listen to me. Zane is lying. You are the only one he ever took blood from without killing."

She touched her throat, suddenly remembering a dream she'd

had in the on-call room. A man, handsome as an angel, had come to her in the narrow bed. *This man.* With a shock, she realized it had been no dream. The man had touched her and then drawn away. He *was* the killer. . . .

He could have raped her, but he had not.

Katie's head swirled with confusion. You decided the killer *had* to be Merrick, she thought, partly because there seemed to be no one else it could be. Now there is. You can believe in Merrick again, if you want to. A strange elation broke through her terror for just a second.

"Oh, Merrick . . . I . . ."

"It's all right," he said. "You couldn't have known."

Zane said, "You don't actually believe him, do you?"

The front door banged open. Zane's face twisted in fury; Katie turned in time to see Art Stratton pitch forward onto his face. She gasped and started toward him, but Zane got there first. He kicked the door shut and knelt astride Art's back. Grabbing a handful of thick blond hair, he jerked Art's head up as he reached to his own back and pulled out a huge knife. Katie screamed as he set the blade against Art's throat.

"Stop!" Merrick's voice cracked like a whip, and Zane hesitated. For a second, Katie saw fear in his eyes, and then contempt.

"Or you'll what?" he sneered.

"Or I'll attack your mind—your memories."

Zane paled but did not remove the knife. "Why haven't you done that already?"

"I should have. You took me by surprise. The man is harmless. He saw nothing and he will remember nothing later."

Zane stared at him. "And if I let him live, you won't try it?"

"I give you my word."

Zane removed the knife and let Art's head drop. Relief flitted through Katie and was gone. Zane got up and looked at her. "So now you know," he said. "Merrick is the good guy and I'm the bad guy. Or so he would have you believe."

"What do you want from us?"

Zane pointed to the phone. "I believe you have a call to make to Doctor Byner. It's after hours, but I understand medical examiners often work late in your fair city."

"Don't do it," Merrick said. "He'll kill you as soon as you're done."

"Not true," Zane said. "But I will most certainly kill your son if you refuse."

Katie knew without any doubt that he meant it. Terror filled her. "If I call, will you leave him alone?"

Zane hesitated, then nodded.

"Give me your word!"

He cocked his head. "You would accept that?"

"Yes."

"Then you understand something about me Merrick does not. I give you my word. Make the call—and do everything else I ask of you—and your son lives."

"He's lying," Merrick said.

Zane whirled on him, his face red. "You think you have a monopoly on honor?"

"I'll do it," Katie said quickly. She hurried to the phone, dialed information, and got the number of the morgue. In a moment more, Byner came on the line. She told him that the killer's blood now looked completely normal—that the membrane must have been the result of some strange chemical reaction that had happened while the body lay in the bushes for two days. She was amazed at how calm her voice sounded. Byner asked her if she had any idea what could cause such a reaction and she said no, and she would keep looking into it if he liked, but the killer's blood was definitely normal, a complete dead end.

Byner thanked her. He sounded relieved.

She hung up.

"You did well," Zane said. He looked as relieved as Byner had sounded.

Against all reason, she felt a grain of hope. "I won't say anything. You can let us go."

"No I can't."

"My son needs his mother."

Zane looked impatient. "Your son will live if you do everything I ask. That is what you agreed to. Or is your word worth nothing?"

Merrick was right, Katie thought. He's going to kill us all. She felt faint with fear. She must do something, now, before it was too late—

The syringe!

Katie slipped her hands into her pockets, taking a step back from Zane. But as her hand closed on the syringe, Zane started toward the kitchen—and Gregory! She thumbed the plastic guard off the needle and lunged at Zane. With an easy motion, he swatted the syringe away and backhanded her in almost the same motion. Dimly, she felt her knees hit the floor. The room whirled, and then a wave of pain rebounded through her. She stayed on her hands and knees, overwhelmed, her last hope gone.

"What was that?" Zane asked. "Some kind of poison?" Before she could answer, he walked into the kitchen and she heard Gregory let out a little cry. It broke her from her paralysis. As she scrambled up, Zane returned from the kitchen with Gregory seated in the crook of his arm. She wanted to lunge forward, tear her son away, but she held herself still, thinking of Zane's promise. Maybe he would keep it.

Zane bounced Gregory lightly against him, as if the child were his favorite nephew. "One more trick like your little syringe, and our deal is off," he said.

"No more tricks," she murmured. "Please don't hurt him."

Zane sighed. "I am going to pick Merrick up now. You are going to walk in front of us to my car, which is parked just in front of yours. You will open the back door and then get into the driver's seat. If you scream, if you do anything . . ."

"I understand."

"Good."

Keeping Gregory in one arm, Zane picked Merrick up with the other as easily as if he were a rolled-up rug and nodded toward the door.

Outside, on the sidewalk, Katie glanced back once. She saw no one behind her, and then Zane let her have a glimpse. She could feel her heart pounding, urging her to action, but there was nothing she could do. She opened the rear door. Someone was already inside on the backseat; Katie stared, too stunned to speak. Jenny Hrluska glanced at her, then looked away. "Hi, Doctor O'Keefe," she said. "I'm really sorry."

The field behind the abandoned farmhouse was screened from the road by a line of trees. A full moon poured down, so bright that Katie could see her shadow ripple across the uneven grassy turf ahead of her. The night air was mild and still, heavy with moisture. Breathless with fear, she walked ahead of Zane and Jenny across the uneven ground, praying that Zane would let Gregory live. *He has to kill me, though. I know too much.* Her stomach lurched, as though she were on an elevator plunging into free fall. Terrified, she stumbled and dropped to her knees.

"Come on, Doctor," Zane said softly behind her. "You can make it. Be brave now."

She remembered almost the same words from the time he'd held the knife to her throat in her lab. "Don't make my son watch," she pleaded.

"No," Zane agreed.

She pushed to her feet and walked on.

"Veer left a little," Zane said, and she veered left. She heard Jenny say something to Zane, her voice too soft to make out the words.

"You know why," Zane answered in a low voice.

Katie felt a dull horror. Jenny had just protested, but Zane had calmed her with three soft words. How did he have such a hold over her? Why had he brought her along to see this? Was an execution of someone she loved a part of her indoctrination into her new life? Katie shivered. Clearly, Jenny needed blood to live now. Nothing else could have changed her so much in such a short time. What an upheaval she had come through. It must be wonderful to feel so good again—and at the same time, hellish to know that the life she had lived, her innocent childhood, was over. Killing someone to drink their blood was not like going in for dialysis. Suddenly, at the age of twelve, Jenny must decide all over again who she was. She wasn't an innocent little girl anymore. She was a . . . a *hemophage,* whether she liked it or not. She had to kill to live. . . .

Or did she?

Katie remembered what Zane had said about taking a few pints of blood in transfusion packs. She realized suddenly that he had been talking about Merrick, mocking Merrick. But if Merrick could do that and survive, couldn't Jenny?

Not with Zane as her teacher, Katie thought.

"Stop," Zane said. "Don't step in the hole."

She stopped. In the moonlight, she saw a blacker rectangle in the dirt, and then she realized it was a deep pit—a grave. She could smell the freshly dug earth. Her mouth went dry with fear. Zane slung Merrick's bound body face down onto the ground a few feet from the grave. He kept his hold on Gregory, who seemed at the moment to be fascinated by the strange play being acted out by these adults.

Zane looked at her. "Get down in the hole."

"Don't do this to her," Merrick said. "I beg you."

Zane frowned. "Don't beg. It's beneath you." He nodded at the grave and shifted Gregory—just the slightest of threats.

Terrified, Katie jumped down into the grave. It was as deep as she was tall, walling her in with the damp dirt and sheared roots. She looked up into Merrick's eyes, only a few feet away. They were filled with such grief and desolation that she had to look away.

Zane sat down on Merrick's back and began amiably bouncing Gregory on his knee. His face looked white as chalk in the flood of moonlight. Beside him, Jenny stood quietly, her expression sad.

Katie remembered the threat Merrick had made against Zane—*I'll attack your mind—your memories.* "If you can do anything to him," she whispered, "do it. To hell with your promise."

Merrick gave his head a slight shake, and she realized there was nothing he could do. He had been bluffing.

"Interesting," Zane said. "You can't attack me now, but you could last night. Why?"

Merrick said nothing.

"Do you expect me to believe I had that memory on my own?"

"What memory?" Merrick asked.

Katie saw a fleeting pain on Zane's face. "That time in Borneo," he said, "when you taught me how to fish."

Merrick closed his eyes. "We capsized and you panicked because you thought you were drowning. You were so young it hadn't really sunk in yet that you couldn't drown."

What are they talking about? Katie wondered. Were they friends, once? Again, it struck her that they looked enough alike to be brothers.

"You must tell Jenny she has a choice," Merrick said.

Zane's expression hardened. He gazed down at Merrick. "What do you care about Jenny?"

"I'd give anything to save her."

"Then why were you letting her die?"

Jenny looked down at him, too. "Yes, *why,* Detective Chapman? I was really sick. All those weeks, and it hurt all the time. You could have helped me. Didn't you want to?"

"With all my heart," Merrick said brokenly.

Of course, Katie thought. Merrick knew Jenny was a hemophage. And yet he didn't try to save her because he knew what she would become. That's why Zane brought Jenny out here, to discredit Merrick. To make her hate him if possible.

But why does he want that?

Katie looked from Merrick's desolate face to Zane's savage look of triumph. *What is it between you two?*

"With all my heart," Zane echoed mockingly. "If you had wanted to save her, you could have done it at any moment. Instead you let her suffer, and you were going to let her die."

"I didn't think she'd want to become a murderer like you."

Zane shook his head. "That's rich. You try to kill me, then call me a murderer."

"It's what you are."

"Don't judge me. I had enough of that from you to last a thousand years." Zane's voice was tight with fury. "We are the lions, Merrick, and these are the zebras." He pointed at Katie and Gregory.

"They are not animals," Merrick said. "Nor are we."

Zane looked amused. "Not animals? Your precious 'normals' kill more of each other every day than we do in a year."

"Why don't you tell Jenny exactly what you do."

"She knows."

"That you kill young women?"

"Before they can breed. I didn't choose young women, the gene did, but I have no problem with it either."

"You kill because you love it." Merrick's voice was heavy with disgust.

"I was *born* to love it," Zane answered. "So was Jenny. You condemn us for being what we are. You want us to be *ashamed*."

Katie watched with dread fascination. There was such antipathy between the two, and yet they clearly cared what each other thought, even now, on the brink of the grave.

Katie felt the panic rising in her chest again. *I'm not ready to die. Gregory needs me. I want to live.*

She glanced down, hoping to see a rock, anything she could use as a weapon, but the bottom of the grave was lost in blackness. Desperately, she looked along the rim—

And saw the slight lump under Merrick's pants cuff.

His ankle holster!

Katie felt a furious surge of adrenaline. There was a chance! But even if she managed to get the gun, Zane was holding Gregory. At the first sudden movement from her, he could twist Gregory's neck, snap it in an instant. And what if she shot at Zane and hit Gregory? No, she must have an absolutely clear shot. If she could distract Zane, get him to look away . . .

But how could she do that from down here?

"I did not want you to feel ashamed," Merrick said.

Zane gave a bitter laugh. "You tried to make me feel like a monster."

"All I wanted was to teach you right from wrong. To give you a chance to love and be loved."

"I love my daughter," Zane said, glancing at Jenny.

My God, Katie thought. Jenny is his *daughter?*

"And I love my granddaughter," Merrick said.

Katie stared at him, astonished.

Jenny leaned toward Merrick, touching him on the shoulder, then looking up at Zane. "Is that true? Is he my grandfather?"

"No," Zane said.

"Don't lie to her," Merrick said.

Zane looked imploringly at Jenny. "Come on, Jenny, would your own grandfather let you die?"

"Maybe he should have," Jenny said softly.

"No," Merrick said. "I was wrong. I didn't know you were my granddaughter then. But I did know you were a sweet, innocent child. No matter what you might become, I should have saved you. And now it's too late. But always remember that I love you very much."

"He doesn't," Zane said. "He's only saying that to—"

"Stop it, both of you!" Jenny screamed. She turned and ran. Zane leapt up, spilling Gregory from his lap, staring after her with a look of anguish.

"Wait!" he cried, but she kept running. Then Zane's head moved slightly, a stiff nod toward his daughter; Jenny staggered to a stop and fell to her knees.

Now! Katie thought. She pulled the gun from Merrick's ankle holster and fired three shots into the back of Zane's head.

THIRTY-SIX

KATIE'S EARS RANG with the shots, BOOM-BOOM-BOOM. She saw blood spray from the back of Zane's head. He pitched forward, out of sight. She realized she was screaming.

"Katie, Katie, KATIE!" Merrick shouted.

She stopped screaming. "Is he down?"

"Yes!" Merrick yelled. "Get out of the grave. Hurry!"

Frantic, she grabbed tufts of weed and grass at the rim of the grave and tried to scramble up. The grass tore free and she fell back, landing hard on her rump. Above her, in the rectangle of milky light, she saw Gregory's face.

"Mommy, can I come down, too?"

"No!" she shouted. "No, sweetie. Get back, please. Just a minute and I'll come up."

"Hurry," Merrick said, "before Zane comes around."

Katie felt another burst of panic. How could Zane survive

bullets in the brain? *Because it regenerates, just like his body.*

"Grab ahold," Merrick said.

She saw that he had squirmed around so that his feet hung over the edge. She grabbed his ankles.

"Hang on," he said and jacked his legs up, lifting her feet from the ground. Her toes banged into the side of the hole; kicking back, she planted her feet and walked up the side, still hanging onto Merrick's ankles. He gave her another tug, and she got a knee on the lip of the grave and rolled out onto the grass. Zane was lying on his face near Merrick. The back of his head was bloody, but not as bloody as it should have been. One arm twitched, and she heard him groan. She jumped to her knees.

"Quick," Merrick said, "the key. Check his pockets."

She scrambled over to him, jamming her hands down into his pants pocket. Her hand closed on the key. In another second she was at Merrick's side, unlocking the padlock. She pulled and tugged at the cable, clumsy with desperation; as his arms came free, he was able to pull the last loops off his legs himself.

Zane groaned again.

Merrick jumped on him, wrapping the cable around his chest and arms first, then his legs. "The padlock!" he said, but she was already there, slipping it through the two loops and snapping it shut again. Merrick took the key and put it in his pocket.

Katie sat down on the grass and hugged Gregory to her.

"Mommy, I want to go home."

She hugged Gregory to her. "Oh, yes. We can do that now. You're a very brave little boy and I love you so much."

"I love you, too, Mommy."

"We're not safe yet," Merrick cautioned.

Katie stared at him in disbelief. "Merrick, I hit his *brain.*"

"I know, but it will regenerate very quickly. He'll be conscious in a minute; within thirty to forty minutes he'll have even the highest functions back—which means he'll be able to strike you down or get into my mind, my memories. We have to hurry. Get my gun again."

Feeling queasy, Katie scrambled across the grass and retrieved the gun from the lip of the grave. When she turned again, she saw that Merrick had hurried away to tend to Jenny, who was still lying in the grass a dozen yards off.

Zane flexed suddenly against the cable, and Katie jumped back, startled. With a frenzied burst of effort, he rolled back and forth, thrashing like a huge shark dragged out of the water. Katie grabbed Gregory up and ran off a few feet, terrified he might break free. At last, he quit struggling and lay on his side, facing her.

"Let me go!" His voice was hoarse with fear.

Katie stared at him, horrified. Gregory began to cry. She felt Merrick's hand on her shoulder and turned. He gave her a quick hug, then said, "Help Jenny, would you? She's still a little weak. I'll carry Zane to the car."

Zane twisted to look up at him, his face suddenly alight with hope. "You're not going to bury me?"

"Not in that hole," Merrick said.

Carrying Gregory, Katie followed Merrick through the woods, worrying about the time. Merrick had driven like a maniac, eighty and ninety miles an hour along the country roads, but almost twenty minutes had slipped by since his warning. She had already felt a few twinges of dizziness. She could not be sure it was Zane trying to interfere with her blood flow, but if Merrick was right, he would be able to strike her—and Merrick—within another few minutes.

And what about Jenny? She was a hemophage, too, and Zane's daughter. Was that why Merrick had left her in the car—so she wouldn't come to her father's aid? She seemed almost catatonic—all right physically, but unresponsive, her eyes dull and far away. How horrible this must be for her—to lose everything she'd known, then to see the only two men who could help her in her new life determined to destroy each other. *Her father and her grandfather.* Katie still could not comprehend it—Zane, Merrick's son! Merrick had given Jenny a big hug and reassured her that everything would be all right, that he would be back in a few minutes and would take care of her. Katie had no doubt he would, but it was what Jenny believed that counted. What if she followed and tried to interfere—or ran away?

"Stay closer," Merrick said over his shoulder. "If you see me freeze, call out to me. If I don't answer, shoot him again, in the head."

Katie moved up quickly, aware of the weight of the gun in her pocket. Her stomach crawled at the thought of shooting Zane again. But she would do it—

She felt another twinge of dizziness. She said, "I think he's trying to get me."

Stopping, Merrick put Zane down and held out his hand. "Give me the gun."

"No," Zane pleaded. "Don't. I won't try again. I swear."

Merrick's hand dropped. He picked Zane up again and ran ahead. Katie hurried after him. In another moment, he stopped in a small clearing, marked at the corners by four big trees. He put Zane on the ground, reached into the grass, and pulled up a trapdoor, and suddenly Katie understood why he had not brought Jenny along. *Not in that hole*—he was going to bury Zane in another hole, one of his own making.

The trapdoor oppressed Katie in some way she could not define. How long had Merrick had this grave prepared? There was no pile of dirt in the clearing, and a trapdoor spoke of careful advance planning.

"Don't," Zane said.

"I'm sorry," Merrick murmured. He picked Zane up. Pressure began to build in Katie's throat, as though the air of the clearing had turned heavy. She buried Gregory's face against her shoulder, but was unable, herself, to look away. Zane groaned, "Father, Father . . ."

Merrick hesitated, his back rigid, then stepped to the trapdoor.

"NOOOOOOO," Zane howled.

Despite herself, Katie felt a stab of pity for him. He's a killer, she reminded herself, then amended it: Zane was a *born* killer. He had a man's intelligence but the heart of a jungle cat. Shaken by his feral scream, Katie saw through the illusion of his human form. This was not a man but a leopard, terrifying but magnificent, howling as it spied the cage.

Zane's wail died with the last of his breath. He gasped, but did not scream again. "I never gave in," he said to Merrick. His voice was suddenly low and controlled, a chilling contrast. "I never did what you wanted. So you lose. Fuck you, *Father*."

Merrick put a foot down into the hole. Zane's gaze roamed wildly, gathering last, desperate glimpses of the world. Merrick hesitated, and Katie could see the agony on his face. "I must," he said. "I *must*."

Merrick carried his son down into the vault, sealing the massive door behind him and giving the inner combination dial a spin. Now, no matter what happened in these final seconds, Zane was locked in. Hurrying with his struggling burden, Merrick stumbled against a leg of one of the deathbeds, wringing a metallic screech from the stone floor. He hoped Sandeman had not heard it. When he'd driven back to Jenny's house to retrieve Sandeman and return him to the vault, the dying phage had seemed exhausted, barely able to speak. Let him be sleeping now, Merrick thought fervently.

And if not, let him hold his tongue.

Hurrying into one of the open perimeter cells, Merrick lowered Zane's bound body onto its cot.

"Don't leave me like this." Zane strained against the cable that bound him. "Please, I need to move. I'll go insane."

Merrick took the key to the cable's padlock from his pocket and dropped it on the bed beside his son. As he turned back toward the door, a gray mist surrounded him. The door shimmered and vanished—

Zane, in my mind!

Merrick lunged toward the place where the door had been, and then he was on his hands and knees, with no sense of having stumbled. . . .

On the stone floor between his braced arms and knees lay the body of a man. The chewed, crimson throat held Merrick's gaze with hypnotic force. The man's blood had stopped pulsing; he could feel its warmth in his belly, soothing away the last of his hunger. The drying eyes of the Baron of Mersey gazed at his forehead, their focus dissolved in death. The bitter self-reproach Merrick always felt at this moment rose like a final noxious breath from the corpse. The baron had had his own vile compulsions, attested to by the small human bones in his dungeon farther down this cold, vaporous hall. *But who am I to judge him?*

"Father?"

Zane's voice behind him broke his gaze from the baron's throat. His son's young face was covered in blood; the soft beginnings of his mustache bristled with faint absurdity in its clotting grip. Impatience burned in Zane's eyes. Having fed first, he was now ready to go. A spasm of worry gripped Merrick. Zane had no remorse at what they had done, no sense of heaviness over it whatsoever. I'm failing him, Merrick thought. And if I fail . . .

Zane—I am burying Zane.

His young son vanished, replaced by the mature one, sitting up on the cot now, working furiously at his bindings, which had begun to loosen. Panicked, Merrick lunged up from his hands and knees toward the cell door—visible again—and through it. Turning, he threw his shoulder against it and twisted the bolt home as Zane crashed, screaming, against the other side.

Merrick slumped down against the door, absorbing the

mighty blows of Zane's fists through the steel, glad for the punishment, which could never be enough. How many innocents had died because he'd given Zane blood? Now he had taken that blood away. It was over.

I am over, Merrick thought.

He realized Zane had stopped pounding. He felt his son's weight slide down the door; sensed Zane's shoulder through three inches of steel, resting now almost against his own. He knows it's finished, too, Merrick thought. With the door locked, there's no further point to paralyzing me in my memories.

Raising his eyes to stare at the thick, stubby wings of the turnbolt, Merrick felt a cold reverberation along his spine. Five hundred years of anguished effort, a hunt that had spanned the globe a dozen times over, had been decided in the end by one quick twist of his fingers.

"My daughter . . ."

A bare murmur, but the steel was not enough to keep it from a hemophage's ears. Was that sorrow in Zane's voice? "I will take care of her," Merrick said.

"Like you took care of me?"

"This time I'll do better."

"She needs her father."

"It's you who needs her."

There was a long silence on the other side of the door. "Yes," Zane whispered.

Merrick's eyes ached in a hot, tearless grief. If he could believe that Zane truly loved Jenny, that Jenny could change him . . .

But no. It was Zane who would change Jenny. And if he allowed that, he would be twice damned. "I'll keep her with her parents for as long as possible," Merrick said. "I'll visit her in the night when it is necessary, and teach her to feed without killing."

"What you will teach her is to *suffer*. To go without what she craves most in all the world, to thirst for a thousand years. We don't just need blood, Merrick, we need to kill. Her dreams, that urge, will never leave her."

"No," Merrick agreed. "But nothing can make her do it. We can live without killing. We can love."

Silence stretched on the other side of the door. Realizing there was, at last, nothing more to say, Merrick pushed to his feet. Turning, he scanned the rows of cots, even though he knew it was unnecessary. He never brought a phage into the commons area until he was sure its muscles were too wasted for movement. None of these withered creatures could lift a finger, much less unlock Zane's cell. And, since the turnbolt mechanism did not go through to the inside of the door, Zane could not pick the lock either, even if he had the tools.

"Good-bye," Merrick said through the door.

"Will you be back?"

"No."

"Good."

Defiant to the last. Against his will, Merrick felt a fierce, pained admiration of his son.

"Jenny will never follow you."

Merrick turned back to the door a last time. "If there is any real love for her in you," he said, "you must hope she does."

Turning away, Merrick drifted in a wretched daze between the cots toward Sandeman's cell, making no sound this time, as though some dark inner grace now guided him. Sandeman lay on his bed, eyes closed, a book on his chest. Merrick called his name. Sandeman did not move. Merrick shook him gently, then harder. No response. Cold with foreboding, he peeled one of Sandeman's eyelids back. The pupil constricted slightly, but did not move to him. A quiet grief welled up in Merrick, and a sense of release, too. Kneeling beside the bed, he took Sandeman's skeletal hand. "It's over. Did I do the right thing?"

Sandeman lay unmoving.

Merrick noticed the book on his chest again. It was by E. M. Forster—*Two Cheers for Democracy*. Merrick started to close it but the bony hand resisted ever so slightly; Merrick saw that one of Sandeman's fingers was inside, marking a page. Careful not to lose the place, he lifted the book from Sandeman's chest, and this time the hand did not resist. A passage on the page had been underlined:

> *If I had to choose between betraying my country and betraying my friend, I hope I should have the guts to betray my country.*

A trembling hand had crossed out *friend* and inked in the word *son*.

Merrick raised his eyes to the ceiling of Sandeman's cell. With a fierce effort he choked down a sob, knowing if he began to weep he would be unable to stop. Gently, he eased one of

Sandeman's eyelids back again. This time the pupil centered on him.

"We will not see each other again," Merrick said. "Good-bye, old friend. Sleep well."

As he dialed the combination to open the massive door above him, Merrick was conscious of each click, each hushed thump of shifting tumblers. Certainly, Zane must be listening, too, his ear pressed to his cell door. Or maybe, despite his panic, he'd been able to memorize the pattern of sounds on the way in. In time, his memory of the sequence would fade, and then all hope would die in him. A mercy, perhaps . . .

No. There was no mercy in this place.

As Merrick pushed up from the vault, tears scalded his eyes, blurring his vision, forcing him to feel his way despite the bright moonlight. Lowering the trapdoor, he groped a covering of leaves over it. Finished, he remained on his hands and knees, unable even to lift his head. Dimly, he felt tears raining on the backs of his hands. Clenching his jaws, he fought to keep the last shreds of control. He could do it. He was no stranger to grief—

But never like this, never so black, so suffocating, so hopeless of relief. He remembered Zane's round, happy face gazing up at him from the cradle with a baby's wide-eyed wonder. A sob broke from his throat, and Merrick wept as he had not since he was a boy running from his village with a stranger's blood on his face, knowing he could never see his mother or father again.

Feeling a touch on his shoulder, he turned with a panicked snarl, smashing the hand away before he realized it was Katie's. He had forgotten her. She knelt beside him, gently putting her arms around him. He let her pull his head to her shoulder. If only he could find comfort there. But there was no comfort. He had just buried his own son alive, and there would never be comfort for him.

THIRTY-SEVEN

KATIE SAT WITH Merrick in the kitchen of his house. It was 3:00 A.M. and the Ritalin, boosted by her own adrenaline, had not faded completely from her system—and wouldn't any time soon, with all the coffee she was drinking now. To hell with it. She would not have felt like sleeping anyway. The nightmare was over and it was good just to be alive, to know Gregory was safe, snugly tucked away in Merrick's guest room.

But there was so much else she wanted to know—*needed* to know.

"More coffee?" Merrick asked.

"Sure."

He hardly took his eyes off her, even to pour, but it was a curious gaze, sweeping her face over and over, never centering on her eyes. He had been this way since they'd gotten back to his house, his ominous silence in the car replaced by this avid gaze. Did he fear that if he looked away from her, his mind would show him Zane? Her heart ached for him. How ghastly his final moments with his son must have been.

"You did the right thing," she said.

He did not answer.

"Would you like to talk about it?"

"No."

Would he ever be able to talk about it? She had the sudden conviction he would not. And perhaps, for him, that would be best.

Katie thought of her own son, sleeping in the other room. Merrick's son, too, and the best cure now for his grief, if only he would take it. Merrick *did* love Gregory, how could she have doubted it, even for a minute? He must have taken Gregory from Meggan's house in case Zane had found out he was there. Zane hadn't, of course—she'd been very careful about that.

Unless she was missing something. The thought that Zane might have tracked Gregory down made Katie cold. She asked Merrick about it.

He gazed at her mouth. For a moment, she thought he hadn't heard her. Then he said, "I had to assume Zane knew, or was close to knowing. Those marks on your throat . . ." He trailed off. Still, it was the most he'd said at once since she'd driven him back here from Jenny's house.

"I don't understand," she prompted.

Again, he seemed not to hear. Fear gripped her as she realized she might be losing him; that he might get up from this table at any moment and disappear into the night and she would never see him again.

"Merrick, talk to me . . . please."

He made a small sound, not quite a groan, then said, "When I found you unconscious on the Hrluskas' lawn, I checked under the bandage. As soon as I saw the marks, I knew Zane had made them, that he had been shadowing you."

"Okay, but I never told anyone where Mom or Gregory were."

"You never called Meggan's from the hospital?"

"Of course, but I always made sure the room was empty. I had a broom and I poked it everywhere."

"The ceiling, too?"

Katie felt a chill as she remembered that eerie night in the on-call room. Waking up and finding the punctures in her throat. Suddenly, she could see Zane in her mind's eye, clinging above her like a great, silent spider, watching her swing the broom into the corners in a panic, then dial Meggan's number. From the number, he could have been working his way to Meggan's address.

Katie groaned in belated terror. "Oh, God. I'm sorry."

"You couldn't have known. I kept you too much in the dark. I was afraid."

She looked at him with new understanding. How alone he always must have felt, a wolf among the sheep—a wolf who had turned into a guard dog, but still alone. He must have thought she would reject him if she knew the truth. He was wrong, but she could not blame him.

"If only I'd known," she said, "I never would have doubted you. When I saw the photo, I'd have understood."

"The photo?"

"Of you and Alexandra." She kept her voice carefully neutral.

Merrick gave a fractional nod. "That man who was nosing around my house."

"A friend of Art's," Katie said. "Art was only trying to protect me."

"He's in love with you."

"I know that."

"He's a good man. Think you could love him back?"

Suddenly, Katie was annoyed. "If you don't love me, just say so."

Merrick's gaze centered finally on her eyes. He reached across the table and took her hands. For the first time since they'd returned to his house, she felt that he was with her. "I love you with all my heart," he said.

Her heart leapt. "Oh, Merrick—"

"But it can't be."

"Why can't it?"

"Because I can't stand the pain anymore, Katie. I've watched too many women I loved die. The human heart can endure that once or twice. I've been through it sixteen times."

Even through her pain, she felt a sense of wonder. "Just how old are you, Merrick?"

"Nine hundred twenty-seven years."

She stared at him, staggered, awestruck. "You . . . you're giving Methuselah a run for his money."

He gave her a joyless smile.

She struggled to grasp it. "You've lived over nine hundred years and loved only sixteen women?"

"I was . . . faithful to each until she died."

Her eyes welled with tears. "How many children?"

"Forty-three."

She hesitated, hardly daring to ask the next question. "How many were hemophages?"

"Only Zane." A wince touched the corners of his eyes, and she knew he could not even say the name without pain.

He said, "I know you can't put it entirely from your mind, but you must try. It's extremely unlikely Gregory will be a phage." Merrick looked away, and she saw his eyes fill with longing.

"What are you thinking?"

"If only I could die."

Alarm filled her. "Don't say that. I love you. I don't want you to die."

"Even if it's the only way we can be together?"

"Surely that's not true—"

"Katie, *listen*." He raised a hand, fingers splayed, as if groping for the right words. "Alexandra was the last before you," he said. "Cancer, in 1962. She was eighty. Our son George died of a heart attack in 1985 at the age of seventy-three. Long before that, in 1928, I had to fake my own death. A few months earlier, Alexandra and I celebrated our twentieth anniversary. Sailing accident, body never recovered. I saw them a few times after that, but obviously I couldn't allow them to see me. I was at Alexandra's bedside the day she died, but I could not comfort her, and she could not comfort me."

"How awful." Despair settled over Katie. Only an hour ago, she'd had such hope. He was grieving, but she would comfort him. And, after all, his dreadful secret was out and she still loved him. Surely, that would be enough to bring the barrier between them down at last.

But love was not enough.

"If you go on . . . feeding, how much longer will you live?"

"The oldest phage I know of lasted fifteen hundred and some years—if his birthdate can be relied on. Memories fail, records crumble to dust. There might have been others who lived longer."

Katie shook her head. Fifteen hundred years—she just could not take it in. After she was gone, Merrick would go on for six centuries. "What if you stopped taking blood? Wouldn't you begin to age?"

"Not in the way you mean. I would go through a period of accelerated aging—a year or so—and then I would sicken with leukemia. It would take me another two years or more to die. I would be in constant agony. I knew of only one phage with the courage to do that."

She sensed there was more, but that she should not ask.

"Does . . . does blood taste good to you?" The question appalled her, but something in her needed to know.

He looked at her for a moment before answering. "It goes beyond taste. . . ."

"You crave it."

"Yes. I don't know if you could understand, but—"

"I could understand," she said.

Merrick's gaze measured her, and she felt a perverse pleasure at having her own small secret.

"Would you excuse me a moment?" she asked.

"Of course."

She went into his bathroom and flushed the remaining three Ritalin capsules down the toilet.

When she returned, he reached across the table and took her hands again. "I love you, Katie," he said softly. "I'd give anything to grow old and die with you. But I have to move on."

Her heart sank. "When?"

"Soon. Very soon. I've been here twelve years. People will start to notice I'm not growing older. And if one of my old colleagues on the force in San Francisco saw my picture in a paper, they'd realize I hadn't aged in almost *twenty* years. . . ."

"But why would your picture be in the paper?"

"Katie, the business of the blood is likely to come out."

"Zane made me call Byner," she reminded him. "And Byner was happy to forget the blood."

"What about Art?"

"What about him? You saw him—he was just coming to when we got back here. He doesn't remember a thing. He knows only what we told him—that I was able to kill Zane with an injection of Fraction Eight, just like we'd hoped."

"Art knows a lot more than that. He helped you study the blood."

"He also knows you saved his life," Katie said. "If he thought the killer was still out there, he might feel he had to go to the police. But people are safe now, and he knows if he said anything, he'd get me in a world of trouble. I don't think he would do that."

Merrick gave her a long, speculative look. "You may be right."

"I *am* right. I know Art."

"Still," Merrick said, "it's only a reprieve. The twelve years without aging is long enough to start raising eyebrows. If the blood story doesn't break, I can stay a month or two longer, but—"

"Fraction Eight!" Katie shouted.

Merrick looked at her as if she'd gone mad.

She gazed back, feeling a sudden desperate hope as she remembered Rebecca's blood mingling with Jenny's under her microscope. *Alpha and Omega.* She realized she was clutching Merrick's hands with all her might. He raised an eyebrow in question.

"There may be a way," she said.

EPILOGUE

KATIE LAY IN bed with Merrick, watching him sleep and listening to the rain. A brisk south wind flung the heavy drops against the bedroom's front window, rattling the panes. The thunder had moved off a ways now, and she could feel a pleasant new coolness in the air as the front moved through. A flicker of lightning showed her Gregory, curled against his father's back, sound asleep now that "Mom" was awake to guard against the storm.

That's right, Katie thought. He called me Mom when he ran in here. What happened to Mommy? He's still only three, for crying out loud.

She stroked his hair gently, considering this new milestone with a mixture of pride and regret. Only a year since the wedding, but she could see profound changes in him since Merrick had moved in. Gregory was more confident, more outgoing—and more spoiled, no doubt about it.

But he was still a good little boy, her sweet angel.

Katie felt a flood of contentment. Life is good, she thought. I have everything I want. . . .

Almost.

If I could just *know*.

Watching the slow rise and fall of Merrick's chest, she permitted herself a small hope. He was beginning to sleep more—wasn't that a positive sign? . . .

Hard to be sure. She'd never had a patient like Merrick before. He had been taking weekly injections of Fraction Eight from Rebecca Trent's blood since before the wedding—more than a year now. At the same time, he'd been supplying periodic doses of his own unique, antigen-free blood for injection into Rebecca—all strictly on the quiet, of course. So far, Rebecca had been the only one to show measurable effects. Her bone density was increasing, she stood straighter; her hair was thicker. She'd been able to graduate to outpatient treatment seven months ago and was doing well at home. It could be hard to detect progress when you saw a patient so frequently, but Rebecca had been in the clinic waiting room a week ago when Art Stratton had paid a surprise visit. He'd seen the difference in her at once.

The memory made Katie smile. Art had taken her aside, and she'd winced inwardly, thinking he was going to tell her how much he missed her. Instead he'd said, "When are you going to write Rebecca up for a journal?"

Ouch!

Art had not mentioned having a new love of his life, but he hadn't needed to. Katie was glad for him. He seemed to be doing great at Boston General. She was not going to write Rebecca up, of course, not unless she could independently synthesize whatever it was in Merrick's blood that was helping her. Even then, she would not become a young woman again. But her clock would have slowed; a day of living would no longer equal a month of dying for her. At an apparent age of seventy, she might have fifteen or even twenty more years of life, instead of one or two.

But what about Merrick?

It kept coming back to that, and every time she thought about it, she felt powerful conflicting emotions. It was so strange to make growing old the goal of a medical treatment. She loved Merrick so much she could not want him to die, ever. But she also knew he really did want to grow old with her. In the past month, with no real evidence he was aging, she'd begun to glimpse the old sadness in his eyes. It made her afraid. If Fraction

Eight did not work, if Merrick could not find his fountain of age, ultimately he would leave, and it would break not just her heart, but his. She would have to go on alone somehow, knowing he was out there somewhere, worrying that he might take up his old life again.

The thought terrified her. When she had given him hope, he had laid down his terrible burden. He'd retired from the police force and was teaching courses in criminology at George Washington. That was good—he knew a great deal about the subject, and he liked interacting with the young—to him, very young—students, but in a way it frustrated her, too. Merrick had been born around the Battle of Hastings. He had seen the invention of the printing press, the voyages of Columbus, the fall of the Aztecs. But he could not share what he had seen without revealing too much about himself. So he must content himself with giving only what a normal man could give.

Still, parts of his old life clung. He never spoke of Zane, but grief showed in his eyes at unguarded moments; once she had walked quietly into a room behind him and found him weeping. So far as she knew, he had never gone back to that terrible place in the woods where he'd buried his son.

The other part of his old life was Jenny, and that, at least, seemed positive, a clear good for both grandfather and granddaughter. Jenny's parents had not been told, of course, that she was Merrick's granddaughter and, for the most part, he avoided them by seeing her late at night. Every two weeks, he drove to her house after midnight, and they went out into the darkness together while her parents slept the deeper sleep that Merrick could still create.

Katie felt a chill. She did not like to think about what Merrick and Jenny did on those nights, but she knew it was infinitely better than what they might have done. No one died. A few dozen people woke up over the course of the year with small puncture wounds in their ankles and a slight listlessness that would pass in a few days. It was all that was left of Merrick's old life, and Katie wanted very much to keep it that way.

Gregory rolled against his father and Merrick hugged him in his sleep. The rain had stopped, and dawn was breaking, she saw. She watched the light brighten on the window, until the sun broke above a shelf of cloud and poured a brilliant, golden light into the room that made the sheets glow and Merrick's hair . . .

Katie's breath caught in her throat. *Merrick's hair!* She

edged closer to him, trying not to waken him, but his eyes popped open anyway.

"What do you think you're doing?" he murmured.

She winnowed through the shock of dark hair on his forehead, searching, searching—there it was! Her heart filled with love and relief and a sadness that was also strangely good. She said, "Did you know you have a gray hair?"

His eyes lit with joy and relief, and then he pulled her to him and kissed away her tears.

*Usually we meet them only in the wilderness of our
dreams, where, before the lion pounces or the cobra
spits or the alligator slithers, we awake, trembling, to
a world we have tamed. . . . Our attitude toward beasts
that kill is simple: We love them—as long as they
don't kill us.*
—George Howe Colt in Life *magazine*

On the ivy-covered Princeton campus, no one suspects that Vincent DeVilbiss is anything more than an unusually charming charlatan. But technology has done a lot to assimilate the modern vampire. Tinted contact lenses hide his amber eyes, sunscreen lets him walk in the daylight, and a mysterious elixir keeps him vital and handsome.

But when DeVilbiss draws beautiful Frederika Vanderveen into the erotic and brutal world of the undead, he makes an enemy of Simon Penn, a young rare-books curator who loves the troubled girl from afar. As Simon confronts a seemingly unstoppable foe, he finds the stakes are much higher than one woman's soul. For DeVilbiss has been sent to destroy an ancient document, before its powers can be turned against him and all the evil he has planned for the world.

THE BOOK OF COMMON DREAD

BRENT MONAHAN

"Easily the best addition to the vampire genre since Anne Rice's _Interview with the Vampire._"
—Indianapolis Star

The scars on her wrists, throat and chest told the story. Somehow Audra Delaney had survived a brutal rape ten years ago, but with her memory of her attacker shattered. Then the unthinkable happens: she hears his voice on the radio, and now all she lives for are dark dreams of revenge.

She was his one loose end—the only one who got away, the only one who can still destroy him. All he has to do is find out her name, so he can silence her forever.

Soon, they're racing neck-and-neck, stalking each other in a world of shadows and evil, where it will take all of Audra's strength and the unexpected ingenuity of a child genius to survive . . .

DEAD EVEN

A gripping novel of psychological terror

EMMA BROOKES

It has been almost a year since Beth Lambert's body was recovered from a ravine on Whidbey, a tranquil island community near Seattle. Now Naomi Wing, a full-blooded Wintu Indian, who turned her back on the old ways to become a high-powered attorney, has returned to her ancestral home, haunted by the tragic death of a girl she had come to love as a daughter—and caught up in a love affair that may have played a role in Beth's death.

What Naomi finds will pit her against Susan, Beth's dangerously unstable mother, and force her to confront the Native American heritage she has denied for so long. On the mysterious, forested shores of Whidbey, she will pursue secrets only the dead can reveal—secrets that lead her to the shocking truth about Beth...and into the dark shadows of her own past.

A DEEP AND DREAMLESS SLEEP
by Meg O'Brien